I0760862

MANIPULATE

PAM GODWIN

Editor: Fairest Reviews Editing Services
Proofreader: Lesa Godwin
Cover Designer: Pam Godwin
Interior Designer: Pam Godwin

Content Warning

Visit my website at pamgodwin.com

The books in the DELIVER series are stand-alones, but they should be read in order.

DELIVER (#1)
VANQUISH (#2)
DISCLAIM (#3)
DEVASTATE (#4)
TAKE (#5)
MANIPULATE (#6)
UNSHACKLE (#7)
DOMINATE (#8)
COMPLICATE (#9)

PART ONE

ONE

Ciudad Hueca, Mexico
Two years ago

What a suck ass day.

To think, it started out so lovely and perfect.

Since Tula Gomez didn't have to go into work, she'd decided to make it a bra-less, drink-wine-at-noon, binge-on-Hellraiser-movies, and masturbate-more-than-once kind of day.

Until her phone rang.

She should've sent her sister's call to voicemail.

She should've let Vera ruin someone else's day.

But she didn't.

She answered the damn phone and surrendered to Vera's demands.

Instead of slumming in her pajamas on the couch, she spent the past six hours on the road, driving toward the last city on Earth she wanted to visit.

When she crossed the New Mexico-Texas border two-hundred-miles back, her mood had spiraled past annoyance and straight into pissed-off.

She eased her Jeep Wrangler forward in the stop-start traffic, trying not to ride the old clutch. If the manual transmission decided to go out, today would be the fucking day.

Wavy lines of heat rose from the scorched asphalt. Horns blared, and some idiot a few cars back blasted his bass so loud it rattled the frame of her poor Jeep.

She grabbed her phone and redialed her sister. "Come on, Vera. Pick up."

As it rang, she inched along with hundreds of other border-crossing commuters lined up at the Mexico port of entry.

The phone continued to ring. And ring. Why wasn't Vera answering her calls?

"Dammit!" Tula gritted her teeth at the sound of the voicemail greeting. "This is bullshit."

She disconnected and gripped the steering wheel, vacillating between turning back home and speeding toward hell.

Home was a one-bedroom apartment two states away in Phoenix, Arizona, where everything in her world was safe, normal, orderly, and stress-free.

Hell was her childhood *colonia* in Ciudad Hueca, Mexico, where Vera still lived. Her younger sister thrived in chaos, drama, and danger—all the things Tula had run away from when she moved to the states.

Her visits to Mexico were infrequent and made only out of obligation to Vera.

She didn't shun her Mexican roots, but it had taken her a long damn time to go through the naturalization process to become a U.S. citizen. She was a proud American and a law-abiding taxpayer, who worked nine to five as a high school Spanish teacher.

Her peaceful, boring life suited her just fine. If she never stepped foot across the border again, she would be just fine with that, too.

But Vera was family. Her only living relative. And her sister needed her.

God only knew what sort of mess Vera had landed in this time. When she called this morning, the shitty connection had chopped up the short conversation into a few staticky words.

Some trouble.

Need you.

Come now.

Bring money.

When the connection had cut off, Tula called back, again and again, with no luck. None of her questions had been answered, and she had very little to go on.

Except Vera's track record.

Last time Vera called, she needed help kicking her thieving loser boyfriend to the curb. The time before that, she'd been abandoned a day's drive from home without money or a ride back. There were dozens of other situations over the years, and Tula always, begrudgingly, came to the rescue.

It wasn't a secret Vera hung out with the wrong people. Living in Ciudad Hueca, it was easy to become entangled with cartels.

Tula's nagging pleas to stay away from them fell on deaf ears, and their relationship became resentful and strained. But at the end of the day, all they had was each other.

She attempted several more phone calls while trudging along in bumper-to-bumper traffic. Rows of cars pressed in on all sides, filled with people whose frustration rivaled her own. Road rage simmered like the summer heat, all of it weighing on her with each passing minute.

An hour later, she made it through the port of entry and took the safest route toward her childhood home.

Not that there was a *safe* route. Ciudad Hueca was going through a volatile time. As a border city, it was perfectly located for drug distribution throughout the United States. This made it extremely valuable to cartels, turning it into one of the most fought-over territories in the country.

Since Vera refused to move to the states, Tula stayed abreast of the local news and crime here. Two violent drug cartels battled for dominance, street by street, to control the lucrative drug-trafficking routes.

Driving through her hometown, alone and unarmed, was dangerous as hell.

She kept pepper spray in her Jeep just for these visits. But no guns. Given her inexperience with weapons, she'd end up shooting herself during an attack.

As a precaution, she'd topped off the gas tank in Texas to avoid an extra stop in Mexico. No lingering. No shortcuts.

The five-hundred dollars in cash she'd stuffed in her purse would have to be enough to fix Vera's mess. Tula planned to stay three hours tops, confirm Vera's well-being with her own eyes, and return to the U.S. before nightfall.

Around three in the afternoon, she arrived at her childhood *colonia* on the outskirts of the city. Rundown businesses, rugged streets, and a few trees encircled the tiny, concrete-block house where she and Vera were raised.

Between the two of them, Vera had been closer to their mother. When they lost their only parent to heart disease five years ago, Vera kept the house.

That was about the time Vera started her downward spiral into trouble.

Tula parked in front of her childhood home and leaned over the steering wheel, inspecting the empty street and surrounding houses. No one lingered around the property. No gunfire nearby or in the distance.

It hadn't always been this unsafe. She left home at age eighteen, and in the ten years she'd been in the states, Ciudad Hueca had grown chaotically. Its tax revenue went to Mexico City, and not much came back. Law enforcement rationed gasoline and bullets. Basic infrastructure—schools, roads, sewers, parks—went to shit.

The city was in a state of disrepair, much like the sagging roof of her childhood home.

She grabbed the pepper spray, her purse, and the house key she still kept on her keyring. Then she bolted to the front door.

The key turned the lock, and she stepped in without knocking. "Hello? Vera?"

Silence hit her, along with the usual weight of nostalgia.

Good times. Bad times. No major tragedy. Just the usual poverty and a mother who was anxious to get Tula grown up and moved out. One less mouth to feed.

She made a quick sweep through the sitting room, kitchen, and two bedrooms before confirming what she already knew.

Her sister wasn't home.

Despite Vera's haphazard approach to life, she maintained a tidy, clutter-free house. Not a single dirty dish in the sink. No dust on the furniture or cobwebs in the corners. Nothing lying around to indicate where she was.

With a sigh, Tula called her again.

No answer.

"Shit." She stared at the front door, tapping the phone against her chin.

Vera usually had a job, but never a steady one. She bounced through employers as fast as she went through boyfriends. If she was at work, Tula didn't know where that was.

Over the next ten minutes, she dared a walk outside, knocking on neighboring houses. Three doors opened for her, and all the responses were consistent.

No one had seen Vera in weeks.

Panic set in.

Why would she tell Tula to drive here, if she wasn't home? Where the fuck did she go?

Indecision sent her pacing through the house, rifling through drawers, and digging in closets. The hunt for clues led nowhere.

"Fuck!" She lowered to the couch and squeezed her fingers around the phone.

Should she leave? What if Vera was on her way here? Maybe she was staying with a new boyfriend and lost her phone after the call dropped this morning?

"Damn you, Vera." Tula slumped deeper into the couch and waited.

And waited.

Three hours later, the sun dipped low on the horizon, signaling the darkness to come.

Vera still wasn't answering the phone. Tula must've left over fifty voicemail messages.

She couldn't risk being caught in the city after nightfall.

Time to go.

Nervous energy trembled through her as she opened the freezer in the kitchen and hid some money in a carton of ice cream. Vera would eventually call, and Tula would tell her where to find the cash.

She kept two-hundred dollars, stuffing the bills into

her back pocket, in case she needed it on the drive home.

Then she left.

Taking the shortest route to the U.S. border, she itched to hit the gas and speed as fast as the Jeep would go. But she forced herself to drive the speed limit and keep a low profile through the rougher parts of the city.

Signs of violence and strife haunted every corner. Roadside memorials, flowers, and lit candles marked sites of death. Young men gathered under awnings, buying and selling drugs. Girls, too young to be out after dark, solicited sex on every street.

These people were survivors. She didn't judge them, but she also didn't trust them.

She didn't trust the local police, either.

The Mexican military had been brought in to put a stop to the cartels and the drug war. But they were all part of the corruption.

Everyone and anyone could've been a target. If a police officer decided to pull her over, she would be at his mercy.

As she drove through the heart of the city, she spotted a sedan with tinted windows in the rear-view mirror a few cars back.

Was that the same sedan that was behind her when she left Vera's house? Her pulse sprinted into a gallop.

Stop it. You're just paranoid.

Following the GPS on her phone, she veered down a side street.

The sedan turned with her.

Her heart thrashed in her ears, and a hot lump formed in her throat.

Why would anyone trail her? She was a nobody schoolteacher from Phoenix, driving a worthless hunk of metal.

She turned down another road to see if the sedan would follow. When it didn't, she released a heavy breath.

"Oh, thank fuck." She wiped a clammy palm on her jeans. "Jesus, Tula. Way to get yourself all worked up over noth—"

A car flew out of the intersection in front of her and slammed on its brakes.

She skidded to a stop, narrowly avoiding a collision with it.

Blinking rapidly, she schooled her breathing and stared at the car.

Another black sedan with tinted windows.

Dread hardened her stomach, and a chill tingled across her scalp.

What the hell was going on?

The sedan blocked her path and didn't attempt to move. The doors didn't open, and the window tint concealed the occupants.

Alarms fired inside her, her instinct screaming to get the hell out of there and fast.

She shoved the Jeep into reverse just as a huge military truck appeared over the hill straight ahead.

Mexican soldiers in helmets, green uniforms, and sunglasses jogged alongside the armored vehicle. They gripped assault rifles and machine guns and headed directly toward her.

She gulped for air, her fingers frozen on the stick shift.

Had she driven into a battle zone? Or was something going down in one of the buildings behind her?

With the gear shift in reverse, she glanced at the rear-view mirror.

Another sedan pulled in behind her, barricading her.

No, no, no.

Her blood pressure careened toward detonation.

She eased out of reverse and dropped her phone into her purse. Hooking the strap over her shoulder, she gripped the pepper spray, prepared to run on foot.

Until the soldiers swept in around the Jeep and raised their rifles.

"Get out!" The man beside her door tapped his machine gun against the window. "Now!"

They were here for her? Why? What did she do wrong?

She dropped the pepper spray and held up her hands, her entire body trembling as she twisted toward him.

Apparently, she moved too slow. He yanked the door open and wrenched her out with his gun in her face.

In a blur of uniforms, she was pushed against the hood of the Jeep, face down with her feet kicked apart. They pawed through her pockets and dug through her purse while other soldiers held her in place.

Her palms slicked with sweat, and adrenaline coursed through her system, shutting down her ability to think clearly.

"What's going on?" she asked in Spanish, her heart pounding painfully. "What do you want?"

"Petula Gomez?" A soldier shoved her passport in her face.

It took her a second because honestly, only her mother had called her Petula. "Yes."

"Gomez?"

"Yes, that's my passport." Ice trickled down her spine. "Why are you asking?"

The man tossed her I.D. into her purse. "Arrest her!"

It happened so fast. One minute, she was bent over the hood of her Jeep. The next, she lay in the cargo hold of an armored vehicle with her arms handcuffed behind her.

Soldiers sat around her, guns in hands, faces stern, refusing to answer her questions.

Terror attacked her in waves, chattering her teeth and locking her joints. She couldn't stop trembling, couldn't catch her breath. She feared for her life.

The truck rumbled into motion, and her heart wanted to rush out of her chest. She'd been pulled into something really nasty, and she had no clue where she was going or what would happen when she arrived.

She traveled five or ten minutes before the vehicle stopped. Cruel hands yanked her out of the truck. When she stumbled, a fist swung from behind and punched her across the face.

Stunned to the pit of her stomach, she gasped through the pain and swallowed down bile.

Another strike hit her tail bone, and she staggered forward, trying to remain upright with her wrists shackled.

Rather than letting her walk on her own, two soldiers dragged her by her arms and hair into an unmarked building.

"Why are you doing this? I didn't do anything!" Her breathing came in frenzied bursts. "Where are you taking me?"

The butt of a gun rammed into her back, knocking the wind from her lungs and sending her to her knees.

She cried out and bit her tongue through the agony. "Please, just give me a second."

She'd been speaking Spanish the whole time and knew they understood her. They just didn't care.

Hoisted to her feet before she was ready, she tried to keep her legs beneath her as they ruthlessly hauled her down a dark hallway.

After a few dizzying turns, they wrenched her into a

concrete room.

A man stood beside an old metal table with peeling paint. He wore the same green uniform as the soldiers, except his was decorated with colorful ribbons and gold medallions.

She didn't need to see the merits to sense his superiority. It wafted from his stiff posture, raised chin, and hard brown eyes. A trim beard outlined his squared jaw and thin lips, accentuating his dominance.

A tremor skated through her, stealing her voice. This man was evil, his rottenness so thick it clotted the room.

One soldier removed her handcuffs while the other tossed her purse to the officer, along with her passport.

The officer studied the I.D. and gave her a clinical once-over. "Remove your clothes."

"What?" Her stomach collapsed, and she clutched the neckline of her t-shirt, holding it tight. "Why?"

"Rápido!"

His explosive roar stopped her heart. She couldn't make her hands move, every part of her frozen in fear.

Did they intend to strip search her? Where were the female soldiers? She didn't remember the law well enough to understand her rights.

A fist slammed into the side of her head, and she collided with the nearby wall. Her skull throbbed. Her eyes ached with tears, and that was when she truly understood.

There was no law here. No justice. No defense for the innocent.

This was military corruption.

"I'll give you one chance." The officer clasped his hands behind his back. "It's up to you if you want to live or die."

There were no options. If she didn't cooperate, they would kill her.

She closed her eyes and swallowed her modesty. Then she removed her sneakers, jeans, and t-shirt. When she met his heartless eyes, she wore only her bra and panties.

The impulse to wrap her arms around herself made her twitch. But she felt the need to make a stand. No one else would be fighting for her here.

Holding her hands at her sides, she pushed her shoulders back, despite the ungodly terror twisting up her insides.

"Where is Hernandez?" He paced a circle around her. "Garcia?"

"I…I don't know—"

He gripped her jaw and yanked it upward at a painful angle, putting his bearded face in hers. "Where's Cortez?"

"I don't know who you're talking about! I live in Arizona. I'm just a schoolteacher. I don't know anyone by those names!"

"Okay." He released her and stepped back.

Did he think she was Vera? How deeply had her sister entangled herself with the cartel? Deep enough to fall into the sights of the Mexican military?

If this was a case of mistaken identity, Tula couldn't point that out and send them after Vera. She'd come to Mexico to protect her sister, not get her arrested.

There had to be another way.

"I gave you a chance, and you didn't take it." He nodded at the soldiers behind her.

"Wait! Let me call someone."

Who? Who the hell would she call? Her boss? A fellow teacher at work? She didn't have friends or family. No one could bail her out of this.

She was on her own.

The two uniforms grabbed her arms and aggressively wrestled her to the table, bending her over the surface with her chest pressed against the cold metal.

In the next breath, her panties were ripped away, leaving behind an ice-cold quake of horror.

This wasn't a strip search. It was sexual assault.

"I want to call a lawyer!" She bucked against their hold, terrified and exposed with her bare butt in the air. "I have the right to an attorney!"

Hands slammed her face down as the other man shackled her arms to the table legs.

Behind her, it sounded like two pieces of metal were being tapped together. Whatever that was shot violent tremors down her legs.

She craned her neck and glimpsed a metal rod in the officer's hand. A wire dangled from it, and she followed the end to where it plugged into the wall.

Ungodly terror crashed down upon her, sitting over her mouth and nose and crushing her chest. A trickle of air slipped through, just enough to keep her organs functioning, but it was crippling, suffocating.

Boots kicked her feet farther apart. Handcuffs tethered her arms to the table. Then she felt fingers, frigid bony digits separating her butt cheeks and the tender tissues around her vagina.

Before she could scream her objections, the metal rod penetrated her rectum in one brutal shove.

A sharp, ripping burn incinerated her anus. The sound of buzzing electricity warped the air as a jarring, horrendous jolt electrocuted her backside.

The pain was so excruciating her bladder released, spilling urine down her legs. Vomit burst past her lips, and her eyeballs felt like they were exploding out of their sockets. As if every drop of life was trying to find a way to escape her body.

She screamed until her vocal cords bled, until she couldn't draw air into her lungs. Snot bubbled from her nose, and tears soaked her face, sticking her hair to her cheeks and mouth.

The torture was never-ending, striking flames through her anal cavity, over and over. Fifteen to twenty jolts. Five seconds each.

He removed the rod, stabbed it into her vagina, and started again. Back and forth he went, reaming that metal device in and out and frying her insides with punishing bolts of lightning.

She cried for him to stop and tried to jerk away from the source of her pain. The pain… It howled through her body and blurred her vision. She couldn't move, couldn't swallow or gasp beneath the agony.

Buzzing, taunting zaps, scuffing boots—all of it grew distant amid the pounding in her ears. Time ceased to exist. Her face stuck to a puddle of vomit, sweat, tears, and snot. Her body lay wasted on the table, electrocuted to the point of death.

She welcomed the end. Willed it to take her from the torment. Yet her heart kept beating. Her lungs continued to suck air. Her body wouldn't die.

Then the buzzing din of static stopped, and the room fell quiet.

A hand stroked over her head, petting her hair. "Are you ready to talk now?"

"Stop." Saliva leaked from her mouth, her voice raw and ruined. "Please."

She didn't have enough energy to lift an arm. Her throat throbbed from screaming and dry heaving. It even hurt to blink.

"We're going to annihilate La Rocha Cartel." His hot

breath brushed her face. "Doesn't matter if you're a small-time player. You need to start talking."

"I don't know anyone in any cartel. I'm. Just. A teacher."

Why were they doing this? Why did they want to hurt her so badly? She hadn't done anything wrong.

"My name is Petula Gomez from Phoenix, Arizona. Please, believe what I'm saying. You have the wrong person."

"You want more?" He patted her cheek. "I'll give you more."

He rammed the rod into her ass and resumed the electrocution.

Fiery waves of voltage shot through her body, causing muscle contractions that were so violent it felt like her bones were fracturing.

Her mind flirted with the edge of unconsciousness, and she reached for it, needing the comfort it would give her. But her awareness hung on, refusing to burn out.

Hours passed. Maybe days. It felt like several lifetimes came and went before they unlocked the handcuffs and kicked her onto the floor.

She lay where she landed, crumpled on her side, unable to move. Silent tears escaped her eyes. Drool tickled her cracked lips, and perspiration clung to her naked skin.

The shaking in her limbs was unbearable, every inch of her drenched in a cold sweat. The pain, the shock, the unholy fear—it gathered in her core and vibrated outward like a jackhammer.

She couldn't escape it, couldn't silence the torment.

Voices sounded from the hallway, and she pried her eyes open.

Three men stood just outside the room—the officer and two unfamiliar soldiers—staring at her passport.

"She doesn't know anything." The officer handed off the I.D. "She's not the woman."

She tried to reach out an arm, form a word, or do something to get their attention. She needed to tell them to call an ambulance.

But they turned and walked away.

The edges of her periphery closed in, shrinking her vision until nothing existed.

She blacked out.

When she woke, the first thing she sensed was the clothing against her raw skin. Someone had redressed her.

The surrounding space felt bigger.

She opened her eyes to a new room, this one filled with at least a dozen people. She lay on the cement floor against a wall. Handcuffs shackled her to the bench beside her head.

They weren't letting her go?

Her chest tightened, her panic deep and internal. The agony between her legs would've made her sob if she'd had the strength. She didn't have enough life in her body to move a muscle.

But she could shift her gaze, and as she looked down, she registered a large amount of drugs in a bag at her feet.

"We apprehended an American." Her torturer stood a few feet away, addressing the room with his hands folded behind him. "Petula Gomez attempted to traffic fifty kilograms of marijuana into the United States."

Her stomach bottomed out.

She had never touched an illegal substance. Never been associated with drugs in any way.

She was being framed.

Incapacitated beyond exhaustion, her body tried to sink back into oblivion. She fought it, desperate to defend herself.

Some of the people in the room tossed out questions. At the edge of her awareness, she sensed the sounds of a flashing camera. A news reporter?

She was too scared, too far out of it to comprehend or open her mouth. Everything inside her felt as if it were slowly dying.

Consciousness slipped in and out. When she woke again, two soldiers were loading her in the rear of an armored vehicle, subjecting her achy eyes to the bright sunlight.

It was morning.

Her heart lurched. An entire evening had passed.

They'd confiscated her purse, phone, and identification. All she had was the clothes on her back.

A twenty-minute drive transported her toward a terrifyingly familiar part of Ciudad Hueca. She knew where they were taking her before the barbed wire walls appeared through the truck's tiny windows.

Jaulaso.

The most violent prison in the nation.

The living conditions in Jaulaso were so dangerous and inhumane there had been several attempts to shut it down. And like many prisons in Mexico, male and female inmates cohabited within its walls.

Her chance of surviving in Jaulaso was zero. Especially as an American woman with no connections or experience. She wouldn't make it the first night without getting raped.

Adrenaline returned to her body, energizing sore muscles and injecting life into her blood. Her heart pumped harder, and her hands clenched in the shackles.

By the time the soldiers dragged her into the crowded halls of the prison, she had enough strength to walk on her own.

The man who booked her led her into a small room with a table and two chairs. He left her there alone, without an explanation or a *fuck you.*

Shivering on the verge of hysteria, she huddled into the metal chair and tried to make sense of what was happening.

Mistaken identity?

That must've been the reason for her arrest. The military had followed her from Vera's house, after all.

She and Vera were only two years apart in age. They shared the same last name, black hair, brown eyes, slender build, and golden complexion. They looked similar.

She couldn't blame her sister for this. The Mexican military fucked up. When they realized Tula didn't know anything, they covered their mistake by framing her.

She was in Jaulaso because of corruption.

What happened to her last night was too overwhelming to process right now. She compartmentalized it, shoved it all down and out of reach.

But she couldn't do anything about the coldness inside her, the deadened sensation in her brain, and her inability to react or function normally. She was in a severe state of shock.

Her gaze drifted to the clock on the wall, and she attempted to calculate the timeline since she'd crossed the border. How long had she been unconscious?

The sandpaper feel of her tongue suggested dehydration, but hunger pangs hadn't set in yet.

It felt like she'd been arrested days ago, though she must've only been detained for one night. Everything hurt. Her body was unresponsive to simple commands, her motor functions clumsy and zapped of life.

After doing some painful guesswork in her head, she

estimated she'd been tortured in that room for eight hours.

She lost another two hours waiting at that table before the door finally opened.

A white-haired, pudgy man lumbered in, wearing a wrinkled collared shirt and a crooked tie.

"I'm the U.S. consular here in Ciudad Hueca," he said without preamble and sat across from her.

"They tortured me." Her voice shivered beneath a strained whisper, and she cleared her ravaged throat. "The military... They...they electrocuted..." She couldn't even say it out loud.

"I'm sorry, but we don't have jurisdiction here in Mexico."

She was empty. Numb. Barely alive. "I need to get a message to my sister."

After he wrote down Vera's contact information, he explained her rights in a bored, repetitive tone.

"How do I end this?" A tear slipped down her cheek.

"Declare yourself guilty. Accept the charges. That'll give you the best chance to transfer to the states and conclude your sentence in the U.S."

"Conclude my sentencc? That's my best-case scenario?"

"Yes." He rubbed his bulbous nose.

"I'm innocent."

What would happen to her job? Her American citizenship?

He arched a brow and tossed her a *that's-what-they-all-say* look. "Your other option is to fight for your innocence in Mexico."

That was the right thing to do. The only option.

"Okay." She might not have been thinking clearly, but she knew she would never plead guilty to a crime she didn't commit. "I'll prove my innocence."

"Fine." His voice drawled with an unnerving lack of care or compassion. "I'll help if I can, but these things take time."

"How much time?"

"Years."

"No. Impossible." Her breathing accelerated. "I'm innocent. I'll be out of here in a month. Two months at most."

"Good luck with that." He heaved from the chair, grabbed his briefcase, and walked to the door without looking back. "I'll be in touch."

TWO

"We have a new one!" The prison guard shoved Tula through the sweaty, packed halls of Jaulaso. "Hot, fresh meat."

Did he really just announce that?

The blatant leering of filthy men pulled her chin to her chest. She folded her arms around her midsection, eyes on the floor, and focused on putting one foot in front of the other.

The lack of strength in her legs made her stagger, her muscles achy and skin feverish as dozens of inmates whistled and screamed vulgarities at her.

Frailty trembled through her and hitched her shoulders around her ears. Tears hit the backs of her eyes, but she refused to cry. She was still standing, still walking on her own. As long as she didn't fall, maybe she would make it to the safety of her cell in one piece.

The immediate future squeezed a fist around her throat. Until she proved her innocence, she would have to fight for her life, every second of every day, and that fight started now.

The scent of vomit clung to her hair, but the air in the hallway smelled worse. The pungency of urine, feces, and body odor polluted every inhale, making her eyes water beyond her need to sob.

The corridor was so crowded she had to step over half-naked people and weave around piles of garbage and discarded clothes.

The darkness accentuated the humid dampness and overall gloom and emphasized how few lights functioned in the facility. Prisoners with working light bulbs squatted in their cells making crafts or preparing food. Others sat in complete blackness.

It was fucking depressing.

Despite the obscurity, men and women of all ages milled around the walkways between cellblocks. The guards were grossly outnumbered, and some didn't even wear uniforms. She struggled to distinguish them from the inmates.

Her escort stopped at a cell, where three men huddled together, whispering. A fourth man rushed out and gripped the guard's arm.

"I'm afraid." His lips pulled back, revealing broken teeth. "My cellmates are gang members. Put me somewhere else. Anywhere."

"Back in your cell." The guard shoved the frail man into the dark cage and continued walking.

She jogged to catch up, craning her neck to check on the man as she passed. The distraction cost her.

The guard propelled her into the next cell, and her weakened, tortured body collided with the grimy wall.

A stained, threadbare blanket lay wadded in the corner. Rodent shit and dead bugs littered the concrete floor.

There was no bed. No sink or toilet. No other

inmates. Nothing in the cell except a blanket she wouldn't touch if her life depended on it.

At some point, she would need to empty her bladder and wash the puke from her hair.

"Where's the bathroom?" She glanced back at the guard.

He gestured down the corridor, slammed the barred door, and strolled away.

The door rattled in the frame and bounced open.

A terrible feeling crept into her gut as she rushed forward and tried to bolt the gate.

No lock. No latch. Nothing to keep the door from hanging ajar.

How was she supposed to sleep? She needed the security of a locked cell. She needed to let her guard down and close her eyes, just for a little while.

Two shady middle-aged men sat in the corridor across from her, watching her hold the door closed.

Averting her gaze, she glanced at her sneakers. Desperation moved her into action.

Five minutes later, she backed away from the door and hugged her waist.

Her shoestrings wrapped around the bars, tied in complicated knots, and cinched tight enough to hold the door closed.

The men in the hall had smirked at her while she did it as if she believed a shoestring could protect her. Of course, it wouldn't stop someone from entering, but it would slow them down.

The task had also kept her mind busy. But now that it was finished, she couldn't escape the fear that seeped in with the clamor of shouting and grunting outside her cell.

The deep, rumbling voices of Mexico's worst criminals echoed off the walls and drove her into the corner of her cell.

Reality enclosed her on all sides, weakening her legs and chopping her breaths. Hands clenching with white knuckles, heart pounding, and muscles painfully rigid, she was helpless against the surge of emotions.

She was in the most ruthless prison in Mexico.

Alone.

Unarmed.

Terrified.

If she didn't survive, would anyone know what happened to her? Her sister, her colleagues at the school, her students… Would they learn she'd been wrongfully arrested and left to die in Jaulaso? Or would she become a missing person, never to be found?

Summer break had just begun in the States. She wouldn't be expected back to work for two months.

No one would look for her until school resumed.

No one would be coming to her rescue.

A horrible choking sound rose from her chest and burst past her lips, heaving the air in a series of sobbing gasps.

Her knees gave out, and she slid down the wall, crumpling into a fetal position. She couldn't hold it in any longer. Horror, sadness, panic, and terrible, uncontrollable fear exploded from her in a rain of tears.

She clapped her hands over her mouth and tried to stifle the sounds that would draw attention.

If only she were invisible. Or a time traveler. God help her, she'd give anything to rewind the clock to yesterday morning and ignore her sister's phone call.

But what if Vera was in trouble? Like life-threatening, abducted-by-cartel trouble? Why else would she have not answered her phone?

What if she was dead?

More tears fell, harder now. Louder. Vicious pain wheezed past the fingers she clamped against her mouth.

Her stomach joined in, growling its reminder she hadn't eaten in over twenty-four hours.

She usually ate at the deli down the street. They made the best grilled cheese sandwich with fontina and mozzarella. The tantalizing scent of fresh baked cookies always greeted her when she walked in.

She wished she could smell that now instead of the putrid stench of vomit and misery.

Nausea rose, chasing away her hunger and replacing it with the crippling weight of exhaustion.

Her eyes fluttered closed, and she sat up, fighting sleep as it forced itself upon her.

She won the battle for an hour, maybe two, hugging her knees to her chest, feeling forsaken and panicked in her war against fatigue.

She was doing good until her head bounced with a jolting nod, kicking her awake.

Fuck, she couldn't risk falling asleep. Not until she better understood how to protect herself in this violent place.

She needed to find a friend in here if that were possible. Someone she could trust to watch her back. But she didn't have the confidence or energy to leave her dark corner. Not yet.

As the night dragged on, her body worked against her. Consciousness abandoned her, and pain-drenched dreams pulled her down, down, down.

She woke to the sound of rustling. Metal clanked beside her, and a gust of hot breath washed over her face.

Oh, God. Oh, God. Oh, God. She wasn't alone.

Her pulse slammed into overdrive, and she scrambled backward in the dark.

A cruel hand caught her thigh. Another latched onto her hip and yanked down her jeans.

Her zipper was already open, her shirt shoved to her neck.

Fear found her, whispering to her in a deranged voice. It told her stomach to buckle, her chest to constrict, and her lungs to slam together.

It told her she was going to die.

A scream ripped from her throat as she shoved against the bulk of nude muscle and sticky flesh on top of her.

Whiskers scratched her cheek, and a hot wet mouth covered hers.

She jerked her head to the side and tried to buck him off, but he was too strong, too big.

Meaty fingers shoved her jeans and panties to her knees and wrenched her legs apart.

"No! Get off me!" She yelled louder, an ear-splitting cry for help as she tried to wrestle her thighs together.

His trousers gathered around his knees, his body twice her size, damp with sweat, and flush against the front of her, pinning her to the floor.

The hard jab of his erection pushed against her inner thigh, seeking the bare place between her legs. Her thrashing, frenzied movements wouldn't hinder penetration for long.

She clawed and spat, screamed and tried to shove him off, her hands digging into hairy skin and flexed muscle.

When she felt the leather strap of his belt hanging free, she didn't hesitate to grab hold and yank it from his pants.

He didn't seem to notice, his movements focused on lining himself up to enter her body.

The belt swung free, and her hands moved on instinct as she looped it around his neck and twisted the ends into a noose.

She wasn't a violent person. Never used her fists. Never picked fights. Except that one time when she woke with a scorpion in her bed.

She'd gone ballistic at the sight of it crawling beside her head and grabbed whatever she could use as a weapon—a lamp, a pillow, a shoe.

Once she'd started attacking it, she was committed. She'd turned into something savage and feral, beating the ever-loving hell out of it long after its guts smeared the floor, pieces of it scattered the room, and the carnage no longer twitched.

She channeled that murderous aggression now, operating outside of her body as every muscle burned to choke, maim, and destroy until he lay as dead as that fucking scorpion.

It was the hardest, most grueling thing she'd ever done. Her arms shook with the effort to cinch the belt as tightly as possible for as long as it took.

He fought with his weight, rolling across the floor in a breathless rage. Elbows landed against her ribs. His massive torso flopped and flailed, crushing her against the wall.

But she hung on, mindless in her need to survive, to follow through until the last trickle of life left his body.

"He's dead." A masculine voice drifted from the cell door.

She flinched, heart racing, and whipped her head toward the silhouette.

Dressed in a prison guard uniform, the man leaned against the metal frame, arms crossed over his chest as if he'd been there a while.

"Why didn't you help me?" She released the belt and stumbled to her feet, yanking her jeans into place. "He tried to rape me!"

Oh, sweet Jesus, she killed a man. Were there consequences for that in Jaulaso?

Murderers probably murdered other murderers every day here. Did the prison guards look the other way? Or did they haul the offenders outside in front of a firing squad?

A tremor raced through her as she stared down at the lifeless body. She did that. One day behind bars, and she strangled a man until he stopped breathing.

"It was self-defense." Gulping to catch her breath, she staggered to the farthest wall, away from the dead man and the prison guard who studied her too carefully. "Were you here the whole time?"

"You're from the States." He tilted his head, and a gray ponytail fell over his shoulder. "And you speak Spanish."

"Yes." She hadn't heard or spoken an English word since her arrest. If she hadn't known the local language, she would've been more lost than she already was.

"Your options are limited, but you have some." He sucked on his teeth, watching her. "Money is one of them."

"What do you mean? Money for what?"

"I'll take you to a better place." He held out a hand. "If you pay."

"Pay?" She blinked at his waiting palm. "I don't have—"

"If it was on you during your arrest, you still have it. The military isn't interested in stealing money."

She shoved a hand into her back pocket and pulled out the two-hundred dollars she'd kept at Vera's house.

Her breath rushed out in relief.

She held out the cash to him, but at the last second, she yanked it back. "Where would you take me?"

"Area Three."

She had no idea what that was. "Would I have my own cell with a lock?"

"Maybe, but it doesn't matter. You'll have protection."

"I don't understand."

"You're too pretty." His gaze dipped, flitting down her legs before returning to her eyes. "Prettiest thing Jaulaso has ever seen. You won't make it a week on this side. Pay me, and I'll take you to a safer, more suitable living environment. Area Three protects its own."

How did she know this guard wasn't just trying to scam her out of money?

He leaned in and lowered his voice. "You'll have many luxuries there, including your own toilet and phone."

"I'll be able to make phone calls? To whomever I want?"

"Yes."

For the first time since she was ripped from her Jeep, her chest lifted with hope.

Maybe he was lying. She wouldn't know for sure unless she accepted his offer, which was inarguably better than waiting for the next rapist to sneak into her cell.

She sure as fuck didn't want to hang around until another guard walked in and found her with a dead body.

"Okay." She handed him the money.

"Come with me."

THREE

The prison guard led Tula through the overcrowded corridors of Jaulaso, seemingly oblivious to the fact that every inch of her was shaking against a storm of doubt and fear.

How could she trust this man, who had just watched her fight off a rapist without stepping in to help? It felt like a setup as if he knew she would be attacked, and he was just waiting for the right moment to make her an offer she couldn't refuse.

But if he wanted her money, he could've just taken it. He carried a rifle, for fuck's sake.

The brutal stress of this waking nightmare kinked painful knots in her neck. Her legs wobbled like jelly as she tried to keep up. The reek of cigarette smoke assaulted her nose, the filth in the air so palpable it made her gag.

How did these people live like this? Sure, they were criminals, and most of them probably deserved to be here. But how many were innocent like her? How many had been forgotten and left here to die?

The backs of her eyes grew achy as she fixed them

on the long gray ponytail of the guard in front of her.

He ushered her through a metal door and into an outdoor yard, surrounded by two-story walls capped in barbed wire.

Nighttime had fallen, dark and humid. Another day lost.

She'd been gone forty-eight hours. Who would collect her mail, water her plants, and pay her landlord for next month's rent?

No one.

Even *if* she managed to reach her sister on the phone, she couldn't trust Vera to pay her bills. Access to her bank account would be too tempting.

Vera would drain her savings. Not that she had savings. She lived paycheck-to-paycheck, and those paychecks would stop if she didn't show up on the first day of school.

Two months.

She would be out of here by then.

The prison guard escorted her across the yard to another door. A young Hispanic man in civilian clothing stood beside it with a rifle resting on his shoulder.

Was he an inmate? She'd heard stories about how the cartels ruled the prisons inside their cities, but she never imagined their presence being so blatant. This guy was staring down her uniformed escort with an automatic rifle in his hand.

Was it true, then? Did the cartel have more power than the prison guards?

Her stomach tilted. Maybe this wasn't her best option.

The armed inmate knocked on the entrance behind him without removing his eyes from her. Deadbolts sounded, and the door opened to a large indoor common area.

Rap music thumped from somewhere inside. Scantily dressed Latina women danced around a table of smiling men and beer bottles. Guys wearing bandannas and wife-beaters played pool. Others stood around laughing among themselves, not paying any attention to the lost woman in the doorway.

There was no stench of death and despair. No overcrowding. Plenty of room to walk around and keep to herself. It looked like a casual house party with friends. Nothing like a prison.

A man stepped into her line of sight, blocking her view. Dressed in a black shirt and trousers, he wore a wreath of gold chains around his thick neck.

"Follow me," he said in Spanish and lumbered away without waiting.

She glanced back, and her prison guard was gone.

Unease gripped her spine. Curiosity tingled her senses. She knew what lay behind her. Whatever waited ahead had to be better.

She jogged to catch up with the guy in gold chains, relieved that the men in the common area didn't leer or try to approach her.

"We have everything here." Her escort guided her through one room after another, gesturing at sectioned-off areas, each serving a different purpose, like a makeshift marketplace. "We have a bar, laundry, restaurant, outdoor gym, health care clinic, recreation area, and canteen that sells food, water, and things for grooming."

The service stations were sad imitations of real places. Each area was pieced together with crates, scrap wood, mismatched furniture, and whatever they could get their hands on to make it work. But the ingenuity behind it was impressive. It almost felt like a tiny mall inside a hotel.

Almost.

As he led her into a maze of corridors, she studied him inconspicuously. His Hispanic features were darker than hers. Darker complexion, browner eyes, blacker hair, and bushy eyebrows.

His whiskered jaw hovered in that awkward stage between a scruffy shadow and a squirrelly beard. Despite his need to sculpt his facial hair, he wasn't terrible looking.

A little bony through the shoulders and rough around the edges, he was probably in his forties. It hadn't been an easy forty years, given the scars marring his arms and peeking through the open collar of his shirt.

"Do you know where you are?" He turned a corner, his strides never slowing.

"Jaulaso." Her brows pinched together.

"Sure, but do you know which side this is?"

"No."

"This is Area Three." He lifted his chin, his expression fiercely proud. "Home of La Rocha Cartel."

La Rocha.

The most aggressive, most organized, most violent cartel in existence.

They were *here*? Inside these walls?

Her shoulders squeezed forward.

The things they did to women… Oh, God. She'd heard stories growing up about how La Rocha members freely raped, maimed, disfigured, and beheaded any female they set their eyes on. They impregnated girls just to crush the babies under their boots after they were born.

She hugged herself at the elbows.

Maybe it wasn't true.

A shiver slid across her scalp. She felt so small, so naive and fearful, just like the helpless, wide-eyed girl she once was, listening to her mother whisper chilling stories meant to scare guileless daughters away from cartel.

"Pick up your feet." The man glared at her from the end of the hall. "Faster."

She hadn't meant to fall behind, but *fuck him*. He was lucky she wasn't sobbing on the floor. That was what she wanted to do. She desperately needed to fall apart.

"Here is your cell." He ushered her into a small concrete room.

In the corner, a mattress sat on a metal frame. Her shoulders loosened at the sight of the fluffy pillow and the clean-looking white sheets folded beneath it.

A blanket spread over the bed with a llama on it. A llama wearing a sombrero and smiling with big teeth. It looked chillingly perverse in the context of its surroundings, but there were no stains or ratty holes in the fabric.

Definitely an upgrade from the last cell.

Moonlight slanted through a tiny barred window near the ceiling. Artificial light flickered from a bare bulb over a single sink that jutted from the wall. Beside it sat a toilet.

The surfaces appeared reasonably clean.

No bugs or mouse drippings on the floor.

No creepy inmates loitering outside the door.

Better yet, the door was solid. She would be able to close it, and no one would see in. "Is there a lock?"

"No." He removed an old cell phone from his pocket and tossed it on the bed. "We control all cell phone use within the prison. That's yours."

"I can make calls to the States? Whenever I want?"

"Yes."

The device was a basic model, the kind that couldn't access email or the Internet. But it would do what she needed it to do. She would be able to call her sister, her boss, a lawyer, and make arrangements for her monthly bills.

She could do this. For a month or two, she could manage her life in Phoenix from the confines of this room. She could keep everything together until she returned. She was going to be okay.

The tension in her body dissolved, muscle by muscle, breath by breath. Until she heard the sound of foil crinkling behind her.

"Now, you pay the rent," he said at her back.

Her heart shriveled, and her lungs lost air. She didn't need to turn around to see the condom in his hand or the expectation in his eyes. She knew exactly what form of payment he intended to collect.

"No." She spun away and stumbled backward across the room. "I'm not doing that. I'll pay another way."

"Maybe you'll come up with something next week, but this is how you pay now." He unlatched his belt. "Get on the bed."

She shook her head wildly, tears rising and burning. This wasn't happening. She couldn't do it. She wouldn't.

"I was promised safety." Her legs trembled uncontrollably, shuffling her away until her back hit the wall. "I paid that guard to bring me to a better place. He said I would have protection here."

She'd been too desperate to believe him, blindly holding onto a grain of hope so that she wouldn't completely lose it.

"You don't like the arrangement?" He charged toward her. "Then you go back." He gripped her hair and hauled her toward the door.

"No! Wait!" She reached for the phone, arms outstretched as the bed blurred by, too far away. "Please, don't send me back. I'll work. I can cook, wash clothes, clean bathrooms. I'll do anything!"

"You do *this.*" He grabbed her hips and ground his erection against her backside. "Or you go back and let a dozen men take a turn with you every night."

Bile simmered in her chest, and her breaths heaved through great, choking sobs.

"No. Please, anything else." She thrashed in his arms, her feet scrambling across the floor as he dragged her into the hall. She needed that phone, the private toilet, the soft bed… "Please, don't send me back."

"You pay the rent or go."

His indifference about whether she stayed crushed her willpower. Fighting him only quickened his strides as if he couldn't wait to be rid of her. He'd given her a choice and wouldn't bend the rules. She wasn't worth the trouble.

She was nothing to him.

A low, agony-soaked sound gurgled in her throat as resignation sucked the life from her limbs. "I'll pay."

He didn't give her time to change her mind. Turning back, he hauled her into her cell and tossed her on the mattress, face down. A zipper sounded behind her, followed by the tear of a condom packet.

Violent, full-body tremors chattered her teeth and rattled the metal frame of the bed.

She couldn't move, couldn't bring herself to look behind her. She just lay there, frozen in shock and horror, aching to be anywhere but here facing what was about to happen.

Her body stiffened with the instinct to protect itself, everything inside her screaming to kick, bite, and come unhinged. But fighting him wouldn't get her that phone.

The device lay inches from her face. Her only way out of this nightmare.

As he wrenched down her jeans and panties, her

fingernails stabbed into her palms.

As he forced himself into her dehydrated body, something broke inside her.

As he pounded the singed, electrocuted flesh between her legs, she swallowed her cries, buried the anguish, and didn't make a sound.

But her silence came at a price.

The only way to hold still beneath the violation was to shed the pieces of herself that cared. With each merciless thrust, she lost her naiveté, her kindness, and her hope in mankind. She carved up the vulnerable parts that wouldn't survive in Jaulaso and let it all go.

Gentle, sentimental fragments of her existence tore away and crumbled to dust, and she knew she would never get those pieces back. Something hard and unfeeling filled the jagged gaps.

Her mind contorted and adjusted, trying to protect itself, to become immune to the damage. She felt herself grow cold and vacant, hardening like a concrete wall.

But she had fractures. God, they were everywhere, letting in the pain from his thrusts, the anguish of being used so despicably, and the fear of tomorrow, and the next day, and the month after that.

She mentally repaired the cracks, stopped the leaks, and shut out the agony. It was a lonely, excruciating effort. As she toughened herself against the stabbing motion of his hips, her edges started to splinter.

The threat of tears burned her throat. It would be so easy to release her grief in a fit of sobbing cries. Maybe someone would hear and take pity on her. Maybe this man would stop hurting her and feel horrible about what he'd done. Maybe, just maybe, her tears would make all this go away.

That wouldn't happen. No one would feel sorry for

her. No one would come to her rescue.

She was in Jaulaso. To survive, she needed to become like them.

Wrapping herself in coldness, she erected shields, closed mental doors, and formed layers of impenetrable resilience.

I will not cry.

I will not show weakness.

I will bear this, bury it, and survive.

A strangled groan sounded behind her, and the weight on her back disappeared.

She looked down at her balled hands and uncurled her fingers. Blood trickled from crescent-shaped gouges in her palms and soaked her nail beds.

The pain didn't register.

She slowly rose, pulled up her jeans with numb fingers, and turned to meet his eyes. "What's your name?"

"Garra." He fastened his pants and ran a hand over his black hair, slicking the strands into place.

"Congratulations, Garra. You forced yourself on an unarmed woman half your size. Your mother must be proud." Her voice echoed in her head with icy detachment. "If you ever touch me again, I'll kill you."

"Welcome to your new home, Petula Gomez." His gaze swept over her with the same detachment. "Rent is due again next week."

FOUR

Austin, Texas
Two years ago

Ricky Saldivar knocked on the front door of Van Quiso's cabin and tore a hand through his hair.

Why had he even bothered styling it? He'd raked his fingers through the gelled pompadour cut so many times on the way here it probably looked like he just crawled out of bed. After hours of fucking.

It was nerves. Completely normal. Not that he was a nervous guy. It was just…

Christ, he was at Van's house. Standing on the motherfucker's front porch. Willingly.

This wasn't normal. Not even in the same realm.

Shifting beneath the overhead light, he squinted at his reflection in the glass door and tried to fix his hair. The longer strands on top spiked in every direction, refusing to be tamed.

Why the fuck was he fussing over his appearance?

Nerves.

Excitement.

Anticipation.

All of it coursed through him in fitful waves.

He knocked again and slipped his hands into his front pockets.

The deadbolt turned. It twisted three more times before the door opened.

Van's wife stood on the other side, wearing a tight red-as-sin minidress and a tremulous smile.

"Hi, Ricky." Amber Quiso chewed her lip, her gaze flitting restlessly over the dark front yard. "Sorry to make you wait. I...I was having a moment. Nothing major. You know, I'm... Sometimes, I slip and... Ugh, save me from this rambling."

"It's good to see you. You look beautiful, as always."

"Thank you." She smoothed her palms down the front of the dress and cleared her voice. "He's waiting."

She didn't move to let him inside, her eyes stark as she directed them at her bare feet.

He'd only met her a couple of times in passing and knew she struggled with some disorders, one of them being a fear of open spaces. Just the thought of stepping outside used to freak her the fuck out. She supposedly had a better handle on that now but still had bad days.

"Amber?"

"Yeah? Shit. Yes. I mean, what?" She seemed to snap out of a simmering panic attack. "Sorry, I was...listening to my heartbeats. *Not* counting them. I wasn't counting. Because I'm okay. Really. I'm just a little off. Not that I'm crazy or whatever you've heard..."

"You don't want to keep him waiting." He nodded behind her, expecting her to let him in.

"He's around back. Outside. I'm supposed to take you." She pointed at the path that led around the side of the house. “The long way. *Bastard.*” She whispered the last word with a huff.

“Okay.” He stepped off the porch and waited for her to join him.

She didn’t move, her hands balling at her sides and her jaw rigidly locked.

Maybe Van demanded this from her as a form of therapy? Or perhaps he just liked to torment her? He was a sadist, after all, which was precisely why Ricky had requested this meeting.

“I assume Van told you the reason I’m here.”

“Yeah.” Her gaze lifted to his. “Are you sure you want this?”

“I know what I need. *Who* I need it with is another story.” He laughed under his breath but didn’t feel the humor in it. “I’d choose anyone but him. Believe me, I’ve tried. But…”

“He’s the best.”

The best at beating, tormenting, and fucking someone into the most violent, life-changing orgasms known to man.

The only other person who would even come close to bringing Ricky to his knees was his best friend, Martin.

But Martin was straight.

And homophobic.

An impossible fantasy.

“Yeah.” He blew out a breath. “Van’s the best at being a real asshole.”

“Oh, but he’s a beautiful, loyal asshole.” She stepped onto the porch and inhaled deeply. “He doesn’t want to hurt you. He only agreed to do this because he wants to *help* you.”

“I know.”

“We’re monogamous.”

He tilted his face toward the night sky and closed his eyes. "Look, I'm not here to steal your husband." He met her gaze. "I don't even like the guy."

"But you're attracted to him."

"He's...compelling."

Even when Van had hurt him beyond his extremely high pain threshold, whipped him until he passed out, and fucked his throat to the point of suffocation, he thought his captor was the sexiest, most viciously captivating male in existence.

Until he met Martin Lockwood.

Martin and his goddamn megawatt smile, Viking warrior build, overbearing protectiveness, and vigilant pale eyes… Everything about the man kindled a roaring need in Ricky, one that wasn't reciprocated and never would be.

Jesus fuck, get over it already.

"He'll give you what you came for." Amber anchored her fists on the toned curves of her hips. "But he won't fuck you."

"Story of my life," he muttered too low for her to hear.

"What?"

"Nothing."

She raised her chin, her tone barbed with ferocity. "No intercourse and no kissing on the mouth. Those are *my* rules."

"Okay…" He cast her a concerned look. "If you're not comfortable with this, I'll go. I don't want to cause problems."

"I agreed to it." She clutched her throat and glanced around before giving him her eyes. "He raped me, too, Ricky. Whatever you're feeling, the filthy things he planted in your head, his taunting voice in your ear whenever you're alone, the shameful memories… I understand all of it. But unlike you, I get to spend every night with him, working through it and repairing the parts he fractured. If you need this from him, I'm cool with it." She shoved back her shoulders. "As long as you remember he belongs to *me*."

"You're a possessive little thing." He grinned.

"With him? You bet your ass."

"No betting needed, considering I'm about to hand my ass over to him."

"Good." She smiled.

"Good." He nodded at the path. "Shall we?"

She breezed past him, navigating the steppingstones with the grace of a beauty queen.

"No one else has sought him out like this." She peered at him beneath her lashes as she made her way around the side of the cabin. "I mean, other than Camila asking him to help with her vigilante work, you're the only one of his…uh…"

"Ex-slaves. You can call us that."

She nodded. "You're the only ex-slave who has reached out to him. He appreciates your trust more than you know, but I'm curious…"

"Why am I here instead of plotting his death like my roommates?"

"Yeah." She padded along the lit path, her expression pinched with wariness.

"Pain makes you stronger, and time heals all wounds. Blah, blah, blah… I'm sure there's truth in that, but to be honest, I sympathized with him and Liv when I found out they were forced into that life."

Back in the day, long before Van met Amber, Van had a hard-on for Liv Reed. He and Liv had made quite the dysfunctional, human-sex-trafficking duo.

Over six years, they enslaved five males and two females. Camila Dias had been their first. Ricky was slave number two.

The night Ricky was captured, he'd taken one look at Liv and followed his dick. The alluring, irresistible beauty had led him out of the dance club, into her car, and straight into shackles with an unspoken promise of fun, kinky, *consensual* sex.

Unbeknown to him, she'd drugged his beer at the bar, which had caused him to black out during the drive. But that wasn't why he ended up in her car in the first place.

He'd wanted her, despite her scarred face, and when he saw Van with a matching scar, he wanted both of them. Separately. At the same time. Any way he could get them.

Apparently, gorgeous criminals were his weakness. He was shallow and reckless like that.

But at the time, he hadn't known what he wanted. Not completely.

"Before Van, I didn't know I was bisexual." He stopped walking and waited for Amber to glance back. "I always knew I wasn't like other guys, but I didn't know how or why until I was chained in Van's attic."

"Oh." She pulled in a slow breath and turned to face him. "He was your first?"

"I'd been with women, but never with a man. Not until him."

"I'm sorry." She cringed. "I imagine he didn't break you in gently."

"No." He laughed with a grimace. "During those godawful months with him… Jesus, he fucked me up so badly I thought I was going to die. But the experience opened my mind. It forced me to examine my curiosities, desires, and all the socially unacceptable things I would've never explored on my own."

"He broke you and put the pieces back together the way they were meant to be."

"Exactly."

It felt good to talk about this, and she seemed to relate to him on a level most people didn't. Because Van had put her through the same hell.

"Had he not subjected me to the things he did…" He gripped the back of his neck. "I don't think I would've ever acknowledged my bisexuality or my need to be dominated in bed. It's crazy that I feel grateful to him for that, considering the nightmares and years of mental trauma he caused me."

But he had time and distance on his side. It'd been eight years since his captivity. Nine years for Camila. Every day was easier than the last.

That was the only reason he was able to face Van tonight.

His roommates—Tomas, Luke, Martin, Tate, and Kate—didn't have as many years to heal. Not yet. They would come around eventually, and maybe someday, they would forgive Van's cruelty.

Even so, the decision to pick up the phone and call Van hadn't been an easy one. It had taken him a year of dialing and hanging up before he let the call go through.

He didn't know if Van would reject him or if he was even ready to take this step with his former captor. He didn't know if he would ever be ready.

"I'm growing impatient." The deep baritone punched from the tree line behind the house, shooting a delicious shiver down Ricky's spine.

Amber must've felt it, too, because her shoulders gave a little shudder.

"It's not too late to change your mind." She squinted

at the trees through the darkness.

Not a chance in hell. But he needed to ask. "Do you want me to back out?"

She shook her head, her lips bowing in a seductive smile. "I've always wanted to know what he's like with a man."

Since sex was off-limits, she wouldn't see Van in all his depraved glory. But one thing was certain. Van would find a way to torture them both, holding them right on that precarious edge between pain and pleasure until they begged for mercy.

"Let's do this." His heart raced as he nudged her across the backyard toward the woods, his gaze probing the shadows, searching for Van's intimidating silhouette.

When he called Van yesterday, they didn't discuss rules or negotiate how this would go, which was ironic considering Ricky had endured months of Van's sexual training bound by a rigid list of requirements. But those had been set by the slave buyer.

Van had no use for rules, laws, principles, or anything that resembled BDSM. He did what he wanted, however he wanted, and it was rarely safe or sane. Tonight, however, it would be consensual.

For the first time, Ricky would surrender to Van's will because he wanted this. He *needed* the relief of an assertive, confident hand.

He'd said as much on the phone when he told Van about his botched dating life, failed foray in the local fetish community, and overall disappointment in male lovers.

He longed to be with someone more alpha than himself. His one-night stands always seemed to fit that mold, until he got them in bed. No matter how many people he fucked—and the list was depressingly long—he hadn't found a lover who could master him on a natural level. It always felt…forced.

After he'd explained all this, he said the words he never imagined uttering to Van.

I need a release, the kind only you can give.

Van's gravelly response had been sharp, swift, and arousing beyond belief.

Come to me.

Ricky shivered as he slowed at the tree line, his gaze connecting with Van's silvery, moonlit eyes in the shadows.

A toothpick lolled at the corner of the imposing man's full lips, his scar etching a monstrous seam in an otherwise flawless face.

As gorgeous as he was terrifying, he was built like a mountain and somehow managed to stare down at Ricky, even as they stood at the same height.

"Van." Blood rushed to Ricky's groin, hardening him behind the zipper.

"Ricardo."

"Don't call me—"

"It's your given name. Grown men don't go by *Ricky*." Van stepped into his space and ghosted the back of a finger across his whiskered jaw. "You've definitely grown since the last time you choked on my cock."

Ricky had added a significant amount of muscle mass over the past eight years. The fact that it hadn't gone unnoticed thrilled him more than it should have.

"Will I be doing that tonight? Choking on your dick?" His breathing quickened, his erection a hot throbbing heartbeat in his jeans.

"No." Van grinned around the toothpick. "I only get hard for my wife. I'll put my hands on you, but you won't touch me. Or her. If you do, we're finished. Understood?"

"Yes, sir."

"Lose the *sir* bullshit. You're not here to stroke my ego."

"God knows it doesn't need to be stroked." Amber stood a few feet away with one brow arched.

Van slowly cut his razored eyes in her direction, and her sassy eyebrow slipped beneath an *oh-shit* expression.

He prowled toward her, gripped her hair, and wrenched her face to his. "How many times did you turn the deadbolt when he arrived?"

Her alarmed gaze flicked to Ricky.

"Don't look at him." Van spat the toothpick on the ground. "Answer me."

She stared up at her husband and licked her lips. "Four times."

"And your knuckles? How many times did you crack them?"

"Zero."

"Good girl." His fist in her hair loosened into a soft, petting stroke.

She nuzzled into the affection and purred so low and profoundly the sound seemed to come from the depths of her soul.

A knot of envy squeezed Ricky's chest, his entire body burning for that soul-reaching touch.

"Sit." Van directed Amber to the edge of a wooden table nestled in the trees.

Ricky hadn't noticed it until now, but the piece of furniture must've weighed a thousand pounds, given the huge chunky legs and wide top. Made of raw wood, the surface was sanded down and sealed with shiny lacquer.

She perched on the ledge, her bare feet dangling above the grass. If she spread her thighs, her pussy would be level with Van's groin. No doubt the height had been designed for exactly that reason.

A closer look at the thick tree trunks around the table revealed hardware—eye bolts, levers, and leather straps—mounted in the bark at varying positions.

With the nearest neighbor miles away, no one would hear a scream on Van's property. The debauchery that occurred here on the regular was probably illegal in most countries.

Amber was one lucky bitch.

Van clasped his hands behind his back and prowled a tight circle around Ricky, penetrating skin and nerves with his intoxicating heat.

"Tell me why you're here," Van breathed against his nape, "instead of at home fucking your best friend."

"Martin?" His pulse sped up. "Why would you assume we're more than friends?"

"Why wouldn't you be? He's the only one in your house who can give you what you need."

"He's straight."

"No." Van laughed, loud and derisively. "He's not."

"Just because you forced him—"

"He hasn't told you." Van tilted his head, his glare sharp and scrutinizing. "Here I thought there were no secrets between you and your roommates."

"What hasn't he told me?" Ricky ground his teeth.

"How he ended up in my attic."

Martin didn't talk about that. Whenever questions were directed at him about his abduction or the time he spent with Van and Liv, he turned heel and vacated the room.

"I assume Liv lured him," Ricky said.

"Guess again."

"You?" His head flinched back. "You took him at gunpoint?"

"I didn't use a weapon or any kind of force."

"What are you saying?" Suspicion tensed his neck. "Did you manipulate him?"

"Not exactly." Van removed a toothpick from his pocket and set it between his molars. "He's your best friend. Ask him yourself."

"I have. He refuses to discuss it."

"Sounds like trouble in paradise." His smirk oozed with ridicule.

"Fuck you."

Van was on him in a blink, an iron fist around his throat and cutting his air as he was slammed face down onto the table beside Amber.

"I'll tell you the real reason you're here." Van ground Ricky's cheek against the wood.

"Enlighten me."

"You want to make him jealous. Ignite that possessive rage he can't control when it comes to you. What better way to provoke him than to return home, flushed and sated in the afterglow of another man's enjoyment? You'll tell him that man was me just to get a rise out of him. He'll shove you into a wall, bruise you with his strong hands, and you'll eat up every second of that physical contact. How am I doing so far?"

That was exactly how it would play out.

"How about you shut the fuck up and hurt me already?" Ricky bared his teeth. "Make me *feel*."

"Put your arms behind you." Van released him. "Cross them against your back and grip your elbows."

His skin heated as he obeyed without hesitation.

He didn't want to think, question, or second-guess this. It was simple. He had an itch and was seeking out someone who excelled at scratching hard-to-reach places.

Heart thundering, he tracked the tread of Van's footsteps through the trees and around the table until the sound paused near his head.

"I'm not going to restrain you." Van bent down, brushing his lips against Ricky's ear. "You are bound by your own will. If you release your elbows, I will stop and send your ass home."

"Got it." He locked his fingers around the crooks of his arms.

"Amber." Van shifted toward his wife. "Lie back. Palms flat on the table."

She moved into position, face up beside Ricky. He remained chest down with his face angled toward her.

Van gripped her waist and pulled, sliding her along the table until her head hung off the edge, upside down.

Ricky knew where this was going, and so did she, given the swallow that jogged in her throat.

Anticipation lengthened his cock, trapping it at a painful angle between his hips and the table. The sound of Van's zipper made him impossibly harder.

Then he saw it, the long stiff evidence of Van Quiso's arousal.

Van rested his erection over her gaping mouth like an offering, teasing the shaft across her lips.

She licked at it, panting and squirming, all while keeping her hands flat on the table at her sides.

A groan escaped Ricky as Van fed her his dick, inch by steely inch. When he reached the back of her throat, she swallowed rapidly without gagging.

Ricky could've done the same. In that soundproof attic, Van had fucked his face until his gag reflex no longer existed.

"Put your fingers in your pussy." Van thrust his hips, his breathing accelerating. "Work it hard. I want a puddle under your ass."

The blow job lasted forever and not long enough.

From inches away, he watched Van's cock sink and retreat, over and over. He lay so close to them the musk of their hunger infused his inhales.

He focused on clutching his elbows and tried to not come. His orgasm hovered right there. If he ground his groin against the table, he would blow.

And this would be over.

Finally, Van pulled free from her mouth and angled toward Ricky. Gripping the base of his dick, he slowly dragged his fist to the tip and squeezed out a bead of pre-come.

He swiped his thumb over it, catching the clear drop, and pressed it between Ricky's lips. "Suck."

Hollowing his cheeks, he sucked Van's thumb the way Van had taught him—hard, consistent, and with a firm tongue.

The subtle tang of Van's essence teased his taste buds. The breathy sounds of Van's groans fueled his need for more.

"Fuck, I haven't forgotten your mouth," Van rasped. "Martin doesn't know what he's missing." He slid his thumb across Ricky's bottom lip. "Don't give up on him."

It was a lost cause. If he pushed Martin much harder, he risked ruining their friendship.

Van circled the table, stopped behind Ricky, and helped Amber into a sitting position.

"So fucking wet, baby." A groan rumbled in Van's chest as he thrust a hand between her legs, fingering her until the squelching sounds of her arousal hit the air. "Jesus, you make me so damn hard. Sit just like that. Don't move."

Van turned his attention to Ricky, divesting him of his shoes, jeans, and everything he wore from the waist down.

A few hard kicks shoved his feet apart, and he didn't fight it. Didn't cower or lose his shit as the sound of Van's leather belt whistled through the air.

The first strike against his ass stopped his heart. He didn't find his breath before the next fiery smack landed on the back of his thigh.

"Fuuuuuck!" He'd forgotten how goddamn hard Van hit.

The son of a bitch didn't hold back, didn't pause for breaks, didn't give a millimeter of mercy. He wailed and whipped and annihilated Ricky's backside until everything burned—his skin, muscle, bone, organs.

With his legs spread so wide and his junk hanging unprotected between his thighs, Van made sure that leather strap caught the back of his ball sac as often as possible. It was torture by fire.

Ricky could release his elbows at any time and put an end to the ungodly pain. Maybe Van would break his promise and keep going until Ricky lay broken and bleeding.

But Amber trusted Van. Camila trusted him, and deep down, Ricky did, too. He wouldn't have come here if he thought he would be powerless.

That was the appeal, wasn't it? To be with Van on an equal playing field? It was something he'd never experienced beneath Van's whip.

But it hurt. Holy fuck, it took everything he had to keep his hands fastened to his elbows and his legs spread, exposing his tender balls.

Just when he thought he wouldn't survive another strike, Van dropped the belt. Clothing rustled, and Van's shirt fell to the ground.

Then the rock-hard terrain of Van's abs lowered against Ricky's arms, where they folded at his back. He wished he were shirtless, too, so he could feel the damp warmth of Van's skin.

Sultry breath visited his ear, followed by the press of Van's erection against the back of his balls, flesh on flesh, heat on heat.

He felt the power in the body mashed against his, the strength of muscle flexing around him. Blood scorched through his veins, a fire Van smoldered hotter and thicker with each drive of his hips.

To accept the touch of a man, appreciate the sound of a deep masculine groan, and long for a presence bigger and more rugged than himself… Ricky hadn't known he coveted these things until Van had shoved his face in it.

Exhibitionism was another turn on, thanks to Van. As much as he despised what had been done to him in that attic, there had been tantalizing moments amid the misery. Moments that had involved Liv.

She hadn't participated in the sodomy, but Van often made her watch. Her presence had changed the dynamics somehow. Made Ricky feel less alone.

He'd started to crave her eyes on him, became addicted to an outsider's attention.

Eight years later, he still hungered for the rare hookup with another couple, when one of them watched for a while before joining in.

Like now.

He angled his neck to steal a view of Amber.

She sat stiffly beside his hips, her gaze fixed on Van's cock and her hand thrusting between her spread legs. Lips parted, she breathed heavily, noisily, breathtakingly stunning in her flushed state of lust.

Leave it to Van to marry the hottest woman in Texas.

What would it be like to spend a night in their bed, naked and grinding between them?

The greedy parts of him ached for a pair of lovers. Wanted them to hold him, kiss him fiercely, fuck him hard, and love him deeply. Rough and sweaty. Raw and honest.

To bask in the unapologetic passion of a man like Van, to experience the possessive love of a woman like Amber… That would be something worth fighting for.

"She's every man's fantasy." Van reached under Ricky's hips and gripped his engorged cock, causing his breath to strangle. "But if you don't take your fucking eyes off her, I'll remove them from your face."

Van squeezed his dick so ruthlessly a roar tore from his throat. It felt as though his manhood—balls and all—was being ripped from his body.

"Okay, stop!" His fingers started to slip from his elbows. He adjusted his grip and turned his face into the table. "Not looking. My eyes are closed. Please, just stop!"

Van's fist relaxed, finger by finger, and began a slow, sensual slide along Ricky's length.

Pain morphed into pleasure as each stroke melted through his groin and tightened his nuts.

"Oh, God." He rocked his hips, thrusting into that strong, confident handhold.

Blissful tremors rippled through him, gathering low and deep, pulsing to erupt. The pressure, the rhythm, and the caress of masculine fingers felt as stimulating as his own hand. Better even. Fucking perfect.

Van had married a woman, but sweet lord almighty, he still knew how to master a cock.

Lowering to a crouch, Van repositioned his grip, reaching between Ricky's legs from behind and pulling his erection backward until it angled toward the ground, parallel with his thigh. Then he stroked harder, faster, twisting his fist along the length.

"I'm not going to last." Ricky grunted, his body

shaking in his effort to hold off his release.

"Yes, you will." Van's gravelly voice brushed across his ass.

That dangerous mouth hovered between his legs, taunting him with heavy breaths.

He rocked his forehead on the table, his chest rising and falling in sync with Van's strokes. The rush of orgasm threatened, throbbing toward detonation.

Right there. Oh, fuck, right there.

Van's hand stopped moving and squeezed right below the head of Ricky's cock. His thumb and forefinger applied firm pressure, pushing back blood and forcing the climax to retreat.

A moan hit his throat and stuck there. He struggled for air, wrestled to keep his arms locked in position, while directing his frustration into the pained expression that strained his face.

Beside him, Amber's whimpers grew louder, faster, and he realized Van's other hand was between her legs.

A moment later, that hand moved to Ricky's backside, and drenched fingers sank into the crack of his ass.

There was no teasing, no warm-up, before Van forced a digit deep inside him, using only the lubrication from Amber's arousal.

With a sharp grunt, he lifted on his toes and choked against the wicked invasion.

Another finger penetrated. Then a third. Stretching, pounding, Van impaled his rectum with one hand while the other jerked him off in twisting, merciless strokes.

The assault scorched flesh and nerve endings, shooting trails of fire through his body in every direction.

Teeth grazed his buttocks. Then firm lips and an aggressively hot tongue. Van's mouth was the sweetest torment, tasting his skin, sucking the welts, and licking the crevice between his flexing glutes.

Feverish currents zinged beneath Van's grip and ignited around the fingers that pushed viciously hard inside him. He unraveled, biting down on his moan with clenched teeth until the sound escaped in a guttural growl.

Goddamn, it felt too deep. Yet he wanted more. Hands and fingers weren't enough. He needed more than a touch, more than a night, more than a borrowed lover.

But Van held him there, working his body toward that blissful edge. His legs shook against the force of pleasure, thrumming to burst.

"Now." Van tightened his strokes and sank his teeth into the back of Ricky's balls.

A titanic surge of ecstasy poured out of him. He groaned and lost his grip on his elbows, slamming his hands onto the table as he emptied himself onto the ground.

He collapsed against the wooden surface, twitching with residual tremors, his breaths gusting past his lips.

Behind him, Van rose and slid a hand down the length of Ricky's spine over the t-shirt.

He arched into the caress, clinging to the unexpected tenderness, needing that simple touch more than anything Van had offered him tonight.

Too soon, Van pulled back, straightening his pants and collecting Ricky's clothes.

Nighttime critters sang softly amid the surrounding trees as Ricky dressed and slipped on his shoes. Then he turned toward the beautiful couple.

Amber hadn't moved from the table, her minidress gathered around her waist. Van stood sideways in the *V* of her legs, with his hip pressed against her pussy, concealing her nudity.

She curled around his side, her cheek on his shoulder and fingers toying with the unbuttoned fly of his jeans. He was still hard, his bulge straining the zipper beneath her roving hand.

They weren't finished. Not with each other.

That was his cue to leave.

"Thank you." He glanced at Amber then met Van's steel-colored gaze. "I needed that."

"Come back anytime you want," Van said. "Though, I know you won't."

He considered arguing and decided against it. "We'll see."

Amber straightened against Van's side. "I'll walk you out."

Van growled at the same time Ricky said, "No. It's cool. You guys enjoy your night."

He ambled away, across the lawn, and as he reached the side of the cabin, her scream shuddered through the darkness behind him.

He paused and peered back, leaning around the corner of the house.

Moonlight illuminated the curves of their silhouettes. Van held her so tightly, so possessively, it was impossible to determine where she ended and he began.

They moved as one, chest to chest, foreheads together, her body on his lap, and her legs hooked around him.

Hungry moans shivered the air. The wet sounds of greedy mouths. They writhed together, enclosed in their own world. A universe where they only needed each other and the fathomless love they shared.

"You won't," Ricky whispered, his chest tight.

Van was right. Ricky wouldn't seek him out again. Not for sex.

What he truly wanted, what he needed, waited for him at home.

FIVE

Martin Lockwood released a slow breath at the sound of Ricky's truck pulling into the driveway. It was anyone's guess where he'd gone tonight. He'd sneaked out before Martin could ask.

Not that Ricky needed a keeper. He was a grown ass man and could do whatever or *whomever* he wanted.

"I can feel you tensing all the way over here." Kate smiled at him from her cozy position on the couch. With her head on Tomas' lap, she tucked her feet against Luke's hip. "I bet Ricky would help you work out that stiffness."

"Kate..." Martin dropped his voice in a warning tone and straightened in the recliner.

"She's right." Tomas absently played with her hair, his gaze glued to the basketball game on TV. "You're glaring so hard I can hear it."

They liked to tease him about harboring romantic feelings for Ricky. It was all in good fun and not even remotely true. He was sick of hearing it.

Luke released a soft snore from the couch, his red hair flopping over his brow with the loll of his head. A mechanic by trade, he'd spent the past twelve hours working on his motorcycle and running errands with Camila.

Camila's voice floated from Tate's bedroom down the hall. She and Tate, always hard at work, were ironing out a strategy to decimate the latest human sex trafficking ring in Austin.

Everyone in this house had a role in their small vigilante group. They had all put in a full day on the current mission and decided to stay in tonight.

Except Ricky. The man had an insatiable sex drive and particular tastes. He was always prowling. Always searching for something.

A key turned the deadbolt, and the front door opened.

Ricky stepped in, and those brown eyes unerringly found and held his.

Martin knew his best friend well enough to discern the meaning behind every expression and subtle movement. The soft look hooding Ricky's eyes confessed he'd just gotten laid. The twitches in his biceps indicated challenge, bracing for whatever Martin might say about it.

Ricky's chest lifted, stretching the tight t-shirt he'd deliberately worn to accentuate his muscled physique. His pretty-boy hairstyle had been disheveled by a night of restless yanking. Not by someone else's hands, but his own. For whatever reason, he'd been nervous.

He was still nervous, yet the cause was different now. He seemed to have trouble holding Martin's gaze.

He was hiding something.

"Hey." He gave Martin a chin lift, smiled at Kate and Tomas, and shook his head at a snoring Luke. "I knew that guy would be passed out before I got home."

"Where were you?" Martin asked casually.

"Out." With a shrug, he headed down the hall.

Frustration curled Martin's fingers against the armrests of the recliner.

Who had he fucked tonight? Where did he meet her? Or him?

Better not have been a *him*.

His heart rammed against the rungs of his ribs, a caged beast trying to escape.

"Three…" Tomas said from the couch. "Two…"

Martin glared at him.

"One." Tomas arched a brow.

He launched from the chair and strode toward the hall, surrendering to his predictable nature with a middle finger in the air. "Happy, asshole?"

"Love you, man!" Tomas called after him, laughing.

He passed the bedroom Camila shared with Kate and paused at the second door, which led to Tate's room. Camila was in there, her voice carrying through the walls as she argued with Tate about which strategy was less dangerous.

She took on more risk than any of them were comfortable with. Hell, they all did. But her mysterious connections made everyone uneasy.

Every time they killed a slave-trading shitbag, some unknown person helped her dispose of the body. Cartel was the most popular assumption, but she refused to confirm it. Tate couldn't even pry the secret out of her.

She demanded they trust her. Which they did. Emphatically.

Martin continued down the hall, stalking through the massive, five-bedroom, ranch-style estate. Tate, Luke, and Tomas had their own rooms. Martin and Ricky shared the master suite.

One of them could've moved into the finished attic,

but after being held captive in Van's windowless hell, no one volunteered.

They sat on millions of dollars—the money Van had collected selling slaves. At any time, one of the Freedom Fighters could buy his or her own house.

No one was in a rush to do that. They were secure here. Happy and comfortable. Not because it was the nicest place any of them had ever lived. It was definitely that.

They loved this house because it kept them together. Close. Like a family.

Family was a concept most of them had never experienced. At least, not in a positive way.

Someday, they might find partners, get married, and move out. Until then, all they needed was one another.

At the end of the corridor, he stepped into the master suite and found Ricky exiting the walk-in closet. Ricky's shirtless chest glowed with a deep natural tan, enunciating the definition in his pecs and abs.

Martin averted his gaze. "What was the skank's name tonight?"

"Is that what you think of me? That only a *skank* would hook up with me?"

"No." A vein of possessiveness ran through him, hardening his jaw.

"You know what I find interesting?" Ricky toed off his shoes and kicked them in the direction of the closet. "You support me in every aspect of my life. You're always there for me, always listening and offering advice on anything… Except when it comes to this. I can't mention dates, relationships, nothing related to sex without you looking at me like I'm disgusting and undeserving of someone's company."

"That's not it at all." Guilt hardened his stomach. "No one is good enough for you."

Ricky's Adam's apple bobbed, and he clutched his nape, glowering at the floor between them. "Right." He let out a hollow laugh and pivoted toward the en suite. "Now you're just being a dick."

"It's the truth." He followed Ricky into the bathroom, simmering with irritation. "As if you don't know the effect you have on people. Women flock to you, with your ridiculously ripped physique and suave smile."

The broad muscles of Ricky's back went rigid as he turned on the water in the shower.

"You're fun to be around. Smart and easygoing." *And painfully good-looking.* Martin gripped the edge of the vanity, taking in the sharp angles of Ricky's jawline. "You put so much damn heart into everything you do it makes the rest of us look bad. I don't say it enough, and God knows I'm an asshole on my best day, but I respect the hell out of you. You deserve more than a one-night stand."

Ricky grunted and slowly turned to face him. "You should've led with that."

"Probably." He rested his hands on his hips, his head down, but his eyes remained locked on Ricky's.

"I don't keep anything from you." Ricky unzipped his jeans and shoved them off. "Ask me again." He reached into the shower stall and adjusted the water temperature. "Ask me where I went tonight."

Steam curled around them, saturating the air and making it difficult to breathe.

The question sat on Martin's tongue, trapped behind teeth and dread.

"Ask me who I was with." Ricky pushed off his briefs and leaned toward him, all nude flesh and chiseled muscle.

No tan lines. Not on Ricardo Saldivar. The gorgeous bastard had been born with skin the color of sand on a beach after it rained.

And some stranger's hands had explored every inch of that flawless landscape tonight.

"Who was she?" He tried to cover the rasp in his voice with a jovial remark. "I bet she was hot."

"He. Not she."

Shards of ice hit his gut, and his nostrils widened with a harsh inhale. He felt like he was going to puke. Or break something.

"Why do you look so fucking repulsed whenever I tell you I was with a man?" Ricky narrowed his eyes. "You think I should only date women?"

"Yes."

"Jesus fucking Christ." Ricky glared at him, utterly unabashed about having this conversation in the nude. "Are you really that homophobic?"

He gestured at the shower. "You're wasting hot water."

"Don't give a fuck. Talk to me."

"What do you want me to say?" His pulse hammered in his throat.

"I have sex with men. Tell me why that bothers you."

He leaned his hip against the vanity for support and constructed a truthful response, without revealing the whole truth. "If you fall in love with a woman, you'll still need someone to shoot hoops, talk about sports cars, and drink beer with. There's a place for your best friend in that equation."

"Sexist much? Women can do all those things."

"Not *your* type. You like your women feminine and your men masculine."

"True."

He could give Ricky everything he ever needed—

friendship, protection, loyalty, and love.

Everything except sex.

"If you get hung up on a dude…" He crossed his arms over his chest and kept his tone even. "Not sure where I fit into that. The guy in your bed would be the guy you're hanging out with. *He* would become your best friend, and I can't stomach the thought of being replaced."

"Do you know how selfish that sounds? What about my happiness?"

"Fuck your happiness." He exhaled a grunt. "Because you know what? Yeah, I *am* selfish. I don't want to lose you, and what kind of friend would I be if I didn't fight to keep you in my life?"

"Okay, well… First off, I'm not falling in love with anyone." Ricky cocked his head. "And do you really believe I would let a lover—man or woman—wreck our friendship? Your reasoning is ludicrous."

Didn't matter if it made sense or not. He felt threatened by every man Ricky hooked up with. Not just threatened. He felt *murderous.*

"Your best friend is bisexual." Ricky's voice cut like a knife, sharp and penetrating. "Don't ask me to be something I'm not."

"I would never… *Fuck.* You're right." He drew in a slow breath and dragged a hand down his face. "I'm such a prick."

"A possessive prick. Could be worse."

"Whatever. I was out of line, and I'm sorry." He turned to leave. "I'll get out of here so you can shower."

"Tell me about your first night with Van. How did you meet him?"

"What?" His breath left him as he glanced back and met Ricky's eyes.

"How were you captured?"

Shame dug in its claws. "It's in the past. Talking about it changes nothing."

"Why is it such a huge secret?"

"Why are you so hellbent on making it one?"

"Forget it." With a scowl, Ricky spun toward the shower.

His back rippled with muscle and strength, tapering into a trim waist and tight ass encased in tanned skin and...

All the air vacated the room.

"What is *that*?" He lurched forward and gripped Ricky's arm, his gaze sweeping over dozens of red welts. "Who the fuck hit you?"

"I asked for it." Ricky yanked his arm free and set his jaw.

"Who?"

"Calm down. You know I like it rough and—"

"Give me a goddamn name!" he roared.

"Van Quiso."

He stopped breathing. "What did you say?"

"You heard me just fine."

"How did he—?" His heart rate careened into the red zone. "Did he force you? I'm going to kill him. I'm going to fucking—"

"I went to him, Martin. Willingly. I drove to his cabin and told him to hurt me."

His arm moved on its own, catching Ricky around the throat and shoving him against the wall.

"The man who held you captive? The motherfucker who tortured all of us? You gave him permission to *hurt* you?" He seethed, pushing Ricky harder against the tiles. "What the fuck is wrong with you?"

"I'm not afraid of Van."

"Did he fuck you?"

"Does it matter?"

"Answer me!" He shoved Ricky higher up the wall by the throat, putting them face to face, chest to chest, hip to hip. "Did. He. Fuck you?"

"No." Ricky pulled at the fist around his neck. "He's married, remember?"

Relief spread through him, magnified by the proximity of Ricky's six-foot-two brawny frame. The shared heat of skin and sinew evoked sensations—tightening, pulsing electricity—that should've felt awkward, not pleasant.

They'd touched so many times his body craved every fist bump, one-armed hug, wrestling scrimmage, and brotherly pat. But never this. He should've cringed away from such close, intimate contact with his best friend.

Yet he didn't.

Hypnotized by the energy in the air, he held Ricky to him. Foreheads drifted together. Breaths mingled. Tension stretched, waiting for that one twitch or sound that would break the trance and snap them apart.

Ricky's dark brown eyes searched his face as if trying to understand what was happening.

Christ, he didn't know. He didn't know what he was doing or thinking. Instinct had put him in this position. The instinct to keep Ricky away from anyone who might take him. The impulse to possess, control, and protect so that no one could ever hurt him.

"Martin." The hungry glare in Ricky's eyes stole his breath. "Either kiss me or let me go."

He yanked his hand from Ricky's throat and staggered backward, reaching blindly for the exit behind him.

"This conversation isn't finished." Ricky stepped into the shower, his gaze stony. "I'll be out in a minute."

With a nod, he strode out of the bathroom and sat on the edge of his mattress.

The spaciousness of the master suite comfortably accommodated two large beds and a sitting area. The need for privacy had never been an issue between Ricky and him. They didn't bring strangers home. No regular lovers or friends with benefits.

None of his roommates were in relationships. Most of them sought out one-night stands. One of them didn't have sex at all.

He shared the latter category with Kate, even though his roommates thought he was a manwhore. He let them believe the lie because the truth was too painful to explain.

Ricky slept around the most and would jump at the chance to fuck him if he so much as crooked a finger. Ricky's interest in him wasn't a secret, but they didn't let it complicate their friendship.

Their bond transcended sexual urges and uncomfortable moments in the bathroom.

Bracing his elbows on his knees, he waited as Ricky finished showering and dressing in the closet. A few minutes later, his best friend joined him on the bed, perching beside him in the same elbows-on-knees pose.

"Tell me what happened tonight." He studied Ricky out of the corner of his eye. "Start at the beginning."

As Ricky talked, it was hard to hear the details. The phone call to Van, the table in the woods, the leather belt, the stimulation of hands and fingers, and the ultimate orgasm... He despised every provocative word, every hitch in his friend's breath, and every jealous reflex that clamped his own airway.

Why was he jealous? Because Van Quiso could give Ricky what he couldn't? His reaction was unreasonable.

"So you'll go to him again?" he asked quietly. "Make

it a regular thing?"

"No. I don't regret it, but it's not what I need."

He didn't expect that and couldn't stop the relief from sighing past his lips. "What do you need?"

"Still trying to figure that out. What about you?"

He grunted. "You know my situation. I can't live like this forever."

Ricky was the only one who knew he hadn't had sex since his captivity with Van. No matter how many times Ricky pressed for an explanation, Martin refused to burden his friend with the horrors of his past.

"You've been celibate for five years." Ricky gave him a sober smile. "What's another five or ten years?"

"Wow. No jokes about you curing my problem?"

"The offer's always there." The words scraped from Ricky's voice. "Wanna talk about it?"

"Nah. Nothing's changed."

Amnesia would cure him. Until then, the thought of sex would continue to turn his stomach with haunting memories.

"What are we going to do?" he asked rhetorically, not expecting an answer.

"We're going to focus on ridding the world of predators." Ricky rose to his feet, his eyes on the door and head tilted as if straining to hear Camila's muffled voice. "Is she still arguing with Tate about his search for her sister?"

"They moved on to arguing about the trafficking ring." He stood and headed in that direction. "Let's go see if they've made progress."

Ricky followed him out, down the hall, and into Tate's bedroom.

"*Hola.*" Camila paced around piles of dirty laundry on the floor, her black hair swinging around her arms where they folded across her chest.

"Hey." Ricky sprawled beside Tate on the bed and propped his head on his hand. "What's on the agenda for tomorrow?"

"Tomorrow," Camila said, "we start trailing Larry McGregor."

"The mailman." Stepping to the desk, Martin traced a finger along the link chart they'd built on a bulletin board that took up the entire wall.

The chart showed people, locations, jobs, crimes, cars, and so on, each one connected by crisscrossing lengths of colored string. Different colors represented different links—family, friend, colleague—between the suspects.

"We're pretty sure the mailman moonlights as a slave trader for this piece of shit." Camila tapped a picture of an average-looking, middle-aged white man. "And he's not even a big player in the operation."

He trailed his gaze along the strings, following each connection until he landed on the man in charge of it all. "All roads lead to Hector La Rocha."

"The notorious leader of La Rocha Cartel," Camila breathed behind him. "God, Martin. He's responsible for thousands of missing women and children. All abducted and sold into slavery."

"If he's our ultimate target—"

"We can't focus on him right now." She waved a hand over the bulletin board. "We need to pick off the little guys, learn what we can from them—"

"Or we can just cut off the head of the beast and bring down the whole thing." Martin flexed his hands and shifted to face the group, expecting the same murderous spirit.

Instead, Tate heaved a sigh and tossed his phone on

the bed. "There's seven of us. What are we going to do? Run into the cartel's city with our little guns and kill his army of thousands?"

"I'll go in." He rubbed his head, thinking through the risks. "Undercover, I can gather intel and scope out the operation."

"And she'll be right there with you." Tate jabbed a finger in Camila's direction. "I can't stop you from risking your life, but I won't let her—"

"You're not my boss, *chingado*." She thrust up her chin, her dark eyes glinting with attitude. "If I want to go—"

"The answer is no." Tate shot her an unwavering glare before setting his gaze on Martin. "We'll work our way up to Hector La Rocha. Right now, we don't even know how to locate him."

Martin shifted back to the link chart, his stomach sinking at the thought of how many children would be lost before they finished this. "It'll take years."

"I know that look in your eye." Ricky appeared at his side, arms crossed, and his gaze on Hector La Rocha's picture. "You'll get him. But you won't be doing it without me."

"Deal."

SIX

Jaulaso Prison
Two years ago

For the next three days, Tula kept her head down and her presence aloof. She trusted no one, evaded everyone, and felt… Her feelings didn't matter, as long as they stayed buried deep beneath her bones.

She dedicated every breath to surviving, proving her innocence, and escaping this nightmare.

The phone became her lifeline, and she used it to make some difficult calls to her landlord, her boss, and countless lawyers.

The principal at her school promised her job would be waiting when classes resumed, *if* she proved her innocence and returned to Phoenix in time. She found an attorney willing to take her case, but she couldn't afford his fees *and* her monthly bills.

She had to let go of her apartment. It hurt like a bitch, but what choice did she have?

The landlord agreed to sell her belongings and use

the money as payment for what she owed. Whatever she had left would go toward legal fees.

Tracking down her missing Jeep was a lost cause. Not that it was worth much.

After paying the lawyer's retainer fee, she was broke. That wasn't even the worst of it.

Vera's phone had been shut off, the number no longer in use. There was no way to contact her sister. No way to leave a message explaining her incarceration or how to reach her.

When she made the call to file a missing person's report with the Ciudad Hueca police department, there was nothing left inside her.

The impatient detective on the other end of the phone made no promises to find Vera and no guarantees to call if her sister turned up, dead or alive.

It was up to her to stay on top of it, and she would.

Area Three was the quietest between the hours of three and four in the morning. That was when she showered.

She crept through the halls, stepping around inmates who had passed out after a night of drinking. In the community bathroom, she quickly stripped and washed in private.

She ate just enough to keep her body alive and spent the daylight hours studying her fellow residents. She lingered along the perimeter, trying to make herself unnoticeable while memorizing faces and eavesdropping on conversations.

Whenever someone approached her, she walked in the other direction. For the most part, the prisoners left her alone.

Except Garra.

He didn't touch her, didn't stare at her suggestively,

and never mentioned his threat about collecting rent next week. But he was always nearby, following her around and talking in her ear.

"The law is here, protected by a wall." He gestured at the two-story concrete enclosure surrounding the outdoor pound. "We are the law, not the government."

She never spoke to him, but she always listened, committing every word to memory. He seemed to know everything about everyone, including her. He knew her name, where she lived, and what she'd been charged with.

There was no telling what else he'd gleaned about her. Did he know she'd been wrongfully imprisoned? Or that she was born and raised in this city? Or that her sister was missing and possibly connected to La Rocha Cartel?

Asking him questions would require her to be civil with him. Being civil meant accepting what he'd done to her.

She couldn't stomach the sight of him, and she sure as hell wouldn't depend on him for answers.

He crouched beside her where she sat on a cement bench. She didn't look at him, didn't react to his nearness, no matter how badly she wanted to cut off his dick.

"That one is no good." He nodded at the men playing chess at a table on the far side of the yard. "The one with the barbed wire tattoo on his forehead. He's a serial rapist with unconfirmed connections to over fifty missing women. Keep your distance."

It wasn't the first time he told her who she could trust and who she shouldn't. Fucking ironic, coming from him.

What was he in prison for anyway? Drugs? Murder? Rape was the obvious answer.

As a resident of Area Three, he was also a member of the vicious La Rocha Cartel. Though, not everyone in here was on the same side.

During one of his one-sided conversations with her, she learned Jaulaso was run by La Rocha Cartel, the González Cartel, and three gangs. They all lived here, cohabiting in their numbered areas, all the while fighting over control of the prison.

It seemed peaceful now, with men standing around, sharing cigarettes, lifting weights, playing cards, and listening to music. But Garra said it could change in a heartbeat.

There were no police, military, or prison guards inside Area Three. Garra claimed everyone needed a gun here because at any moment, hell could break loose.

Two nights later, it did.

She woke to the sound of gunshots reverberating in her chest. The bursts boomed outside her cell, too loud, too goddamn close. Her blood ran cold.

She leaped out of bed as the frantic din of footsteps and shouting erupted in the hall. Bullets pinged against her door, knocking dust loose from the cracks in the ceiling.

The pauses between each gunshot grew shorter and less frequent, until all she heard was the constant report of full-blown magazines being emptied.

What the hell was going on? Why were they shooting at one another? Was this one of the cartel wars Garra had warned about?

The clothes on her body—jeans and a shirt—were all she had to her name. Everyone in here owned a gun except her. Not that she wanted one. But dammit, she might've felt brave enough to peek her head out if she had a weapon in her hands.

A moment later, the door to her cell swung open.

"We're going to have a riot." Garra leaned in, captured her eyes, and returned his gaze to the sights on his rifle, which he aimed into the hall. "The González Cartel is trying to take control of Area Three."

A riot? Images of fires, hostages, breakouts, and bloodshed caved in her chest. Without the aid of prison security, who would contain it?

The mayhem of stomping boots and gunfire grew closer. Her pulse exploded, and her hands slicked with sweat as she hunkered down and covered her head.

They could kill one another for all she cared, as long as she didn't get hit in the crossfire. This wasn't her fight.

"It's safer upstairs," Garra said calmly and fired off a few rounds down the corridor. "Go!"

Then he was gone.

She clenched her fists. He wanted her to go out there without a gun? Shots were firing from every direction. Why couldn't she just stay here?

Fear trembled through her as she inched toward the open door. A peek into the hallway gave her a view of the stairwell thirty feet away. Beyond that, crowds of inmates ran left and right, plowing one another down.

Some faces she recognized. Others she didn't.

The unfamiliar men swept along the corridor, spraying bullets into every cell they passed. It wouldn't take them long to reach hers.

Paralyzed by panic, she ducked back into her cell. Adrenaline coursed through her system. She couldn't catch her breath.

The attacking cartel would consider her an enemy merely because she was in Area Three. She was a sitting duck.

Dropping to her hands and knees, she poked her head into the hall, waited for a clear break, and scrambled for the stairwell.

Bullets whizzed by overhead, and one tore a hole in

the wall right beside her. A scream escaped her throat, and she might've peed a little. She couldn't feel her body amid the violent pounding of fear.

She bustled across the floor, crawling, sliding, falling, and dragging her legs. Her lungs heaved a frantic pace, chopping her breaths and burning her chest.

Almost there. Almost there.

With a knee-grinding lunge, she flung herself through the gap in the open doorway of the stairwell. Her elbows banged against concrete, and her head hit the wall. But she made it.

"Fuck." She released a heavy exhale and flew to her feet, pivoting to race up the stairs.

Gunshots rang out overhead. Multiple shooters. Angry shouting. A firefight waged right above her.

Her stomach flipped inside out.

Goddamn Garra! She couldn't go up there, and she couldn't risk running back to her cell.

Fucking fuck, fuck!

She spun in a circle, jumping at the deafening pops of guns. Shooters were in the stairwell, in the corridor, and she was caught in the middle.

"What are you doing?"

She whirled toward the deep voice in the hall.

Across from her, the door to a cell stood open. An older man with silver-black hair leaned a shoulder against the door jamb, arms hanging at his sides, his expression as calm as could be.

"I…I don't know." She'd seen him a few times in the common area but hadn't learned his name.

"Do you know how to use a gun?"

No. She nodded jerkily.

He removed a pistol from his waistband and tossed it across the hall to her. "The safety's off."

She palmed the heavy weight of metal, turning it over in her shaking hands.

The sound of his door jerked her head up.

He'd returned to his room. *Shit.* She should've told him the attackers were shooting into all the cells.

The stampede of boots broke out in the corridor, stomping in her direction. The report of gunfire on the stairs above her resounded in her ears. At any moment, she was going to get shot.

But she had a gun.

Clutching the grip in both fists, she hunkered low to the floor between the corridor and the stairs and tried not to throw up.

Her nerves wound so tightly the pistol rattled in her sweaty hands. She'd never even practiced on a paper target. How would she shoot a moving person? She didn't have the guts or the skill.

Except she'd strangled a man with his own belt.

Surely, a bullet would be easier. Quicker.

The thought steeled her spine as an army of González members ran past the stairwell.

She backed into a shadowed corner, out of view, and held her breath.

Some of the footsteps slowed at the doorway, but the sound of gunfire upstairs sent them continuing down the hall.

All but one.

A young, lanky guy with a rifle stopped at the door to the old man's cell and tried the handle. It didn't open.

Her pulse rushed in her ears.

The armed man stepped back, trained his rifle on the door handle, and fired.

The bang stopped her heart and echoed in her eardrums so loudly and painfully she wondered if they'd ruptured.

Ten feet from her hiding spot, the shooter raised his gun to fire into the now open doorway of the cell. He intended to kill the old man.

What if the old man had given her his only weapon? She couldn't just stand here with his gun and let him die.

Three running steps brought her into the hall. The shooter swung his gaze over his shoulder and met her eyes. His mouth opened, but she was already squeezing the trigger.

The explosive bang kicked her arms back and jarred her insides. But the bullet aimed true, hitting her target in the back, dead center.

He dropped to the floor.

The gun blast echoed in her head, her hearing momentarily lost as she stared at the unmoving body.

She'd taken another life.

Guilt tried to work its way in, but her relief was too big. All around her, the sounds of gunfire had fallen silent. She was still alive.

So was the old man.

He stood in the doorway of his cell, his expression etched in surprise and gratitude.

Would he want his pistol back? She tightened her grip on it, unwilling to surrender the only thing in this place that made her feel safe.

"It's yours." He thrust his chin at the gun and gave her the first warm smile she'd seen in days.

"Thank you."

With a nod, he retreated into the darkness of his cell.

"It's safe now," someone shouted from down the hall. "You can come out!"

Bodies were pulled away. Furniture was straightened, and stashes of alcohol emerged out of nowhere.

While she was the only female inmate in Area Three, there was no shortage of women. Prostitutes came and went at all hours. Especially tonight. They filed in by the dozens, and with them came the sharp scent of weed.

Music blared. Cocaine covered the tables, and the aroma of grilled food permeated the air.

An hour after the riot ended, an enormous party swung into full force.

She stood in a quiet, shadowed alcove off the main common area, taking it all in with disbelief.

These men narrowly survived a bloodbath with a rival cartel. They lost fellow inmates. People fucking died. Yet here they were, laughing, banging hookers, and getting high.

A familiar presence moved into her space, darkening her corner. She ground her teeth.

"You survived your first riot. Well done." Garra leaned a shoulder against the wall beside her. "The boss wants to see you."

Boss? She scanned the crowd of drunk criminals. A leader lived among these assholes? Who?

"How long is this silent treatment going to last?" Garra tapped his fingers on the wall above her head. "It was just sex. Nothing personal."

Her hand moved to the pistol in her waistband, her fingers itching to blow a hole in his stupid face. But if she killed him, every man in this room would fire a bullet in her direction.

He shook his head, scrutinizing her. "You have no idea who runs this operation, do you?"

Evidently, she was about to meet him, and the prospect chilled her to the bone.

She'd listened to enough conversations over the past

few days to know what made people nervous around here.

They didn't trust newcomers. Convicts often paid their way into different areas of Jaulaso to gather information and keep tabs on enemies.

What if the boss thought she was a spy from another gang? Would he confiscate her gun? What if he didn't want her here and kicked her out?

"Come on." Garra strode in the direction of her cellblock.

She followed on shaky legs as he led her away from the party and crowds. He entered the corridor where she slept, and her steps slowed with shock.

"Here we are." He stopped at the old man's cell.

Confusion pulled her mouth into a gaping frown.

The door had already been replaced with a new handle and lock. Well, not *new*. It looked as though the parts had been taken from someone else's cell.

He inclined his head. "This is the private quarters of Hector La Rocha."

Her breath caught in her chest. She couldn't have heard him correctly.

"I see you know his name." He narrowed his eyes. "Do you know he has absolute control of the prison and the city?"

That nice old man? The one who had given her the gun? *He* was Hector La Rocha? How was that possible?

His name alone struck fear in the hearts of every man, woman, and child in Mexico. With an army that outmatched the Mexican military, he was responsible for thousands of deaths every year.

How did he maintain such an atrocious reputation from prison? And why didn't she know he'd been incarcerated?

Oh, God. Even if he didn't expel her from Area

Three, how would she sleep at night knowing his cell was only thirty feet from hers?

"Don't be afraid." Garra tsked. "You are here because he allows it. He wants to get to know you."

Why? She wanted to ask, but her lips were frozen in terror.

Garra knocked, and a muscular man with a mean scowl opened the door. Intimation deepened the shadows on his face and oozed enough menace to make her heart rate explode.

Was *he* the cartel boss?

With a grunt, he turned and lumbered into a room that was four times the size of her cell.

She stepped forward, and Garra closed the door behind her, shutting himself out.

Her feet carried her into the dark quarters, her senses shuddering at the overwhelming scent of spicy food and cigarette smoke.

Some of the interior concrete walls must've been removed to expand the space, though she couldn't imagine how it would've been done.

The first ten-foot section was arranged like a dining room. At the center, the old man sat at a small table, surrounded by platters of steaming burritos, *carne asada,* and rice.

Random pieces of furniture encircled the space. Wooden bookcases, filing cabinets, and antique chairs—the furnishings were nicer than anything she'd seen in Jaulaso.

Stockpiles of guns and ammunition filled what would've been a neighboring cell. Beyond that, a heavy drape hung from the ceiling. The edge of a bed peeked out from behind it.

The scowling wall of muscle returned to the door and stood with his back to it and his arms crossed.

Was he a guard?

"Don't mind Luis." The older gentleman wiped his mouth with a linen napkin, his Spanish thick and hypnotic. "He's my security."

Where had Luis been during the riot? Had he been in here the entire time? Or out there killing people? Maybe she didn't want to know.

"Okay." Her hands trembled at her sides. "I…um… My name is—"

"Petula Gomez." The syllables rolled off his tongue with old-world eloquence.

He knew her name.

The most feared man in Mexico knew who she was.

Her pulse quivered as reality crashed in.

She was talking to Hector La Rocha, standing three feet away from him, in the room where he slept. Sweet merciful hell, her mother must've been rolling in her grave.

"What do I call you?" Her voice sounded stronger than she felt.

"Call me Hector." A smile touched his gentle eyes. "Please…" He gestured at the seat across from him. "Sit. Eat with me."

Her stomach bucked with nausea. If she ate, it would all come back up.

"I'm sorry. I… I wasn't prepared for this." She rubbed a clammy palm on her jeans and lowered into the chair. "I didn't know you were here. *In prison.*"

"Very good." He lit a cigarette, watching her through a curl of smoke. "I pay a lot of money to a lot of people to keep my location a secret."

Made sense. It would be easy for his enemies to send assassins into Jaulaso. Hector could only run as far as the prison walls.

She stared at his cigarette with longing. She hadn't

smoked since college, but the urge crept up sometimes.

It would calm her nerves, maybe make her look tougher than a high school Spanish teacher.

He tracked her gaze and held out a pack of smokes. "Go ahead."

She couldn't hide the tremors in her hands as she lit one. Somehow, she managed not to cough through the first drag.

Silence stretched between them, and he didn't seem to mind. There was no expectation in his warm brown eyes. No judgment in his relaxed posture.

He was nothing like she'd imagined.

The stories she'd heard growing up had painted him as a raping, murdering, blood-thirsty tyrant. Maybe that was true when he was younger. But now? All she saw was a soft-spoken, unassuming gentleman in his sixties.

Silver streaked a full head of black hair, and the few wrinkles fanning from his dark eyes made him look mature and distinguished. Modestly dressed with a lean physique, he was too debonair to be a cartel leader. Too pleasant and fragile looking to fit in with the uneducated, vulgar gangsters who roamed the halls of Area Three.

His cream-colored shirt buttoned neatly over his narrow chest with the collar undone. No flashy necklaces or rings. Nice teeth. Clean hair. Smoothly shaved jawline. He took care of his appearance without coming across as pretentious.

He didn't radiate cruelty like his guard at the door, and there wasn't a trace of sexual interest in his gaze.

So why was she here? Maybe it was a test, one that would cast her out of Area Three if she failed.

But if she were allowed to stay, Garra would attempt to collect rent. She meant what she'd said. If he touched her again, she would kill him.

She desperately needed to belong to a structure that would keep her safe. To survive, she needed to be part of a group, a circle of trust that would support her when she defended herself and protect her when she couldn't.

If Hector La Rocha truly owned Jaulaso, she needed him on her side.

Scanning his belongings, she searched for something that might help her connect with him and wriggle into his good graces.

An old record player sat in the corner next to a stack of vinyl records. Old-fashioned paintings colored the walls in Mexican landscapes. Handwoven rugs brightened the floor, and countless books lined the shelves. Books with Spanish titles about politics, war, technology, and religion.

If he actually read those texts, he was an intellectual. Probably the only person in Jaulaso she could engage in deep conversation. The cleanliness of his private quarters suggested a tidy mind. If nothing else, perhaps she could offer him some mental stimulation.

"How long have you been here?" She took a long drag on the cigarette, savoring the lightheaded calm of nicotine.

"I've served eight years of a life sentence."

"Oh."

"You should eat."

"Thank you. I wish I could. Everything looks so delicious, but my stomach doesn't feel well."

He nodded, and his silver brows knitted together. "I didn't have this as a child." He waved a hand over the aromatic platters of food. "Sometimes, we didn't have anything to eat at all."

"Makes you appreciate it." She crushed out the cigarette. "So much more than someone who has never felt hunger pangs."

"You know this from experience?" He tipped his head, his expression attentive and thoughtful.

"Sure." She lifted a shoulder. "I was raised by a single mother in the throat of Ciudad Hueca. She did her best to provide for us. Some years were better than others."

"The struggle made you stronger." His eyes locked on hers, and a slow stream of smoke trickled from his nose. "You saved my life."

"I don't know about that." She glanced at the cases of guns and ammunition. "You have an arsenal in here."

"Yet I didn't need it."

He watched her with an indiscernible emotion pressed between his lips. Tenderness softened the creases around his eyes. Admiration, even. It made her feel warm and uncomfortable at the same time.

She returned her attention to the bookcases, skipping over manuals, textbooks, and heavy tomes. "You're interested in learning."

"A man is only as great as his knowledge."

As an educator, she appreciated that sentiment.

Her gaze snagged on a beginner's book of English grammar. "You speak English?"

"I trying learning," he said clumsily in English. "Speak little."

There it was. The connection she needed. Her *in*.

She lifted her eyes to his and took a leap. "I'm a teacher."

His face held no reaction.

She didn't want to offend him, but she had to go for it. A chance to win his trust.

"I teach Spanish in the States. I know it's not the same thing, but maybe I could teach you English, if you want to learn."

His nostrils widened with a deep inhale, his

expression unreadable.

Crap. Her hands clenched on her lap. "I didn't mean to presume—"

"Yes. You will teach me to speak, read, and write English like a gringo." A smile broke across his face. "You will work for me."

Her relief lasted a fraction of a second before panic swept in.

Work for Hector La Rocha? What had she done?

Once a cartel member, always a cartel member.

But there was no turning back from this. Refusing him would be a death sentence.

Was she in a position to bargain? Probably not, but she had nothing to lose. "Does Garra work for you?"

"Yes."

"I'll teach you, but I ask one thing in return."

"Anything." He stretched out his arms, indicating all his possessions.

"Castrate him." She sat taller. "Remove Garra's manhood."

Silence. Stunned, agonizing silence. He let it build for so long she couldn't feel anything but the ice forming on her spine.

Then his hand slammed onto the table. She jumped a foot off the chair as he burst into laughter.

"Oh, you are a delightful surprise!" He slapped the table again, rattling the dishes.

"You'll do it?"

He blew out his cheeks with a heavy sigh. "Castration is too messy."

"Your reputation suggests otherwise."

"You think so?" He rested his forearms on the table and leaned forward, his eyes hard and unblinking.

"I know so." She stared back with a knot in her

throat.

"Luis." He didn't take his gaze off her. "Send in Garra."

Within seconds, the man she hated most in the world stood at attention before Hector.

Nervous energy skittered through the room as Hector puffed on his cigarette. Was he going to do it? Cut off Garra's balls right here in front of her? Or was the whole conversation just a way to fuck with her? Give her some hope, let her relax a little, then cut her throat?

She stopped breathing.

"There's been a change in the ranks." Hector exhaled a cloud of smoke, his gaze on Garra. "Petula works directly for me, and you now work for her."

Her heart stammered.

"Yes, boss." Garra's voice didn't carry a hint of surprise, but the flex of his hand affirmed his displeasure.

"She pays rent to me," Hector said. "You will not touch her or anyone else unless she allows it. No sex, starting now. You will be celibate like a eunuch, yes?"

"Understood." A muscle feathered across Garra's whiskered cheek.

This wasn't castration, but it was emasculating, nonetheless.

She might've sagged with happiness if her insides weren't gurgling with foreboding.

Hector had given her what she'd asked for, but in return, she would be indebted to the notorious leader indefinitely.

"If you want to fuck a woman, you must have Petula's permission." Hector reclined in the chair, his tone chillingly calm. "She is your number one priority. Whatever she needs, you will provide it. If she's in danger, you will protect her with your life."

She couldn't believe what she was hearing. Hector wasn't just removing Garra's manhood. He was demoting the man, binding him into service to her.

A personal security guard would give her more protection than the gun in her waistband or a lock on her door. But tethering Garra to her side was the last thing she wanted.

"It will be my honor." Garra clasped his hands behind him and shifted to face her. "I'm at your service, Petula."

His eyes connected with hers, and in that look, she glimpsed his contempt. It was there and gone in a blink, leaving behind an empty expression.

Hector's command was law. Didn't matter if they liked it. Neither of them could refuse, and they both knew it.

"We will begin English lessons at sunrise tomorrow." Hector struck a match and lit another cigarette. "You may go."

Garra followed her into the hall and along the thirty-foot walk to her cell. At the doorway, she turned toward him.

His face contorted, a furious scowl twisting at the center.

"Could've been worse." She rested her hands on her hips. "I told him to castrate you."

A seething breath slipped past his clamped teeth, and he tried to rein it in.

With a forefinger and thumb, he pinched the bridge between his eyes and dragged in a string of deep inhales. Each one grew slower, calmer, until his shoulders relaxed.

Then he lowered his hand and met her gaze.

A thousand words clashed between them, none of them voiced. In that defining moment of silence, he accepted his role as her guard, and she came to terms with her new reality.

She'd joined the most ruthless cartel in Mexico.

The very cartel her mother warned her against her entire life.

She'd passed the point of no return.

PART TWO

SEVEN

Jaulaso Prison
Present Day

The fun-size package of sex in tight jeans stole glances at Martin from beneath her dark lashes. He didn't have to look at the Latina beauty to feel the caress of her exotic eyes along his skin. But goddamn, did he look. He couldn't stop.

She sat at a table on the far side of the common area, bent over an open book. Each time her gaze lifted, he openly stared back, savoring the view.

Monochromatic tattoos sleeved her arms in a blend of illustrations too detailed to make out at this distance. Perky tits formed an enticing valley in the *V*-neck of her shirt. Full lips begged to be kissed, no matter how hard she pressed them together.

Large brown eyes perused him up and down, taking his measure, weighing his worth. With each pass, her expression softened as if, in her attempt to analyze him, she'd inadvertently let her guard slip.

After a moment, she looked away. Whatever she decided about him made her pull in a breath. Her chest rose with the inhale, squeezing her perfect rack in the confines of her shirt.

Fuck, his dick.

For the past seven years, the thought of having sex again had tortured him into a celibate existence. But after two days in Area Three, watching this alluring woman react to him, he couldn't control the swelling torment between his legs.

He wasn't prepared.

Not for her.

He and Ricky had trained nonstop for months, focusing on combat, weaponry, and cartel politics. In addition to their daily workouts, they spent a good part of the year perfecting their Spanish.

Going into this assignment, they knew the score.

Coke, marijuana, meth… Name the drug. It was here. Prison guards didn't enter this nasty, dark corner of hell, where inmates carried high-powered submachine guns.

Drug dealers with Uzis.

And they were all at war with one another. If a *vato* so much as looked at someone wrong, he was dead.

He and Ricky had three months to complete the mission while living among the worst of the most violent, crazy, and disturbed men on the planet.

According to their intel, there weren't supposed to be female prisoners in Area Three. And certainly not one as hot as Petula Gomez.

"Stop staring, dipshit," Ricky whispered behind the loose curl of his hand.

"Only reason you're not is because your back is to her."

Being bilingual proved exceedingly useful. Since no one in here seemed to know English, he and Ricky used it in their private conversations.

"How did we not know she existed?" Ricky tossed two cards onto the table between them, maintaining the ruse of playing poker.

Matias Restrepo had been their primary resource for information. As the capo of the biggest cartel in Colombia, he kept tabs on all his rivals. When he married Camila earlier this year, her vigilante group of freedom fighters had gained a powerful ally.

Without Matias, they would've never located Hector La Rocha.

Their target.

Matias and Camila had arranged the arrest that planted Martin and Ricky in Jaulaso. Before they were detained, Matias had given them a few instructions.

Pay a prison guard to move you to a nicer area.

Request Area Three.

Try not to get shot or raped in the process.

Never wander off alone.

So far, so good.

In three months, their bogus drug trafficking charges would be dropped. Whatever deal Matias and Camila had negotiated with the Mexican government guaranteed their release from Jaulaso.

They had three months to steal as much information as possible. Vital information, like the location of the *comandante* who runs the cartel's multinational sex trafficking operation.

That intel would be handed over to the Mexican government and used to put Hector La Rocha out of business.

Martin would give his left nut to kill the crime boss

himself. Not an easy feat, considering Hector was surrounded by hundreds of La Rocha members in Jaulaso. Attacking their leader would be a suicide mission.

Not only that, a dead cartel leader would only give rise to a new one. All the heads needed to be removed, and that required cunning.

Penetrating Hector's inner circle was the first step. Martin had a sinking feeling that circle included the female inmate they knew nothing about.

"She's a deviation." Ricky kept his whisper beneath the din of chatter around them. "Deviations from the pattern are never good."

Through extensive profiling prior to the mission, they'd compiled a list of every officer in La Rocha Cartel. All of them were men.

How did no one outside these walls know about her? Who was she?

Rumors on the inside were rampant, leaking from every mouth in Area Three. In the two days he'd been here, he'd heard she could outmatch any inmate in a knife fight, drink the biggest man under the table, and knew every closely guarded secret in La Rocha Cartel.

Some said she strangled a man with her bare hands on her first night in Jaulaso. Others claimed she'd saved Hector La Rocha's life during a prison riot.

The stories were too outlandish to be true. She carried a weapon on her person at all times, but that didn't mean she had the strength to take down a two-hundred-pound convict. She was just a little thing, half the size of the smallest man in here.

His skin prickled, the electric touch of her gaze making it damn difficult to sit here and ignore her. He was confrontational by nature and wanted nothing more than to charge across the room and talk to her.

That, as he'd learned on the first night, was not allowed.

When he and Ricky had entered Area Three, a man named Garra met them at the door. After Garra informed them they would be sleeping on the floor in the common area, he left them with a warning.

Any man who approaches Petula Gomez without permission is a dead man.

Two days of observation confirmed the threat carried weight.

Her fellow prisoners tracked her with hungry eyes, injected her name into conversations, and boasted about all vulgar ways they would *tear up that pussy*. But no one made a move on her.

No one approached her. No one talked to her. Every man in Area Three gave her a wide berth.

Except her ever-present guard dog.

Rumor had it that Garra was her lover. The only one, given the possessive way he stood between her and everyone else. When he wasn't glaring, growling, and pissing a circle around her, he was poised at her side with his mouth moving at her ear.

She didn't speak, not to him or anyone, but her posture maintained an alertness that suggested nothing slipped past her notice.

"Jesus." Ricky stomped a foot on the ground and lifted it to reveal a pile of bug guts. "Is it just me or are the roaches unnaturally large here? Why are there so many? I don't even know where they're coming from."

"We've been here two days and haven't seen the boss. We have no weapons, no way to contact anyone on the outside. We're surrounded by the most brutal drug cartel in Mexico, and you're bitching about roaches?"

Their eyes met, and a rush of warmth filled his chest.

Ricky's mouth curved upward, his handsome face gentling with affection before tensing again.

The impulse to rescue his best friend's smile pulled him forward.

"Remember when we first started sharing a room?" He leaned across the table, erasing the distance. "I changed our Wi-fi name to *I Can Hear You Masturbating.*"

"Yeah." Ricky's hard angles softened, and he bent in, closing the last few inches. "The next morning, I changed it to *I Know.*"

"It was funny at home, but not here." He trapped his grin behind a feigned glower. "Your chronic fist fucking will attract unwanted attention."

"What are you saying?" Ricky asked, playing along.

"Seeing how we're in pound-me-in-the-ass prison and sleeping out in the open…" He nodded at the corner of the common area, where they'd crashed the past two nights. "You need to cease and desist the nightly hand parties."

"A little self-gratification never hurt anyone." Ricky's mouth twitched.

"Shooting venereal excitement all over the place?" He couldn't stop his cheeks from rising. "Definitely bad for the environment."

Ricky chuckled. "I don't need your permission to beat off."

"No, but you want it."

Ricky's smile slipped.

Fuck, he shouldn't have said that. It'd been all joking fun until he inadvertently hit on the truth.

Silence crept in, and unspoken words caught and held between them. Neither of them looked away.

Throughout their seven-year friendship, he'd accepted his best friend's sexual interest in him. It was never shoved in his face, and he didn't let it make things weird.

They were too close to ever feel awkward around each other. Even now, as Ricky stared at him in a way he couldn't reciprocate—eyes hooded, pupils dilated, lips parted—he didn't resent his friend for it.

But he wouldn't send mixed signals, either.

"Ricky." He hardened his voice. "I didn't mean—"

"I know." With a forced smile, Ricky steered them back to the safety of their banter. "So no solitary sex? For three months?"

"I advise against all sex." He glanced around at the scarred, tattooed faces of Mexico's hardest criminals. "Considering your pool of potential dates."

"What about the smokin' hot chili pepper at your ten o'clock?"

His gaze shifted, instantly locking on her deep brown eyes.

She was watching his interaction with Ricky, a frown pinned on her gorgeous face and the turned page of her book forgotten in her hand.

He could've looked around the room and determined how long each man had been here by the dimness in his eyes. The light in hers hadn't completely faded, but fractures distorted the glow. Broken memories of a different life.

She bore tattoos, carried weapons, smoked cigarettes, and scowled at everyone. But beneath the tough exterior lurked an innocent sort of curiosity that didn't fit in Jaulaso.

Maybe he was wrong, but she hadn't been here very long. Not as long as most of these men.

Her attention pinged between her book and her surroundings, lingering on Ricky and him more than anyone else in the room.

"She's watching you, isn't she?" Ricky asked.

"Watching *us*." He shared a smile with his friend and returned to her.

Her brows gathered, her expression incredulous.

"She looks confused." He smiled bigger. "Like she's never seen a happy person."

"Maybe she hasn't. Certainly not in this shithole." Ricky scanned the perimeter. "Nothing but gray walls and breathing corpses."

"I wonder how long she's in for."

A lot of the prisoners came here to rot, and they carried that hopelessness in their bones.

This was the hardest assignment he and Ricky ever attempted, but it was temporary, just a job, not the end of the road for them.

"We need to talk to her." Ricky put away the playing cards. "Find out who she is."

"We don't need to do anything."

"Because she'll come to us." Ricky sat back and carved a hand through his thick black hair.

"Yeah." Holding her gaze, he gave her a wink.

Her shoulders tightened, and she shut the book. Then she pushed away from the table and strode out of the room.

Garra straightened from his post against the wall. Instead of following her, he made a beeline to their table.

"Incoming," Martin said beneath his breath.

Ricky slowly twisted in his chair, his expression hardening into granite.

He was one of the most laid-back guys Martin had ever met, but when the situation demanded it, he could switch on his primitive drive and turn into one scary motherfucker.

Garra towered over their table, dressed head-to-toe in black, resembling a forty-year-old Antonio Banderas, without the congeniality or charm.

"We're not interested," Ricky said in Spanish, exaggerating the trill of his *R*s.

"Not interested?"

"Gold necklaces." Ricky motioned at the heavy chains draped around Garra's neck. "Are you not a jewelry salesman?"

"Stupid fucking *gabacho*."

"It's a joke, not a dick. Don't take it so hard. And for the record, calling me a *gabacho* isn't entirely accurate. I'm at least one-eighth Latino."

As if. Ricky might've been born in the U.S., but his mother was an illegal immigrant from Mexico.

With a growl, Garra turned toward Martin and leaned in, his eyes like black marbles. "I don't like the way you look at her."

"What way is that?" Martin rose to his feet, forcing the man to step back.

"You want to fuck her."

"Every man in Jaulaso wants to fuck her. Look around."

Garra didn't move his eyes. He didn't even blink.

"What I want is a meeting with her." Martin knew the answer before it punched through the air.

"No."

"Just tell me one thing." Ricky drew out a long pause, probably just to fuck with the scowling man. "I'm trying to get a jump start on my Christmas shopping and noticed she likes books. What was she reading?"

"200 Ways To Gut A White Boy."

Ol' Garra didn't miss a beat, but neither did Ricky. "If the rumors are true, she doesn't need a book to do that.

I hear she's terrifying with a knife."

Ricky didn't believe the gossip any more than Martin did. He was fishing for the truth.

"If you want your balls to remain attached to your body," Garra said, "you'll heed those warnings and stay away from her."

"The depths of your concern make me feel all tingly," Ricky deadpanned.

Garra shot him a parting glare and ambled out of the room.

Martin returned to his chair and switched back to English. "Gonna go out on a limb here and say—"

"Garra has no friends?"

"He's not going to tell her we want a meeting."

"He won't have to." Ricky leaned back and laced his hands behind his head.

She'll come to us.

"So we wait." Martin rubbed the tension in his neck. "And try not to get killed."

EIGHT

A swarm of emotions chased Tula through the halls and caught up with her in her cell. The sharp burn hit her sideways, stabbing through her throat and gathering behind her eyes.

Most days squeaked by without worry or dread or the threat of tears. She'd become one of them, a member of Hector's inner circle, and with that came safety. Any harm directed at her had to go through Garra.

Two years in Area Three and she hadn't sustained so much as a scratch.

She had nothing to fear.

No, that wasn't true. She feared it would all be taken away. If something happened to Hector, she would lose his protection. She would also lose a friend.

She'd developed a close bond with him. Enjoyed his company, even. He never leered at her, touched her inappropriately, or gave her any reason to think he would hurt her.

She trusted him.

But every once in a while, a bad day sneaked in. A familiar scent or melody would spark a memory, and she would wake from the numbness, sweating and gasping for air. In those moments, the veil lifted, and old hurts came rushing back—how she'd arrived here, the decisions she'd made, and everything she'd lost.

Today was one of those days.

It was the new prisoners. They reminded her of home. Not just because she hadn't seen another American in two years. But because they were different. Smart different. Full-of-life-and-hope different.

With their drawling accents and tattoo-free skin, they looked more like the guys she used to date and less like hardened convicts.

They radiated confidence, not arrogance. Their muscled physiques promised pain if provoked, but they didn't seem like the type of men who bulked up because they had something to prove.

Christ, they were gorgeous, the blond hair and blue eyes of one contrasting with the black hair and brown eyes of the other. Together, they were an overload on the senses. Too much testosterone in one place. Too much lethal beauty.

Area Three didn't see a lot of attractive men. There was plenty of brawn pumping iron in the yard, but those honed bodies were attached to twisted expressions, vile tongues, and depraved minds.

The new guys belonged on the cover of a magazine, but that wasn't what captivated her.

It was the endearing bond between them, the way their gazes connected and held so easily. She envied that closeness. Envied how they weren't alone in this place.

Were they brothers? Best friends? They didn't touch each other with the familiarity of sexual intimacy, so probably not lovers.

Whatever their relationship, they'd arrived here

together. That meant they were probably together at the time of their arrest. What crime had they committed?

The blond carried himself with a stern sort of reserve and control. The Hispanic guy was more expressive, smiling brighter and scowling darker than his friend.

They kept to themselves and navigated their new surroundings as a single unit—their *own* unit—with no clear loyalties to a race or group.

That was a problem. The white guy was too white, and his friend was too *pocho*. The fact that they weren't born and bred in Mexico was a strike against them. They made it worse by not sucking up to the shot callers.

It was only a matter of time before they got *heart checked*. The biggest predators would start circling them, sizing them up, seeing if they would fight or cower. Respect was established by being fearless.

Maybe they *were* fearless, but unless they gained four-hundred pounds of muscle, punched like Mike Tyson, and grew eyes in the backs of their heads, they might not survive the week.

Then there was Hector. The boss kept tabs on everyone, and if he suspected them of doing anything against his cartel, he would deal with them painfully and permanently.

That bothered her. For the first time in a long time, she felt something other than indifference. Part of her wanted them to make it through this, and not because they were good-looking.

Well, maybe partly because they were good-looking.

She'd spent the past couple of hours in the common area, basking in the glow on their handsome faces and pretending they weren't dangerous criminals. She wanted to sit at their table and make believe they were just a couple of cute, harmless guys in a restaurant. A real restaurant with real utensils.

They would talk about how hot the Arizona summers were, laugh about the silly things they did as kids, and end the night with a kiss that promised another date.

She missed that. Not a date with two men. That was just a fantasy.

She missed dating. And teaching high school, paying rent, grocery shopping, answering calls from her sister…

Vera.

God, she ached to hear Vera's voice.

Two years with no news, no leads, no nothing. The loss of her sister left a hurt inside her so profound and excruciating it was more than she could bear.

Anguish surged through her chest, and her eyes caught fire.

Stop it.

Gulping deep breaths, she pushed it down, shoved it away, locked it up.

No tears. It's a waste of good suffering.

It was her favorite quote from her favorite book. She glanced down at it in her hand, smoothing a palm over the hardback cover.

The Hellbound Heart.

The rare 20th Anniversary Edition had been signed by Clive Barker himself. God only knew how much it was worth.

Hector had given it to her four months after her arrest. A condolence gift, he'd called it, for the news she'd received from her attorney.

She'd been sentenced to five years for smuggling marijuana. The court made the decision without her being there because that was how the penal system in Mexico worked.

Her devastation had been inconsolable.

The attorney tried to get an *amparo,* an appeal designed to protect the rights of the accused.

It was denied.

In the weeks that followed, she'd fallen into abject despondency. She didn't leave her cell, couldn't eat, barely breathed.

She was innocent, serving a sentence for a crime she didn't commit. She was stuck in a cold, dark place of uncertainty and violence with five years on her shoulders.

Then Hector showed up with the book.

Before Jaulaso, she'd never read the literary draft of her favorite Hellraiser movie. But there it was, a signed copy in his outstretched hand.

More books followed. He filled her cell with novels of all her treasured horror movies. In return, she made a full commitment to the structure of the cartel.

Teaching him English had been her first job, but it wasn't the last.

Three years from now, she would be released from prison. But she would never be released from Hector La Rocha.

She could blame him for trapping her, for manipulating her into a life of crime. She could hate him with every fiber of her being. But it wasn't his fault.

The military put her in Jaulaso. They turned an innocent schoolteacher into a criminal cartel member.

There would be no going back to Arizona or her high school teaching job or the American citizenship she'd worked so hard to obtain. She was in too deep.

A tear slipped from her eye, and she swatted it away.

Crying about it didn't change a damn thing.

And no more fantasizing about the new guys. If

there was any goodness inside them, this place would beat it out. Only the meanest, ugliest souls survived Jaulaso.

There was a reason she kept her distance. No investments. No attachments. No losses.

Footsteps sounded in the hall, and she recognized the tenacious gait. Expected it.

She took her time returning her book to the crate with the others Hector had given her. Locating her cigarettes, she struck a match, took a long drag, and another.

Then she gave Garra her attention. "Are you spreading more rumors about me?"

"I do what is necessary to protect you."

"Someday, all those lies will backfire. You need to stop."

"I am one man against two hundred." He stabbed a finger at the doorway. "Two hundred men who want to fuck you, kill you, and fuck you again when you're dead."

She flinched.

"The rumors add a layer of defense." His gaze lowered to her arms. "Just like your tattoos."

"It's just artwork." She ran a hand along the intricate black swirls that held no special meaning or significance.

"They camouflage your softness. Isn't that why you got them? To make you look tougher? Harder? To fit in?"

He was right, of course. One of the things she learned early on was that inmates with smaller builds and passive dispositions became victims of daily beatings and sexual slavery.

She heard the screams, saw the bruises, and knew exactly how deep that pain went.

If a man didn't come into the prison fighting with fists and teeth, he became someone's fuck toy. As such, he was loaned out to other inmates for sex in exchange for commissary goods, such as soup, cigarettes, and other things that replaced currency.

She had no power to stop it, but as long as she had Hector's protection, it wouldn't happen to her.

If she lost Hector…

She shivered at the memory of her first night in Jaulaso. Her tattoos wouldn't replace the shelter Hector provided, but they helped hide her fragility. They gave her confidence.

"The boss called a meeting." Garra glanced back into the hall. "They're starting to gather."

She took a drag on the cigarette and crushed it out. Her presence was required at every cartel meeting. She didn't always participate in the discussions, but sometimes her opinions were demanded.

Sometimes she was assigned a job, small tasks, such as eavesdropping on a conversation, delivering a verbal message, or overseeing a drug trade.

Hector never made her enter another area in the prison, touch an illegal substance, or take a life. But she was part of his criminal operation, contributing to its corruption.

Violence was necessary to maintain order in the cartel. She'd grown numb to it, started to justify it, because it was for the common good of Area Three.

Pulling in a breath, she followed Garra into the corridor. She didn't have to ask why this meeting had been called.

The González Cartel was recruiting people, convincing them that La Rocha Cartel was losing power. Every person who stepped foot in Area Three was under the microscope, even if it was just a short visit.

Most of the men who came in wanted to join this side and vocally declared their allegiance. Others weren't as transparent about their intentions.

The two American prisoners had shared nothing about themselves. No one knew their cartel affiliations or their reasons for coming to this side of Jaulaso.

Were they recruiters for the González Cartel? Spies from one of the gangs? Or random nobodies like her, just looking for a safer place to sleep?

They were the reason Hector had called this meeting.

Their fate was about to be decided.

NINE

The meeting began with updates on business outside of the prison. Tula stood with her back to the room and thumbed through Hector's vinyl record collection, half-listening to the cadence of deep voices.

Behind her, Hector sat at the table with his closest advisers—Garra, Luis, and a loudmouth, heavy-set *vato* named Simone. Hector's eclectic taste in music fascinated her far more than Simone's complaints about a missing shipment of heroin.

As they argued back and forth, she dug to the bottom of the record stack. His collection included everything from Renaissance composers to Latin American pop, but the majority of the albums covered the breadth of 1960's British bands.

She flipped quickly through the ones she'd seen before. *The Beatles, The Who, The Kinks, The Rolling Stones…*

Wait.

She jumped back to the previous record and slid it from the pile.

On the sleeve, a blond lady with bouffant hair

smiled beneath the title, *Petula Clark's Greatest Hits.*

Who was Petula Clark?

"The new arrivals are Martin Lockwood and Ricardo Saldivar." Hector's soft melodious Spanish drew her gaze over her shoulder. "They were booked on drug trafficking charges."

"Are they cartel?" Garra rested his forearms on the table. "Did González plant them?"

She abandoned the records and drifted toward the conversation, her attention piqued.

"I don't know." Hector met her eyes and gave her a gentle smile before shifting his gaze back to the group. "We don't have anything on them."

That was always the case. The moment a convict was booked into Jaulaso, the prison guards notified Hector. He was given a name and little else.

Funny how La Rocha Cartel knew their shit when it came to drug peddling and illegal firearms, but when they needed to investigate a guy, they were at a loss.

So they did what they did best. They resorted to violence.

"I don't care who they are." Simone ran a finger along his thick mustache. "We need to get rid of them."

He wasn't talking about eviction. They rarely kicked a man out of Area Three. The rejection wouldn't just send a prisoner away mad. It would incite him to join sides with the enemy.

La Rocha needed to grow its numbers, not send potential members to the other side.

"Remember what happened the last time we killed a new arrival?" Garra arched a black eyebrow. "We can't risk another riot."

Her thoughts exactly. When they made inmates disappear without justification, it caused unrest in Area

Three. The inmates started questioning their own longevity within the structure, wondering if and when they were next. That kind of uncertainty bred low morale and weakened loyalties, which often led to an uprising.

After narrowly surviving three riots in two years, she shuddered at the thought of another one.

She paced behind Hector until he pulled out the chair beside him and motioned for her to sit.

"Thank you." She lowered into the seat.

"We need to take them out without anyone knowing it's us." Simone drummed his chubby fingers against his thigh.

"Check this out." Luis leaned in, eyes glimmering. "We'll have a big party. Once the two *gabachos* are drunk out of their minds and everyone else is passed out, I'll go in there and beat them to death."

Everyone laughed but her.

These guys loved to party. A lot of women, cocaine, and alcohol. More than that, they loved to spill blood.

"I'll make it look like one of the inmates did it." Luis smiled proudly. "It's a good idea, yeah?"

More laughter. Several head nods. Everyone seemed on board.

Brawls between inmates were accepted as the norm. Broken bones and knife wounds determined pecking orders and gave the caged animals an outlet to burn off steam. While infighting didn't usually result in death, sometimes it happened.

Luis' ham-handed plan would probably work, but it should be a last resort.

"You don't even know these guys are with the rivals," she heard herself say.

The room fell quiet, and glares hit her from every direction.

Except Hector. He studied her in that fond way he did, with admiration and respect. "You have a better idea?"

She blew out a breath. "You need to be recruiting potential members, not killing them."

"True, but we don't know if the enemy planted them here. We can't rule out the possibility of espionage."

"Then find out who they are and where they're from."

"What do you suggest?" His dark eyes glinted with amusement. "Shall we ask them?"

The room exploded in another round of laughter.

Of course they couldn't ask a spy if he was a spy. She wasn't stupid.

Her teeth clenched. "Tell one of your guys in the city to investigate them."

The ability to access the Internet in Jaulaso was nonexistent, but Hector had endless resources on the outside. Anyone with a web browser could perform an identity search for him.

"I already had a background check done." His lips thinned. "There is no background. No arrest records. No traffic tickets. No history. Nothing on the dark web. Their identities have been wiped."

Oh.

Her stomach sank. "If they're big-time traffickers, they probably paid off people to wipe their identities and make them untraceable. Doesn't mean they work for an enemy cartel."

"Doesn't mean they don't."

"They know Spanish." Simone tightened his fists on the table. "But they whisper in English, so we can't understand what they're saying. They're hiding something."

"Maybe they're just being cautious." She turned back to Hector and asked quietly, "So you're just going to kill them?"

"Yes." He cocked his head, studying her. "Unless you think you can coax them to talk."

"Me?" She jerked back.

"Yes! I like this." Simone heaved forward on his chair, physically interjecting himself. "Put her in a short little dress that shows off her ass and legs with her titties out to here." He cupped the air in front of him. "Send her to the common area, and call up the *gabachos*. When they see her… Boom! They'll want it. They'll want all up inside it."

"No! Absolutely not!" Garra jumped to his feet, his eyes wide and pleading with Hector. "This is not an option."

Her fingernails dug into her palms, her breath stuck in her throat, as she waited for Hector's reaction.

He lit a cigarette, his thoughts hidden behind a blank expression.

"When she gives it to them, she'll pull them in real deep, if you know what I mean." Simone gripped an imaginary body on his lap and thrust his hips.

She clutched her midsection with cold fingers, willing Hector to put an end to this humiliating conversation.

"It's brilliant." Luis slapped Simone on the shoulder and laughed. "A man will do and say anything in a beautiful woman's bed. We'll get them drunk on the pussy and make them talk."

"Stop." A rush of anger swept through her, burning up her cheeks. "I won't—"

"She's not doing it." Garra shot them a harsh squint, his chest thrust-out and jaw tight. "It's too dangerous."

Simone and Luis talked over him, their postures perking up and voices rising as they described the manipulative powers of the vagina.

Luis pulled on Simone's sleeve, dragging him closer. "She can tell them she plans to desert the cartel and needs two strong men to protect her."

What the fuck? She tried to capture Hector's gaze, but his attention remained fixed on his men.

Simone nodded, his eyes flickering. "She'll earn their trust in bed, and they'll be desperate to help her. If they have connections, they'll bring her into their fold and share their confidences."

"What if they're nobodies?" She inhaled through her nose to calm the tremble in her voice.

What if they were innocent? Victims of the wrong place and wrong time? *Just like her.*

Every inmate in Jaulaso claimed to be innocent. Every. Single. One. The Americans would probably say the same thing, and there would be no way to prove it.

"If we confirm they're not working against us," Simone said, "we'll tell them they passed the test and keep them. That'll add to our numbers, just like you said."

She wanted no part of this half-cocked misogynistic plan. Forget the fantasies she had about the new guys. Appreciating their good looks from afar wasn't the same as manipulating them with sex.

They were locked up in the most violent prison in Mexico. Because they were criminals. *Not* the type of men she invited into her bed. Even if it was for the common good of the cartel. Even if they were innocent. Especially if they were innocent. It was too deceitful, and she wasn't a deceitful person.

But she didn't need to vocalize her objections. Garra did it for her, vehemently rejecting every point with a *No,*

Fuck No, and *Over my dead body.*

His duty was to protect her, but his loyalty lay with Hector. Because of that undying allegiance, he was an overachiever in his job as her guard.

The three men continued to debate the advantages and dangers of the proposed plan. Through it all, Hector remained quiet and still, pensively puffing on his cigarette.

Surely, he wasn't considering this? She felt safe with him and trusted he would never force her into doing something as heinous as fucking a man for information.

Within minutes, the conversation shifted from casual to heated. Simone and Luis leaped from their chairs and faced off with Garra, who refused to hear anything they had to say. Volumes rose. Words sharpened, and faces turned red hot.

"What's your problem, Garra?" Simone sneered. "Afraid you'll lose your spot in her bed? She can still fuck you on the side."

The tingling heat of embarrassment crawled up the back of her neck and across her face. As much as she hated Garra's rumors, she never denied them. The pretense of belonging to a powerful man like him discouraged sexual advances.

But, for whatever reason, Simone's accusation sent Garra into a seething rage.

His lips pulled back, and the cords in his neck strained against his gold chains. "Say one more word about that, and I'll kill—"

"Silence." Hector's chillingly calm tone snapped the room into stillness. "Get out. All of you."

She started to rise, but he put a hand on her arm, staying her.

The others left without hesitating, speaking, or glancing back.

The primary rule of Jaulaso was that Hector La Rocha made the rules. His word was law, and disobedience was a capital crime. Anyone who rebelled—like the González Cartel—was considered a sworn enemy and killed if caught.

The Americans... What were their names? Ricardo and Martin? If she slept with them and learned they worked for an enemy, they wouldn't just be executed. Their deaths would be theatrically and gruesomely staged to serve several purposes.

One, it would reassure the residents of Area Three that they were under the protection of the cartel. Two, it would give pause to any rival considering a raid. And most importantly, it would send a message to everyone.

Obey, or you'll end up like this.

She didn't know if Ricardo and Martin had wives, children, or legit lives at home in the States. She didn't know if they were heartless, murdering drug smugglers or clueless tourists framed for a crime they didn't commit. Whomever they were, she didn't want to be responsible for their deaths.

But that wasn't the only reason this plan made her sick to her stomach.

She turned toward Hector and sat taller. "I'm not a whore."

"No." A slow smile built as he switched to perfect English. "These old eyes see an intelligent, respectable woman, who is a pleasure to talk to and easy to trust."

His compliment slipped beneath her guard and softened her voice. "You want me to do this."

"Yes, but I won't demand it." He touched a firm finger beneath her chin and lifted her gaze to his. "It's your choice."

"If I don't do it, you'll have them killed."

"Yes." He lowered his hand.

Either way, their blood would be on her hands.

Unless they were innocent. If they weren't here with nefarious agendas, they would be allowed to stay. She had the opportunity to save their lives.

"You've never concerned yourself with the business." He tilted his head to the side. "Why do you care if the gringos die? Because they're handsome? Mysterious? From your United States?"

"As far as we know, they've done nothing wrong." She lifted a shoulder and looked away. "I don't want to cause the deaths of innocent men."

"So sensitive and delicate. I would protect you from all the ugliness in the world if I could."

He had a way of saying that without sounding condescending. Her ethics were considered a weakness here, but he never patronized or belittled her for it.

She melted in the glow of his warm gaze. "You make it hard to say no to you."

"That's what I hear." He leaned back with a content smile playing at the corner of his lips. "Is that a yes?"

"Yeah." Her pulse quickened. "But I don't have a clue how to do this. What if I can't get them to talk?"

"Then we'll go with Luis' idea."

Throw a party, wait until they're drunk, and beat them to death.

"Super." She gave him a deadpan smile.

"I want updates on your progress."

"Yes, of course." She stood on shaky legs and wiped her palms on her jeans. "Have you heard… Are there any updates on Vera?"

"No. I'm sorry." His eyebrows pulled down, darkening his expression. "My men won't stop searching until they find her."

When she'd told him about her missing sister's possible connection to his cartel, he vowed to look into her disappearance.

"Okay," she said. "Thank you."

As she trudged toward the door, his quiet timbre whispered over her shoulder. "Petula."

She glanced back. "Yeah?"

"You're stronger than you think. You have the courage to do this job, just like when you saved my life. I have faith in you."

Each word loosened the cement around her heart, chipping away jagged pieces until she felt the slow leak of an unfamiliar emotion.

She'd always been grateful for his friendship but hadn't realized how much she needed his approval.

Her mother had kept her at a distance, and she'd never had a mentor or elder to look up to and ask for advice. She needed that. Needed someone to offer guidance on her choices and praise her accomplishments.

Who would've thought Hector La Rocha would fill that role? She should've been terrified of him, but their relationship wasn't like that.

He wasn't a crime boss with her. He was her friend.

The sincerity in his eyes steeled her with determination. She refused to fail. Couldn't bear the thought of disappointing him.

"Thank you." She gave him her fiercest smile. "I won't let you down."

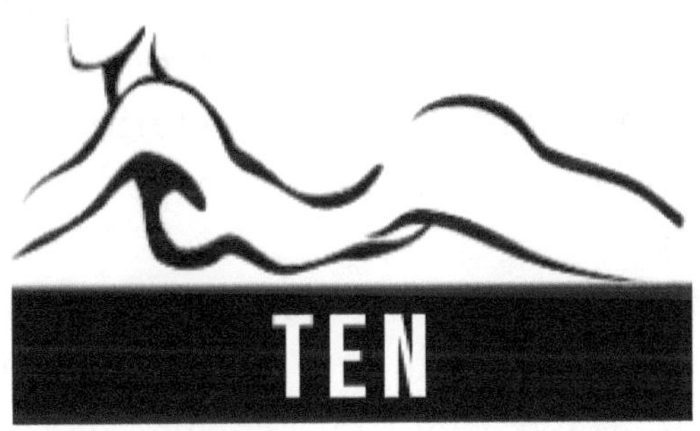

TEN

Back in the hallway, Tula found Garra waiting for her with his arms crossed. She didn't need to tell him what had been decided in Hector's quarters. One look at her and concern sank into the grooves around his eyes and swallowed his glare.

"Don't say anything." She strode down the hall, past her cell, and headed toward the yard for some fresh air. "I get it."

"You get what?" He chased after her, huffing passive-aggressive breaths down her back.

"If something happens to me, you fail your job, and you can't stand the thought of that."

"It's just a job."

"Not to you." She paused at the door to the yard and peered through the grimy window. "See those guys over there covered in tattoos, with the three dots around their eyes and the faceless clocks on their necks? They'll be running in the opposite direction of the trouble you'll be running straight toward. That's why Hector respects you. Because you fear God more than man. You run into battles, outnumbered and undaunted by the outcome, with only loyalty in your heart to your leader."

"That almost sounds like a compliment."

"It's the truth." Her gaze jumped to the gunshot wound on his shoulder, the scarred welt partially covered by his black tank top. "I haven't forgotten, Garra."

He'd taken that bullet for her. During a riot that broke out a year after her arrest, he leaped between her and the shooter.

Before that happened… God, how she'd hated him. She'd made sure he knew it, too, barely speaking to him and forcing him to live that first year like a castrated servant.

When he saved her life, she decided to let go of the past. No more grudges. No more revengeful punishments. She let it all go and gave him a free pass to have sex with whomever was willing.

Maybe that made her a softie. Compared to everyone in here, she was. But when she thought about the compassionate, naive schoolteacher who was arrested two years ago, she knew that woman was gone. None of those soft, sentimental parts remained inside her.

Not even when it came to the man who had taken a bullet for her.

Garra had only been doing his job, and now, she needed him to step back and let her do *her* job. A job that would put her in the arms of a criminal.

Two criminals.

Ricardo and Martin could've been rapists, pedophiles, serial killers, or rival cartel members on a mission to take out anyone close to Hector. She'd agreed to learn who they were by spending an indefinite amount of time with them. Intimate time. *Alone.*

It would be hard enough to manipulate them into

trusting her. If Garra were with her, hovering and watching and listening to every word, they would never open up.

She had to do this on her own, through a series of private moments, away from the watchful eye of her guard.

Garra had already come to this conclusion, given the worry lines etched on his face. He knew the gun on her hip would come off during sex, and she wouldn't be able to defend herself.

Not while she was naked.

Spread beneath a hard body.

With a dick thrusting inside her.

Her breath caught. Her pulse sprinted, and a sudden rush of heat throbbed between her legs.

She clenched her thighs together.

Christ, where did *that* come from? She hadn't experienced arousal since before her arrest. She'd almost forgotten what it felt like.

Two years without sex, and now she was supposed to be some kind of femme fatale? It felt impossible.

"I hate this as much as you do." She opened the door and stepped into the sunlight, grateful for the cool breeze. "You don't want to disappoint Hector by failing at your job, and neither do I."

A fire burned in her belly as she crossed the yard toward her favorite bench. She would tackle this challenge with the same tenacity that got her out of the slums of Ciudad Hueca.

She'd put herself through college, graduated with honors, and immigrated to the U.S. all on her own.

She could do this.

What were the first steps? She needed to approach the Americans, let them know they could interact with her.

Then she would need to talk to them, without coming across as obvious or desperate.

Where should this happen? She glanced around at the dozen or so inmates in the yard. Not here. Too many ears.

"Garra." She met his eyes over her shoulder. "Why don't they have their own cell?"

"They haven't earned it."

No one paid rent the way she had when she first arrived. She'd realized later that Garra had arranged that special moment in hell just for her.

She turned to face him and lowered her voice to a whisper. "I can't do this with everyone watching and listening. Give them a cell."

"No."

"Then move two beds into mine."

It was a hollow demand. She would never willingly share her cell with a stranger, let alone two strangers. She also knew Garra would never agree to it.

"I'll find them some space," he growled.

"A private cell. With a lock." If this turned into a sexual thing, she didn't want anyone walking in.

"Fine." His nostrils flared.

"Today. Right now."

He drew in a sharp inhale and scanned the yard, likely searching for inmates who might threaten her. A moment later, he stormed off.

She treaded in the other direction. As she neared her bench, a pack of five men came into view around the corner.

All muscle, tattoos, and menace, they walked with cocky swaggers and eyes locked on wherever they were headed.

She followed their gazes to a table, where the two

Americans sat alone.

Shit.

Ricardo and Martin were about to meet the welcoming committee, and it wouldn't be gentle.

Her muscles tensed, and she glanced in the direction Garra had headed. No luck.

Even if he were here, he would never interfere in a yard fight. And she had no power or authority over anyone, which was why Garra didn't like to leave her side.

She had no choice but to let this play out.

Her bench sat within hearing range of the confrontation. No one looked in her direction as she lowered onto the sun-soaked seat.

"Hey, *gabachos.*" A huge bald man known as Papá approached the black-haired guy, who she assumed was Ricardo. "I have a list for you. Make sure we get everything on it by tomorrow."

The wrinkled paper in Papá's fist probably demanded things like cigarettes, soap, underwear, and other goods that could be purchased or traded at the canteen.

"Sure, can I see it?" Ricardo asked in fluent Spanish and slowly stood.

As Papá handed over the list, Ricardo slammed a fist into the huge man's nose.

"Oh, fuck." Her hand flew to the grip of her gun, knowing full well they would kill her if she interfered.

In a blur of bodies, five men with sledgehammer arms slammed into the Americans.

She expected them to fall beneath the beating. Or run for their lives. Either option would've labeled them as cowards and turned them into permanent punching bags. Or worse.

But they didn't cower.

They hit back, furiously, expertly, and without fear. Even more incredible was the awareness they had of each other. They worked in tandem, one of them punching high while the other kicked low. Their strikes were synchronized, their arms and legs moving as if controlled by one mind.

The way they predicted each other's movements was mind-boggling. They must've trained together. A lot.

Their bodies carried the muscled strength and coordination of men who had dedicated some serious time to the heavy bag. Biceps flexed with every punch. Pectorals contracted and heaved against the stretch of their shirts. Powerful legs delivered blows that sent a massive man like Papá into a stunned lurch of discombobulated limbs.

Make no mistake, the new guys were getting their asses kicked. But through it all, they shared secret smiles as if they weren't engaged in a fight they couldn't win.

She held her breath as the sounds of meaty knuckles pounded flesh, cartilage, and sinew. Grunts rent the air, and Papá's team started to stagger. A couple of the men stumbled out of the throe, bleeding from cuts on their faces.

The instant Ricardo and Martin dropped to the ground, the battle was over.

They lay on their backs, sweating into the dirt and gasping for breaths. Their attackers wiped away blood, straightened their clothes, and limped out of the yard.

There was no heckling, trash talk, or cheap shots as they departed. The silent exit was a form of praise to the new guys for having enough heart to fight a battle they knew they would lose.

She released a sigh of relief then silently scolded herself for caring.

Ricardo and Martin had just earned respect, but that

didn't mean there wouldn't be more tests and harder fights.

Martin pushed into a sitting position, his expression strained, scowling beneath a sheen of blood.

"For our first prison fight," he said in drawling English, "that wasn't bad."

His friend dropped a forearm over his eyes and groaned. "Yippee-ki-yay, motherfucker."

She felt a tic in her cheek. An unfamiliar emotion.

I like them.

The sentiment was neither here nor there. She had a job to do, and it started now.

Drawing in a deep breath to calm her heart, she stood from the bench and made her way toward them.

Martin noticed her first and rose to his feet with a grace that didn't match his rugged, banged-up physique.

He looked like hell, with a bloody nose, fat lip, and his shirt hanging in shreds around his sweat-slick neck. She'd never seen anything sexier in her life.

His blond hair was short on top and even shorter on the sides. He wore dark fitted jeans that hung low on narrow hips and a thin layer of scruff on his chiseled jaw.

His lashes, thick and golden, hooded his deep emerald eyes as he perused her from head to toe.

An unexpected shiver slid across her skin.

"You must be Martin," she said in English and shifted toward the man lying on the ground at her feet. "And Ricardo."

Ricardo moved his arm from his face and stared up at her with velvety brown eyes. "Ricky."

Ricky and Martin.

"Livin' la Vida Loca?" The instant she blurted the question, she felt awkward.

Ricky shot her a stony glare, and Martin's eyebrows

gathered.

Of course, they were confused. She'd ignored them for days, and now she was poking fun at them.

Two years in this place and she'd completely forgotten how to socialize.

"Ricky Martin. You know, he sang that song…?" She shook her head. "You do speak English, right?"

"We thought we were the only ones," Martin said in English.

Perfect. That was the language she would continue to use with them. Maybe it would help them connect with her.

"To what do we owe the pleasure?" Ricky rose to his full height, stretching over six feet of gorgeous masculinity. "Petula, is it?"

Well, hello, Tall, Dark, and Handsome.

He was as tall as Martin, dark where Martin was fair, and just as gorgeous close up. She loved the trendy look of his thick black hairstyle, the way the strands tumbled loosely and disorderly on top and faded beneath a severe side part into shaved sides.

Neither man bore visible tattoos, piercings, or track marks from heroin use. No wedding rings, either.

Maybe they were carrying assassination orders in their back pockets. But at first glance, they seemed like they would show up on a first date with flowers. *And condoms.* But not guns.

"It's Tula, and you two look like you could use a drink." She turned away, tossing an order over her shoulder. "Walk with me."

She didn't wait for them to follow, and after a few steps, her nerves tightened. Dammit, they weren't coming.

Way to make a fool of yourself, Tula.

She was in over her head, but she kept walking, one

foot in front of the other, chin up.

Then the sound of shoes scuffed behind her. They grew closer and flanked her on either side, invading her senses with testosterone and body heat.

Her eyes wanted to steal greedy glances at them, but she trained them forward and planned her next step.

If they were going to tell her anything, they would have to trust her first.

She needed to make herself vulnerable. Because what man didn't trust a vulnerable woman?

Blood dripped from head wounds and multiple cuts on their bodies, and Martin's swollen lip looked pretty painful. She had the supplies to clean them up and the alcohol to numb the aches.

In her private cell.

That was where she would take them.

For the first time in two years, she was going to open herself up and invite someone in.

She just hoped they wouldn't hurt her the way Garra had.

ELEVEN

Pain coughed through Ricky's battered chest, and every step aggravated his throbbing shins. He had a few scrapes, some cuts, and a bruise on his ego. Nothing he couldn't handle. After a stiff drink and full night's sleep, he would be back in business.

His partner in crime lumbered along with a slight limp, sporting two sexy shiners on his face and a fair amount of blood on his shirt.

Tula strolled between them, setting an unhurried pace with her shorter legs.

He and Martin had noticed her in the yard right before the muscle squad showed up. Just what a guy wanted—a beautiful woman watching him get his ass kicked up between his shoulder blades. Good times.

As she led them deeper into the maze of hallways, he eyed her up and down in his periphery.

The graceful dip of her waist flared into a round, tight ass. The sinuous line of her neck, small tits, and toned thighs in denim formed an irresistible shape.

Everything about her was delicate, from her petite

height and slender tattooed arms to her pert nose and small feet. It would take no effort at all to lift her with a hand around her throat and pin her against Martin's chest. Before she could sputter an objection, he would have her separated from her gun and restrained between him and Martin, with his mouth on her lips and Martin's teeth scraping her neck.

Could she take them at the same time? Or was her pussy too tight? They would have to go slow, give her time to adjust to the stretch of two cocks.

Goddamn, just thinking about it made him hard.

Watching her walk next to Martin, seeing them side by side, it was the *only* thing he could think about. Martin's blond hair, chiseled features, and broad chest towering over Tula's head of long black hair, vivid brown eyes, and dainty figure… They were balls-grippingly gorgeous.

She veered into the corridor a few steps ahead of them, and he exchanged a look with Martin.

His friend raised an eyebrow as if to say, *This was too easy.*

He gave Martin a shrug. *Roll with it.*

"We're almost there." She escorted them down a long run, with a two-story wall of cells on one side overlooking a dining area on the other.

Rectangular tables lined up in rows, and large pots of beans simmered on the stove. The scent of kerosene, grease, and cigarette smoke pervaded the air, and rotting garbage strewed the floor where inmates ate.

He and Martin had managed to avoid that unventilated, windowless shithole, choosing instead to buy watery onion broth and tortillas from the canteen.

"How are you making it in here?" she asked.

Jaulaso lived up to its squalid reputation, with its racist cliques, petty hall fights, inedible food, and endless hours of soul-sucking misery.

He grunted. "It's a lot like high school."

"With guns and knives." Martin glanced at the group of armed men they'd just passed.

"This is your first time in prison?" Her dark eyes flicked between him and Martin. "Both of you?"

"Yup." He stepped around a Jurassic-sized cockroach on the floor and shuddered.

"Your ability to throw hands made an impression in the yard." She glanced at Ricky. "That right cross you caught Papá with made his knees go out."

"You mean the bald-headed diesel?"

"Yeah. You hit him so hard he wobbled away like a baby giraffe." She stopped at a cell door and met his eyes. "There's a saying around here."

"Don't drop the soap?"

Her pretty red lips formed a tense line. "An ass whipping washes off. A coward isn't forgotten." She opened the door and waved them in. "Let's get you cleaned up."

His position in the hall gave him a view of women's jeans and shirts hanging from a pipe in the ceiling and floral hair products lined up on the small sink. A single bed sat in the corner, piled with folded blankets.

This was her private cell, and she was inviting them inside? Where was her surly, overprotective guard?

Martin wore an expression that matched the unease in Ricky's gut.

Why had she brought them here alone? Was it a trap she and Garra had set up? Or maybe she'd waited until Garra was distracted so she could lead them here without his notice? For what reason? To fuck around behind his back?

He and Martin knew better than to touch another

man's woman, especially in prison.

"Where's your boyfriend?" he asked.

"What?" Her eyes widened. Then she exhaled past a frown. "You mean Garra. We don't... We're not together. He just watches out for me."

"You should tell *him* that." Martin glanced up and down the hall as if expecting Garra to leap from the shadows. "He dishes out threats to anyone who looks at you, like you're his property."

"He wishes." Her mouth relaxed, and the corners curved upward. Her cheeks rose, and her lips parted, setting free a blinding, dick-hardening grin. "That asshole takes his job way too seriously."

Christ, her smile. It possessed her entire body, pushing away the tension in her muscles and illuminating the golden streaks in her brown eyes. Fucking beautiful.

"Asshole, huh?" Martin braced a hand on the wall above her head and leaned down to imprison her eyes. "You're the only female inmate in Area Three, and you're telling us there's no boyfriend? No lovers or anyone who might feel compelled to pump us full of lead for talking to you?"

"There's no one. Even if there was, *I* decide who talks to me." Her smile flattened between clamped lips. "I'm offering you a drink, medicine for your cuts, and amicable conversation." She narrowed her eyes. "Kindness is rare around here. I wouldn't pass it up if I were you."

"Why do you have medical supplies in your cell?" Ricky crossed his arms.

"Since Garra is determined to block every challenge aimed at me, the least I can do is keep supplies on hand whenever he eats a fist."

"That happens often?" Ricky asked.

She shrugged.

Every item acquired in Jaulaso was earned, traded, or bought with prison currency, such as cigarettes or food. It would've taken her months, if not years, to collect alcohol and medicine. And she was offering her invaluable stash to two strangers.

Why? He trusted her about as much as he trusted everyone else in Jaulaso, but she might be their only access to Hector La Rocha.

The cartel boss didn't let women into his dirty fraternity. But he made an exception for Tula Gomez. She must've been important to him.

Ricky entered her cell with a tingle of apprehension between his shoulder blades. Martin followed, and she shut the door behind them.

"What about you?" She stepped toward the small sink and rummaged through the supplies on the floor. "Any spouses or committed relationships waiting at home?"

"Nope." He stood beside the cot, scrutinizing the claustrophobic space.

Several crates of books, cartons of cigarettes, a portable cooking stove, and an old cell phone summed up her belongings. She'd definitely been here a while.

He and Martin only had the clothes they were wearing and the cash in their pockets. Everything else had been confiscated during their arrest, as expected.

"Tequila?" Crouched beneath the sink, she held out a bottle behind her.

"Thanks." Martin lifted it from her hand and removed the cap, glaring at the gold contents as if hesitant to drink.

"I don't have cups. Are you not used to slumming it?" She snatched the tequila and sipped straight from the bottle. "Where did you say you were from?"

"We didn't." Ricky grabbed the bottle and swallowed a long pull, savoring the smooth burn of agave before handing it to Martin. "Where did you learn to speak English so well?"

"College. I'm a Spanish high schoolteacher in the States." She paused, and her eyes lost focus as if she were rearranging her thoughts. "I *was*." She blinked. "Never dreamed I'd end my career with a prison sentence, but here I am." Her fist gave an unenthusiastic pump in the air. "Killin' it."

"What are you in for?" Martin lowered onto the mattress and rested his elbows on his knees, watching her from beneath the bloody gashes on his brow.

"Drug smuggling."

Why did you do it? Did *you do it?* The silence exhaled the questions so loudly they didn't need to be voiced.

"I'm innocent." She grabbed some gauze and a bottle of antiseptic solution. "Same thing every prisoner says." She held up the supplies. "Who's first?"

He nodded at Martin. "This guy needs all the Band-aids you got. He's been holding back tears since we left the yard."

With a swollen-lipped scowl, Martin flipped him off.

"Take off your shirt." She peered at Martin from beneath her lashes. "I'll soak it in the sink and try to get the blood out."

This would be interesting. Martin wasn't exactly the touchy-feely type, especially around strangers.

"Don't bother. It's ripped to hell." Martin reached behind his head with a pained grimace and pulled off the shirt.

Ricky lowered onto the bed beside Martin and examined the defined cuts of muscle he'd been drooling over for seven years.

Martin had always been fit, but the past six months of training had turned his body into a chiseled work of art.

He and Ricky had spent several grueling hours a day together, rolling around on a mat, boxing in a ring, and lifting weights. The torture hadn't just been physical.

His hands knew every inch of Martin's body, and it wasn't enough. The urge to reach for Martin plagued him constantly, to feel all that strength against him, the press of hot skin, and the gust of frantic breaths as their bodies moved as one.

"How do you know each other?" She poured the antiseptic solution onto a swath of gauze and inspected Martin's swollen eyes. "I assume you were arrested together?"

"It's a long story." Martin angled forward, putting his face within an inch of hers.

"We have nothing but time." She didn't try to reclaim the personal space he penetrated. "Get it? Time?" She sighed. "Prison joke."

"Why are you helping us?" Martin leaned back and pressed his scowl to the lip of the bottle, taking a swig.

"Why are you here?"

"Drug trafficking," Ricky said.

He and Martin could be honest about everything except their alliance with the Restrepo Cartel and the assignment that put them here.

"Let me guess." She touched the medicated gauze against the cut above Martin's eye. "You're innocent."

"We're guilty of many things." Ricky grabbed the tequila and slugged it back.

She glanced between them, and her eyebrows gathered. "Are you lovers?"

The alcohol went down the wrong pipe, and he tried his damnedest to stifle a coughing fit.

"No." Martin glared at him. "Why would you ask that?"

"You seem close. I don't know." She shrugged. "The way you look at each other... It's intimate."

"I'm attracted to him." Ricky calmed his gag reflex and took another drink. "He's attracted to women. At the end of the day, all that matters is our friendship."

"Oh. That..." She moved the gauze to the cut on Martin's lip. "Sounds complicated."

"We don't make it complicated." He winked at Martin, coaxing a soft smile from that handsome face.

"Such a guy thing to say." She gave him a dissecting look, up, down, and through the heart. "Are you only interested in men or do you—?"

"Don't worry, Tula." His direct eye contact made her swallow. "You're definitely my type."

"That's not what I—"

"Then why did you ask?"

"Just making conversation." She gathered more gauze.

"Asking a man his sexual orientation is one way to make conversation." He rubbed his jaw. "Tells me where your mind's at."

Her mouth opened, closed, and opened again. "You brought it up."

"No, *you* did when you asked if we were lovers."

With an annoyed inhale, she rolled her eyes to the ceiling. Then she turned back to Martin. "Your friend's a pain in the ass."

Martin bit back a smile, likely anticipating Ricky's response.

"Darling," Ricky said in a low voice, "if I was in your ass, *pain* would be the last thing you'd feel."

The bottle of antiseptic fell from her hand.

"Shit." As she leaned down to recover it, her gaze found Martin's. "I can't tell if he's a smartass, a badass, or just an ass."

Martin grabbed the bottle before she reached it. "Most people don't know how to take him."

"It's kind of a gift." Ricky devoured the view of her backside as she bent to examine Martin's chest for wounds.

"How long have you known each other?" she asked.

"Seven years." Martin handed her the antiseptic. "I needed a place to live. Ricky and the others had a spare bed."

"The others?" She wiped away a smear of blood on his chest.

"We have a few roommates."

"Is that the long story you mentioned?"

"Everybody has one." He squinted at her. "What's yours?"

"Wrong place. Wrong time." She edged closer, her eyes fixed on his lap as she reached for a splotch of blood on his waistband. "Looks like you got hit—"

Martin sprung from the bed in a blink. His hand seized her throat and slammed her back against the wall before Ricky could process what was happening.

TWELVE

"Martin!" Ricky's heart rate doubled as he jumped to his feet. "What the fuck?"

Tula jerked against Martin's hand at her throat and went for the gun in her waistband. Ricky beat her to it and tossed it out of reach on the bed.

"Hey, man." He put his face into Martin's line of sight without touching him. "Snap out of it."

Martin bared his teeth through a feral grimace. His green eyes glazed over with a faraway look, one he wore whenever he fell into the mysterious black hole of his past.

It could've been his time in Van's attic or something from his childhood. Whatever haunted him had been set off when Tula touched his waist.

"Let go!" She thrashed beneath his grip and shoved uselessly at his chest. Her wide eyes darted to Ricky, the brown depths pooling with fear. "Get him off me!"

"Martin, look at me." He hardened his tone. "Right now."

Slowly, Martin turned his head. His lashes lowered and lifted through a long blink, and he dropped his hand.

She clutched her splotchy neck and gulped for air. Her cheeks went from pale to an angry shade of red, and her eyes zeroed in on the gun.

In the next breath, she launched for it, but Ricky caught her around the waist.

"Hold up." He didn't have to restrain her or use much force to guide her slight weight in the opposite direction. "Martin, how are you doing?"

"Fine." Martin paced away, dragging his hands down his face.

Muscles rippled along either side of his spine, and he rolled his shoulders as if trying to shake off his demons.

The impulse to erase the distance and comfort Martin gripped him hard, but it would only end in rejection.

Breathing heavily, Tula backed away, her eyebrows squished in confusion.

Ricky turned to the mess that had been made during the scuffle and used Martin's ruined shirt to wipe up the spilled antiseptic solution. Thankfully, the bottle of tequila still sat upright on the floor.

"What did I do wrong?" She picked up the scattered gauze and approached Martin cautiously. "Tell me so I don't repeat it."

"Nothing." Martin shifted to the sink and rested his backside on the edge. His hand went to his brow, rubbing restlessly as he blew out a breath. "You did nothing wrong."

"Liar." She stepped right up to him and gazed into his eyes. "I touched your waist. Or was it your hip? Is there a no-touch zone?"

"What?" Irritation vibrated through his tone.

"What?" she snapped back.

They seemed to be feeding off the tension in the air

between them, but there was something else going on.

They scrutinized each other, not in a confrontational standoff, but in some kind of intense, wordless conversation.

Whatever Martin read in her eyes started to calm the storm in his. Her expression softened, growing solemn. After a suspended moment of eye contact, she spoke.

"When I was arrested two years ago, the Mexican military tortured me with…" Her chest hitched. "I don't know what it was. They electrocuted me with a rod, vaginally and anally, for eight hours straight."

Ricky's insides turned to cement.

She stared into Martin's stark green eyes. "Then they transported me here, and on the first night, an inmate attacked me." Her hands flexed and released at her sides. "I strangled him. I don't know how, but I killed him."

The rumors were true? Maybe she was lying, but if so, she had a damn good poker face. He'd never seen a woman look as vulnerable as she did now.

With her shoulders curled forward and the dull sheen over her eyes, she appeared to be drowning in a violent ocean of memories.

"I gave a prison guard all my cash to bring me here." Her voice wobbled, and she pressed the heel of her palm against her stomach. "Area Three was supposed to be safer. I didn't know I'd have to pay rent for this cell."

A chill spread across Ricky's scalp. Martin said nothing, but his stony expression spoke volumes. They both knew what sort of payment would be demanded of a beautiful woman in prison.

"That same night," she said quietly, "I had to pay with my body. It felt like rape. Or *worse* because I couldn't say no. I had to just lie there and take it." Her gaze slipped to the bed before jerking back to Martin. "I killed a man for trying to rape me, yet the one who succeeded still lives. He's not a threat to me anymore, but I struggle with…what he did to me. Maybe someday, I'll forgive him, but I doubt it."

He glanced between her and Martin, his chest tight as he processed her words. Not only had she been tortured by electrocution, but within hours, someone had forced himself inside her injured body.

Was it Garra? He seemed to be the property manager around here. If he raped her, that would explain his possessiveness, as well as the standoffish way she interacted with him.

Ricky's pulse elevated, and his blood heated to punish that son of a bitch.

"What about you?" She drifted closer to Martin, leaving a sliver of space without touching him. "Is the source of your pain still alive?"

Ricky leaned forward, holding his breath.

She might've figured out Martin had a tortured past, but she would never be able to draw the details out of him. He wouldn't even talk to Ricky about it.

Seconds filled the silence, each one stirring a disquiet through the room as she watched Martin, waiting for an answer.

Ricky was confident his friend wouldn't respond.

Until Martin reached for her hand.

"I killed the first one." Martin closed his fingers around her tiny, tattooed wrist. "The second one still lives, and like you, I doubt I'll ever forgive him."

Ricky's heart stopped, and pinpricks stabbed the base of his skull. The one who lived was Van Quiso. But who was the first one?

He'd suspected something terrible had happened to Martin before Van captured him, but Martin had never given any indication he'd killed someone.

Someone who had caused him pain.

Was it a relative from his childhood? A stranger on the street? Was the murder premeditated or self-defense? Had he been alone? What happened to the body?

Martin had given Tula—a woman he'd just met—more insight into his past than he'd ever offered Ricky. Why her? Because she'd shared a tragic story? He didn't even know if she was telling the truth.

Ricky tried to rein in the hurt that smoldered in his gut, but it only magnified as he watched them look at each other with mutual understanding.

Unbelievable.

He could actually feel the beginning of something spark and hold between them. Made him feel like a goddamn third wheel, interloping on a private moment.

Jesus, get a grip, you jealous fuck.

He and Martin were here for a job. If the sexy little vixen had a thing for his best friend, they could use that to ply her into spilling secrets about Hector La Rocha.

Screw it. They could eye fuck each other for as long as they wanted.

He reached for the medical supplies and tended to his wounds. But after a few irritating swipes of the gauze, he couldn't stop his gaze from gravitating back to them.

Martin guided her hand to his waist and pressed her palm against his skin, proving he didn't have an issue with touching.

Very few people invaded his personal space because of those fuck-off vibes he exuded. But she'd reached right through that when she touched him the first time.

That must've been what triggered him. He wasn't used to physical contact. Except she'd put her hands on his face to clean his wounds. He hadn't flipped out until she went for his pants.

Now that he'd given her permission to touch, she splayed her fingers against his nude stomach, lingering there for a long moment. Then she explored the mouthwatering grooves that carved a *V* from his hips to the low-waisted dip of his jeans.

Ricky imagined all that honed power flexing against his own hand—the corrugated ridges of abs and the heat of life pumping beneath warm, smooth skin.

A surge of hunger raced through his veins, and his body hardened as he indulged in an unobtainable fantasy where the three of them fell into bed together. In the heat of passion, Tula gave them the locations of the cartel's major players in the sex trafficking ring. Martin realized he wanted Ricky as deeply as Ricky wanted him. They vowed to protect the woman in their arms and fucked one another in every position imaginable for the rest of their lives.

"I was going to check the bleeding here." She glided her palm toward the red splotch on Martin's waistband.

"It's not my blood." Martin watched her from mere inches away.

"Oh. Okay, I might be able to wash it out."

"I'm not taking off my pants."

"No, of course not. I…" Her fingers brushed the flat expanse of his abs as she withdrew her hand. "I'll check your back if you turn around."

Ricky clenched his teeth and twisted away to clean the broken skin on his knuckles.

The bottle of tequila on the floor caught his eye, and he nudged it closer with his foot. As he finished patching up his hands, he poured the potent drink down his throat, hoping to escalate the *D* in drunk. Or the *E* in *ebrio,* if he wanted to be really Mexican about it.

A moment later, the soft sound of her footsteps

approached, bringing with it the feminine scent of her shampoo or soap or whatever the hell she used to make her body smell so damn delicious.

"Want me to clean that cut on your face?" She tapped her fingers on her denim-clad thighs.

"Already took care of it." He rose and stepped around her, headed toward the sink.

Martin shifted out of his way. He didn't look at those green eyes as he washed his hands and face, but he felt them burning into the back of his head.

Her cell was too small for the three of them, and ignoring Martin made him feel hot and itchy in his skin.

If he looked at Martin, there would be a confrontation, and this wasn't the time to clear the air between them. Not with Tula cataloging everything. He didn't trust her.

A knock sounded on the door.

She opened it, and lo and behold, her scowling guard stood on the other side.

"Their cell is ready." Garra glared at him and Martin before giving Tula a possessive once-over. "Number 24. Right above you." He flicked a finger toward the ceiling.

When he strode away, she closed the door and turned.

"You got us our own cell?" Ricky dried off his face with the hem of his shirt.

"Yeah." Her attention dipped to his exposed abs, and her lips parted.

He lowered the shirt, his thoughts stuck on why and *how* she arranged a room for them.

"Explain how the rent works." Martin approached her, voicing Ricky's chief concern.

If Garra expected sex from her or them in exchange for a cell, he could eat his own dick. They would continue sleeping on the floor in the common area.

"There's no rent." She raised her chin.

"How?" Ricky asked.

"I have some leeway here."

"How?" He asked again, harder this time.

She drew in a breath and released it. "I work directly for the boss."

"You work for Hector La Rocha?" Martin crossed his arms over his chest. "A little thing like you—"

"Go ahead and misjudge me. That'll be fun."

Martin barked a derisive sound of laughter that immediately cut off as she shoved the barrel of her pistol beneath his jaw.

Ricky froze, and his training kicked in.

Her finger wasn't on the trigger, and most of her weight rested on one leg. He could sweep that foot and redirect the gun before she fired. One miscalculation, however, would put a hole through Martin's head.

How the hell did she even recover the gun without them noticing? She must've grabbed it when she answered the door?

"Tula," Ricky said slowly and captured her eyes. "The rumor that your boss doesn't employ women is clearly incorrect. As for the gossip that you can defend yourself against men twice your size? I can dispel that rumor, too." He looked at the gun and back to her. "You absolutely can."

She searched his face, her huge eyes shining with distrust and perhaps a hint of appeasement.

He held still, letting the moment work itself out as he drank in her incredible beauty.

Black satiny hair tumbled to her elbows. Tawny skin radiated beneath swirls of ink on her toned arms, and rosy lips pursed with suspicion. She reminded him of fire, glowing in warm hues of red, gold, and black against the cold gray cement of her cell.

Finally, she lowered the gun and opened the door. "Use the stairwell on the left. Your cell is on the second floor. Above mine. Number 24."

His chest tightened. She was kicking them out.

With a glance at Martin, he stepped into the hall.

"Thank you for getting the cell." Martin followed him out and turned back. "Why are you helping us?"

"Not for the reasons you think."

"What are—?"

She shut the door in his face.

THIRTEEN

Ricky made a choking sound in the dark, windowless concrete cell, wishing he hadn't just taken that weary breath. The sweltering, roach-infested space reeked of human waste and poor life choices.

The socket above the sink didn't have a bulb, but the door had a lock. Not that he would close it right now and block the only light from the hall.

Two mattresses sat side by side on metal frames, leaving a small walkway to the toilet.

This was where he would be sleeping with Martin for the next three months.

On the bright side, it was a step up from the floor in the common area. The lock on the door would allow them to sleep with both eyes closed.

Martin glanced up and down the empty hallway and stepped into the cell. In two long-legged strides, he reached Ricky's side.

His bruised face closed in, and his green eyes burned for a fight. "What the fuck is your problem?"

"*My* problem?" Ricky whispered harshly. "You're

the one who lost your shit. Why did you attack her?"

"It won't happen again. Can you say the same?"

"About what?"

"You know what." Martin scraped a hand over his head. "Jesus, fuck, Ricky. You can't get butthurt whenever I talk to her."

"Why did you tell her about your past?"

"I told her *one* thing. Nothing important."

"It was more than you've ever told me."

"This is exactly what I'm talking about. Your fucking jealousy—"

"Who did you kill?"

Martin's head drew back stiffly, his lips flattening in a stubborn line. Then he narrowed his eyes. "I've killed several men with Camila. You were there."

"Before her. Before the Freedom Fighters. Who did you kill?"

His silence stabbed with refusal.

"Why her?" Ricky slumped against the wall and wiped the pain from his expression. "Why now?"

"There's something… Shit, I don't know. She has this pure sort of openness about her that compels me. Not just her story, but the look in her eyes, the sadness in her voice." Martin bowed his head, causing the shadows to shift across the sharp angles of his features. "She gave me a vulnerable moment."

"I've never given you that?"

"No." Martin braced an arm on the wall beside Ricky's head. "There's nothing vulnerable about you. You're confident in your skin and strong as hell. Look at how you handled Van. You and I endured the same hell in his attic. Yet you overcame it without looking back. Fuck, I admire that and expect nothing less from you." Martin touched Ricky's jaw. "I wouldn't want you any other way."

"You don't want me in *any* way." He turned his neck, jerking away from the extraordinary touch.

"That's not—"

"Forget it. I'm just being a dick."

He'd mastered the art of pretending Martin's rejections didn't hurt, but every interaction hit hard and dug deep. For seven years, he suffered in silence, shouldered the agony of wanting what he couldn't have, and buried the ache whenever Martin rubbed up against his space.

Like now.

He pulled in a breath and focused on the mission. "She's not as vulnerable as you think."

"No, she's not." Martin's mouth hovered an inch away, his voice low. "She survived this place for two years on her own."

"An American high school teacher, and she works for Hector La Rocha. It's too unbelievable to be a lie. I mean, if she's going to feed us bullshit, she'd make it easier to swallow, right?"

"Exactly. She hasn't lied to us." A muscle twitched at the corner of Martin's swollen lips. A smile. Barely. But a smile, nonetheless.

"You're attracted to her."

"That's an understatement. But…" Martin's gaze darted to the hall, and he tipped his head as if listening for footsteps. Then he bent in and put his mouth at Ricky's ear. "*You* are going to fuck her."

Sudden, raw desire spun up his pulse and caught his skin on fire. The gravelly command in Martin's voice, the heat of Martin's body against his, and the thought of fucking Tula Gomez while Martin watched—all of it gripped him between his legs, tightening his balls and lengthening his cock.

He pressed himself against the cold concrete wall, fighting the impulse to kick his hips forward and mindlessly grind against the gorgeous man leaning into him.

Martin seemed to sense his inner battle and started to move away.

"Wait." He gripped Martin's waist, holding tight to hard muscle. "Let me have this. Just… Just let me feel us for a second."

The cost of having feelings for Martin had left him needy and destitute. He had no romantic relationships, no interest in finding someone else. His heart wanted Martin or no one at all.

He braced for the bane of his life to push away, his mind already closing itself off to the possibility of a stolen moment.

Martin shifted and stretched an arm toward the door. His fingers caught the edge, and he swung it closed, blanketing them in darkness.

Every cell in Ricky's body thrummed to acute awareness.

With a long, heavy exhale, Martin slowly eased his weight against the front of Ricky's body. Chest to chest, hip to hip, Martin let him feel the press of hot skin and six feet of carved masculinity.

He fisted a hand in Ricky's hair and rested their foreheads together, breathing softly, comfortably, sinking into the bond.

Goddamn, the divine torture. The blissful hell. It was everything and not nearly enough.

He dug his fingers into Martin's waist, his cock throbbing in his jeans, trapped between the crush of their hips.

Martin didn't rock against him or jerk away in repulsion. Ricky's need was front and center, a bulging rock between them, conspicuous and unrequited.

"I'm sorry I can't give you what you need." Immersed in blackness, Martin tightened his fingers in Ricky's hair and flattened his other hand on the wall. "If I'd met you before… Before my head got all fucked up, I would've made you mine."

Ricky's heartbeat went off the deep end and crashed into a pool of chaotic hope.

"You mean—" He choked on a leaden tongue. "You're open to being with men?"

"I never told you I wasn't. You made assumptions."

"You never told me you *were.*" An overload of ecstatic hope consumed him. "If you can be with men…"

"I'm broken, Ricky. Incapable of being with anyone." With a sigh, Martin removed his touch and stepped away. The mattress squeaked, signaling his distance in the dark.

"Why? Because of the man you killed?"

"Never said it was a man."

"You didn't have to."

Ricky was tempted to open the door so that the hallway would shed light on Martin's expression. But maybe the concealment of darkness would make it easier to expose secrets.

"Tell me what he did to you." A pang gnawed in his chest as he imagined the level of hurt Martin would've endured to push him to kill someone. "How does it connect to Van Quiso?"

"I can't talk about this."

"Why not? I'm your best friend. The person you trust more than anyone else."

"Because everything that happened…" Martin's voice dropped to a raspy whisper. "It was *my* fault. *My* ignorant choices. I'm fucking ashamed of it, and I won't… I refuse to change your perception of me."

"I would never—"

"Drop it. I'm done discussing it."

His heart collapsed. "I need to say one more thing." At Martin's silence, he pushed off the wall and glared into the rancid darkness. "It doesn't matter who you open up to about your past. If it helps you to talk to Tula, I won't get butthurt over it."

When Martin said nothing, he opened the door and surveyed their dismal cell in the light. They needed to eat, but he wasn't in the mood to scrounge up their next unsatisfying meal.

Instead, he tackled the filthy mattresses. Martin helped him drag them into the hall and beat the dust out of them.

Once the beds were put back together, he cursed his sore ribs and surveyed the darkening bruises on Martin's face.

As Martin reclined on one of the mattresses, his movements were slow and stiff. An indication he was in more pain than he let on.

Today's fight in the yard wouldn't be their last physical altercation. The inmates were walking powder kegs, ready to explode and looking for a target. If he and Martin limped into the common area in search of food right now, they would probably be attacked again.

They needed to sleep, give their wounds time to heal, and discuss Tula Gomez.

"Can you wait until tomorrow to eat?" He gave the quiet hall another glance.

"I'll manage."

He closed and locked the door and lay beside Martin in the foulness of their pitch-black cell. His mind churned through everything that had transpired today and stalled on something Martin had said.

"Why did you tell me to fuck her?"

"She's our way in, and women never refuse you."

"I could say the same about you, but your damn self-imposed celibacy—"

"It's not an option."

"Fine, but she might not know anything about the sex trafficking operation."

"She works directly for Hector and has the means to find out. The first step is getting her to trust you."

"In bed."

"Yeah."

His cock twitched, ready to jump on the idea. "Fucking her doesn't guarantee she'll switch sides. Hector probably sent her to us to figure out where our loyalties lie."

"We'll tread carefully." Martin shifted, creaking the mattress springs. "Keep in mind, if we convince her to work against the cartel, it'll no longer be just our lives at stake."

Good point. The cartel thrived on its draconian rules. If she turned her back on them, they would kill her.

He and Martin would be released from Jaulaso in three months, but Matias wouldn't be able to free Tula.

Maybe she was a conniving murderous cunt and planned to gut them while they slept. But deep down, he agreed with Martin.

There was something about her. Like a shyness beneath the tattoos. Uncertainty behind the gun. He'd detected sweet, straight-laced schoolteacher vibes long before she told them her career.

Turning on his side, he strained to see Martin in the blackness. "What will you be doing while I'm with her?"

Matias Restrepo had been adamant about them never being alone in Jaulaso. As long as they stuck together, they had twice the eyes and double the strength.

"I'll try to help," Martin muttered.

"What?" A shocked laugh erupted from his chest, and he sat up, reeling in the dark. "You're going to help me have sex? How would that work?"

"Fuck off, asshole. I'm not fucking impotent."

"Are you sure? You haven't used your dick in seven years."

"My dick works fine. It's my goddamn head that—" Martin grunted. "Doesn't matter. Let me worry about it."

The thought of Martin watching him having sex was a glorious turn on. But if Martin participated? Holy fuck.

"I can hear the direction of your thoughts." Martin whacked him across the head. "Shut that shit down and get some sleep."

Swallowing a groan, Ricky stretched out on his back and closed his eyes.

He should've gotten laid before the arrest. Between the daily training for this mission, the horrifying disappearance of his roommate, Kate, his move to Colombia to work with Camila, and Kate's rescue two weeks ago, his downtime had been nonexistent.

How long had it been since he'd had sex? Six months? Longer?

On that thought, he slipped in and out of restless sleep, his senses piqued for sounds in the hall.

The second floor seemed to be the quietest section of Area Three. Whoever resided in this cellblock didn't spend a lot of time in their rooms. Most inmates kept to the yard and common area, where drugs, whores, and parties coalesced every night.

After an endless hour, maybe two, he lay wide

awake, listening to someone's footsteps pause just outside the door.

"Martin," he whispered.

"I hear it."

They stood at the same time as a fist rapped on their door.

Martin rested a hand on his shoulder and squeezed, silently telling him to go ahead.

He shook out his arms and loosened his muscles for whatever waited in the hall. Then he opened the door.

Stark light poured in, and he shielded his eyes.

Tula stared up at him, holding a large box in her arms.

"No light bulb?" She squinted into their dark cell.

"No." He glanced back at Martin and winged up an eyebrow.

Martin slid his hands in his pockets, his face expressionless.

She set the box on the floor and dug through the contents.

"Hopefully, this works." She removed an old dusty bulb and held it out.

Martin took it from her and screwed it into the socket. Rusty metal squeaked with each turn until light flooded the room.

As Martin returned, Ricky leaned a shoulder against the doorframe and gave her a questioning look.

"So..." She pulled in a breath and released it with a rush. "You're from the States, and I miss my life there. You speak English, and I miss that, too. You don't have track marks from drug use or tattoos that celebrate the kills you've made. You don't have *any* visible tattoos. Not that I have anything against ink." She held out her tattooed arms. "Obviously."

He exchanged a look with Martin.

"From what I can tell, you guys don't belong in a place like this. Neither do I." She bent down and lifted the box, hugging it to her chest. "You seem like... I don't know. Maybe if I'd run into you in a park or at a bar, we would've been friends. Maybe not. But I could really use a friend *here*."

He stared at this inviting woman, with her black hair twisting around her slender arms, and her makeup-free face angled upward, unguarded and staggeringly beautiful. Eyes of molten brown were steeped with susceptibility—an attribute he and Martin would either learn to trust or use against her.

"I guess what I'm trying to say is..." Her gaze drank him in and slid to Martin. "I'm lonely." She lifted a stiff shoulder. "That's why I'm helping you."

FOURTEEN

Tula bit down on the inside of her cheek.

She did it. Against Hector's advice, she'd spoken the truth and put herself at the mercy of two intimidating, potentially dangerous men.

After Ricky Martin—*yeah, she referred to them as one entity*—left her cell, she went straight to Hector and gave him an update.

He wanted her to move forward under the ruse of turning against the cartel. He believed if she pretended to be a traitor, they would be more inclined to confide in her.

But since he left the plan up to her, she decided to do it her way. She was already uneasy about the job. Putting on an act would've turned her into a blubbering nervous wreck.

Coming here alone was the scariest thing she'd ever done. If they worked for another cartel, they would likely kill her before she figured out who they were.

The smart thing would've been to keep her mouth shut and let Luis get rid of them quietly. But her conscience couldn't accept murder as a solution until she knew for sure they were bad men.

So here she was, standing before them on the microscopic chance she was saving their lives, which would only happen if they joined sides with La Rocha Cartel.

Martin folded his arms across his shirtless chest, the valleys between his abs obscenely deep in the glow of the dingy light bulb.

The swollen bruises around his eyes didn't diminish his hotness. His square jaw bore a speckle of darker hairs in an otherwise blond five o'clock shadow.

The golden hair on his head was short enough to maintain order while Ricky's spiky black strands stuck up in every direction.

Ricky took the heavy box from her, and the sight of veins and sinews bulging in his sculpted forearms swept a tingling heat through her.

God, had she ever seen anything sexier?

Arms. She was drooling over forearms.

"Come in," Martin said, making the invitation sound more like a command.

She stepped in and locked the door behind her, scrunching her nose at the putrid stench of sewage.

"There's a scented candle in the box." She coughed against her fist. "It might mask the smell."

They stared at her with blank expressions. Maybe her spiel about needing a friend had been too honest? If they didn't believe her, they might kill her on suspicion alone.

The gun in her waistband felt hot against her tailbone. She wasn't a good shot, and Ricky had already disarmed her once. She was out of her league.

"Smells like you brought food." Ricky turned to the box and removed the candle, followed by plastic containers of pork *pozole* and Mexican rice. "This is for us?"

"Yeah. Everything in there is yours." She rubbed her hands on her jeans. "I gathered what I could."

The box included basic supplies, such as clothing, soap, shaving razors, toothbrushes, towels, blankets, toilet paper, cutoff plastic milk cartons to use as dishes, powdered milk, instant coffee, and her only cooking stove.

Martin removed a stack of shirts and cotton pants. "How did you get all this?"

"I bartered a few things. Some of it I already had."

Home-cooked meals were brought in by families of the inmates, and she knew who to approach to trade for it.

Ricky dug through the box, the muscled column of his neck stretching into sloping shoulders and taut ripples of brawn along his spine.

Her cheeks heated.

"This is incredible, Tula." He lit the candle with a match and located a plastic spoon for the *pozole.*

She glanced at Martin and found him watching her with a glint of suspicion in his emerald eyes.

Her mouth dried. "I promise I didn't poison anything."

His expression hardened.

She returned his glare. "If I wanted to kill you, I would've just let you starve."

"Eat." Ricky smacked the container of rice against Martin's chest and turned to her. "Come here."

Two uncertain steps carried her the short distance. She craned her neck to look at him.

Lord have mercy, he wasn't even touching her, yet she felt him up and down the front of her body. As she swayed into his force field, his dark masculine scent curled around her.

The light press of his knuckle lifted her chin, igniting

tiny shocks of electricity across her skin.

"I'm going to thank you now." His rich brown eyes darkened as they dipped to her mouth.

Oh, God. He was going to kiss her. She ached for it as much as she dreaded it. He scared her. This scared her. She didn't know what the hell she was doing.

Her teeth sank into her bottom lip, causing his breathing to accelerate. He angled in and pressed his thumb against her lip, tugging it from her bite.

His cheeks rose with amusement. Or pleasure. Maybe both. Then he grabbed her and crushed that heart-melting smile against her mouth.

Warmth flooded her chest, and her pulse burst into a gallop. It wasn't just the hot glide of his lips. It was him, breaking through the walls she'd erected two years ago.

His hands tingled down her spine and skimmed around the shape of her butt. They rested on the backs of her thighs, his fingers tucked between her jean-clad legs. He used that grip to hold her tight against him.

He didn't open his mouth to deepen the kiss, but a promise breathed past the seam of his lips. *When* he decided to take her, it would be explosive and unstoppable.

"Thank you," he murmured against her mouth.

Her entire face tingled as she stepped back.

Martin's presence felt like a pulsing beacon in the small space. When she peeked at him, she was surprised to see a soft smile in his eyes.

"I brought a bottle of tequila to wash that down." She motioned at the spoonful of rice he lifted to his mouth.

He took a bite and chewed slowly, his throat bouncing as he swallowed. Watching him eat felt strangely suggestive. The flex of his jaw and the groan in his chest conjured images of twisted sheets and whiskers scratching inner thighs.

"It doesn't need to be washed down. It's really good." Martin passed the rice to Ricky.

"Okay, well..." She reached for the door. "If you need anything else—"

"Stay." Ricky gripped her hand.

"Oh, I—" A tremble hijacked her voice. *Damn nerves.* "I thought I woke you."

"We couldn't sleep." He tugged her away from the door and removed the blankets from the box.

Within minutes, they had the beds made and the food devoured.

"You guys were starving." She sat at the end of the mattress, watching Ricky sort and stow the supplies.

"Not anymore, thanks to you." He grabbed the tequila and three plastic cups. "Let's drink."

Ricky projected a smile no woman could refuse. She wanted to feel it against her lips again. And other places. *All* the places.

She squeezed her thighs together.

"Confession." He sat beside her on the bed and poured three shots of alcohol. "Before today, I only consumed tequila using the lick-swallow-suck method."

"How very American of you."

"That's not how you drink it in Mexico?"

"No way. We don't need salt or lime. No licking or sucking. We sip it straight—"

"Say that again." Martin shot her a good hard stare.

"What?"

"Licking and sucking." He curled his lips around the words, drawing out each syllable in his sexy American accent.

Her pulse pounded in her throat, and Ricky fell still beside her.

A palpable hum charged the air, skittering along her arms and rousing the tiny hairs on her nape.

"Sip." She reached for one of the cups and took a deep breath.

Ricky followed suit, holding his up. "One…"

"Two…" She lifted the shot toward her mouth.

"Wait. Martin's not ready."

Martin, who sat on the other mattress looking underwhelmed by the prospect of drinking, picked up the third cup.

"One…" Ricky grinned at him. "Two… Three."

He and Martin threw the tequila down their gullets and gagged.

She sipped hers, and her throat closed in protest. She swallowed the rest and breathed through her nose as the liquid burned all the way to her stomach.

"Shit." She slammed down the cup and wiped the tears from her eyes. "That's horrible."

"What the fuck is this?" Ricky inspected the faded half-torn label on the bottle. "It tastes nothing like what we drank earlier today."

"What you had earlier is almost gone, so I got a new bottle, which is always hit and miss. Sometimes, it's watered down. Other times, it's mixed with something."

"This one's laced with paint thinner." Martin tossed his cup toward Ricky.

As the fiery burn faded from her throat, she breathed a sigh of relief that it was over.

Until Ricky announced, "Another round!"

They repeated the process again and again. With each round, the tequila went down smoother, and their smiles grew bigger.

Innocuous conversation filled the pauses between choking laughter. Embarrassing moments in school, favorite music, theories on dinosaur extinction—they covered a safe and wide range of topics.

As the bottle of turpentine neared its final drop, her memory began to blank, and her skull pounded as if she'd been hit in the back of the head by a shovel.

She remembered tipping into Ricky's lap, laughing hysterically at something he said. Martin had cut them both off from drinking sometime before that, but not soon enough.

She woke hours later.

Lying face down in the running position, her brain wailed, *Why, why, why?*

Oh, God, her stomach, her head, her unfortunate split ends… Everything hurt.

Never again.

She cracked open her eyes, immediately blinded by the light bulb over the sink.

Martin lay on the other bed beside her, his oh-so-pretty features void of the tension he carried when awake.

The weight of Ricky's arm rested across her back. She took up most of his bed, forcing him to squeeze between her and the wall. He pressed so close to her side his soft snores ruffled her hair.

The intimacy of it startled her tequila-addled brain. She did a mental inventory of her body. Still fully clothed. Still armed with the gun in her waistband.

They could've forced themselves on her, beaten her, or killed her. But they didn't.

They still could.

No, they were good people. Except they were convicts. More importantly, they were the sexiest men who ever walked the Earth.

Hang on. What did that have to do with anything? And why was she thinking in English? Wait, that was

Spanish.

Shit, she was wasted.

With slow, dizzying movements, she crawled out from between them and swayed on her feet.

The room spun, and saliva rushed over her tongue. She was going to be sick.

Neither man stirred as she opened the door and backed into the dark hallway. No lights. That meant it was sometime before dawn.

Her senses heightened as she stumbled toward the stairway. It wasn't safe to wander around alone.

She always showered around three in the morning while everyone slept, but never when she was hammered. Her clumsy movements and foggy head made her paranoid and jumpy.

As she rounded the corner to the stairwell, the sound of a pained cry hit her ears.

A child's cry.

Her heartbeat banged in her head, and she staggered sideways, catching herself against the wall.

She gulped down the next breath and held it in her lungs, listening, shivering, waiting.

Nothing.

Sometimes, she woke in her cell, convinced she heard a weeping child. The nightmare felt so real she often ran into the corridor, searching for an actual kid, only to realize she was chasing the haunting remnants of memory, the echoes of the little sister she once had.

She heard it again and froze. The cry sounded so small, so scared and sad. She spun, overshooting her steps and crashing to her knees.

Vera, Vera, Vera.

Goddammit, she missed her sister so fucking much.

A sob crawled up, and she pushed herself into the

stairwell, teetering, lurching, unable to escape the crushing pain.

Tears spilled free as she wobbled on the top step. The stairs rippled beneath her blurred eyes. Maybe she would fall and break her neck.

Awwwwesome.

Would the eternal darkness welcome her? She was already in hell. What could be worse than this?

Shouldn't she have a legit reason to die, though? She needed a valiant cause with a colorful flag that she could wave as she rode off to face her death.

She had no flags, no causes, no reason.

But hey, if there was nothing worth dying for, there was nothing worth living for, either.

She should just take that final step into the bowels of yonder stairwell and find out what came next. Maybe Vera would stop crying.

A hand gripped her shoulder, and she jumped, releasing a yelp as she whirled.

"Tula." Ricky yanked her away from the stairs and clutched her shoulders, steadying her. "What are you doing?"

"Shhh." She tried to press a finger against his lips. Her hand knew roughly where to aim, but it landed on his jaw. "Do you hear her?"

"Who?"

"My little sister."

Her balance felt off because seriously, two legs weren't sufficient in keeping a person upright in a wave. The thought made her thirsty. Could she get dehydrated while swimming? Why was she swimming?

She wriggled her lips into the shape of a grin. "I'm drunk."

"No shit. You were about to take those stairs face

first and…" He gripped her jaw, forcing her to meet his eyes. "Were you crying?"

She touched her cheek, and her fingers poked through a soggy cloud. "I can't feel my face. But…" She leaned in, and her nose collided with his concrete chest. "You should know that if I had a grilled cheese sandwich, I would most definitely, positively, accurately hit my mouth with it."

Laughter shook the warm wall that held up her head. "That so?"

"Mm-hmm. A Ricky Martin sandwich would work, too, but I call the middle." She gasped. "Oh, no. We lost Martin."

His hand guided her face to the hallway. She blinked, focusing hard until three blond Viking gods merged into one.

Oh, dear lord, Martin was magical.

He reclined against the wall a few feet away, fingertips resting in the front pockets of his jeans, looking for all the world like he could strip away her panties with only the intensity of his eyes.

"Don't do it." She pointed at him. "Don't you dare. My panties are *mine*."

"All right, *querida*. Here we go." Ricky hooked his arms under her and cradled her against his chest.

She floated down the stairs in a haze.

"This is nice." She hugged his neck and breathed in his intoxicating male scent. "Except whoa… My brain is moving slower, I think. By a half-second or so."

Ricky chuckled softly at her ear. "Slow down a little more, and you'll be thinking at Martin's speed."

A glance behind him gave her a direct view of Martin. He trailed at a distance, his gaze sweeping the perimeter.

"Am I the only one who drank too much?" She dropped her hundred-pound head on Ricky's shoulder.

"We all drank the same amount, but Martin and I are a lot bigger." He touched his lips to her brow. "You're going to hurt tomorrow. I'm sorry."

He lowered her onto a bed, and she looked around, recognizing her room.

Martin sat beside her feet and removed her shoes.

"Don't forget the toes." She stared at the rotating ceiling and gagged on the toxins gurgling from her stomach.

"What about the toes?"

"They need polish. It's been too long. I'm a girl, dontcha know?"

"Yes, I'm fully aware you're a girl."

Was that Martin talking?

"The strong, silent type." She waved a heavy hand at the silhouette beside her feet. "You just sit there and look pretty."

She lost Ricky in her periphery, but after a few long blinks, he was there again.

"Drink." He pushed her potable water jug into her hands, forcing her to suck it down.

"My jeans…" Her waistband constricted her stomach, making her restless and itchy. "I can't sleep in this."

"No, wait." Ricky caught her hand on the zipper. "They need to stay on." He cleared his voice. "For protection. Just keep them on."

"Protection is good." She sank into the bed and drifted into a spinning, nauseating half-sleep.

"Tula." Martin's rumbling drawl popped her eyes open. "Why did Hector make you a member of the cartel? How did that happen?"

"I saved his life." She closed her eyes against a hammering headache. "Then I taught him English. If you want to join La Rocha, I'll make it happen. Just tell me you want in."

A hand stroked through her hair, brushing strands away from her face. "How long are you in for?"

"I have three years left in prison. Forever with La Rocha Cartel."

"Are you involved in their human sex trafficking operation?"

"It's drugs," she mumbled. "And guns. That's what they smuggle. I stay out of that stuff."

"Hector abducts women and children, Tula." Ricky's voice penetrated her fuzzy mind. "He sells them as slaves. You know that, right?"

"No, he doesn't." She tried to laugh, but holy hell, she felt severely tired and sick to her stomach. "He's a nice old man and respects women. He respects *me*. Tula Gomez. A high school Spanish teacher from Phoenix. I was just a teacher, you know? I didn't do anything wrong. I tried to help my sister, and she…" Tears burned her scratchy eyes. "I lost her. I lost Vera."

A sob swelled in her throat, but she didn't have the strength or focus to give into it.

"Hey." A strong pair of arms pulled her into a blanket of heat. "You're not alone. Not anymore."

As it turned out, she had the energy to cry after all.

Bracketed between two hard bodies, she wept until the pain faded into darkness.

FIFTEEN

"We disproved one rumor." Martin lay face down on his cot, his limbs heavy from sleep. "She can't drink the biggest man under the table."

"It's also safe to say…" Ricky rose from his bed and stretched, wearing only a pair of boxers. "She doesn't know Hector's secrets."

"Maybe not, but she knows *him*."

"It's weird how she looks up to him like she's forgotten he's a cartel boss and all-around horrible human being." Grabbing his toothbrush, Ricky lumbered to the sink. "Do you think she's brainwashed?"

"I don't know."

The sight of all that flawless, nude skin made him lose his train of thought. He turned his face into his folded arms beneath his head and tried to concentrate on something other than his best friend's half-naked body.

They'd stayed in Tula's cell until dawn, watching her sleep and keeping her safe in her inebriated state. Before Area Three began to stir, they'd hurried back to their own cell, relieved that none of the supplies she'd given them had been stolen.

Slumber had come quickly and sucked away most of their day.

They should go check on her, make sure she was okay. It was his first thought when he woke, a stabbing instinct in his gut.

Was she still asleep? Did she have pain medication to soothe a hangover? Was she drinking water? Was anyone bothering her?

Imagining her venturing out in her weakened state among two-hundred male inmates made him feel goddamn feral. He needed to be at her side, protecting her the same way he and Ricky watched out for each other.

But she wasn't his responsibility. No one had forced the alcohol down her throat. Even so, they'd deliberately coaxed her into drinking too much.

When she'd told them she brought tequila, the idea had popped into his head. He saw the same plan formulate in Ricky's eyes right before he started pouring shots.

Getting her drunk had been easy. Loosening her tongue had been even easier. But watching her cry herself to sleep? That had been fucking brutal.

Her longing for her sister had bled through his skin. Her hiccuping cries lingered in his bones. Her tears fused her pain with his and messed with his head.

He hated that she was hurting, and there was nothing he could do to stop it.

Ricky spat toothpaste into the sink. "We need to see how she's doing."

"Yep." Instantly on his feet, Martin brushed his teeth and splashed cold water on his face.

They dressed and stepped into the hall. The short walk to the stairwell and down to Tula's cell led them past throngs of glaring inmates.

He didn't look at the floor or aggressively return the menacing scowls. He kept his eyes focused straight ahead, determined to reach Tula's cell without being attacked.

When they arrived at her door, his relief was short-lived. Ricky's knock was met with the violent sounds of retching on the other side.

They stormed into her room. Martin scanned the empty space as Ricky raced to her kneeling position.

Bent over the toilet, she dry-heaved uncontrollably. Tremors shook her shoulders, and her cheeks glistened with tears.

Martin felt that unnerving instinct again. The one that compelled him to protect her from anything that might cause her pain.

It wasn't an unfamiliar urge. He experienced it every day with Ricky—the imperative to shelter, comfort, and take care of his best friend.

Crouched beside her, Ricky slid a hand in her hair, holding the velvet curtain away from her face. His other arm supported her midsection as she continued to gag into the toilet.

There was nothing left in her stomach.

"You need to try to eat something and sleep it off." Martin collected some of her clothes and located her toothbrush. "We're taking you upstairs."

Ricky touched his brow to the back of her head. "You're not alone."

"Okay." She breathed out a ragged sound. "Thank you."

For the rest of the day, she drifted in and out of sleep in Ricky's bed, curled up against his chest.

As Ricky dozed with her, Martin warmed a can of broth on the portable stove and indulged in the pleasure of watching them.

Ricky's long, hard body fit possessively around her petite form. His black hair made hers look brown where it caressed its way down her back, reaching toward her firm ass.

There was a caginess about her, too much hesitation in her movements and caution in her eyes. Even as she slept, she exhaled a whimper and squirmed uncomfortably. She wasn't used to being handled so intimately.

After spending an entire night with her, he'd gained a lot of insight into her personality and circumstances.

Her tattoos gave her a bold, edgy look that stood out against her bronze skin, but she hadn't sleeved her arms to honor a memory or express her individuality. Last night, she said it was her armor, to look the part of a hardened prisoner.

Beneath the artwork lurked a sweet, modest woman, one who shied away from attention and avoided chaos and drama. Hours of unguarded, drunken conversation had revealed a gentle soul. She adored children, teared up when she laughed, and dreamed of a simple, quiet life.

She was in the most violent prison in the nation, right here, only feet away, but it was so easy to see her in a classroom wearing a conservative dress, her hair gathered in a low bun, and pink lipstick on her beautiful, patient smile.

She didn't belong here.

She did, however, look perfect in Ricky's arms.

If she let him, Ricky would treat her like a queen.

Like Martin, Ricky had been sexually trained by Van. Whoever was lucky enough to share Ricky's bed reaped the benefits of that training. And his expertise was only one of his strengths.

Ricky was, quite simply, the most selfless and

dependable person Martin had ever met.

He trusted Ricky with his life. Those brown eyes were his home, and whenever they rested on him, he never felt more whole, more peaceful, or more healthy.

But there was something else there, too. A physical attraction that compelled him to stare too long, too hungrily. Seeing Ricky and Tula together only magnified his desire, doubled the temptation.

A deeply buried need pricked at the edges of his awareness, taunting him with what-ifs.

What if he gave in and finally tasted Ricky's lips? What if he put his hands all over Tula's delectable body? What if he buried his damn nightmares and joined them in bed?

It was only a matter of time before Ricky stripped Tula down to her skin and charmed his way between her legs. The thought hardened Martin's cock and made his blood run hot.

When he imagined them in the throes of passion, he was right there with them, commanding their movements, devouring the union of their sinful bodies, and taking himself in hand, stroking, groaning, and coating their flesh with his come.

Ricky's hard lines against her delicate curves, his muscled arms holding her carefully, protectively, and their expressions soft with sleep—they were painfully beautiful and mesmerizing in their stillness, like a sculptured masterpiece of the gods.

His attraction to them was visceral, but his desire went deeper. What he felt was the start of a much-needed inhale that pulled through his senses and sank into his chest. It was a starved breath that turned into a hypnotic hum as it hit his blood and fed his soul.

He could watch them forever—sleeping, talking, and

Christ, he ached to watch them fuck.

Damn if that didn't make him feel like a predator.

It made him feel like Jeff.

Jeff and his heavy fists, ruthless demands, and his taking, forcing, breaking…

His stomach hardened, killing the warmth in his groin.

If he had to do it again, he would. He would pick up that hammer and bash the motherfucker's skull over and over and over.

He scrubbed his hands down his face and looked up.

Ricky's gaze met his, catching and holding. He tucked Tula tight against his chest and ran his nose through her hair. Without looking away, he skimmed a hand down the back of her leg and tangled the other in her hair.

His brown eyes glimmered, teasing.

Come here, they said. *I dare you.*

Martin squinted sternly, his voice low. "Hungry?"

"Always."

"Dinner." He held up the warmed can of broth.

A groan vibrated from the beauty in Ricky's arms. "I feel like death."

Ricky grazed his lips along her slender neck. "If death looked as good as you, suicide would be all the rage."

"Oh, God, stop." She pushed against his chest and rolled to her back. "I need a shower."

He and Ricky tensed.

Privacy didn't exist in the communal showers. How did she wash without getting assaulted? Is that where Garra came in? Did he clear out the bathroom while she showered?

"Where's Garra?" Martin shifted down the mattress,

erasing the distance to hold out the broth to her.

"I relieved him from his job." She sipped from the can and handed it back.

"Why?"

"I wanted to talk to you, get to know you. I couldn't do that with him breathing down my neck."

He detected truthfulness in her words, but not the whole truth.

"You gave up your protection." He bent toward her, propping his forearm on his leg. "You think that was wise?"

Her face reddened. "I came here last night, hoping for friendship. Showing up with a guard doesn't exactly engender good will. Was I naive to think I don't need protection from you?"

"Yes. Extremely naive." Ricky gripped her arm when she started to pull away. "You know nothing about us. We could've hurt you."

"But you didn't." She yanked her arm free. "I trusted my gut, and it didn't steer me wrong."

He met Ricky's eyes over her head. She preferred their protection over Garra's, and they both knew why.

"How many times did Garra rape you?" The question burned like venom from his throat.

"Just the one time." She struggled to look up, but after a moment, she summoned enough courage to meet his gaze. "I'm tired of being alone."

They were leaving in three months. Where did that leave her?

Here. Alone. For three more years.

"You're safe with us." Ricky touched her chin, guiding her face to his. "But I'll be honest. The prospect of you showering in a bathroom full of hard dicks is horrifying. We can only fend off so many men."

"Oh, I…" She picked at a frayed hole in her jeans. "I always shower between three and four in the morning, when everyone's asleep."

Martin nodded, impressed with her adaptability. "We have a few hours to wait. How do you feel?"

"Better. I haven't been that wasted since college." Her eyes narrowed. "I don't know whether to be mad that you got me drunk or thankful you stuck around to clean up the puke." She slumped back on the bed. "How many secrets did you wheedle out of me?"

"Only your dirtiest, darkest ones." Ricky leaned his back against the wall and lifted her denim-clad legs to rest across his lap.

"I'm serious. What did I tell you?"

He appreciated her directness and couldn't think of a reason to lie to her. "You described your first few weeks in Jaulaso, how your relationship with Hector came to be, and why he made Garra your personal guard. You asked Hector to castrate him? That was a risky move."

"I was desperate." She stared down at her lap and bit her lip.

"We know you have three years left on your sentence." He waited for her to look up. Then he let his eyes convey his sincerity. "You're serving time for a crime we know you didn't commit."

"None of that is a secret." She shrugged.

"You told us you lost your little sister." Ricky traced a finger along her calf.

"Oh." Her shoulders hunched forward. "I vaguely remember her crying last night. I dream about her sometimes and wake up thinking she's here. As a child. It's fucked up."

"What happened to her?"

"Wish I knew. The morning I was arrested, Vera

called me. She was in trouble again…"

She talked through the events that led to her arrest, her sister's possible connection to the cartel, the mistaken identity, and how the military tortured and framed her for drug smuggling.

"I've kept in touch with the detectives at the Ciudad Hueca police department." She hooked an arm around her waist. "There have been no leads, no body, nothing. She just…vanished."

Ricky gave him a knowing look.

Yeah, they knew a guy. Cole Hartman had a specialized skill set and a military background that connected him with a lot of unsavory people. He located Camila's missing sister and rescued Kate when she was abducted. If anyone could find Vera Gomez, it was Cole Hartman.

But they couldn't contact him. Not until they were released.

Matias Restrepo had warned them that all cell phones in Jaulaso were strictly controlled by La Rocha Cartel. The inmates tracked transmissions and monitored every phone call.

Cole Hartman was tied in with Restrepo Cartel, a sworn enemy of La Rocha. Calling him from any phone would expose their loyalties.

"Hector's looking for her." She folded her hands on her lap.

"Is that right?" He cocked his head, unable to decipher her stony expression. "What else does Hector do for you?"

"What does that mean?"

"Does he touch you?"

"No!" She gasped. "Never. He's not like that."

Something was off about their relationship. Why

would Hector treat her so kindly? What did he gain from it?

"Does he talk to you about his human trafficking operation?" Ricky asked.

"Oh, my God." She sat ramrod straight, her eyes igniting with fire. "You *did* say that last night. I thought I dreamed it." Her hands balled into fists. "You don't know what you're talking about."

"It's true, Tula." Ricky reached for her.

She jumped back and scrambled off the bed.

"He's kidnapping women and children in the U.S." Martin moved to the edge of the mattress, prepared to grab her if she went for the door. "He smuggles them across the border and sells them as slaves. Thousands of *children*."

"He wouldn't do that." She snatched the toothbrush he'd brought from her cell and moved to the sink. "I sit in all his meetings. I would've heard them discussing it." She tackled her teeth in a frenzy, scrubbing and spitting. "I was just like you before I met him. His reputation terrified me, but I was wrong about him. He's a good man."

"By *good man*, you mean nine levels of vicious, terror-reigning, mass-murdering tyranny."

"No." She spat into the sink.

"He's a cartel boss."

"That's a job title, not a character trait."

Hard to argue that. Matias Restrepo actively hunted down and decimated slave operations across Latin America, and he was the leader of the biggest cartel in Colombia.

Hector La Rocha, however, did nothing of the sort.

Their vigilante group, the Freedom Fighters, had been collecting evidence against him for years. But he couldn't share that with her without revealing his connections.

"Are you *procesados*?" She leaned a hip against the sink and crossed her arms. "Or *sentenciados*?"

Under the Mexican Constitution, pretrial defendants whose cases were still in process—*procesados*—were to be housed separately from prisoners who were serving sentences—*sentenciados*.

The same Constitution prohibited the blending of male and female prisoners in the same facility.

Jaulaso was one of several cartel-controlled prisons that gave the Constitution the middle finger.

"We're still in process." He glanced at Ricky and returned to her. "Why?"

"You'll be charged within four months. That's the law. And they'll do it without your presence in court, even if you have a good attorney."

"Is that what happened to you?" Ricky stroked his jaw, his attention fully engaged.

"Yeah."

They didn't need an attorney. They had the Mexican government and a resourceful cartel boss on their side.

"How do you want to do your time?" She ran a hand through her hair. "Do you want the welcoming committee to extort a pound of flesh from your bodies every day? Or do you want to be one of the guys in the welcoming committee?"

"I think," Ricky said, "I'll just pass my time making macaroni necklaces for my eight kiddos at home."

Her mouth dropped open.

"Ricky." Martin pinched the bridge of his nose. "Neither of us has kids, nor do we have any desire to be involved in cartel politics and disputes." He met her eyes. "That's what you're suggesting, yeah? You want us to work for La Rocha?"

"You either work for them or against them."

"Did Hector send you to us with that sales pitch?" He glared at her. "Or are you just looking out for us as a *friend?*"

Her spine straightened. "Hector doesn't trust you, and it sounds like that goes both ways. Look…" She lowered onto the bed beside him, her expression open and pleading. "I don't condone the violence, and if I could quietly do my time and stay away from all of it, I would. But that's not an option in Jaulaso. Trust me on this."

He trusted her motivations, but she wasn't telling them everything.

"What does he know about us?" Ricky clenched his teeth.

"Nothing. That's the problem." She rolled her bottom lip between her fingers. "Why were your identities wiped?"

Ah, so Hector La Rocha had them investigated.

He and Ricky didn't have living relatives and were never reported as missing persons. They were, however, responsible for the murders of some very bad people—rapists, slave traders, and over the last two years, they'd taken out several big players in La Rocha Cartel.

It was paramount that Hector didn't discover the latter.

They could've entered the prison system with fake identities, but that wouldn't have stopped a skilled investigator from linking them to their real names. So they took the safest route and had Cole Hartman erase them from existence. Good thing, too.

"We have enemies from a previous life." The rehearsed lie rolled off Ricky's tongue. "That's none of Hector's business."

She blew out a heavy sigh. "I'm trying to protect you."

"From Hector?" Martin's neck stiffened.

"From everyone."

"Tula." Ricky crooked a finger. "Come here."

Her throat bounced with a swallow, and she shook her head. "I don't think that's a good idea."

The subtle squeeze of her thighs contradicted her words.

If he had to guess, she was attracted to Ricky, but she feared that attraction.

Shifting toward her, he rested his fingers on the back of her neck and guided her gaze to his. "Tell me what you're thinking."

She cut her eyes to Ricky and back to him. "He's going to try to kiss me."

"There's no *trying* involved." Ricky stretched his legs across the bed and reclined against the wall, all lean muscle and confident male.

"And?" He ghosted the backs of his fingers down the curve of her neck, making her shiver.

"We just met yesterday. I don't know either of you, and I never kiss on the first date."

Fucking hell, this woman. She was such a precious rarity, so guileless and straightforward. His chest squeezed at the thought of someone as innocent as her being locked up in this hell for five years. It was fucking unfair.

"I held your hair while you puked last night," Ricky said. "Pretty sure that skips like five dates."

She didn't look convinced.

Martin didn't want to force the issue, but the urgency of a three-month timeline pressed down upon him.

If they couldn't seal a kiss with this girl, there was no way they would convince her to do anything else, like steal information from Hector.

They needed her trust because right now, she was the only angle they had.

"Tula." Martin put his face in hers. "Give that man your mouth. Swear to God, it'll be the best kiss you've ever had."

Her breath hitched. "You know that from experience."

"I know *him*." He didn't look at Ricky, but those dark eyes burned a trail of heat across his skin.

Her eyes flashed. "*You* kiss him. If you do it, I will."

A shifting sensation squeezed a sharp pang near his heart. Nerve endings tingled along his thighs, and the sudden acceleration of his pulse sent a surge of blood to his groin.

As his body revved up, his mind bristled at her words, making his tone sound meaner than he intended. "That's not how I operate."

"I knew it. You're one of those." She studied her fingernails, baiting him.

"Finish that thought, Tula."

If she made a homophobic comment, he would bend her over his knee and redden her ass.

"I've dated guys like you." She pushed back her shoulders. "Bossy. Controlling. Always has the last word."

He laughed in surprise. "Your point?"

"The thought of kissing him doesn't repulse you. What raises your hackles is someone telling you to do it."

The accuracy of her words hit him directly in the stomach.

He didn't take orders from anyone. Never again.

Memories—a year's worth of sick, brutal memories—unfurled from a desolate place in his mind. He was no different than the son of a bitch he'd killed so brutally.

The pitch-black fantasies he'd kept locked down erupted all at once, spilling from his subconscious in ribbons of depravity.

Restraining, choking, whipping, forcing, using, ripping open, bleeding out, hard and ruthless, unsafe and unwilling, no hole left unpunished—everything Jeff had done to him was exactly what he craved to do to Ricky and Tula.

Violent sex was all he knew, and it aroused him so deeply it terrified him.

A hand rested on his shoulder, warm and familiar. He turned toward Ricky, and their eyes met and held.

Despite the disturbing direction of his thoughts, he found peace in Ricky's gaze. It wasn't where Ricky looked that was important. It was where he didn't look.

Those eyes didn't slide down Martin's body, indicating lust. They didn't stare at his lips, demanding a kiss. They didn't lower to his groin, signaling a desire to touch.

Ricky stared right at him, into him, wordlessly confessing this was more than sexual desire. Ricky didn't just want to fuck him. He wanted it all—friendship, love, intimacy, forever.

It was just a look shared between best friends, but it was powerful enough to punch through Martin's memories, sink past heavily guarded walls, and fuse with the longing he couldn't hide from Ricky.

This wouldn't end with a kiss.

He would hurt them beyond repair.

"For fuck's sake." Tula leaned in, infusing the air with her sweet, feminine scent. "If you two don't kiss after staring at each other like that, I'm going to lose all respect for you."

A delicious shiver slid beneath his skin and froze his

lungs. His body might've forgotten how to breathe, but it knew exactly how to take what it wanted.

His hand went to Ricky's nape, a merciless grip that yanked Ricky's head where he wanted it.

Then he took what belonged to him and devoured Ricky's mouth.

SIXTEEN

A vicious fire roared inside Martin, unleashing a dormant need to plunder and consume.

After seven years without sex, he didn't have any restraint left to ease into a kiss. He hauled Ricky against him and mauled that perfect mouth with sharp teeth and bruising lips.

Ricky opened for him with a guttural groan, and Martin swept his tongue inside, hunting and licking every hidden wet crevice between teeth and cheek.

He'd denied himself too long, but that wasn't the only reason he felt so reckless and desperate.

Ricky wasn't just an exceptionally trained kisser. He kissed passionately, feverishly, with every breath, every beat of his heart, and every muscle in his body.

"Sweet Jesus." Ricky gasped and slipped greedy fingers beneath Martin's shirt and along his back.

Blood flowed, and muscles trembled beneath the diabolical caress of masculine hands. His hunger rose in a flood of heat, throbbing between his legs and skyrocketing his heart rate.

They pressed closer, chests colliding, arms winding, and bodies entwining as they frantically deepened the kiss. It wasn't enough.

He hauled Ricky against him and took him down to the mattress, falling atop him in a grinding crush of hips and swollen cocks.

Fucking goddamn, his familiar taste. It was the first time they'd ever kissed, but he recognized the dark, crisp flavor of Ricky's mouth as if it were his own.

The scent of Ricky's hot skin seeped into his lungs. The firmness of Ricky's lips permanently imprinted the moment on his heart. He melted into the sensations, clinging tight to the pleasure as Ricky grunted and thrust beneath him.

"I need you." Ricky gripped his ass and bit his lips. "Please. Fucking touch me. Hurt me. Put me out of my misery."

The intensity of that surrender vibrated the muscles beneath Martin's hands, but the words gave him pause.

Hurt me.

Ricky didn't know what he was asking.

Gutting memories invaded his senses and coiled his insides into a bloody knot of horror.

How was he supposed to separate the damage he endured with Jeff and Van, the pain Ricky craved, and the hurt he desperately needed to inflict? There were levels of right and wrong, willing and unwilling, and gray areas in between. He didn't know how to navigate intimacy with one person, let alone two.

All he knew was he didn't want to stop.

Lashing his tongue wildly against Ricky's, he indulged in Ricky's surrender. With his hands fisted in Ricky's thick black hair, he bit, sucked, and kissed savagely and mindlessly with abandon.

Until nausea hit his stomach.

He pushed away before it became too much, before he lost himself in the past and puked his guts out. Or worse, before he became the monster he feared.

"Tula," he rasped breathlessly.

She was already there, lips parted, nipples pebbling beneath her shirt, and the burnt umber of her gorgeous eyes glittering around dilated pupils.

"He's waiting." He sat beside Ricky, breathing heavily as he tried to reel in the unraveling mess of his thoughts.

He just needed a breather, and she seemed to read that in his expression.

With a nod, she turned to Ricky and said softly, "That was exciting."

"You liked watching us." Ricky sat up and lifted her onto his lap, arranging her legs to straddle him.

She shook her head and blinked.

Ricky kissed her, just a tease of lips, before boldly pinching one of her hard nipples. "These don't lie."

She batted his hand away and touched her brow to his. "You kissed like you've been lovers for years." She feathered her fingers along his whiskered jaw. "You're in love with each other."

The precision of her words zapped every molecule in the air. Ricky felt it, his eyes locking onto Martin's like beams of energy, holding him stationary in time and space. They emitted a thousand words that didn't require voice or explanation.

Lines had been crossed.

Boundaries erased.

Everything had changed.

"Thank you." Ricky touched his lips to hers. Then he did it again. "You opened a door."

"And now she was walking with demons." Her mouth twisted. "A quote from *The Hellbound Heart*."

Must've been one of the books in her cell. Martin wasn't much of a reader, but the sexy, nerdy, schoolteacher persona she hid from the other prisoners turned him on like nothing else.

"I don't know that one, but I can give you this." Ricky cleared his voice and belted out a familiar tune, "Her lips are devil-red, and her skin's the color mocha. She…will…wear…you…out."

"Livin' la Vida Loca." She threaded her fingers through his hair. "That has me thinking…"

"What's up, *querida?*" Ricky trailed his mouth along her jaw.

"There's no Tula in Ricky Martin."

"Wanna bet?" He nipped at her throat and met Martin's eyes. "I've fantasied about this for years. I want to watch him with you. I want him to watch you with me. I want the three of us together, joined in every position, fucking and ravaging without hesitation or caution."

Christ, the way Ricky just threw that out there in his gravelly voice… His confidence was sexy as hell.

"How could you always want that when you just met me?" she asked.

"In my wildest fantasies, the woman between us was faceless." Ricky inclined his head, edging closer to her lips. "Not anymore." He cupped his hands around her neck. "God help me, I never imagined you'd be this beautiful. Every time I look at you, it fucking hurts."

"Ha." She laughed nervously. "Such a charmer. Men and women everywhere must fall at your feet."

"Not the ones who matter." His hands slipped down around her waist, pulling her hips against his.

She leaned back, and her mouth drew into a straight

line.

Her reluctance made Martin tense, but he understood it. He wrestled with himself every second he spent with Ricky. Desire battling fear, the present always at war with the past. It was easier to shut down and pull away. It was safer.

Ricky caught his gaze, and in that moment, they shared the same thought.

She didn't need seduction. She needed compassion, connection, and security—everything he had with Ricky.

Martin rose to his knees and moved in behind her, straddling Ricky's legs and loosely sandwiching her between them.

"I will never disregard what you've been through." He swept the heavy length of her hair to one shoulder and rested his lips against her graceful neck. "Nor will I abuse the trust you gave me when you told me about the electrocution and Garra's assault. You haven't been touched by a man in two years?"

"No."

"Any lasting damage from the torture? Anything I need to be concerned about?"

"No, I'm healed."

She eased a shivery sigh as he kissed a winding path to her upper arm and back again, lingering beneath her ear.

"Tonight, your clothes stay on." He ran his nose through her hair, breathing in the soft scent that was uniquely her. "No pressure. No expectations. No venturing into places you're not ready to go."

"Okay." She rested her hands on his thighs, where they bracketed her hips.

"Are you ready to experience the best kiss of your life?"

"Good God." Her fingers dug into the denim on his legs. "How can you top the kiss I just experienced between you two?"

He locked eyes with Ricky over her head. Their gazes hung, tangling and fusing, neither of them moving.

This was just the beginning. Once she got a taste of Ricky, she wouldn't be able to stop.

It would be a long night of clothes-on torment, but he could handle the kissing. In fact, he couldn't wait to feel her soft mouth against his.

He didn't want to fuck this up. If he stayed right here in their space, reaching for Ricky's gaze, breathing the feminine fragrance of Tula's hair, their bodies aligned and mouths sealed together, he could do this without losing his shit.

"Tula." He reached around her and gripped the back of Ricky's neck. "Give him your mouth."

SEVENTEEN

Ricky's body thrummed to life as Tula leaned in and offered her mouth. She did it slowly, with nervous starts and stops, which only made him want her more.

As the sweetness of her breath quivered across his lips, everything inside him went taut with need. But Martin's hand on his nape reminded him to go slow and keep himself in check.

Dear God, desire looked sinful on her, heating her cheeks and stretching her pupils until her brown eyes turned black.

Her lust-soaked expression was exactly what he wanted to see on a woman before he took her mouth.

With Tula, he started with light teasing sips. Then he sucked faster, more assertively, licking and drinking the hesitation off her soft lips.

"Ricky." Her hands found his hair, tugging him closer as greedy little noises escaped her throat. "More."

That was all the invitation he needed. He trapped her in his arms and kissed her harder, opening her hot mouth with his tongue and delving deep.

Martin tightened his grip on Ricky's neck and lowered his lips to her shoulder. The potency of his presence, the weight of his gaze, the collective sounds of their breaths—all of it coursed blood to Ricky's groin.

Christ, he loved being watched. Never in a million years did he think Martin would participate in something like this. And the woman in his arms? They couldn't have found a better match.

She was submissive and fierce, honest yet cautious, and because he was a man, he had the biggest fucking hard-on for her perfect body.

Holding this sexy, exotic creature on his lap, he knew he would never get enough of her.

He savored her with deep-reaching strokes, ravishing her more aggressively, his pulse singing in his veins as flavors exploded in his mouth. Her clean minty taste, the wet warmth of her breaths, and the honeyed essence of her innocence… He gorged himself on everything soft and feminine and sensual about her.

His hands roved over her shirt, memorizing every elusive dip and beautifully toned curve underneath. He wanted to rip away the cotton and bask in the feel of her satiny skin. But she wasn't ready.

Neither was Martin.

He retreated from the wet heaven of her mouth to steal a glance at his friend.

The emerald facets of Martin's eyes flickered amid the shadows of their small cell. There was a war going on inside that head, an inferno of want raging against a torrent of pain. Whatever happened to Martin years ago had severely messed him up.

Ricky would give anything to teleport through time and save that boy from the horrors he'd endured.

Maybe he and Martin shouldn't have kissed, but he

didn't detect a trace of regret in Martin's gaze. Their friendship was too solid, their bond too tight. No matter where they went from here or how they fit Tula into their relationship, they would only grow stronger together.

The hot little vixen between them shifted on his lap, peeking at him from beneath heavy lashes before turning to Martin.

She licked swollen lips and touched a finger to the deep grooves between Martin's brows.

Stretching her spine put her mouth a hairsbreadth from his, and she waited there, eyes wide and unblinking, silently offering her vulnerability.

He glanced at Ricky for a fraction of a second before capturing her lips. He pressed in gently, then harder, sliding his wicked tongue through her mouth.

The sight of them melting into each other stole his breath. The weight of their bodies straddling his lap sent feverish tingles across his skin. He hooked an arm around her waist while his other hand traveled over the thick bones and sinewy thews that sculpted Martin's torso.

His possessive hands remembered Martin's body on the training mat. The corrugated terrace of abs, ripped biceps, and muscled legs locked around him, slick with sweat, and flexing with domination as they grappled and rolled across the floor. All testosterone, agility, and infinite power contracting and heaving beneath tanned skin.

Martin's hands had the strength to grab him and pin him to the wrestling mat without mercy. But as he watched Martin with her, he noted the gentleness in every touch, the way those ruthless fingers slipped through her hair and let the tresses fall slowly, strand by strand, as he kissed her at leisure.

They made a tantalizing couple. Martin's hard jaw gliding against the pixie-shape of her face, their tongues rubbing together and sending soft licking sounds through the room. Panting breaths. Rustling clothes. Pleasure-drenched moans. It was the most erotic thing he'd ever witnessed.

Martin held the bulk of his weight off Ricky's thighs while she sat fully on his lap. With her legs straddling Ricky, she had to twist at the waist to kiss Martin behind her. She felt like a feather on his legs, but she couldn't have been comfortable.

"Lie down." Ricky tapped her thigh.

With the beds pushed together, they stretched out across them with Tula in the middle. Martin lay on his side, propped up on his elbow, mirroring Ricky's position.

A long, deep breath nuzzled between them, silent and content, but there was a slow build in it. It started quietly, stirring the energy in the air.

Inhales chased exhales, the cadence of breaths growing faster, louder. Toes curled against the mattress. Chests rose and fell in tandem, and Martin drifted imperceptibly closer as if he wasn't aware he was doing it.

Tula's warm fingers rested against Ricky's chest. He covered her hand with his, holding her to him, but he didn't look at her. His gaze was confined by Martin's stare.

Spiritual closeness lived and breathed through their eye contact. But it was no longer just a platonic connection between friends.

A fire had been kindled, stoked with a brazen kiss. He couldn't brush it off as a smoldering moment of lust. A cold shower wouldn't douse this.

Their hunger for each other was a waking volcano that had been burning too deep and too long beneath the surface. It would never die out, never grow cold. Not without total devastation.

Face to face, gazes locked, they held onto each other

the way they always had. With their eyes, their history with Van, and the trust they'd forged over the years.

Except now, Ricky needed more.

He needed to hold Martin in his arms and wrap his mouth around Martin's cock while thrusting deep inside Tula's body. He needed her right here with them, between them, under them.

"I love the way you look at each other," she murmured. "It's like you're having a whole conversation without moving your lips, like you're reading each other's thoughts."

"I read his expressions." Martin traced a finger along the waistband at her hip. "And the way he holds himself. His body language is loud."

"Is that right?" A smirk pulled at his lips. "What am I thinking?"

Martin angled over her and clutched Ricky's neck. "You're choreographing all the positions you would arrange her in while I fuck your ass."

Sharp, penetrating heat shot along the length of his cock.

"Is that true?" she asked.

"Yeah." He felt wired and overheated as he studied the dark prisms of her eyes. "Since I don't know your expressions yet, tell me what you're thinking. What do you want?"

"This." A small smile trembled at the corner of her mouth. "Two nice, gorgeous, experienced men who kiss like…" Her lips pouted out with a pushed-out breath. "I don't even know. I've never experienced anything like it. You *both* have this incredibly magical, mind-numbing way you kiss, like you were born from the same womb or something." She squinted. "You're not brothers, are you?"

"No." Ricky laughed. "That would be awkward."

"Good, because if you're asking me what I want..."

"I am."

"I want to live in your kisses. For the next hour. For the rest of the night. For as long as we're here. Watching your mouths move together..." Her breath stuttered. "It's freeing. Makes me forget I'm in prison."

The electricity in her words fueled the fire inside him. A fire that burned for his best friend.

His gaze lifted, but Martin was already leaning in. Bent over her chest, he grabbed Ricky's neck and slammed their lips together.

Their tongues met and retreated. Then they clashed again in a possessive duel, whipping and licking and cutting with teeth.

Martin went wild, feeding the flames that roared between them. His fist pulled Ricky's hair as his tongue thrust frantically, relentlessly, fucking Ricky's mouth with brutal strokes. Desire rose and swelled, untamed and ravenous.

Then he broke away, his chest heaving, and his face contorted in torment.

His distress was a knife through Ricky's heart.

"Are you okay?" She reached for Martin.

"Yeah." He let her touch his jaw, and the contact seemed to chase his demons back to wherever they came from. The shadows in his eyes receded, and the cords in his neck relaxed.

No wonder he was celibate. He was navigating around a switch inside him. When it flipped on, it went full throttle, barreling him into a vicious sexual rage.

Ricky wanted him rough, ruthless, and out of control, but not if it caused Martin pain. He needed to figure out how to ease Martin forward without taking too many agonizing steps back.

"I know you said you don't have an issue with touching." She leaned up on an elbow, her brows knitted as she searched Martin's face. "But you have a past like mine, don't you? It helps to talk about—"

"No." Martin glared at her.

She drew back, her shoulders hitching toward her ears.

Ricky shot Martin a disapproving look. "It's not you, Tula. He hasn't told me anything about his life before I met him. He keeps that shit locked down."

"Until he's in an intimate situation." Her eyes darted through the room before returning to Martin. "Does it affect *all* your sexual relationships? Or is it just us?"

Martin's nostrils flared, and Ricky held his breath.

"I'm sorry." She cringed. "That was too personal."

"Don't be sorry." Martin softened his expression and tucked a lock of hair behind her ear. "It's not you. But there's definitely something about you. I don't know what it is…" He stared at her as if utterly gobsmacked. "I haven't had sex in seven years, and I can't for the life of me figure out why I just told you that."

Compassion soaked her quiet eyes, her face a portrait of unguarded trust.

"That's why." He trailed a finger along her cheekbone and looked up at Ricky. "You see what I see?"

"Yeah, I see her."

She was too trusting. While it was a trait that made overprotective guys like him and Martin want to throat-punch any man who looked at her, it didn't belong in a place like this.

Trusting the wrong person in Jaulaso would get her killed, and she put a helluva lot of trust in Hector La Rocha.

"See what?" Her voice lowered with suspicion.

"What do you see?"

"You're an inherently good person." Ricky stroked her hair. "Because of that, you see goodness in others, even when it doesn't exist."

Her eyes flared. "That's another way of calling me naive."

She sat up and started to scramble out from between them.

Martin gripped her leg and yanked her down to her back as Ricky bent over her.

"Don't overreact." He nipped at her lips.

"I'm not," she growled, twisting her hips in Martin's hold.

"You're overreacting." Ricky curled a hand beneath her jaw. "No one said you're naive. I'll reserve that label for our conversation about Hector's sex trafficking operation."

Anger sparked in her eyes, and her mouth opened. He silenced her with a finger against her lips.

"Not tonight." He slid his hand down her neck and traced the hollow of her throat. "Tonight, we're going to give you what you want."

Her swallow bobbed against his touch. "You think you can subdue me with kisses?"

"Totally."

She flung a questioning look at Martin.

"My money's on Ricky," Martin said.

"Do you even have any money?" She cocked a brow.

They had millions in the bank because of Van, but that was a detail they couldn't share.

Martin answered her with a mysterious smile. He didn't share those smiles often, so when one appeared, it was disarming.

She sighed beneath it. "I don't understand how the

two most attractive men on the planet ended up here, in prison, with me. It defies the laws of the universe. Can you explain it to me?"

She would lose her mind if she saw all the Freedom Fighters together.

Van Quiso and Liv Reed had handpicked every single one of them based on the slave buyers' specifications. Physical beauty was always a requirement.

Ricky didn't give a fuck what he looked like, but he appreciated her compliment and showed her as much by stealing a kiss.

The featherlight touch of lips gave way to another, then another, until the flames lit and the slide of their mouths caught fire.

Martin settled in beside them, his face inches away. When Ricky leaned back, Martin moved in and twisted a hand in her hair.

Watching Tula and Martin together was a feast for the eyes. They stared at each other, their lips not quite touching as their tongues reached and slid together in the space between their open mouths. She angled her head to take him deeply, and he dove in, their hands clawing and gripping with equal urgency.

When Martin's breathing lost rhythm, and his biting became too aggressive, Ricky crowded in and took his place.

Back and forth they went. Kissing her. Kissing each other. Three mouths vying for affection. Three pairs of legs tangling together. Hands grasping and wandering over clothes, and the sounds of panting groans rising into a crescendo.

Martin worked them into a feverish frenzy, and Ricky slowed them down, drew it out.

Between stretches of breathless kissing, they talked

and laughed about nothing and everything.

When their lips fell still, they curled up in the cozy silences, content with their thoughts.

Hours later, the clock on her phone struck three in the morning. She still wanted that shower.

Ricky led them through the dark, eerily vacant corridors to the communal bathroom on the ground level.

He and Martin took up posts by the door, listening to her clothing fall on the floor followed by the sound of water sluicing over her naked body. He only needed to take two steps into the bathroom, and he would have a direct view of her around the corner.

"Don't even think about it." Martin crossed his arms over his chest and held up the wall with his back.

"Don't act like you're not tempted."

"I've had enough temptations for one night." Martin's gaze dropped to Ricky's mouth and shifted toward the sound of splashing water. "She's…"

Exquisitely sweet. Sharp as a whip. Sexy as fuck.

"The whole package." Ricky dropped his head back against the doorframe.

"Yeah." Martin lowered his voice. "The next three months are going to fly by."

"And she has three years after we leave."

They couldn't lengthen their sentences or shorten hers. It was an impossible situation with a nebulous outcome.

If she changed her plea to guilty, she might be able to transfer to a prison in the States. She would be safer there. But would she be willing to carry a guilty conviction for the rest of her life?

It was too soon to predict how her priorities might change or where the three of them would go from here. He didn't know how deep her cartel loyalties ran or if she would be able to leave those ties behind after prison. What if she couldn't escape Hector's control?

Bottom line, he and Martin were here for one reason, and they needed her help.

Once they convinced her Hector was rotten to the soul, they would have her spy for them, whether it be listening to conversations, digging through documents in Hector's private quarters, or using her sweet personality to coax information directly from Hector's mouth.

She didn't know it yet, but she was going to help them bring down La Rocha's sex trafficking operation.

Involving her, however, put her life at more risk than it already was. In Jaulaso, working against the cartel was more dangerous than working for it.

But that was where he and Martin drew the line. They would never join La Rocha. Sure, it would make their time here easier—fewer bruises and bloodied knuckles. Becoming a member, however, went against everything they fought for.

As cartel soldiers, they would be required to sell drugs, trade guns, collect money, and kill traitors. All of that shit contributed to a despicable machine that sold women and children into slavery.

He and Martin didn't plant themselves in prison to make La Rocha Cartel stronger. They were here to demolish it.

"I needed that." She stepped around the corner, her long black hair dripping down her tattooed arms, dampening her clean yellow shirt. "If you want to take a shower, this is the best time. There's no one around if you drop the soap."

With a nod, Martin breezed past her, yanking off his shirt as he headed toward the showers. "I don't want you out of our sight."

"I'll wait by the door." She combed her fingers through her wet hair.

Ricky shook his head. "You don't have to watch us, but we need to be able to see you." He pointed at the bend in the bathroom. "Stand there. It'll give you a line of sight to us and the door."

"Why do I need to wait around at all?" She glanced at the exit. "It's late."

"You're sleeping with us from now on." He stepped into her space and pressed his lips to hers. A small touch with a significant message. "The moment we kissed you, you became ours. Our girl. Our responsibility. Ours to protect."

Her eyes softened, and she slipped her hands into her back pockets. "That's a nice thing to say." She turned her face away, her voice thready. "It would really suck if you guys are playing me."

"That goes both ways."

The shower sounded around the corner. In a few seconds, he would rest his eyes on Martin's naked body in a way he'd never been able to before.

Focus, Ricardo.

She raised her chin and gave him direct eye contact. "Do you have an alliance with another cartel or gang?"

The Freedom Fighters weren't just aligned with the Restrepo Cartel. They were married to it, literally, by way of their leader, Camila Dias-Restrepo.

A pang of guilt pinched his stomach. He hated keeping secrets from her, but one thing he wouldn't do was fill her head with lies.

"I can feed you reassuring words." He hooked his thumbs under the front of his waistband, deliberately keeping his hands to himself. "I can kiss you until you melt. Touch you until you scream my name. Or God's name. Same thing." He winked. "But I can't force you to trust me. That requires a valiant act of heroism, and I'm fresh out of those at the moment." He shrugged. "So this—you and me and Martin—this trust we need to build between us? It's going to take time. You know what they say in prison?"

"We have nothing but time."

She believed they had at least three years together. It broke his fucking heart.

"Put your ass where I can see you." He smacked a kiss on her mouth. "And don't move."

She tried to shape those fuckable lips into a scowl, but a smile broke through. "What am I going to do with you?"

He pulled off his shirt and stared down at the fly of his jeans. "You can start with—"

"Stop right there." She held up a hand and stepped to the spot he'd directed her.

"I was going to say…" He tossed his shirt at her. "Bury your nose in that and get used to my scent. You're going to be covered in it from now on."

"Overly optimistic, aren't you?"

"Confident, *querida*." He approached the showers, and his breath ran away from him.

Martin stood under the spray of water, his palms flat against the wall in front of him and defined arms bracing his upper body.

Rivers of water followed the carved grooves in his torso and trickled over the flanks of his tight ass.

"I can feel you staring." Martin lifted his head.

Their gazes collided, and he had to remind himself to breathe.

Distractions were out of the question. No flirty eye contact. No thinking about hand jobs in the bathroom.

Even at three in the morning, this was a dangerous place for a man to get caught with his pants down.

He glanced back at Tula.

She stood stiffly against the wall, her body angled slightly away. With her eyes on the door, she held his wadded shirt against her chest.

If anything happened to her…

He couldn't let his mind go there.

Stripping his clothes, he joined Martin under the warm spray.

A bar of soap served as shampoo and body wash. He lathered and rinsed quickly, trying his damnedest to ignore the heated glances from the man beside him.

His cock, however, ate up the attention, swelling with blood and rising toward his abs.

"Your timing sucks." He scrubbed his hands over his whiskered face. "You've had years to look, man."

"I did look. I devoured every inch of you when you weren't paying attention."

His dick throbbed. "Why didn't you tell me?"

"I didn't want to lead you on." Martin shifted to stand in front of him, keeping Tula in their periphery. "But now… I don't know. The rules are different here."

The rules changed because of a beautiful woman. Between her and the kiss she dared them to share, there was no turning back.

"Finish up." Martin leaned closer and put his mouth at Ricky's ear. "And keep your hands off your cock."

Martin slammed a palm against Ricky's ass, echoing a *smack* through the room and shooting shockwaves through his body.

"Killing me," he muttered and finished the shower in record time.

Back in their cell, he lit the scented candle to battle

the sewage smell and shut off the light.

The flame cast shadows over her and Martin, where they lay diagonally across the two mattresses. She burrowed into the den of Martin's body, her arms around him, and her eyes already closed in sleep.

Crawling in behind her, Ricky folded an arm around her waist and rested his hand against Martin's chest.

Those glittering green eyes found him across the space above her head. Hooded and warm, they looked content, happy even.

"Feels good, doesn't it?" Ricky whispered. "To be held. To be needed."

"Yeah." Martin rested his mouth against her head.

"I've always needed you."

"I know."

The silence that followed churned with their wants, their fears, and everything in between.

They had to earn her trust, navigate Martin's demons, steal Hector's secrets, and try not to get raped or killed in the process.

But right now, they had this. Skin, heartbeats, and breaths aligned in an unbroken moment. A moment to fight for.

EIGHTEEN

The next week dragged Ricky through the nine circles of hell. Between bone-bruising fights with inmates, lusting after the two people in his bed, and his guilt over hiding secrets from Tula, he felt as though he were running backward in a race against time.

Adding to that was the festering misery of prison life. The despair, the restlessness, the destruction of bodies that the inmates never seemed to grow sick of—there was an abundance of self-hatred in Jaulaso.

But for all the violence, guilt, and torment in limbo, there were glimpses of heaven. They dwelled in the slide of soft lips and hungry tongues.

Christ, the kissing. He'd never devoted so much time and attention to another person's mouth, but holy fuck, that was where it was at.

All those years of dating, countless lovers, Van's sexual training… How had he not discovered the sinful pleasure in a kiss?

He was addicted to it now. Good thing, because after a week of sharing a bed with Tula and Martin, kissing was all they'd done.

Martin had intimacy issues. Tula was hellbent on them joining La Rocha Cartel, and Ricky was left with a crumbling plan, two blue balls, and a black eye.

His busted face was a gift from a four-hundred-pound inmate in the common area two days ago. Martin had managed to escape that particular fight unscathed. The other times, however, he hadn't been so lucky.

Since they only ventured out among the prisoners while Tula was in meetings, she hadn't watched them get their asses kicked over and over. But she was always there to clean them up afterward.

"She's been gone too long." Martin bent over the sink in their cell, scraping a razor against the stubble on his jaw.

She met with Hector a lot. Sometimes it was a meeting with his advisers. Other times, she slipped away, saying she needed to check in with him.

She swore up and down he never touched her, never hurt her in any way. Didn't stop Ricky from chewing a hole in his cheek. He fucking hated every second she wasn't within eyeshot.

The reclusive cartel boss rarely left his private quarters. In the ten days they'd been here, they'd only spotted the old man twice. When they passed him in the hall, he was surrounded by guards and didn't spare them a single glance.

But he knew they were there. Tula didn't spend all that time with him without talking about the men she shared a bed with every night.

Was she talking about them right now?

Ricky lowered onto the mattress. "With any luck, we planted a seed of doubt in her head, enough to make her question every interaction she has with him."

"She's smart. If she's suspicious of him, she'll dig, ask questions, and find her way to the truth."

"That could work against us, too. If Hector doesn't trust us—"

"That's a given." Martin set the razor aside and rinsed his face.

"Then he's putting the doubts about us in her head."

If she discovered their loyalty to Restrepo, she would feel betrayed. Not just because they worked for a sworn enemy, but because they'd kept it from her.

The sooner they got her on their side, the better.

"You need to seal the deal." Martin inspected his face in the mirror, searching for stubble he'd missed.

"Meaning?"

"Fuck her, Ricky." He turned and folded his arms across his chest. "A woman like that doesn't have sex with a man she doesn't trust. If you open her legs, you'll open her heart."

"That sounds like a great plan. Love her then leave her in three months."

"If we succeed here, we'll be saving thousands of women and children. She'll understand that."

"Maybe." He studied Martin's expression, resenting the secrets lurking behind those eyes.

"Whatever's on your mind, just spit it out."

"You want me to fuck her, but she wants both of us. How can I convince her to trust me enough to sleep with me, when I can't even convince my *bisexual* best friend to do that?"

"It's two completely different things."

"It's the same fucking thing." Frustration burned through his veins as he rose from the bed. "It took all *three* of us to start this relationship, and we can't move forward unless all three of us are committed to it. I know you see that. You're just..." He pulled in a breath. "You're too fucking scared."

"Yeah?" A dark shadow passed across Martin's expression.

Then he attacked. Both hands hit Ricky hard enough in the chest to send him flying backward and crashing onto the bed.

"I'm scared, you fucking asshole." Martin followed him down and unleashed a sharp, backhanded blow across his face. "I'm scared *for you.*"

"What the fuck?" His jaw stitched with pain as he raised his arms to defend against the next strike.

Martin aimed low, punching him in the ribs. Ricky grunted in shock and dropped his hands against the hurt, realizing too late he'd exposed his neck.

A muscled forearm slammed against his throat and nailed him to the mattress. He gulped for air, pulling nothing into his lungs.

He clung to the arm at his throat, his fingers digging into muscle as he tried to dislodge the choking hold. But beneath the constricting pain stirred a dark desire.

Martin's crushing weight, cruel scowl, and unbending restraint—all of it heated Ricky's blood and tightened his balls.

"You want me to hurt you?" Martin seethed in his face. "I promise you don't want my brand of hurt."

Give it to me.

He tried to choke out the words, but they hit the air without sound or breath.

With a guttural growl, Martin shoved his free hand between them and gripped Ricky's erection through his jeans.

Oh, God. Don't stop.

His pulse roared. Black spots bloomed across his

vision, and all the heat in his body rushed to his dick. He'd never been this hard.

Martin's fingers curled around his nuts and squeezed with agonizing pressure. "You'll beg for death before I'm finished with you."

Martin would cut his own arm off before he crossed a line that couldn't be fixed. To prove it, Ricky shoved his neck against the iron bar of Martin's arm, seconds from passing out.

A knock sounded on the door.

Something passed over Martin's expression, and he blinked. His features softened, and his eyes looked brighter, sharper.

He pushed off the bed, and Ricky gulped for air, dragging starved breaths through his bruised throat.

Martin stabbed his hands in his hair. His chest heaved, and his jeans bulged with the long, engorged evidence of his arousal.

A second—more impatient—knock rapped on the door.

"Fuck." Martin reached for the handle and stopped.

Glancing down, he adjusted his erection and straightened his shirt in an attempt to hide what was too large to be concealed.

Ricky moved to the edge of the bed as Martin unlocked the door and opened it.

Garra stood on the other side, holding a paper bag. He glanced between Martin and Ricky before pushing his way inside.

"Come on in," Martin snarled in Spanish.

Ricky jumped to his feet, and the paper bag dropped on the mattress.

Garra pointed at it. "Use those. *Every* time."

Curiosity moved Ricky toward the bag. He dug his

hand in and pulled out a fistful of condoms.

Not what he was expecting.

He dropped the rubbers, unable to conceal the contempt in his voice. "Did you use one when you raped her?"

"Yes." Garra shoved his shoulders back.

No cowering with this one. No sense of self-preservation, either.

Ricky sent a fist into the motherfucker's nose. The wet sound of breaking cartilage accompanied a gush of blood.

Red trickled down Garra's lips and splattered the gold chains around his neck. He didn't roar in pain. Didn't throw a counterstrike.

The son of a bitch smiled.

"If you do that out there…" He stabbed a finger at the hallway, his Spanish thick and nasally. "You might keep her alive."

What the fuck was happening?

Garra pivoted and strode out the door. When he reached the corridor, he turned back. "Before you stick your dicks in her, picture this… Her belly round with your child while she sleeps on a filthy cot, scavenges for prison food, and gives birth on the floor surrounded by violent criminals." He spat a glob of blood in the hall and nodded at the paper bag. "Use the condoms."

Then he was gone.

Martin shut the door and leaned against it. "That isn't a man who's *just doing his job*."

"You don't say."

"Does he love her?"

"He delivered condoms to two men he doesn't know." Ricky cocked his head. "To use with the woman he loves? I don't think so."

"Good point." Martin stepped to the bed and peeked into the bag. "Nice right hook. You broke his nose."

"I should've broken more than his nose."

"He solved the condom issue."

"We didn't have a condom issue." Ricky had intended to hustle prophylactics from one of the prostitutes. He would've used flattery, charm, a couple cans of soup, whatever means necessary to obtain protection for Tula. Except sex. Tula was the only woman he wanted.

Garra saved him the hassle, but he still wanted to kill the guy.

"Where the fuck is she?" Martin shoved a hand in his hair.

"We need to go find her." He moved toward the door.

"Can you avoid a fight?"

His stomach tightened. The fights found him, not the other way around. "No promises."

NINETEEN

Something by The Beatles hummed from Hector's record player and caressed Tula's senses. She danced slowly in place, one hand on Hector's shoulder and the other resting in the loose curl of his fingers.

The warm cadence of the song calmed her heart. Or maybe it was the warm gaze stroking her face.

"There's just something about the sound of vinyl." She stepped when he stepped, letting his expert foot movements guide her through the slow dance. "It's richer, more authentic."

"You get those little scratches and pops in the records, the hum of the turntable motor, the tactile touch of the needle to the vinyl, and physical friction of the two."

"Listen to you. Your English is so elegant it's poetic. I can barely hear an accent."

"I had a good teacher." He spun her around, making her laugh.

"I'm getting better at this, right?" She pivoted on clumsy toes and straightened her slouching posture. "Lie if you have to."

"I've found you're good at everything, Petula. A natural talent."

"Except recruiting." Her heartbeat quickened. She drew in a long breath and released it. "They said they want to spend their time here quietly and stay away from cartel politics."

"Because they don't like cartels? Or because their loyalties lie elsewhere?"

"The first one, I think."

"If that's the case, they can't be here."

Her insides turned to ice. "Don't kill them."

He narrowed his dark eyes. "You like them."

"I don't know them well enough to feel one way or another, but I want the opportunity to see if I *would* like them."

She was hedging. The truth was she liked them too much, and she was afraid to admit that to Hector.

It was that damn accusation they'd planted in her head.

She wanted to ask Hector about the alleged human trafficking, but if it were true, he wouldn't tell her. Not if he'd concealed it from her for two years.

Asking him outright would make her look like she was siding with the enemy, which she would be doing if Ricky Martin were right.

She couldn't afford for Hector to be suspicious of her. He needed to trust her, and she wouldn't give him any reason not to.

But she wouldn't turn a blind eye, either. Hector La Rocha wasn't a benevolent man. He was a cartel boss with a nasty reputation, one he'd probably earned.

Except he wasn't nasty to her. He treated her like she meant something to him, like she was an important part of his world. He'd always kept her safe, and her life depended on that protection.

In return, all she had to do was remain loyal.

As the song ended, he released her and walked the short distance to the record player.

With his back to her, he lifted the needle and powered off the turntable. "Have you had sexual relations with them yet?"

Her face heated. "No. I need more time."

"And they haven't elaborated on why their identities were wiped? Other than the mention of enemies in a past life?"

"No." A nervous twitch skittered down her spine. "I know it doesn't seem like I'm making progress, but I spend every minute with them, feeling them out and earning their trust. They haven't done anything to make me believe they're a threat."

He shifted to look at her. "Except for their refusals to join me."

And their accusations about his business affairs.

"Give me more time." She squared her shoulders. "They're young and athletic, smart and skilled at fighting. They would serve you better alive than dead."

A grin stole over his mouth, and he ran a hand through his silver-black hair. "Take all the time you need, Petula. You have my confidence."

"Thank you." She needed to return to the guys but couldn't leave without asking, "Have you found anything on Vera?"

His face fell, and his head shook imperceptibly.

"I'm so sorry." He stepped forward and rested a warm hand on the side of her face. "One of these days, I'm going to give you a different answer."

A lump swelled in her throat, amassing with a horrible combination of doubt and hope.

Vera had been gone too long to be alive. His news would likely come with the discovery of a body.

But that would be better than not knowing. She needed closure, so she could finally grieve.

"Thank you. Again." She stood taller. "Why are you so kind to me?"

"You saved my life." He sat at the table and lit a cigarette. "You taught me English, and I enjoy your company." His eyes twinkled as tendrils of smoke curled from his nose. "Why are you so kind to me?"

She laughed, relieved by his answer. "You keep me safe. And I enjoy your company, too."

"Very good." He shooed her away with a hand. "Go recruit the gringos before I change my mind and kill them."

His teasing tone made it possible to walk calmly to the door. But as she stepped into the hall, the threat in his words closed a fist around her heart.

She made a beeline for the stairwell and faltered at the bottom step, her senses buzzing at the commotion of a nearby crowd.

The din of shouting and squeaking footsteps drifted down from the second floor. Something was happening in the stairwell directly above her.

"Fuck you!"

Her heart stopped.

She knew that American accent.

She knew it when it was gravelly with desire, sharp with frustration, and now stony with anger.

Her hand went to the pistol in her waistband. She flipped the safety off and took the first set of steps two at a time.

At the landing between the flights of stairs, she whipped around the corner and slammed to a stop.

A dozen men were gathered on the steps above her, and more spilled out of the top floor. At the center of the throng, Ricky lay on his back beneath four inmates, his body pinned to the steps.

On the landing above him, Martin fought four…five…six men and counting. Every time his fist connected with a body, he received three or more punches in return.

Her pulse exploded as she aimed the gun at the crowd and shouted in Spanish, "Get away from them!"

"Don't interfere, little girl." The man closest to her stepped into her space and crossed his arms. "This isn't your business."

Two more prisoners flanked him.

No guns were drawn, but if she fired her weapon, she would be staring down the barrels of a dozen or more guns.

One of the inmates holding Ricky's legs rose to his full height.

Her stomach turned inside out.

It was Trog. The large, hairy man was known for having a huge penis and a harem of unwilling bed partners.

A zipper sounded, and Trog whipped out his two-foot dick.

"Suck on this, bitch." He wrapped his hand around it, guiding it toward Ricky's clamped lips.

Outrage blazed in Ricky's eyes, his entire body flexing with murderous aggression.

He'd been disrespected by Trog *and* his dick. If Trog raped him, it would be the beginning of the end.

Once a bitch, forever a bitch.

"Name your price." She glared at the men in front of her. "And get the fuck out of my way."

Bribing them for their cooperation shouldn't cost more than thirty soups or a couple packs of cigarettes.

On the top floor, Martin grunted and punched his way through a half dozen prisoners. Outnumbered and losing ground, he would never reach Ricky in time.

Ricky renewed his efforts to escape as his captors held his head immobile. They pried their fingers into his mouth and stretched his jaw open to accept the massive erection angling toward him.

Panic chased her heart to her stomach. Her spine slicked with sweat, and the ringing sound of her fear thrashed in her ears.

She jerked her attention to the men blocking her path. "I need an answer."

TWENTY

Ricky bit down on the fingers in his mouth and tried to summon his nonexistent gag reflex. If he could puke on these motherfuckers, it might give him a fleeting moment to escape.

"You have options." The grizzly-bearded bastard with the donkey dick glared down at him. "While you're staring at it, you can hit, kick, whimper, cry, lick, suck, spit, or swallow."

What was funny about this was that the scaly, bulbous organ jutting toward his face was the ugliest goddamn dick he'd ever seen. What wasn't funny was the likelihood of it ramming into the back of his throat.

"Or you can roll to your stomach, and I'll visit China," the grizzly man said. "I'll leave it up to you and your personal survival instinct. But let's be honest. You're getting it one way or another."

His survival instinct had been honed by six months of training.

An outpouring of adrenaline hit his system, boosting his heart rate and blood pressure. A surge of muscle strength made him feel invincible, but he knew he wasn't.

No amount of training would get them out of this. There were too many men, and they were out for blood.

But he sure as hell wouldn't lie here and take it quietly.

He jerked his head to the side, coughing away from the body odor as he said in Spanish, "Someone's deodorant isn't working."

"It's not me," one of the dumbfucks said. "I'm not wearing deodorant."

A round of laughter erupted, and he used the distraction to twist his arms and break free from the restraining hands.

With a hard shove of his feet, he gained some distance, moving his position two stairs closer to Martin. Then more hands fell upon him, holding him against the steps.

Rough fingers opened his fly. Others joined in, yanking his jeans and boxers to his knees. There was even a goddamn one-armed man in the mix, slamming his only fist into Ricky's abdomen.

He tried to fight them off, wrestling and punching for a dominant position, but he was outmuscled and outnumbered.

With his groin exposed, he couldn't stop them from grabbing and smacking his junk.

He trapped a roar behind his sealed lips. His vision clouded. His ears pounded, as the increased blood flow to his extremities energized his strikes, powering his punches harder, faster, with the intent to kill.

He tried to track the sounds of Martin's fight above him. God knew how many men he was fending off. He was going to get himself killed.

Was Tula still standing at the bottom of the stairs?

He'd heard her voice amid the shouting but couldn't see her.

He didn't want her anywhere near this shit show. He couldn't protect her. Couldn't breathe. Couldn't do anything but fight for his life.

He fell into a zone, locked in tunnel vision and moving on instinct. Arms, legs, the core of his body—his muscle groups worked together to defend his most vulnerable areas and keep that hairy prick away from his mouth.

Until they flipped him over and shoved his face against a concrete stair.

Multiple bodies dove onto his back and legs, smothering him in the ripe stench of unwashed armpits. The rest of them restrained his arms above his head.

He was fucked, and in a few seconds, he was going to be fucked in the literal sense.

Never mind the diseases he would contract from the grotesque erection jabbing at his ass crack. He would probably survive the rape. He'd endured this before with Van.

It would be an agony that rivaled death, but that wasn't what terrified him the most.

If they won, he would have to endure it again and again. It would earn him a label no prisoner wanted in Jaulaso. For the next three months, he wouldn't be able to freely walk the halls. They would drag him out of his cell and sell his body for a can of soup.

He couldn't let this happen.

Renewing his efforts, he fought with all his strength to escape the thick press of bodies.

The noise from every direction was deafening—inmates yelling, stomping, and slamming fists. The stairwell was as hot as Hades, dampening his skin and making it easier to slide out of sweaty grips.

But there were too many men who outweighed him. He was overpowered.

The moment he felt greasy fingers separate his buttocks and expose his anus, he knew it was over.

Countless hands prevented him from moving. Sweltering breaths pommeled his neck and back.

He closed his eyes and tried to squeeze his glutes together, fighting the vise of fingers between his buttocks.

The stab of hard flesh pressed against his opening.

No, no, no.

He dug deep and summoned another surge of strength. If he could…just…pull…his legs free—

A gunshot rang out, reverberating in his ears and ricocheting through his chest.

Stunned silence gripped the stairwell for a millisecond. Then chaos broke loose.

The men around him flew to their feet, and the weight on his back tumbled off. The grizzly man's head landed next to his, and he came face to face with a bullet hole. Right through the temple.

His heartbeat convulsed, thudding slowly, thickly through his veins before speeding up and losing control.

"Don't fucking move," Tula screamed.

She stood above him, eyes wild as she waved a gun at the crowd.

Oh, God. Oh, fuck. What had she done?

She shot one of them. She fucking killed a cartel soldier in front of his army.

Weapons appeared in every hand, all of them aimed at her.

He yanked up his pants as he rose in front of her, blocking her body from the Uzis trained in her direction.

She hadn't thought this through. There wasn't a man

in this stairwell who would let her walk away after interfering in their business and killing one of their own.

He pressed in and circled his arms around her back, unable to shield her from all sides. He didn't obstruct her ability to fire her gun, but she would only get off one round before they were both dead.

His pulse thundered. Then it redoubled as Martin appeared behind her, with his chest against her back.

With a grimace, Martin blinked through the pools of crimson in his eyes. Blood gushed from everywhere, coating his hair, face, mouth, and chest. Fucking hell, he looked horrible.

But he was alive. For now.

The prisoners stood in a stand-off with their fingers all over the fucking triggers. As soon as the first shot fired, every gun would go off. It only took one dumbass to sneeze or twitch, and the entire stairwell would light up like fireworks.

He met Martin's blood-drenched eyes, and his heart sank with dread. They weren't going to survive this.

"Lower your weapons," someone said calmly in Spanish.

Ricky turned his neck toward the unfamiliar voice.

The sea of inmates parted on the stairs, and Hector La Rocha stood at the bottom, staring up at the crowd.

Then one by one, every gun descended, dropping out of view and tucking into waistbands, including Tula's.

Heads bowed in respect, and tense silence crept in.

Garra leaned against the wall behind Hector, his posture deceptively casual. Ricky didn't miss the small gun tucked in the curl of his fingers. Or the bandage taped across his broken nose.

Hector clasped his hands behind his back and swept his gaze over his soldiers.

He reminded Ricky of Fred Rogers from *Mister Rogers' Neighborhood.* It wasn't just the thin cardigan, buttoned-down shirt, silver-streaked black hair, and warm expression. There was a gentle frailness about him, a sense of unruffled patience in his demeanor.

Was it a ruse? Or was the cartel boss just old and tired?

"You." Hector looked at one of the inmates on the stairs as if randomly calling him out. "Tell me why guns were aimed at Petula."

"She shot Trog, boss." The man pointed at the dead body. "This wasn't her business and—"

"It is her business," Hector said softly. "Trog has been stealing cocaine from my supplies, and I told Petula to deal with it."

A wave of exhales rippled through the room.

Was that true? Ricky didn't think so.

Hector La Rocha hadn't interfered to save Martin or Ricky. Hell, he wouldn't even look at them. They refused to join him, and that made them the enemy.

No, Hector had come here for Tula, to protect her and keep her safe.

"Get rid of this and move along." Hector gestured at the dead man.

A whirlwind of motion erupted around him. Within seconds, Trog's body was dragged away, and every prisoner vacated the stairwell.

Garra pushed away from the wall to leave, but Hector didn't move.

Tula gripped Ricky's bicep as she wriggled out from between him and Martin. Her gaze went to Hector, and they stared at each for an eternity.

Whatever passed between them didn't end with a word, an expression, or a nod. Hector simply turned away and vanished around the corner with Garra on his heels.

She spun toward Martin and Ricky and gave them both a quick once-over. Her features looked molded in plastic, unmoving and lifeless, as if she'd sent her emotions far below the surface.

"Can you walk?" she asked Martin.

"Yeah."

"Follow me." She headed down toward the ground floor.

Where was she going? Their cell was upstairs.

Ricky lunged after her and grasped her arm, yanking her around. "Wrong way. We need to get Martin—"

Martin swayed, and his knees started to buckle.

"Shit." Ricky caught him before he fell down the stairs.

Two-hundred pounds of muscle and dead weight strained Ricky's exhausted, battered body as he leaned Martin against the wall.

Her expressionless mask cracked, releasing a well of tears in her eyes. She quickly wiped it away and pushed back her shoulders.

"I need to…" She coughed to clear her trembling in her voice. "I need to get you both into the showers, wash off the blood and the—"

Her gaze slipped to Ricky's backside and darted away.

"Hey." He held Martin against the wall with one hand and used the other to guide her face to his. "He didn't rape me."

Her eyes widened in disbelief. "He didn't?"

"No, baby. You put that bullet in his head just in time."

Her hand dropped to the railing, bracing her upper body as she sucked in gulps of air.

Beside him, Martin let his head fall back against the wall.

"I thought..." She raked her fingers through her hair and composed herself. "God, that's such a relief." Her eyes flitted to Martin. "I need to get you under the water. Really we all need showers since we'll be holed up in your room until you're healed."

"We can't fend off another attack right now."

"No one will bother us in the bathroom."

"You don't know that." Martin slurred past swollen lips.

"After what just happened..." She rubbed her head and whispered under her breath, "Hector *never* gets involved in fights. By defending me the way he did, he just established my position in the cartel."

"What does that mean?" Ricky asked.

"No one will mess with me for a while. Maybe not ever. And lucky for you, whenever you're with me, no one will fuck with you, either."

Ricky looked at Martin, and his friend gave a stiff nod.

TWENTY-ONE

Two hours later, Tula trudged to the sink in their private cell and rinsed out a bloody towel. Her neck ached from bending over, and exhaustion weighed down her bones.

She'd done what she could for the gruesome gash on Martin's head. It had bled so damn much—through his shower, during the walk back to his cell, and the entire thirty minutes it took her to stitch it closed.

His skull had been slammed into a concrete wall. At least, that was what he thought had happened. He was struggling to focus. Hell, he was doing well enough to stay conscious.

Given his dilated pupils and staggering gait through the halls, she worried he had a concussion. Didn't that mean he needed to stay awake? Or was that a myth? She wasn't taking any chances.

She'd cleaned and stitched the laceration on his head the best she could. She didn't know what else to do. It would leave a thick scar along his hairline, but at least the bleeding had stopped.

It could've been worse.

Her mind rewound the scene in the stairwell, shoving her in and out of horrifying moments. She'd watched a dozen men beat Martin into a bloody pulp and listened to Ricky's agonized grunts as he fought off violent, raping men. She'd wanted to die right then and there and take every single one of those bastards with her.

A torrent of grief rose through her chest and seared the back of her throat. She gripped the edge of the sink and tried to choke down the emotion, but she couldn't. She'd been holding it in for hours.

What if she hadn't been able to bribe the men on the stairs to let her pass? What if she'd missed and shot Ricky in the head instead?

Her terror had been so all-consuming it had rattled her grip on the gun as she pulled the trigger.

"I could've missed." A sob tore from her throat, and she clapped a hand over her mouth, knowing better than to cry in this unforgiving place.

"Tula." Ricky's arms surrounded her, and his shirtless chest blanketed her in heat. "What's wrong?"

"I could've shot you."

"You didn't." He lifted her, cradling her body against him as he sat on the bed. "You had perfect aim."

Only because she'd been standing three feet away. A blind person would've hit that target.

"I don't cry." She wiped the back of her hand across her damp cheeks and pulled herself together. "Not since I've been here. I hate that I feel so weak right now."

"You cried the night you were drunk, and you're anything but weak. You saved my ass. Literally."

More tears hit her eyes, and she buried her face in the warm, smooth skin on his shoulder. "I can't believe I drunk-cried."

"You were so beautiful that night." He lifted her chin

with a knuckle and kissed the wetness on her cheeks. "Just like now."

She melted against him, forehead to forehead, nose to nose. "Thank you."

"Thank you for helping us." Another kiss. "How did you get past the men at the bottom of the stairs?"

"I traded my gun."

"You what?" He jerked back and swept his hands around her waistband, searching in disbelief. "You used it when you shot Trog."

"That was the deal I made. If they let me by with it, they could have it after the fight. They came to the bathroom when you were helping Martin into the shower." She shrugged stiffly. "I passed it off to them when you weren't looking."

"Goddammit, Tula." His nostrils flared. "I wish you hadn't done that."

It wasn't ideal. Weapons were the most valuable commodity in Jaulaso, and a gun was worth a lot more than the price of a toll. Hector had given her that pistol two years ago, and even though he had an arsenal in his cell, she wouldn't ask for another one.

She was already indebted to him up to her eyeballs. After he lied for her in the stairwell, she owed him more than her life. Now she owed him the lives of Martin and Ricky. She would never be able to settle that debt.

"Rumor is you're good with a knife." Ricky squinted at her. "Where is this knife they speak of?"

"I exchanged it a week ago."

"For what?"

He was going to be angry. It was already bubbling in those milk-chocolate eyes as he anticipated her response.

She blew out a breath and patted the cotton pants on his legs beneath her.

"You traded your knife for our clothes?" The cords in his neck went taut, and his jaw turned to granite.

Yep, he was pissed.

She had no weapons left, but after the boon Hector had given her today, maybe she wouldn't need any.

"Yes, your clothes," she said. "And your razor, toothbrush, blankets… It bought all the supplies I didn't already have." She shoved at his chest. "You're welcome."

He pulled her close and ran his nose through her hair. "Thank you."

With a satisfied sigh, she peered over his shoulder to check on Martin.

He lay on his side, breathing evenly, the swollen skin around his closed eyes already darkening with bruises. He always looked so badass after a fight, all banged up on the surface while his intimidating fuck-off demeanor still vibrated underneath. Even with his eyes closed, she would think twice before creeping up on him.

Wait. Was he asleep?

"Martin!"

"I'm awake." He rolled to his back and hissed in pain. "Are you wet?"

"What?" She flinched.

"He's asking about your clothes." Ricky twisted to glance at Martin behind him. "She's soaked."

That sounded so dirty her belly fluttered with heat.

The three of them had showered together. With the guys naked and the bathroom in constant use by other inmates, she'd left on her bra and undies.

The whole ordeal had lasted less than three minutes. There had been nothing tantalizing about scrubbing blood out of Martin's hair while he knelt beneath the spray of water and fought to remain conscious.

She'd kept her eyes above their waists, and as far as

she knew, they hadn't stolen glances at her half-naked body. They'd been too busy trying to get through the shower as quickly as possible without an altercation.

The inmates who had passed in and out of the bathroom had stared menacingly and made threatening comments. Nothing unusual about that. But no one had bothered them.

After the shower, she'd hurriedly yanked on her clothes over soggy underwear and had been itchy and wet ever since.

"Take off your clothes and get into bed." Martin's head lolled toward her.

Despite the injuries that crisscrossed his face, his eyes glinted with unbending authority.

She sucked in a breath.

Normally, when she needed to dress or use the toilet, they stepped into the hall and gave her privacy. Asking them to do that now would be ridiculous, and honestly, she should've dropped the timid act days ago.

How many prisoners shared a bed with a woman for seven nights without molesting or attacking her while she slept?

She'd bet her life that Martin and Ricky were the only two in Jaulaso. They respected her modesty and had been nothing but patient with her.

Maybe she didn't trust their accusations against Hector, but she one-hundred-percent trusted them with her body.

"If I lie down with you…" She crawled off Ricky's lap and knelt beside Martin, inspecting his eyes. *Still dilated.* "You can't fall asleep."

"You'll keep me awake." He lifted the blanket beside him in invitation.

What an invitation. Beneath the covers, he wore only

a tight pair of black briefs. The sight of his chiseled body and all its divinity drove her insane.

When her gaze returned to his, he used his tongue to trail an unspoken command across his lips.

Come here and taste.

Her body reacted.

Heated.

Throbbed.

Liquefied.

Movement sounded behind her. Then the light bulb went dark, leaving only the dancing flame of the candle.

She turned, and holy shit, if there was ever a time to swoon, this was it.

Her eyes feasted on Ricky's masculinity, indulging in every inch of his sharply honed anatomy.

He'd stripped to his boxers, revealing a body that was sculpted so flawlessly not even Michelangelo could recreate it.

Her brain stopped working as she drank in the shadowscape of his square-cut jawline, the thick column of his neck, and every beckoning ridge and valley that shaped his torso.

Six feet of ripped muscle towered over her. Not a pinch of fat or a single imperfection. She knew those bulging biceps delivered bone-crushing strikes. His powerful legs carried two-hundred pounds of strength.

And the hard outline in his underwear told her how badly he wanted her.

Little tight pulses gathered between her legs. Her thighs quivered, and her inner muscles clenched with empty spasms, aching for penetration, needing him and Martin, both at the same time.

Good God, she had to physically shake herself out of a building orgasm.

"You can close your mouth," Ricky rasped.

She snapped her jaw shut and dropped from her knees to her hip on the bed. "Not fair."

"What's not fair?" He sat beside her and played with the ends of her hair.

"You. Him." She peered at Martin. "You look like models, fight like Gladiators, kiss like porn stars—"

"Porn stars?" Ricky arched a dark eyebrow.

"I don't know. That's what I see when I replay it in my head."

He trapped a smile between his teeth. "Continue. Please."

Why not? She was on a roll.

"You have all the confidence, none of the fat, and you smell like the best sex I've *never* had." She flopped back on the mattress beside Martin and stared at a patch of mildew in the ceiling. "I feel like a whimpering virgin around you guys because I… I've never…"

Ricky stretched out beside her, sandwiching her in between him and Martin. "You've never…?"

"I've never been with someone like you. Either of you. I've certainly never dated more than one man at a time, and the ones I've been with… They were nice, normal, average. Average bodies. Average jobs. Average conversations."

"They sound horribly boring," Ricky said. "Bet they were average in bed, too."

"I was okay with that." She closed her eyes. "I wanted normal and quiet. I loved my average life."

"And now?"

She wanted a life. With them in it. She wanted them so badly it scared her. "You're way out of my league."

Their silence vibrated against her, prompting her to open her eyes.

"Bullshit." Ricky glowered down at her, his dark, beautiful expression twisting in outrage. "Have you looked in the fucking mirror?"

She didn't have a complex about the way she looked. She had a small chest, but it never bothered her. Two years of poor nutrition had eaten away her figure and dulled the shine from her hair, but she was still pretty.

"Look, I'm not insecure. I know I look fine. I'm just not…" She waved a hand over him and Martin. "I'm not insanely, heart-stoppingly, drop-dead gorgeous like you two."

Martin leaned across her and touched Ricky's lips. Then he trailed his fingers down Ricky's neck, defined pecs and abs, and lingered on the strip of dark hair that vanished beneath Ricky's waistband.

"All of this is for you, Tula." He closed his hand over the swollen outline of Ricky's cock.

Ricky made a strangled sound in his throat, rivaling the loud gasps pushing past her lips.

She trembled to slide her hand over Martin's and stroke that thick hardness with him. But he moved his touch, and in a blink, he closed his fingers around her neck.

"Take off your clothes." His green eyes swirled with intensity. "I won't tell you again."

The only aphrodisiac she needed was the command in his voice. Hearing his salacious order and knowing he expected her to obey, she didn't realize until now how much she wanted to be dominated by a man she trusted.

Not just any man.

These two men.

Martin wasn't just telling her what he wanted. He was telling her what *she* wanted because somehow, he knew better than she did what that was.

His hand gave her throat a warning squeeze and slid

away.

Lying on her back between them, she toed off her sneakers. As they thumped to the floor, excitement charged the air.

Martin pushed himself into a sitting position and rested back against the wall. His eyes hooded as they honed in on the wetness between her legs. Wet from the shower. Mostly.

She released the fly on her jeans as her other deeper wetness turned into an inferno, throbbing to be extinguished.

Sadly, there would be no sex with them tonight. Not without birth control. It was a frustrating thought, but she wouldn't let it kill her mood.

The denim was the dampest around her butt, making it awkward to slide the material down her legs. Ricky helped her pull it off. Then he tackled her shirt, ripping it over her head before she could stop him. Not that she would have.

"Goddamn." He pried her thighs apart and knelt between them. "Be still. Just let me digest this for a second."

A voracious tremor rippled through her, and her rabbit heart pattered toward certain death.

She peeked over at Martin to see hungry green eyes studying her from beneath golden lashes. He tipped his head in admiration, angling for a view of the fabric between her legs.

A whoosh pulled through her stomach as his searing gaze drifted along her inner thighs. His expression was as predatory as his posture. Casual and confident, patient and threatening, he reminded her of a lazy lion, watching his meal, waiting for it to come a little closer before he played with it.

She ripped her eyes away as a finger traced the tattered strap of her bra.

Ricky followed the edge where the broken lace met the upper curve of her breast.

"This is what I put on…" A stinging memory clogged her voice. "The morning Vera called me. The last time I talked to her. I threw on some clothes and raced out the door. I had no idea the mismatched bra and undies I absently chose would be the only ones I would wear for the next five years."

His brow pulled down over the shadows collecting in his stricken eyes. He gently caressed the off-white bra cups, carefully touching the unraveling holes along the underside.

Lowering his hand, he glided the backs of his fingers down the faded purple triangle that covered her pubic bone.

She closed her eyes, savoring the sensation of his expert touch. "I had this one set that was burgundy satin with lace trim. The flirty panties were low cut, lots of cheek peek with a cage-back. You know, with the crisscross lattice that shows off the top half of the butt crack?"

"No. Jesus." He groaned. "I have no idea what that is, but it sounds sexy as fuck."

"Yeah. It was." Regret pinched her chest. "I wish I would've thrown on that set before I rushed out the door. Now it's gone, along with everything else in my life."

"I'm here." He lowered onto her, chest to chest, and braced his weight on his arms. "Martin's here, and we're going to make you very happy that we are."

"Martin? Are you sure?" She peeked around Ricky to lift a brow at the quiet, watchful man in question. "He's selfish with his body. He lets us look, but no one's allowed to touch."

"I'll work on him, but right now, I'm going to work on you."

He kissed her long and deep, sending languorous curls of fire through her veins. The warm glide of his tongue ignited her pulse. The hard press of his muscles melted her limbs, and the heady buzz of his presence made her want. Oh, God, how she wanted him.

He released her mouth to trail a scorching path of kisses down her neck. His hands slipped beneath her and deftly removed her bra. As he bent over her breasts, his pink tongue slid between his lips. She wanted it between her legs, and the thought made her hot and restless.

He licked her nipples, and she struggled to remain still. He nibbled and bit, torturing her, making her gasp. She tried to squirm away, but not really.

She needed him. Needed every atom in his body. She wanted to fuse with him at a molecular level so that nothing or no one could tear them apart.

Not just him. She craved them both.

Martin raised his heated gaze from Ricky's mouth on her breast and met her eyes. His fingers moved along his thigh, drawing a winding line as if he were tracing her body. It was profoundly seductive, fucking with her breathing and setting her skin afire.

"How's your head?" she panted.

"Fine. How's your pussy?"

She moaned. "Wet. Come here."

"Lie still and shut up."

She gave him the side eye.

"Do as you're told." He gripped her panties and yanked one side down her thigh.

Ricky took over, sliding the threadbare cotton off while being mindful not to rip them.

Then she was bare, totally nude and utterly exposed

beneath the weight of their eyes. They took in the dark hair between her legs, their nostrils pulsing and expressions burning with desire.

Her body was completely natural and all her. No creams, perfumes, polishes, powders, dyes, waxes, surgeries, or enhancements of any kind. But they liked what they saw, and she kind of loved them for that.

"Open your legs," Martin said.

She submitted without hesitation, relishing the way he controlled her. Both her and Ricky.

Ricky was domineering in his own right, but when he was with Martin, he let his friend take the reins. She adored the dynamic, loved that they didn't compete against each other for attention or dominance.

Each of their roles in this threesome felt natural, fitting together seamlessly, effortlessly, without alterations or compromises.

Nothing in her life had ever been this easy or felt this right. It was as if some cosmic force had decided she deserved a chance at happiness, and *poof,* here they were, molding her into a woman who would never want anyone else but them.

"She's lost in her head," Martin said. "Rectify that."

Ricky stretched her legs open and fit his wide shoulders between her thighs. Her heart stuttered as he lowered his mouth to her pussy.

The first touch of his lips bowed her back. He did it again, and she gulped uselessly for air, choking and trembling.

"Breathe." Martin crawled in beside her and brushed her hair from her face. "Deep breaths."

She inhaled slowly, unable to stop her thighs from squeezing around Ricky's ears. "It's been so long."

"I know." He dropped a kiss on her mouth.

He did know. Seven years without sex. She needed to understand why, but she wouldn't push him. Not tonight.

"I don't know if I can have an orgasm." She stared down her body to find Ricky's waiting gaze, the depths glimmering with promise. "I can do it on my own, but I haven't tried in two years."

"Give me your eyes," Martin said.

She looked up and fell into a crystal green ocean.

"You've never come with another person?" He stroked a finger across her lips.

"No."

"Lick her, Ricky. Do it slowly and draw it out."

"I love it when you're bossy." Ricky grinned.

Then he buried that smile between her legs.

The firm, wet warmth of his tongue made her gasp. Martin caught her lips between his, kissing her soundly as Ricky brought her body to life with skillful licks and soft sucking pressure.

Her arms encircled Martin's neck, and she kissed him back, hungrily eating at his mouth while pulling him closer, tighter. She wanted him on top of her, inside her, deep and hard and *more.*

His dark, manly scent drugged her inhales. The potency of his hot skin on hers evaporated her brain cells. The taste of his breath pulled her hips up, spurring her to flex and grind against the diabolical swirl of Ricky's tongue.

Two mouths worshiped her, kissing in sync and catching an urgent rhythm. Her entire body throbbed beneath the pure expertise of their tongues, and that was when she knew she would come.

Pleasure rose from dormancy, bursting from her core with a vengeance. There was no slow build or warning tingles. When the orgasm sparked, it blasted across her vision in Technicolor and shot full-body compression waves through her nerve endings, shaking her down to her soul.

She screamed their names, cursed them in four-letter words, and Martin devoured every syllable with his mouth over hers.

"I just died a thousand deaths." She shivered against the lingering twitches of the best orgasm she'd ever had.

Ricky crawled up her body, his lips swollen and wet and curved in a breathtaking smile.

"You're the reason the gods invented oral sex," she said to him. Then she glanced at Martin, unable to ignore the massive bulge straining his briefs. "You should let Ricky use his mouth on—"

Martin grabbed a fistful of Ricky's hair, and their lips collided. The kiss skipped slow and gentle and plunged straight into ferocious.

She scooted out of the way as they rose to their knees and crashed together. Their mouths moved violently, rabidly, sucking, biting, groaning, panting. Hands pulled at hair. Fingers clawed down backs. Their hips slammed, cocks grinding. They were fucking each other with only the barrier of underwear between them.

It was so beautiful, so utterly staggering it made her heart hurt.

Martin ripped his mouth away and stared at Ricky's lips. Then he dove in again, his hand tangled in Ricky's hair as he licked around Ricky's open mouth, curling his tongue into the corners and the undersides of Ricky's lips.

She stopped breathing as it dawned on her. Martin was lapping her come from Ricky's face.

Martin leaned back, his gaze unfocused. "Fuck, she tastes..."

"Like resurrection."

Her heart fainted. Then it hammered anew as she watched them stare at each other. The penetrating glares, stiff necks, and swollen need between their legs… The passing seconds hardened and condensed between them.

They weren't finished.

She silently willed them to fall into each other and fuck until they passed out. But she didn't say a word, didn't move a muscle, afraid she would break the spell.

"Let me touch you." Ricky looked down at Martin's strained briefs. "Let me send you into ecstasy."

"Tula." Martin held Ricky's gaze as he said to her, "Lie on your back and spread your legs."

TWENTY-TWO

Ricky's pulse thundered in his ears as Tula moved into position.

With her thighs open and tits heaving, she lay like an erotic buffet spread out before him. He was five seconds from blowing a load in his boxers.

"You're fucking gorgeous." His gaze raked over her sensual body, making her shiver. "Can't wait to bury my cock in your cunt."

"Kneel between her legs." Martin smacked Ricky's ass so hard his breath cut off.

His lips pulled back, releasing a groan of pain, and his entire body tensed to spin around and punch Martin in the face. But he didn't.

A sense of peace stole over him as he obeyed. And there was something else. *Hunger*. It raised his body temperature, accelerated his breaths, and blazed more blood to his cock.

His erection strained harder, taller, tenting his boxers and producing a wet spot at the crest.

Martin moved in behind him and curled a hand

around his rigid length.

Fuck, he would never get used to the feel of that fist on his cock. He'd dreamed about it for so long it didn't seem real.

Martin swiped his thumb over the crown, rubbing the slippery wet spot as he bit and licked along Ricky's nape.

"Don't stop." Ricky dropped the weight of his head forward and groaned.

The sharp bite of teeth sank into the juncture between his shoulder and neck. Maddening pain gnawed through the muscle there, stabbing so hard and deep he was certain Martin drew blood.

The agony centered him, and his balls tightened in anticipation.

Beneath his bent position, Tula's jaw dropped an inch, her eyes wide and glistening. "You're hurting him."

"Shhh." Ricky slid his palm between her breasts, holding her to the mattress. "I like it. We both do. But Martin would never force you into edge play."

"If you think I'm playing…" Martin grabbed Ricky's nuts. "You don't know me at all."

That fist clenched viciously, squeezing without mercy. Black spots strobed across Ricky's vision, and his stomach twisted with nauseating pain.

"Are you man enough to make me scream?" Ricky choked out.

"I'm mean enough to make sure you can't." Martin released Ricky's testicles and cuffed his throat, instantly cutting off his airway.

Cruel fingers tightened without care, digging into his vulnerable esophagus as if intending to yank it out.

"You're scaring me." Tula's face paled. "Let him go." She jackknifed upward and pulled uselessly at Martin's arm. "He can't breathe!"

"I didn't tell you to move." The chilling calmness in Martin's voice made her freeze.

Martin's other hand imprisoned Ricky's cock, stroking him ruthlessly, vigorously toward orgasm. He tried to shake his head, to tell her he wanted this, but he had no voice, no air, and no power to move.

She clutched her throat, her eyes watering as she looked down at Martin's pumping fist.

The urgency to come had never felt so terrifyingly pleasurable, and she must've seen that in Ricky's expression because she dropped back on the bed, her gaze lasering on his cock.

Martin's fingers loosened on Ricky's neck, allowing him to drag delicious gulps of air into his lungs. The instant he could breathe without choking, the hand cinched again, strangling his next inhale.

Tula watched with lust-filled eyes as Martin jerked Ricky off, stroking him expertly toward release. Right as Ricky reached the pinnacle, Martin stopped. The vise of his hand squeezed beneath the head of Ricky's cock and stifled the orgasm, causing Ricky's body to shake uncontrollably.

And so it went. Martin tortured him for an eternity, bringing him to the edge of climax, asphyxiating him to the brink of unconsciousness. Then he paused, gave Ricky air, and started again.

Each time grew rougher, harder, and more reckless until Martin started to go too far. Ricky felt a real fear of death beneath the hand on his throat. Midway between desire and unconsciousness, self-preservation kicked in, and he started to fight.

Martin released him and tangled that brutal hand in his hair, wrenching his neck at a painful angle.

"I'm going to fuck your ass." The voice at Ricky's ear

spoke without emotion or familiarity. "I'll do it dry while you're tensing in fear. Once you're nice and bloody, I'll shove the handle of a hammer into that ruined hole and ram it hard." Martin ground his erection against Ricky's backside. "Every blow will drive so deep you'll feel it in your stomach. The pain will own you, make you so fucking weak you'll try to puke it out. I'll shove your face in the vomit, make you lick up your own filth. When you start crying, because you will, motherfucker. You'll cry like a goddamn faggot, and I'll piss all over those whiny lips."

A sickening feeling punched Ricky in the gut and sank to the pith of his stomach.

Van Quiso hadn't put those images in Martin's head. This was the creation of something much more sinister.

"Oh, no. Martin." She rose to her knees and pressed a trembling hand against her mouth. Tears poured from her eyes as she shook her head in horror. "Who did that to you?"

She stole the words out of Ricky's head. His dick started to shrivel as he yanked his boxers back in place. Then he turned toward his best friend.

Martin's arms lowered to his sides, and he went hauntingly still. His expression froze, vacant and eerie, as his glazed eyes stared off into the distance.

"Martin." She touched his jaw, her voice thick with tears. "How old were you?"

His brows pinched together, and his breathing lunged into a wheezing panic.

He shoved off the bed and pivoted toward the wall, flattening his palms against it.

Heart racing, Ricky moved to comfort him.

"Don't." Martin dropped his head between his braced arms and sucked heavy gulps of air. "Stay there. Please."

The *please* locked Ricky's limbs. The desperation in Martin's voice gutted him. Martin never pleaded. Never asked. Whatever compelled him to do it now held Ricky in place.

A sob sounded beside him, and he hooked an arm around her, pulling her onto his lap.

He clung to her, suffocating in the wake of Martin's pain as he helplessly watched Martin put himself back together.

Agonizing minutes passed before Martin straightened and stepped toward the bed. Stitches and bruises marred his gorgeous features, but none of it detracted from his strength.

He stood tall and powerful, wearing only briefs. He didn't need the armor of clothing or the security of a masked expression. He let Ricky and Tula see all of him—the soft bulge between his legs, the bobbing swallow in his throat, and the indelible memories of abuse in his eyes.

"How badly did I hurt you?" Martin asked.

"It was nothing that I didn't want or couldn't handle." He shifted to one end of the pushed-together mattresses, taking Tula with him. "I know you don't want to talk about why you—"

"I can't."

"Can you tell me about your parents?"

Ricky had asked that question numerous times, and the only answer he'd been given was Martin had a dad, as in *once had* but not anymore.

Had Martin's father molested him? Was that the man he killed?

His silent glare confessed nothing, his lips refusing to answer.

"I never knew my dad." Tula pulled the blanket over her, covering her nude body on Ricky's lap. "And my mom couldn't get rid of me fast enough. I don't know why. I never gave her any trouble and always did well in school. She and Vera were close, but she kept me at an arm's distance. When I turned eighteen, she begged me to leave. To leave the city. The country. To just go away. So I did." She sucked on her quivering bottom lip and released it. "She died seven years ago, and I miss her so much."

Ricky slid a hand into her hair, raking his fingers along her scalp as he pulled her against him.

"I'm sorry, *querida*." He kissed her head, his eyes locked on Martin, waiting.

"My mother left when I was two." Martin lowered onto the far end of the mattress and leaned against the wall at his back. "I grew up on a small farm in Texas with my dad. He was a good man. Hardworking. He died from a stroke when I was fourteen."

Orphaned at fourteen.

His heart caved in.

Based on his own experience, Ricky could draw conclusions about what happened to Martin. "I was given up at birth and spent my entire childhood in foster care. Fortunately, I was always placed with nice families." He softened his voice. "No pedophiles or abusive foster dads."

"I wasn't put into foster care."

"Orphanage?"

"No."

"Then what—?"

"Fucking drop it, Ricky."

All three of them had been victims of rape, and they coped with it in different ways. Martin's experiences had been the worst by far, and Ricky knew he hadn't heard the half of it.

He could be patient, but he would never stop trying to help Martin.

Tula adjusted her position on his lap. With her back to his chest, they faced Martin with the length of the mattress between them.

"I know you don't want to talk about it." She kept the blanket clutched to her chest. "But what *do* you want? What do you need?"

Martin's eyes flashed. "Lower the blanket."

"Oh." She tensed against Ricky's chest. After a reluctant moment, she tossed aside the cover.

"*That* is what I need."

"You need my…?" She looked down at her breasts.

Ricky knew the answer before her head popped up.

"My obedience," she breathed.

"Yes." Martin inclined his head. "And your trust. Open your legs."

After what she just witnessed, her trust was a helluva lot to ask for. The mood had been decimated, replaced with a stifling gloom in the air, but that didn't stop Ricky's cock from swelling again. The damn thing couldn't ignore the gorgeous, naked woman on his lap.

Martin bent over the edge of the bed and reached for the box of supplies on the floor. The crinkling sound of a paper bag told Ricky what Martin was doing, and his body hardened in anticipation.

Tula gave him a look over her shoulder, one that said, *I know that's not a banana in your pocket.*

"We don't have condoms." She turned back to Martin and stared at the foil packet he set between her legs. "Okay. Where did you get that?"

"Garra." Martin returned to his perch against the wall. "He delivered a bag of them earlier today."

"Garra?" A sound of surprise left her lips. "That's why he has a broken nose. Which one of you punched him?"

"It might've been the one-armed man." Ricky pressed his grin against her neck.

"I don't care that you hurt him. I'm guessing Hector sent him with the condoms. I don't think Garra gives a shit if I get pregnant."

She was wrong. Garra had a lot more interest in her than what she believed, but Ricky didn't want to talk about that bastard right now.

"Who does this belong to?" He cupped a hand between her spread legs and met Martin's eyes.

"Ricky Martin." She dropped her head back on his shoulder and chuckled. "My pussy belongs to Ricky Martin."

Ricky slapped the silky, damp flesh, making her yelp. "You're going to put that condom on me. Then you're going to slide down in this exact position so Martin can watch your pussy lips stretch and suck on my cock."

"Jesus, you're dirty." She melted against him, sighing. "Why does that turn me on so much?"

"Because you're dirty, too." He slid his touch along her slit, slowly working it up and down, teasing her.

Fuck him, she was tight and wet. He sank two fingers into her velvety heat and stroked her clenching muscles. His other hand cupped her breast, kneading the soft weight.

As she grew slick around his fingers, he curled them into a beckoning motion, again and again. She writhed and panted on his lap, and he turned his mouth toward hers, biting and licking and grunting at her sweetness. So fucking sexy.

"Get the condom." He slipped his fingers from her body and caught her tight little clit, rubbing it until she moaned.

She twisted around and delivered a hungry kiss to

his lips. Then she climbed off his lap.

He scooted to put his back against the wall that sat perpendicular to the one Martin leaned against. Then he removed his boxers and widened his legs. One foot touched Martin's hip. His other rested on Martin's ankle.

The position would give Martin the best view of her body as Ricky slid in and out of her cunt.

The thought sped up his pulse and pooled warmth in his balls, drawing them closer to his body. He needed her. *Now.*

Then she was there, kneeling beside him with the condom ready.

He grew impossibly harder.

As she rolled on the latex with small, warm fingers, he flicked his gaze between her and Martin, reveling in their presence and absorbing the moment.

Martin's blank expression started to gain color and life, the pain he carried inside him retreating from his eyes. He was a ticking time bomb, that guy. He thought he could keep it all locked up, but Ricky had just found the key.

It was probably going to hurt like hell, but Ricky was confident that sex would set Martin free.

"I think I did it right." She peered up at him, her eyes round and dark with desire.

"Straddle me, facing Martin."

She threw a leg over his lap, giving him a brain-scrambling view of her curvy ass. He gripped her hips, holding her over his cock, keyed up and so damn ready to fuck.

The weight of her petite frame in his hands, the feel of her satiny skin beneath his palms, the deep pulses at the base of his dick… Everything suspended, waiting on Martin's command.

For a handful of heartbeats, Martin simply watched

them. He bent a leg and draped his arm over his raised knee. His cock lay semi-hard beneath his briefs. Then it twitched, moving the fabric.

Dark stormy energy rotated around him, his green eyes aglow in the shadows of the flickering candlelight. Hell only knew what kind of thoughts were swirling in his head.

"Give me her orgasm, Ricky," he said in a rock-grinding voice. "I want to see her face as she forgets every man who came before us."

"What other men?"

Ricky heard the smirk in her response right before he pressed the tip of his cock inside her.

The tight ring of her opening stole his breath. Her hands went to his wrists as he held her waist, hovering her over him and making her squirm on that first inch.

He pushed deeper, and they moaned together. He extended the torture, turning that initial stroke into the slowest and longest in history. With every inch he worked in, he felt her wrapping around him, constricting and pulsing and stoking his need into electrifying chaos.

He wanted to see Martin's expression, but it was all he could do not to drive himself, hard and fast, inside her. When he finally reached the back of her cunt, he sucked in a breath and began to fuck her deeply, languidly, savoring the sinful feel of her strangling heat.

"Martin." He groaned. "She's so fucking tight."

A masculine groan rumbled in answer, and the mattress squeaked as Martin shifted his weight.

Ricky's control only lasted so long. She felt too good, too damn warm and sweet. He knew her scent, her taste, and now he knew the depths of her sex. He was in heaven.

She squeezed down on him, grinding her ass each time he buried himself to the root. Eventually, he released her hips and let her move on her own.

Reaching between their legs, she cupped his balls and scratched her nails up and down his scrotum. He grunted at the wicked sensations and thrust his hips harder, jerking himself off in her slick pussy.

His blood pressure went up, and his heart rate increased as he rapidly approached the point of no return. He wanted to come inside her while staring into her eyes.

But first, Martin was going to see the face she made as Ricky made her explode.

He snaked his hand into her hair and turned her neck, locking her into a kiss. She undulated on his cock, driving her hips to meet the slamming force of his thrusts.

Her mouth opened for his lashing tongue, and the kiss morphed into a mauling of lips and teeth. He was too hungry, and his thrusts were bouncing her too fast. They couldn't keep their mouths connected amid the panting, groaning, full-on fucking.

Using his grip in her hair, he angled her face toward Martin and sealed his lips to her neck. She clenched her inner muscles, and his eyes rolled back into his head. He wasn't going to last much longer.

With a hand between her legs, he tortured her clit. She cried out in pleasure, spreading her legs wider. He circled his fingers around and around the little nub, making her thighs tremble and breaths come faster, harder.

"Look at me." Martin's deep voice penetrated his chest.

He knew Martin was talking to her, but he looked anyway, tilting his head to get a direct view of those green eyes in front of her.

Martin stared at him with the force of fire, stirring the embers of a rising heat. Ricky worked his hand harder around her clit, flexing his hips and spinning them into delirium.

Martin balled and released his fist, and a muscle bounced in his jaw. "Give it to me. Now."

"Tula first." Ricky drove deep, desperate to send her over.

Martin leaned forward, giving her the force of his daunting glare. "Now."

She doubled over and gripped Ricky's knees, bearing down on his cock as she met Martin's eyes. Her hips jerked once, twice, and she let out a throaty roar, growling and panting through clenched teeth. She continued to grind, gasping and milking her release to the last drop.

Ricky didn't breathe through the entirety of her full-minute orgasm. Didn't wait for her to find her bearings. Didn't spare Martin a glance. He didn't stop to do anything as he tossed her onto her back and slammed himself into the tight sheath of her body.

Pinning her pretty tattooed arms above her head, he captured her lips and thrust his tongue deep. All control gone, he hammered his hips, dipping in and out of her slick cunt and spurring them into wild madness.

He couldn't let up, couldn't slow down. He gave and took, raw and mindless, kissing and fucking to within an inch of their lives.

"Holy fuck." She moaned against his mouth, her face radiating with the afterglow of her orgasms.

"That's right, baby. What's my name?" He pounded into her.

"Oh, God." She clawed at his back.

"God is good, aren't I?"

"So good."

She made him feel like a god. In her arms, under Martin's heated gaze, he caught fire.

He'd never felt like this—free, wanted, happy, exactly where he belonged. With her. With Martin. Coming his fucking brains out.

"Fuck, fuck, fuuuuuck!" He stared into her eyes as muscular spasms attacked his body, starting at his face and quaking down to his toes. Even his rectum contracted, squeezing in rhythm with the pulsing spurts of his cock. Heat and sweat spread over his skin and penetrated deep, saturating his insides from his balls to his nipples.

On a squeaky rusted cot, in the most violent prison in Latin America, he experienced the best orgasm of his life.

He rolled to his back, taking her with him. As she settled onto his chest, both of their heads turned toward Martin.

The brutal intensity of Martin's eyes raked over them, stroking more than their bodies. He felt Martin reach inside him and curl around his soul.

He depended on that connection. He needed the completeness of all three of them, and he was so close. Tula reciprocated every touch, and Martin no longer felt like an impossible dream.

She lifted her hips, letting his softening cock slip out of her. "You annihilated my orgasm-less existence."

"I would gladly do it again, every day, for the rest of my life." He removed the condom and tossed it at the bag of trash in the corner.

Her gaze drifted back to Martin, and she tilted her head. "Do you…?" She glanced at his semi and returned to his eyes. "Masturbate?"

Martin's lips bounced before surrendering a grin. "Yes, Tula. I'm quite proficient at it."

"Do you want to do it now? Or I can—?"

"If I need to come, I'll come." He pushed off the wall

and crawled to her. "You were devastatingly perfect tonight."

He kissed her, nudging her onto her back as he bent over her. Soft and slow, he licked and nibbled and took his time.

Then he turned to Ricky and placed his hands on either side of Ricky's head. His bright eyes filled with equal amounts of apology and affection. Then he pulled Ricky close and slid his tongue in Ricky's mouth.

The languorous kiss curled warmth through Ricky's chest, and by the time it finished, Martin left no doubt in Ricky's mind that they'd only just begun.

They slid in on either side of Tula and twined their limbs with hers. Martin's hand brushed Ricky's bare hip, curled around his buttocks, and stayed there.

Ricky basked in that touch, in the nearness of this man and woman, in the three of them together.

As he drifted into sleep, *forever* sank into the crevices of his soul.

TWENTY-THREE

The next month was the happiest month in Tula's memory.

There had been no attacks on her or the guys. Hector's security guard, Luis, had been released from prison. That meant fewer cartel meetings and more time with Martin and Ricky.

Her sex life had gone from nonexistent to nonstop, and the sex…

Sweet mother of Himeros, Ricky had unending stamina and talent. He was inside her every day, multiple times a day, in every position. Slow and fast, hard and gentle, they went at it so frequently she had to ask Garra for more condoms.

She'd never felt such uncontrollable desire for a man, let alone two.

Martin kissed her and Ricky as often as she and Ricky had sex, but he never allowed himself relief. He never let them touch him sexually, and after that first night she and Ricky were together, Martin stopped touching them, too.

She knew he didn't want another violent episode

after the one he had with Ricky. So he sat on the sidelines, seemingly content to watch her and Ricky fall apart at his command.

Behind his tightly controlled bearing, however, simmered a bottomless well of pain and frustration. He tried to bury it, but it burned from his eyes and scorched the air around him whenever he was aroused.

Sex was his trigger, and it made him viciously mean. She couldn't fathom the abuse he'd endured.

Pressing him to talk about it only made him coil tighter, and whenever he lashed out, his fury was loaded with accusations.

Accusations directed at her.

She left him and Ricky in bed this morning, telling them she had a meeting with Hector. The lie made her chest hurt, but dammit, she knew they weren't being truthful with her, either.

She sat in her own cell, on a mattress she didn't use anymore, and pored over everything they'd said over the past five weeks.

Martin's distrust resided with Hector, steeped with the notion that Hector's cartel snatched children off American streets and sold them into slavery.

Though Martin never admitted it, she knew he'd been a victim of sexual abuse as young as fourteen. His stance against child slavery wasn't just a moral one. It was personal.

That wasn't the case for Ricky. No, he just flat-out hated Hector.

They had no evidence against Hector's involvement in human trafficking. Their claims came from alleged news reports and rumors they'd heard in the circles they ran in. Or so they said.

That was where her suspicions really niggled. What

circles? Who were Martin Lockwood and Ricky Saldivar really? Where did they come from? Why had they paid their way into Area Three if it wasn't to join La Rocha Cartel and take advantage of that protection?

She didn't know all their truths or the details about their pasts. They maintained they were innocent of their drug trafficking charges, which she believed. They were too high-minded and honorable to fuck around with narcotics.

So why were they arrested? She didn't buy their bullshit story about a Mexican vacation gone wrong. The military didn't just scoop up American tourists and throw them in prison.

Except that was exactly what happened to her.

With a self-pitying groan, she dropped her head in her hands.

She cared about them deeply, possessively. They'd taken her from feeling nothing to feeling everything, and it wasn't just lust and orgasms. It was more profound and soulful. She thought of them as hers. Hers to hold and support and love.

She didn't know if she loved them. There was so much about them she still hadn't discovered. Not just the secrets they kept from her, but who they were outside of prison. What did they do when they woke every morning? Where did they go? Who were their friends?

All this could be derived from a conversation, but she wanted to experience it herself. She wanted to be with them outside of these claustrophobic walls, and that couldn't happen for at least three years. Maybe longer, pending their sentences.

Even then, when she was released from Jaulaso, she would never be released from Hector.

Hector.

Her loyalty to him was all tangled up in her feelings for Ricky Martin.

Whenever she asked Martin what he wanted her to do about the accusations he threw around, he told her to find the truth.

Open your mind. Be skeptical. Investigate your boss.

If she could be suspicious of Martin and Ricky, why couldn't she be suspicious of Hector La Rocha?

Because she was scared.

Terrified.

Fear had kept her from poking around, but here she was, prepared to do just that.

Her hands slicked with sweat, and her pulse tapped neurotically in her throat. She was a nervous fucking wreck.

Another five minutes passed before she heard footsteps in the corridor.

She rose soundlessly and darted behind the partially opened door to her cell. No one would suspect she was in here. Her cell had been empty for a month.

She held her breath as the movement in the hall passed by without stopping.

Tiptoeing around the door, she peeked out to see the backs of Garra and Hector as they made their way around the corner and out of view.

She blew out a quiet breath.

With Luis out of prison now, Hector had become wary about his personal security. Garra had stepped in to do the job until Hector could find someone permanent to trust with his life.

In the meantime, he reduced the number of meetings in his private quarters and kept to himself more than usual. But he still had to shower, and he did it like clockwork, every other day at eight in the morning.

She stepped into the empty hall and silently raced the thirty feet to his cell. The handle turned. Unlocked.

Only someone with a death wish would enter his space without his permission.

Her heart banged so hard in her chest she thought she might pass out.

She didn't know how long he would be gone. Ten minutes tops. She slipped inside and went straight to the filing cabinets. She'd never seen inside the drawers and expected to find paperwork when she opened them.

Nope. Every drawer held nonperishable food. Pork rinds, bread rolls, cereal, rice, tequila, and enough soup to feed an old man for twenty years. No wonder Hector rarely left his cell.

Her nerves tightened as she stepped toward the rear of his quarters. Behind a heavy drape sat a small bed with folded linens and a soft pillow.

This was the first time she'd ever been back here, and she hoped it would be the last as she ran her hands under the mattress and rummaged through every nook and cranny.

She found a knife under his pillow and left it there. There were no documents. No diaries. Nothing that might incriminate him. Where the hell would he hide his secrets?

Something rustled behind her. Her heart rate exploded as she spun around.

A massive cockroach darted across a paper bag and squeezed into a crack in the wall.

"Fuck!" She pressed a hand against her chest, trying to soothe her wailing heart.

He could walk in at any moment, and she didn't even know what she was looking for. She just needed...*something*. Proof that he was or was not trafficking women and children.

Five running steps carried her to the bookshelves. She thumbed through every text and novel, shaking them on their sides to see if anything fell from the pages.

Nothing.

She continued along the shelves, removing and returning the books. How long had Hector been gone? Four minutes? Five? She needed to go.

"What are you doing?" His soft voice drifted from the door, paralyzing her lungs.

She forced herself to breathe. Then she turned slowly, willing the tension from her neck and shoulders.

"Hey." She pinned a timid half-smile on her lips. "Sorry I was digging through your books. I knocked, but you weren't here." She motioned at the shelves behind her. "I was looking for something new to read."

"Have I not given you enough books?" He remained near the door, his face concealed by shadows.

"You've given me too much."

He'd given her more than anyone else had in her life, and she repaid him by snooping through his shit.

"Any updates on the gringos?" He set down his bath towel and toiletries and joined her at the bookshelf.

She grasped desperately at the change of topics. "Not since last week. We've been…"

"Making use of the condoms?" He lifted an eyebrow. "Garra told me you needed more."

Oh, Jesus. Her face heated, and she looked away.

"You're enjoying yourself." His tone lacked judgment or suspicion. "There's very little pleasure in Jaulaso. Take it when and where you can."

"I'm definitely doing that."

Talking about her sex life with Hector La Rocha creeped her out. But she preferred this conversation over a discussion about trespassing in his private quarters.

"Thank you for letting me have this time with them," she said. "They're…nice. I know that's not enough, and I'm still working on—"

"You're distracting them."

"What?"

"If they intend to take action against me or my cartel, their plan is going nowhere as long as you're with them, keeping them preoccupied."

Was that true? She hadn't meant to distract them. She didn't even know if they had a plan.

He swept his gaze over the bookshelves. "What are you looking for?"

"Non-fiction, I think." She studied the Spanish titles on the spines, disinterested in the contents. "Something educational or—"

"You didn't come here for a book, Petula." The musical rhythm in his voice tingled a chill down her spine. "*What* are you looking for?"

This time, she couldn't turn and look at him.

She couldn't hide the perspiration forming on her skin, the tremors in her hands, or her inability to blink or form a coherent answer.

Lying would only dig her grave deeper. He saw straight through her.

Was he capable of hurting her? Definitely. Would he? She didn't know.

"I sit through your meetings and hear you talk about trafficking drugs and weapons and all the wars over the smuggling routes." She pulled in a shuddering breath and met his gentle eyes. "Why haven't you mentioned trafficking humans or sexual slavery? I mean, all the other cartels do it."

"Not all the cartels. In fact, the Restrepo Cartel in Colombia actively fights *against* it." He clasped his hands behind his back and canted his head, scrutinizing her. "Human trafficking isn't a lucrative business. I make more money in narcotics and guns."

Alarmed by his response, she drew her head back. "If human slavery had better profit margins, you would do it?"

"I answered your question. Now answer mine."

What are you looking for?

Deep down, she'd come here for more than an answer to the human trafficking accusation.

She was looking for validation that he was a good man. A man she could trust not to hurt her. She needed to know she hadn't been wrong about him.

If he was willing to sell women into slavery for the right price, what was his intention with *her*?

"I'm looking for an answer." She stared into his eyes. "Why am I the only female inmate in Area Three?"

"I've waited two years for you to ask that question." He ambled toward the record player.

"I thought it was because I saved your life." Her neck stiffened.

"That came *after*." He lit a cigarette from his pocket and removed an album from the middle of the stack. "Do you know this one?" He held out *Petula Clark's Greatest Hits*.

She shook her head. "She has an unusual first name."

"Yes, she does. She's been my favorite singer for as long as I can remember." He extended the album toward her. "Go ahead."

Tula just happened to share this woman's name? That couldn't have been a coincidence.

Her mind spun as she moved toward him, her steps laden with nerves. She lifted the record from his hand and reached inside the cardboard sleeve. Her fingers slid along the grooved surface of the vinyl and bumped papers.

She glanced at his unreadable expression and removed a handful of documents.

A smaller paper fluttered to the floor, and she reached for it.

And stopped.

Three photographed faces smiled up at her.

Her heart stuttered as she grabbed the photo and brought it closer to her eyes.

It was a snapshot of Hector in his late-thirties or forties with his arm around a beautiful young woman with black hair.

With a baby on her lap.

The woman.

The baby.

She knew those faces, but her brain struggled to process what she was seeing.

"That's my mother." Her voice cracked, and her heart pounded in her ears. "That's me. We're… We're in a photo with you? How are we—?

She glanced up at his affectionate eyes. Brown eyes like hers. A narrow face like hers. Small bones, petite height, bronze skin… He looked like her. She looked like him. How had she not seen it?

"Oh, my God." She swayed as the strength in her legs deserted her.

"Sit." He guided her to a chair, the cigarette dangling from his lips as he examined her expression. "Are you calm?"

"I'm a little freaked out."

She had a father.

Hector La Rocha.

The notorious crime boss her mother warned her

against all her life.

Her mother had sex with him?

Holy.

Fucking.

Shit.

He was her father.

He took the seat beside her and stared at the photo in her trembling hand. "When I saw your name booked in Jaulaso, I had a prison guard bring you to Area Three."

That prison guard had watched her kill a man. *Then* he offered to take her to a nicer part of the prison. His timing had been impeccable.

Because Hector had orchestrated it.

"When he brought me here, Garra raped me." Her throat closed. "If you knew I was your daughter, why did you let that happen?"

"I made it happen."

Her heart collapsed, and a surge of anger raised her voice. "Why?"

"My enemies go to great lengths to try to kill me, including sending a woman by the name of Petula Gomez into my territory. I had to confirm your identity. So I sent Garra to collect your DNA."

"I don't understand." Her hands flexed on her lap. "He could've stolen a strand of my hair or taken my saliva from a cup."

"Vaginal fluid has a high DNA content."

The condom.

Garra had taken it with him after he…

What the fucking fuck? It had all been a setup?

She felt sick to her stomach.

Hector tugged on the forgotten paperwork in her hand, drawing her attention to it.

She stared down at a paternity test. It listed her

name as the child and Hector La Rocha as the alleged father. Beneath all the columns of numbers and medical explanations, she read, *Probability of Paternity: 99.9998%.*

Her chest squeezed as she flipped to the header page and found the date.

Two years ago.

He'd known for two years.

Her jaw set. "Why didn't you tell me?"

"Just because you're my daughter doesn't mean you're on my side. I didn't trust you." He huffed at her scowl. "Don't give me that look. You didn't trust me, either. Maybe you still don't."

"I feel manipulated."

"Because of the Garra thing?"

"Yes," she hissed. "Because you had Garra rape me." She leaned back in the chair and stared at Hector with new eyes. "I can't believe you were with my mother."

"For only a couple of weeks." His expression turned wistful. "She was extraordinarily beautiful. But she hated me. Hated the cartel life. She forbade me to come around when she discovered who I was. I only saw you once after you were born." He nodded at the photo. "The day that picture was taken."

"What about Vera?"

"She's not mine. You're my only daughter, and I have four sons." He smiled sadly. "I miss them."

She had four brothers she'd never met, a missing sister, and a father, who had felt like a father since the day she'd met him.

Because his name was written in her genetics.

She looked down at the paternity test, and the sight of the record album beside it clicked another clue into place.

"*You* named me." Her eyes snapped to his. "After

your favorite singer."

"Yes."

The signs had been there all along.

Her mother had hated Hector La Rocha with a seething passion. It was the hatred of a scorned lover, and over the years, that hatred transferred into resentment of the daughter who shared his DNA.

Hector, on the other hand, had doted on her from day one. He'd opened up his protective circle to her, the only woman in Area Three, and kept her safe.

But he was still Hector La Rocha, a cartel boss who didn't think twice about sending his only daughter to seduce his potential enemies, Martin and Ricky.

That didn't sit right with her. Did he know more about them than he was letting on? Did he want her to spend time with them, not to gather information, but to distract them from something? But from what?

She felt used, deceived, manipulated. At the same time, she felt connected to Hector in a way that finally made sense.

He protected her because she was his blood. He was kind to her because she was his daughter. He cared for her, but did that mean he would never hurt her?

He pulled the Petula Clark album off her lap. "Want to hear it?"

More than anything, she wanted to race back to Martin and Ricky and tell them everything. She felt the safest in their arms, in the cage of their possessive eyes, and in the reassuring words she knew they would give her.

She itched to run, but she owed Hector her life.

So she nodded. "Sure. I'd love that."

TWENTY-FOUR

"We've been here for forty-five days." Martin gripped the edge of the sink in their cell, digging his fingers into the porcelain as he tried to curb his pent-up rage. "Forty-five fucking days, Ricky. We're halfway through our time, and we're no closer to the goal than we were at day one. We need a new plan."

"Give her more time." Ricky raked a hand through his hair.

They'd been arguing since Tula left this morning. Cooped up in this tiny goddamn cell. Sitting on their fucking hands. Wasting precious hours.

Martin's frustration with himself, Tula's inability to see what was right in front of her, and Ricky with his laid-back demeanor and cock-hardening kisses—all of it was coming to a head because Martin couldn't do it anymore.

He couldn't pretend that watching Ricky and Tula fuck each other wasn't killing him.

He couldn't ignore the fact they would be leaving her alone and unprotected in this place in forty-five days.

He couldn't run from his vicious need to restrain,

choke, whip, and mark them until they bleed.

He couldn't touch them without spreading his filth all over their perfections. But he *needed* to touch them. And love them. He just didn't know how. When he allowed himself happiness or pleasure, his impulses took over and turned everything into pain.

His pleasure and their pain. One didn't come without the other.

"Did you hear me?" Ricky rose from the bed and approached him.

"Yeah. You want to give her more time, so you can continue getting your dick wet."

"Banging her was your idea, you fucking prick." Ricky seethed in his face.

"And it's been a real hardship for you." He shoved Ricky away.

Seven years of celibacy was nothing compared to the past month with Tula and Ricky. Looking without touching. Kissing without fucking. The sounds of their groans, the sight of their joined bodies, the scent of their raw, unbridled arousal in his lungs—it was ecstasy and torture, heaven and hell, death and resurrection.

He coughed to mask an unbidden groan as hunger flooded his body, pulsating and shooting flames low in his belly. The physical need he'd denied himself for so long hardened and swelled between his legs.

He didn't have a second of privacy to fuck his own hand, and he refused to do it in front of them. The shame would've been more than he could bear. Not to mention his unraveling control. He didn't trust himself around them. Letting go while they were within reach was too risky.

If he hurt them, he would never forgive himself.

"Your pissy mood has nothing to do with the

mission." Ricky closed in, blocking Martin's view of everything except the glaring frustration in his brown eyes. "You know I'm having the best sex of my life, and you would be, too, if you could get it up."

Martin swung.

The punch crashed across Ricky's face, powered with all the torment and desire that was unfurling inside him.

Ricky hit back, landing a jaw-cracking blow that whipped his head to the side. Blood filled his mouth, and he spat it into the sink. Then they lunged at the same time.

He slammed Ricky against the wall and attacked his mouth with tongue and teeth. "I fucking hate you."

Ricky smacked him, ringing his ears. "I love you, you stubborn cunt."

In a practiced sweep, Ricky's leg shot out and hooked Martin's ankle, taking him to the floor. Martin's shoulder rammed into the frame of the bed on the way down, sending a screech of metal through the room.

They grappled in the narrow aisle, punching with elbows and knees, grinding and twisting for the top position. Slick with sweat and grunting in pain, they rolled over supplies and overturned jugs of water, destroying everything within reach.

Martin boiled from the inside out, burning to fight and fuck, ruin and devour, punish and possess. His mouth glanced off Ricky's lips, trying to capture a kiss that turned into smacking teeth and lashing tongues.

"Say it again." He latched a leg around Ricky's thigh and flipped them, putting himself on top. "Say it, you little bitch."

"I love you." With a furious glint in his eyes, Ricky tore a hand through Martin's hair, ripping it at the roots. The other shoved between their hips and fisted Martin's erection through his jeans. "I need you. Fucking Christ, Martin. I need this cock inside me."

An agonized, animalistic sound escaped Martin's throat as he ground against that firm grip, working his hips into a frenzied rhythm.

"Take off my pants." Ricky ravaged Martin's mouth, biting and sucking and demolishing the last thread of Martin's control. "Fuck me. Give it to me, goddammit."

There was a reason he shouldn't, but his mind emptied. Lust and primal instinct consumed his body. The drive to fuck moved his arms and hips as he wrenched Ricky onto his stomach and shoved Ricky's flimsy cotton pants out of the way.

Ricky's rock-hard glutes filled his hands. He wedged his fingers into the crevice, spreading muscle and flesh to expose the tight, dark hole within.

His dick throbbed with its own heartbeat, jerking against the restraint of his jeans. He stabbed a thumb into Ricky's anus, twisting it as deep as it would go, digging past nerves and muscles that were bone-dry and begging to bleed.

Ricky gasped, and his entire body went taut, strung like a bow. "Fucking spit on it."

"Shut the fuck up." He yanked his thumb out and impaled Ricky's ass with two dry fingers. Then he added a third and thrust.

A low, distressed groan strangled in Ricky's throat, but he didn't fight. Martin rammed harder, faster, stretching Ricky's anal cavity with fiery friction and ruthlessness.

Ricky lifted his hips, flexing into the deep penetration as he wedged a hand beneath him and jacked himself off.

With each piercing stab of his fingers, Martin felt the

scorching burn in his own rectum. He felt the hot panting breaths on his back and the river rocks grinding beneath his knees as he flailed beneath excruciating pain.

Memories flogged him, pounding his body and contorting the windowless prison cell into the thick woodland of the Texas wilderness.

He found himself lying on a riverbed, his face in ice-cold water. A huge hand forced his head into the stream as a stiff penis tore things inside him, making him bleed from his butt.

It was his first time camping. Two months after his dad died. Jeff lived in an RV and told him that night they needed to go to the river to catch fish.

He'd lied.

Martin lost his virginity with his face submerged underwater. Before he passed out, he was given air. When he screamed, he was dunked again.

There had been no lubrication or spit to lessen the brutality. Not that day nor the four-hundred-and-twenty-six days that followed.

But there was always blood. All of his underwear was stained with it. Dark brown reminders of the damage inside him.

He felt that damage now as he forced dry muscles to suck his thrusting fingers. Heavy groans penetrated his ears, so very different than soundless screams he'd kept trapped in his throat.

Blinking rapidly, he yanked his hand away and stared at it. No blood. No damage.

"If you want me to bleed, you're going to have to try harder." Ricky glared at him over his shoulder. "My ass is conditioned to take a pounding."

Van Quiso had ensured that. When he'd fucked Martin and Ricky, he taught them how to take it without tensing. Van knew what he was doing. He was merciless and depraved, but when it came to sex, he was a master. He knew how to thrust without tearing skin, how to whip without leaving a scar, and how to ride that delicate line between pleasure and pain.

Martin had been trained by Van, but he didn't have Van's sophistication. His fourteen-year-old mind had been molded by a savage monster, and that was what he became whenever he tried to have sex.

His cock lay swollen and trapped at an uncomfortable angle in his jeans. He only needed to release it, and in the next breath, he could be deep inside Ricky.

He would lose his mind, his inhibitions. He would go fucking crazy, rutting and humping and undulating his hips until he was spent. Like a feral dog.

Just like Jeff.

He pushed to his feet and stumbled to the sink to wash his hands and clear his thoughts.

"So that's it?" Ricky stood and yanked up his pants. "I know you want this. The proof is straining your zipper. Why don't you at least try?"

"I did try, and I made myself sick." He kept his tone tempered as everything inside him buzzed and throbbed for relief.

Ricky's expression fell, and his gaze thickened with disappointment. "I'm going to take a cold shower." He pointed at the bulge in Martin's jeans. "Take care of that before I get back."

He grabbed a towel and soap and didn't give Martin a backward glance before charging into the hall.

The door closed with a resentful smack, and an iron band wrapped around Martin's chest, squeezing tight.

Ricky shouldn't be out there alone, but it was for the best. They hadn't been attacked since that day in the stairwell, and Martin posed more of a danger to him than anyone else.

He glared down at his raging hard-on and unzipped his pants. This was the first time he'd been alone in almost two months, and he wouldn't waste it.

Releasing his cock was a relief in and of itself. He fisted a hand around it and flattened his other on the wall in front of him. Then he stroked. Long hard pulls from base to tip.

Pre-come lubed his grip as he flexed his ass and thrust aggressively. The sounds of smacking flesh distracted him. They were lonely sounds, echoing inside a lonely man.

He adjusted his feet, making his stance sturdier and leaning into each pump. If Tula were here, he would shove her to her knees and make her swallow his entire length. He would hit her throat, trigger her gag reflex, and fuck her face until she couldn't breathe, couldn't scream—

The door creaked open. Fuck, in his lust-drunk haze, he'd forgotten to lock it.

"Sorry." Tula stood in the doorway, her gaze glued to the angry, swollen erection that pulsed in his fist. "I—I can leave?"

Her fingers clenched briefly at her sides, and she parted her lips. Her nipples beaded beneath her shirt. Denim hugged her hips and legs, highlighting the curves he longed to mark with his teeth.

His hand started moving on its own, rubbing hard flesh and mimicking the strokes he ached to give her. She was right here, breathing heavily and silently asking with those huge, guileless eyes.

"Come here," he heard himself rasp.

She stepped in and closed the door. Her hand lingered on the handle, trembling as she locked it.

"Where's Ricky?"

"Shower."

A glance around at the scattered supplies on the floor raised her eyebrows. She didn't know what she'd walked into, but she was about to find out.

Her next two steps put her within arm's reach.

He grabbed a handful of her hair and pushed her to her knees. "Suck me."

"Martin—"

He rammed himself into the hot haven of her throat, making her gag on the first drive of his hips. As he pulled back, she yelped, catching him with her teeth.

Tightening his fist in her hair, he angled her head where he needed her and fucked her mouth with vigor. In and out, hard and harder, he slammed into the back of her wet throat, pistoning his hips, grinding against her face, and chasing his release.

Until he looked down and saw her glistening gaze.

Tears rolled from the corners of her eyes. Her hand clutched his thigh, her fingernails buried in the skin. He didn't register the pain until now, but that wasn't what snapped him out of his madness.

Her other hand was between her legs, massaging the denim seam against her clit.

She was turned on. By him.

He shoved into her throat, over and over, savoring the sounds of her choking cries. "You like that shit?"

Her head nodded, and the hand on her pussy moved faster.

"Such a dirty slut." He grunted at the sensation of her tongue, the tight ring of her lips, and the stunning look in her hungry eyes. "Feels so good. Fucking love your mouth."

If her mouth felt this sinful, he couldn't imagine

what her pussy would do to him.

He pulled out and hauled her to her feet. "Turn around and hug the wall. I won't be gentle."

"Martin, wait—"

"How badly do you want my dick?"

"I do. Very much. But can we lie on the bed? I want to see your eyes." She placed a warm hand on his cheek. "I want to help you."

"Here's how you help me." Anger spiked through his blood. "Put your fucking face against the wall and lift your ass in the air."

He didn't wait for her to obey. With a grip on her inked arm, he flung her into position.

"I knew if you did this, if you finally took this step, it would be painful." She pressed her palms against the wall and exhaled. "So I'm not going to say no."

"In a few seconds, you won't be able to make an intelligible sound." He crowded in against her back, released her zipper, and shoved down her jeans and panties.

A tremor skated through her, shaking her luscious body against his.

With an arm holding her to the wall, he glided his other hand over her fine ass. As he reached through the apex of her legs, he grabbed her soaked pussy from behind.

"So fucking wet for me." He pushed three fingers into her tight clasp, making her lift on her toes.

Her breathing quickened, fueling his thrusts. As he fingered her cunt, he stretched his thumb back and impaled it into her asshole.

She gulped, and her buttocks tensed spasmodically.

"Have you ever been fucked here?" He pushed his thumb harder inside her anus while holding his fingers in her pussy.

She cried out. "Don't do this. You're not *him,* Martin."

"You don't know who I am. Answer the question."

"Yes, I've had anal sex."

"Because you're a filthy cock-hungry whore."

"Yeah, I'm a whore." She rammed an elbow into his ribs. "Why don't you fuck me bareback and catch a disease? Or you can believe the truth. I had a lover who enjoyed it."

"Is that what you were doing with Hector this morning? Letting him enjoy your tight little asshole?"

"What?" She gasped, straightening her spine. "No! Hector and I aren't like that!"

"I need names and locations of all the high-ranking officers in his human trafficking operation." He removed his hand from her and freed his cock.

"Why are you—?

"Stop bullshitting me, Tula. I want the truth."

"He's not in that business. He says it's not profitable and—" She went still, filling the silence with the sounds of her labored breaths. "Are you undercover? With the military?"

"Hardly." He slid his length between her legs from behind, rubbing the head along her slick folds.

An inferno rose beneath his skin, his reaction to her body instantaneous. Sweating, panting, teasing himself as much as he teased her, he needed her like he needed air.

She shuddered as he pressed the tip against her entrance, barely penetrating. Then he pulled back to give her back hole the same torture. She pushed against him, grinding and tilting up her ass, begging for it. Fuck if that wasn't the hottest thing he'd ever seen.

Her legs opened for more, and he indulged himself

in her perfections, sliding through her decadent arousal as she melted around him, dripping down his length. He dipped in and out of her folds, stroking but not breaching, desperate for her, and denying them both.

If he fucked her, he would ruin her with his filth.

He needed to push her away and keep her at the same time.

"Ricky lets you ride his cock for free, but you have to pay for mine." He gripped his shaft and stirred the crown around the opening of her drenched pussy. "I want names and locations. Give me that, and I'll give you the dick."

He stepped back and stuffed himself away, his muscles shaking with the force of his desire.

"What?" Her ragged gasp cut through his chest. She yanked up her jeans and turned around, her eyes glassy with unshed water. "You're using me? You got close to me because you wanted me to leak information to you?"

"Isn't that what you're doing? Crawling in bed with us every night and running to Hector in the morning to tell him our secrets?"

"No." She shook her head, knocking a river of tears free. "I don't even know your secrets!"

"Because we know better than to tell you anything."

Her chin trembled, and she looked away, trying to suck down a choking inhale.

Stabbing pain hit his gut and burned through his throat.

"You're hurting me, Martin. Fucking breaking me. Right here." She clamped a hand over her heart. "Not just because you're destroying us. But because you're destroying yourself."

She turned to the door, and as she opened it, Ricky walked in.

He looked at her face and shot a murderous glare at

Martin. "What did you do?"

She breezed by him.

"Tula, wait!" Ricky grabbed her arm. "Whatever this is, I'll fix it."

"You want to fix this?" She jerked free. "Fix *him!* I'm done."

As her footsteps faded down the hall, Ricky stabbed a hand through his wet hair and sneered at Martin. "What the fuck have you done?"

"I warned you." His heart felt cold and dead in his chest. "You don't want my brand of hurt."

TWENTY-FIVE

Martin slumped onto the mattress, listening to the sound of Ricky's footsteps chase Tula down the hall. His stomach hardened as he waited for the sound to return, knowing it would.

One minute.

Five minutes.

Ten minutes.

There it was.

Ricky stormed back into the cell and slammed the door, locking it. "She told me what happened and refuses to see you. As much as I want to drag her back here like a caveman, I think she's been abused enough for one day."

"I fucked up."

"Yeah, you've been doing that a lot lately." Ricky removed his shirt and kicked off his shoes. "Give me a rundown of your sexual history."

Now there was a subject that should be locked in a vault and dropped in the deepest ocean. He held up his middle finger.

"Listen, motherfucker." Ricky bent over him, eyes

flaring. "You're going to lose every person you ever cared about. If that matters to you, you'll figure out a way to make that mean mouth form the words *yes* or *no* to every question I ask."

Fuck. This was happening, whether he wanted it to or not.

Ricky straightened and shoved off his pants, leaving the boxers on. "Have you ever had consensual sex?"

"Yes."

"With a woman?"

"Yes." He'd had a handful of one-night stands in the few years between Jeff and Van. None of them were memorable.

"Have you had consensual sex with a man?"

There it was. Sharp and malignant, the pain cleaved through his airway and smothered his senses. "No."

"Then you've only ever been the bottom? Forced to take it?"

"Yes."

"You've never fucked a man in the ass?"

"No."

"Okay." Ricky swiped a hand down his face and sat beside him. "Have you had anal sex with a woman?"

"Yes."

"The sex you've had willingly… Was it always rough and angry?"

"Yes."

"Did you hurt them?"

"No. I was just a teenager." Young and horny. Broken beyond recognition but not as complicated as he was now. Every year he put between Jeff and him added another layer of anger, resentment, and depravity. "If you think I won't hurt her—"

"You already hurt her." Ricky shifted to face him.

"You hurt her with words. With rejection. She feels betrayed and manipulated." Ricky's dark eyes connected with his, solidifying their bond instead of cutting it off. "I can't fix this thing that happened to you. I can't tell you how to cope with it. But I can get you past this one obstacle, which is preventing the three of us from moving forward together."

"If you're talking about sex—"

"Shut up and pay attention." He stood and pushed the last of his clothing to his feet.

His cock hung semi-hard between muscular thighs, thick and heavy and growing by the second.

"This is the last time I will offer myself to you." Ricky knelt at his feet, speeding up his pulse. "We'll do it slow and easy, or not at all."

A swallow stuck in the back of his throat. "I don't know how."

"I know, and I've been part of the problem." Ricky sat back on his heels. "I always tell you to hurt me, fuck me hard, and make me bleed." He shook his head. "The thing is I've had every kind of sex imaginable. Soft, rough, sweet, wild… I've experienced the gamut, and I know what I like. But you haven't. You've never had sensual, affectionate, tender sex."

A quiver of grief skittered along Martin's jaw and burned the backs of his eyes. He fisted his hand in the bedding, fighting the longing that swelled inside him.

"Let me give you that." Ricky lowered his head and placed a kiss on Martin's denim-clad thigh.

He tried to imagine what Ricky was offering, but he couldn't picture it. He didn't know what it looked like or how he would handle the intimacy. But he wanted to know. Every nerve ending in his body pulled toward the idea.

"Tell me you'll try." Ricky rose on his knees and gave him an expectant look.

"I'll try." His mouth dried. "But Tula should be here."

She was the gentle one.

He needed to make sure she was safe. She deserved so much better than him, but that wouldn't stop him from groveling, pleading, and fighting for the rest of his life to get her back. He couldn't lose her.

"One problem at a time." Ricky slid his palms up Martin's thighs. "She promised she wouldn't leave her cell tonight."

"I don't want her sleeping—"

"Shut up."

"I can't do this if you intend to top me." He gestured at the soft bulge of his crotch. "Does nothing for me."

"You think I can't make you hard?" Ricky winged up a sexy brow.

"Not if you're bossy."

"Take off your clothes."

With a sigh, Martin stood and stripped. His briefs hit the floor last, and a masculine sound rumbled deep in Ricky's chest.

As Martin lowered back to the bed, Ricky didn't wait for an objection. He knelt between Martin's thighs and slowly sucked the soft length of him between those talented lips.

"Ah, fuck." His hand went to Ricky's hair, clenching hard.

Ricky released him with a *pop* and shook his head. "Soft and easy."

"Fine." He braced his hands behind him.

Returning to his cock, Ricky licked along the shaft from balls to tip, sending languorous ripples of pleasure through his groin. Ricky went at it assertively but not aggressively. Soft unhurried sucks and teasing licks filled him with blood and quickened his breaths.

"I've wanted to do this for years." Ricky swirled his tongue across Martin's scrotum.

"You've done it a million times in my head, and swear to God, it's never felt this incredible."

"And you're not even punching the back of my throat."

"The urge is there, but…"

Ricky sucked on the crown, flicking his tongue along the underside, where all the nerves resided. "Feel that?"

"Fuck yeah, I feel it." The stimulation of his glans spread electricity through his body. Feverish chills. Breathless invigoration. Every sensation was new and different.

"You don't experience that when you're pounding someone's mouth like a jackhammer." Ricky blew a soft breath along his length. "Don't get me wrong. There's freedom in letting go, but there's so much sensuality in a kiss."

He proceeded to kiss Martin's cock with firm lips and an agonizingly talented tongue. The sensuality Ricky mentioned was a slow burn. A fusion of feelings. A different kind of energy, emotion, and artistry.

His legs shook against a building orgasm, and just when he thought he might come, Ricky's glorious mouth abandoned him.

"Lie back." Ricky patted his thigh.

Martin stretched out across the two beds, and Ricky crawled over him, kneeling between his legs.

"You're so goddamn arresting." Ricky caressed a hand down Martin's chest. "Seeing you laid out like this, aroused and bare for me…" The roving caress continued along his hip and down his leg. "Every inch of you makes me hard."

"Show me."

Ricky rose up on his knees and lazily stroked his cock. Tall and stacked with muscle, the man was fucking gorgeous.

Leaning back down, Ricky angled his hips and aligned their dicks side by side. Then he rubbed them together, gliding his hand up and down the lengths, slowly jacking them off.

There were no words after that. No race to a finish line. No mindless, uncontrollable thrusting. Ricky fondled and explored with expert fingers solely for the pleasure of touch and affection.

Martin saw it in Ricky's eyes, felt it in every loving stroke. Ricky intended to make love to him, and the prospect filled him with a need that went beyond physical lust.

Ricky moved up his body and worshiped him with lips and tongue. A kiss on the scar on his head. A nibble on his ear lobe. A lick across his mouth. Then he slid downward, paying homage to skin and muscle. By the time he finished, he'd kissed every part of Martin's anatomy he could reach.

The adoration left Martin panting and twisting on the bed. Blissful heat bloomed around his perineum and disseminated through his balls and anus. He felt Ricky everywhere, around him, against him, inside him, and they hadn't even had sex.

The eternal buildup had produced the deepest, most intense feeling in his body. The fire Ricky had stoked howled into a conflagration. Martin needed to fuck, and he didn't care how. Hard, gentle, fast, fierce—it was going to happen.

He pushed up, wrapped his arms around Ricky, and flipped him face down on the bed.

"Stop." Ricky didn't move or raise his voice. "I'm not going to fight you, but I need you to listen."

"I'm listening." Martin gripped his ass and speared three fingers between his hard cheeks. "You can talk while I'm fucking you."

"Face to face." Craning his neck, Ricky glared back at him. "I'm going to roll over."

His spine tensed as his mind spun to understand the position. He knew it could be done, but why?

"Martin." Ricky shifted to his back and opened his legs. "Come here."

The heat in Martin's groin evaporated, and his body chilled with unease.

"You've never had sex this way?" Ricky widened his eyes. "Not even with a woman?"

He scoured his mind, digging through old memories—quick fucks, stolen moments, up against a wall, bent over a piece of furniture, doggy in the backseat of a car. Sex had always been a means to an end. A hard, fast release.

"No." His answer fell on a choked breath.

"My tortured, beautiful man. I couldn't be more in love with you." Ricky gripped his hand and pulled him down.

Martin lowered on top of him, chest to chest, cock against cock, and let his weight rest in the cradle of Ricky's powerful body.

Their lips met in a soft caress. A nibble here. A sip there. He inched back to see the lust in Ricky's eyes and closed in again, kissing and breathing as one. His hips rocked in a languid motion, swiveling, grinding, and feeding the heat between them.

He stretched his mouth wide, reaching deeper, and Ricky opened for him, angling his head and licking away doubts and reservations. If sex with Ricky was as poignant and passionate as this, Martin wouldn't be the same afterward.

He'd never felt so wanted, so loved, so damn alive.

His heart sputtered beneath the heavy emotion, and he broke away, panting and clinging to Ricky's dependable gaze. Then he dove back for more, his tongue moving in a dreamlike state, a higher level of oneness. Every touch lifted them in harmony. Every lick burned him hotter.

By the time they came up for air, he was ravenous.

He sat back on his knees and stared down at their cocks. Engorged and leaking from the tips, they jutted across Ricky's abs, side by side. They looked so fucking sexy together.

"I need to be inside you." He grabbed Ricky at the root and stroked. "Right now."

"Keep your eyes on mine." Ricky flexed his hips in Martin's grip and groaned. "No rushing to the end. We're going to enjoy this."

Martin gathered spit in his mouth and angled his head over his aching cock. Parting his lips, he let his saliva trickle out and run down his length.

"I'm going to come just from watching you do that." Ricky shifted restlessly beneath him, clawing at the blankets.

Collecting more spit, Martin lathered his fingers and massaged them against Ricky's anus.

"This is happening." Ricky stared up at him in awe. "We're doing this."

"I don't know if *slow and easy* will be good for you." He lined himself up with Ricky's opening. "I don't know what I'm doing."

"You've been kissing me for a month. I don't think you realize how incredibly affectionate you are."

He was?

The sucking of lips, the drugging sweetness of breaths, the whispered words… Ricky and Tula were under his skin, expunging nightmares and replacing them with dreams.

Dreams of a future with the two people he would give anything to keep.

Ricky pulled his knees toward his ribs, opening himself wide. "Eyes on me."

Falling into that heated gaze, Martin pushed his hips and sank into the nirvana of Ricky's body.

His breath cut off, and Ricky moaned deep in his throat. They trembled together, adjusting to the overwhelming sensations.

Ricky's hand flew to his cock, stroking himself. Martin slid out and pressed back in, his eyes rolling back in his head.

"Seven years." He thrust, digging deep, catching a desperate rhythm. "It was a long fucking time to wait for this. But so worth the wait."

"Holy fuck, Martin." Ricky panted, quickening the pump of his hand. "You're huge. I feel you in my stomach. Fucking feel you everywhere."

Martin wrapped a fist around Ricky's grip and quickened the pace of his strokes, sliding their fingers up and down in sync with the frantic drive of his hips.

"Slow down." Ricky gasped, flexing his glutes and using his legs to meet every thrust.

"I own you." He grabbed Ricky's waist and slammed himself deeply, mercilessly, stuffing that ass, making damn sure Ricky felt him. "You're fucking mine. Every touch, every kiss, every drop of your come belongs to me."

"I love you."

Ricky's quiet words breathed into him, resuscitating him from the darkness. The tempo of his hips faltered, and his blood hummed with life.

The solid body beneath him anchored him to the present, providing dependable, stable footing. Ricky had been here all along. Martin's compass in the storm.

"No one's ever said those words to me." Martin assumed his dad had loved him, but it had never been voiced.

"I'll never stop saying it." Ricky grasped his neck and hauled him in for a kiss. "Fucking love you."

His tongue slid against Ricky's, curling and flicking with the depth of his feelings. He was infatuated with the taste of Ricky's mouth, the feel of his magnificent physique moving beneath him, the heat of his skin, and the sexy Latino glow of it.

More than that, he was addicted to Ricky's devotion, his commitment to their friendship, and the effort he put into it.

He loved everything about this man. Always had. Always would. He'd loved Ricky for seven years.

With an arm between them, he took Ricky in hand, stroking him, grinding into him, desperate to give himself entirely to this.

"I need your come." He rubbed Ricky harder, savoring the friction of Ricky's clenching ass as they locked eyes. "Give it to me."

Ricky's mouth opened. His pupils dilated, and his cock pulsed in Martin's hand.

"Martin, oh, fuck. Oh, Jesus, I'm coming!" Ricky ground his hips, bearing down on Martin's thrusts as he ejaculated ropy strings of come across his chest.

Martin followed him over the edge, hammering erratically while staring into his eyes. "Always loved you. With everything I am."

The intensity of his climax stole his breath and exploded stars across his vision. He came and came and came until there was nothing left. All of him was in his best friend—his body, his love, and his life.

"Definitely worth the wait." Ricky rolled them, putting them on their sides, nose to nose, legs entangled, and breaths mingling.

"I don't deserve you." He took Ricky's mouth, their tongues rubbing through a satiated kiss.

"I'll remind you of that the next time you're a dick."

"Don't I know it." He kissed Ricky again, devouring the intimacy. "Thank you."

In the isolation of their prison cell, he sank into Ricky's embrace in a way he never had before. Hands roamed. Lips touched and held. Cocks brushed. Gazes caressed, and Martin fell. Mind, body, and soul. He gave it all to Ricky, and Ricky gave in return.

In that lazy span of an hour, they had more than they could've ever wanted. But they weren't complete.

"I'm going to get our girl." He slid out of bed and grabbed his jeans.

"Our girl isn't going to listen to you." Ricky joined him, pulling on his own clothes.

"She will." He shoved on his shoes. "I'm going to explain everything."

"Everything?"

He turned and looked his best friend in the eye. "We have a decision to make."

TWENTY-SIX

Martin entered Tula's cell without knocking, his pulse steady, his gait determined, and his eyes set on his goal.

Tula sat on the end of the bed, smoking a cigarette. She glared at him, her face a beautiful shade of fury, before turning away and denying him the view of her eyes.

Martin couldn't remember the last time she'd smoked. She kept some cartons around to use as currency to buy meals and supplies, but she'd dropped the nicotine habit when she started hanging out with him and Ricky.

Ricky followed him in, shut the door, and leaned against it.

As Martin approached her, he marked her stiff spine, rigid jaw, and the flex of her fingers. She had every right to be pissed at him, and he would let her have her anger as long as she listened to what he had to say.

He knelt on the floor before her. "I'm sorry."

She took a long drag without looking at him. Then she met his eyes and released the smoke in his face.

In a calm, calculated motion, he gripped her hand and twisted it in an unnatural direction at the wrist. The technique caused her just enough discomfort to release the cigarette from her fingers.

She yanked her hand away. "Why did you—?"

"I can't be fixed. Not overnight. Maybe not ever." He squashed out the cigarette beneath his knee. "But Ricky and I just had sex."

Her glower darted behind him to Ricky. Her eyes softened for a moment then returned to him, reigniting with fire. "You came here to rub that in my face?"

"No." It probably wasn't the best thing to lead with after teasing her and rejecting her just hours earlier. But he was laying it all out on the table, and having sex with Ricky was the easiest part to confess.

Now came the hard part.

He dragged a hand over his head and centered himself on the presence behind him. Ricky didn't know what he was about to say, but Ricky's strength gave him the resolve to continue.

"His name was Jeff. The man I killed." Martin inched closer on his knees and rested his hands on the mattress on either side of her. "He raped me every day for over a year, starting when I was fourteen. He was my dad's brother. My uncle."

Her posture stooped, and the anger in her expression melted into concern.

A reassuring masculine grip landed on his shoulder and squeezed. Then Ricky sat beside her.

"After the shit I said to you, to you *both*, I owe you my story. It's not an excuse for my actions. I should've been more open with you, but I…" Dread curled in his stomach. "The one and only time I ever told someone about Jeff, it ended very badly."

Ricky caught his gaze, studying him intently as if trying to make a connection.

"I'll tell you about it." He met her eyes. "If you still want to hear it."

"I do." She leaned forward but didn't touch him.

"My history doesn't just include Jeff." He rested a hand on Ricky's knee, his heart pumping with purpose.

They'd made a decision before leaving their cell, one that changed their mission, and with any luck, it would change hers, too.

They trusted her with their lives and would choose her over all else. No matter what happened, she was their priority.

"We're vigilantes." He touched her face and pulled her close to whisper at her ear, "We work to punish and eradicate human sex traffickers. It's personal for us. The way Ricky and I met, everything we do, the reason we're here—it's all entangled with our vigilante group and our alliance with the Restrepo Cartel. We strategically arranged our arrest to come here and gather enough intel to take down Hector La Rocha's operation."

"Jesus." She sucked in a breath. Then her expression tightened with indignation. "That's where I come in."

"You were our angle, yes. But not anymore. Now you're our purpose."

"Your purpose?" Her face reddened. She glanced at the closed door and lowered her voice to a furious whisper. "You're aligned with a sworn enemy and working against Hector. He won't just kill you when he finds out. He'll have you tortured and make a spectacle of your deaths. This is *exactly* what he wanted to know about you, and you just handed me a confession."

Martin absorbed the flux of emotion that crossed her face, fascinated by her thought processes. He wasn't concerned about her ratting them out. She loved them. She just didn't know it yet.

Her brows knitted, and her gaze bounced through the room before landing on him. "Why would you trust me with this? You already figured out that he sent me to you to learn your secrets, and you know I tell him everything. You're not just throwing away your mission. You're risking your lives by telling me."

"Yes, we are."

"We choose you, Tula." Ricky tucked a lock of hair behind her ear. "Over the mission. Over everything."

Her lips parted, and she shook her head. "But you don't know if I'll choose you."

"You already have," Martin said, hoping to hell he was right.

"How's that?"

"I told you I wanted the names and locations of high-ranking officers. You had the past several hours to pass that information along to Hector. But you didn't, did you? You didn't even consider it."

"No. I…" She touched her throat, and her gaze turned inward. "I learned something about Hector today, and I'm still trying to process that."

"What is it?" His pulse sped up. "His human trafficking operation?"

"You first. I want to hear your story. About your uncle." Her fingers slid over Ricky's on the bed. "How you and Ricky met. Your vigilante work. All of it."

"Not here." Martin stood and offered his hand. "In our cell."

If he was going to cut himself open and expose his miserable fucking shame, he wanted to do it in a place where he felt more secure. Despite the stink and gloom of Jaulaso, the cell he shared with her and Ricky was where he'd experienced the happiest moments of his life.

Not to mention, their cell had a lock on the door.

"Okay." She gripped his fingers and followed him into the hall.

When they reached their destination, they kicked off their shoes and climbed into bed together. Tula and Ricky sat with their backs against the wall. Martin stretched out in front of them.

With a leg bent and an arm resting on his knee, he braced himself for the pain and let his mind travel back in time.

"When my dad died, the state sent me to live with my only living relatives. Jeff was an estranged uncle I'd never met. My dad never talked about him. Jeff lived out of an RV in Texas, and he had a son two years younger than me. Ford was his name."

A hot ember formed in his throat, and he swallowed past it. Ricky laced his fingers around Tula's, their gazes soft and watchful.

"Jeff had been a schoolteacher, and he taught me how to fish and build fires. He home-schooled Ford and me as we traveled from one campground to another throughout Texas. He waited two months—" His voice broke, and he tried again. "I was with him for two months before he raped me the first time. Then he did it again, every night, for the next four-hundred-and-twenty-six days." A torrent of anguish welled up in his chest. "I couldn't leave. He told me if I did, he would go to Ford to take care of his physical needs. His own fucking son. I believed him."

The nightmare tore through him, shaking his shoulders. Instead of fighting it down, he breathed it out. "Ford was only twelve. He didn't know what his dad did to me every night when he led me into the woods. Jeff kept it from him. I kept it from him. But Jeff got careless. He was drinking the night he sodomized me with the handle of a hammer."

Tula cupped a hand over her mouth, her eyes soaked with tears. Ricky moved toward him.

"If you touch me right now…" He would break down. "Let me get through this."

"Okay." Ricky sat back and wrapped his arms around Tula.

"The hammer…" Martin inhaled, exhaled, and let the pain lance through him. "Ford watched it happen. He found us in the woods, and I'll never forget his face. The damage to his young mind, the horror of seeing his father doing such a despicable thing… He ran off into the trees, and Jeff was too drunk to chase him. So he sent me. But I was injured, bleeding down my legs from what he'd done to me. I could barely walk. It took me all night and into the morning before I…"

His eyes burned, and his throat closed up. He covered his face with his hands and felt the tears dampening his cheeks.

"Martin…" Ricky's voice fell over him, soothing. "You don't have to finish."

He needed to finish it, purge it from his mind. "I saw him on the railroad tracks not far from our campsite. He just laid his neck on the rail and let a train run over it. That's how I found him. Without his head." His guilt over that night cut him to the bone. "If I'd walked faster, searched harder, I could've stopped him."

"It wasn't your fault."

"I returned to the RV that morning. Jeff was passed out drunk in his bed. His leverage over me was gone. Ford was… He was gone. So I searched for that goddamn hammer, and when I found it, I beat Jeff's skull in with it. Then I ran."

Ricky's arms came around him, and Tula crawled

onto his lap. He let the tears fall as they held him. Then he forced out the rest.

"I was fifteen, homeless, and on the run. Over the next two years, I stuck to the border towns in Texas. Found odd jobs in the ghettos. I slept with women, but not often. My depraved urges started to scare me. Then I met a man." He drew in a breath, lost in the memory. "He was sitting alone at a club I used to frequent, and he had a gruesome scar on his face."

"Van," Ricky breathed.

Tula shifted on Martin's lap, confusion furrowing her brow as she glanced between them.

"I don't know if it was the scar that got me. It was obvious someone had hurt him, and I thought maybe he'd been hurt by someone like Jeff. He was also the most gorgeous man I'd ever seen. I was instantly captivated. He bought me a drink, and we shot the shit. Then he asked me if I wanted to get out of there. I didn't hesitate. We walked aimlessly along the dark, quiet streets. I felt comfortable with him. He was easy to talk to. I had never told anyone my story, but that night, I told Van. I told him everything, and he listened without judgment or pity. When I finished talking, he kissed me. And kissed me. The son of a bitch kissed me until I couldn't think straight. I had never willingly had sex with a man, but that night, I willingly went home with Van Quiso. Only he didn't take me to his bedroom. He chained me in his attic, beat me, and raped me for ten weeks."

Ricky knew the rest of it, but Tula didn't. So he talked through the series of events that led from Van's sex trafficking operation to the creation of the Freedom Fighters and the mission that planted him and Ricky in Jaulaso.

By the time he finished, his eyes were dry, and his

chest seemed lighter. The pain was still there, branded forever in the marrow of his bones. But it felt different. Duller. Softer. Maybe this was the beginning of catharsis. An opening for the poison to slowly escape.

Tula held him tight and gave him comforting words. As they settled on their sides, she prodded him for details about his sexual training, his relationships with his ex-captors, and the evidence the Freedom Fighters had compiled against Hector La Rocha over the years.

He and Ricky answered all her questions, and the three of them talked late into the night, sharing painful moments, happy stories, and everything in between.

Then she told them about the paternity test.

In a monotone voice, she explained what had happened in Hector's room this morning—why she had gone there and everything Hector had told her. She'd learned he was her father moments before she'd walked in on Martin with his dick in his hand.

She'd come to him for comfort, and he'd treated her like a whore.

"I'm so fucking sorry." He shifted her to face him and studied her expression.

Emotional exhaustion weighed down her lashes and fanned lines from the corners of her eyes. Despite the events of the day, she looked devastatingly beautiful in the glow of the candlelight.

"How are you taking this?" Ricky curled around her back and kissed the top of her head.

"I don't know. Hector has always been kind of a father figure to me, but after everything you told me about his disgusting operation..." Her voice cracked. "I'm sickened and confused, and I have no fucking clue what to do about it."

"There's been too much thrown at you today."

Martin scooted down, putting them at eye level. "You don't need to do anything right now but sleep. Let us worry about what to do next."

Her expression turned pensive for a handful of heartbeats. Then she tensed.

"You said you arranged your arrest." She popped up on an elbow, her eyes wide and alert. "Does that mean you arranged your release?"

His heart stopped, and he met Ricky's anxious gaze over her head. "Yes."

"How long?" She looked between them, her fear palpable. "When do you leave?"

He clenched his hands. They didn't have a solution for the one thing that mattered most.

Her safety.

Who would protect her after they left? Because they *would* be leaving her. There was no way to stop it.

They would hire the best lawyers, pull every connection they had, and fight like hell to shorten her sentence. But the likelihood of success was terrifyingly low.

Martin reached for her, holding her tight as he choked out the words. "We leave in forty-five days."

For the next two days, Tula sank into an ebb and flow of heartbreaking conversations, heated arguments, and quiet introspection. She had a lot to mentally and emotionally process, and Martin and Ricky were right there with her, holding her in bed, showering with her at night, and putting together meals from the stores of food they kept in their cell.

She only had forty-three days left with them.

Deep down, she'd suspected they would leave Jaulaso before her. She didn't know how or why, but her heart had tried to keep its distance, expecting their departure.

Her heart had failed, though. They'd crashed right into it and woven themselves into the very essence of her existence. When it came time to sever those ties, it was going to hurt like hell.

They finished a dinner of canned chicken soup, and she lay curled up in Ricky's muscular arms, staring at Martin's back where he sat on the edge of the other bed.

Her quiet, tormented man had been more subdued

than usual today.

The absolute hell he'd endured in his short twenty-four years had obliterated her anger with him. Her hurt feelings were nothing compared to the hurt he carried inside that powerful frame.

He'd cried several times over the past forty-eight hours, and she and Ricky had cried with him, holding tight to his trembling body. It was progress. He was finally talking about it, letting it out, openly and painfully.

The details of his life were difficult to hear, but she sensed the promise of healing in his voice, saw it in the clarity of his crystal green eyes. It would take time, *years*, to recover from his trauma, but he was moving in the right direction. He was trusting people to hold him through his pain and bear some of the burden.

He would always have Ricky for that, and maybe she would be there, too.

In three years.

Ricky mentioned trying to stay in prison with her by doing something asinine like attacking a prison guard or starting a riot to extend their sentences. She'd laid into him for even thinking it and quickly shut him up.

They wanted to help her shorten her sentence, but they couldn't do that if they were locked up. Nor could they risk getting stuck in Jaulaso for life. She only had three years left. It wasn't forever.

Maybe they would still want her when she was released. Perhaps they would be waiting for her at the gate the day she gained her freedom.

She fantasized about that moment, about starting a life with them outside of prison.

Her debt to Hector, however, was a lifetime sentence. Didn't matter that they shared DNA. He'd told her on several occasions she would be expected to work for the cartel after her release.

Given Martin and Ricky's resources and connections, perhaps they could help her escape Hector's organization. If they let her, she would join their vigilante group and work with them to take down La Rocha Cartel.

Her loyalty to Hector had taken a hard hit. He'd sent Garra to rape her, kept his parentage from her for two years, and looked her right in the eyes and lied to her about his involvement in human trafficking. What else had he been dishonest about?

She didn't trust him, but she still cared about him. Not just because he was her father, but because he'd always been kind to her, always protected her. She found herself clinging to the idea that he'd been dishonest with her because he wanted to protect her from the terrible things he did.

She talked through all of this with Martin and Ricky over the past couple of days. Together, they speculated and plotted, smiled and cried, argued this and agreed on that.

But at the end of the day, she was left with a crushing inevitability.

They were leaving.

"We can still focus on your mission," she murmured into the silence.

"No," they said in unison, firm and unbending.

"He's kidnapping women and children."

Children who would go through the same abuses Martin had suffered. Her stomach turned inside out every time she imagined it.

"We should've never involved you." Ricky ran his nose through her hair. "Thinking about you in his room and rummaging through his belongings when he walked in… It makes me want to bend you over my knee and beat your fucking ass. But it's *our* fault. We pushed you to investigate him and put our damn mission over your safety."

"You didn't know me when you arrived here. You couldn't have predicted what would happen between us."

"What's happening between us?" He coasted a finger along her collarbone, teasing the neckline of her shirt.

"Sex. Really good sex."

"It's more than that, Tula. I need to hear you say it."

Love was a landslide of sorrow and dread, swallowing her chest in the ruin of its unavoidable end. "It hurts. My heart knows you're leaving, and it's trying to protect itself. Please don't make me say it."

"Okay." He pulled her close and rested his forehead against hers. "Fuck, I hate this. It's fucking killing me."

She couldn't bear the pain in his voice. So she steered the conversation back on topic. "I was your best option to get those locations from Hector. It was a brilliant plan, really. Seduce the woman he's closest to and win her over with the best orgasms of her life."

"The best in her life?"

"Don't get cocky." She cupped the side of his face, holding his gaze. "I could talk to Garra—"

"No."

"We haven't tried that angle. I wouldn't be obvious about it."

"I said no."

"I could eavesdrop on his conversations with Simone. If they know the details of the operation—"

"Fuck no." Ricky gripped her chin, forcing her to meet his glare. "The mission is forfeit. We're going to lay low, keep our asses in this cell, and let our time go by. Just like this. *Together*. Then, after Martin and I are released, we're going to get you out of here."

Hector ruled over the city and the prison. If he couldn't get himself released, Martin and Ricky wouldn't be able to do shit for her. But she didn't refute him.

It was the best plan they had.

She wanted every second she had left with them to be in this bed. She wanted their kisses, their hungry breaths, their bodies moving inside her and each other, shaking and groaning in pleasure.

Amid the revelations of the past two days, there had been no sex and no discussions about the sex between Martin and Ricky.

They needed to talk about it. Or better yet, they just needed to do it.

As often as possible.

Because in forty-three days, they wouldn't just be taking her broken heart with them. They would be taking away the only pleasure she'd ever had inside these walls.

Her attention drifted to the silent man sitting on the other bed. With his back to her and his feet on the floor, he braced an elbow on his knee and held his face with a hand. He cried that way sometimes.

Two days ago, the dam broke inside him, drowning him in a ten-year flood that needed to run its course.

But right now, his relaxed posture and steady breaths told her he was deep in thought, not grief.

She shared a look with Ricky and pressed a hand against his shirtless chest, silently asking him to stay. Then she crawled across the beds and knelt behind Martin.

He wore only his briefs and didn't move as she rested her mouth on his shoulder and her fingers on his nape.

She remained in that position for a long time, breathing with him and indulging in the potency of his presence.

"Want to talk?" She ghosted her lips along his neck and inhaled deeply, savoring his masculine scent.

"No."

"Want to fight?"

He grunted. "No."

"Want to make love?"

His head slowly lifted and turned in her direction. His mouth parted, and the tip of his tongue wet the corner.

"I want to know what you feel like inside me." She kissed his strong jaw. "I want to see what your face looks like when you're buried inside Ricky."

"You want my filth in your pussy?" His voice was stony, laden with antagonism.

"At least forty-three times."

"And your ass?" He folded his arms around her and dragged her onto his lap to straddle him.

"Yes." She found Ricky's hooded eyes over Martin's shoulder.

Martin gave her a troubled look and touched their foreheads together. "We only have forty-three days."

"Spend them inside me." She brushed her lips against his, drawing a groan from his chest.

When she pulled back, he chased her, capturing her mouth in a starved kiss. His hands went to her hair and slid down her back, pulling her closer as he worked their tongues into a delicious tangle.

"I don't want to hurt you." He trapped her arms behind her and ground her body onto his hard cock. "I'm fucked up."

"Aren't we all? We're fucked-up people living fucked-up lives with no access to medication or therapy. But we have one another."

His soft laughter filled her mouth.

She breathed in the sexy sound and held it in her

chest. "I'm keeping that."

"What?" he rumbled against her lips.

"Your laughter. I'm collecting all your happy moments, just so you know."

"They're yours." He glanced back at Ricky. "And his."

"Promise me something."

"Anything."

"When you get out of here, don't push him away. No matter how hard it gets or how many setbacks you have. Let him make you happy."

"Tula." His expression hardened. "We're going to get you—"

"Promise me."

His gaze shifted to Ricky and held. "I promise."

"You love him."

"Yes." He tucked a finger under her chin, lifting it. "And you. I love you."

A heavy pang hit her heart, and oh, God, the wonderful wretchedness of it. This harsh, deliciously damaged man was worried he'd hurt her with his cruelty. But it was his love that would leave the deepest scar.

He wanted her now, but would he love her in three years? Would she even be the same person by the time she walked out of here?

She couldn't predict the future, but the present was directly in front of her. This moment, right now, was within reach, and she grabbed onto it with both hands.

Their mouths came together. Their chests collided, and they fell onto the mattress in a rolling grind of bodies.

His weight pressed down on top of her, and his kisses turned ravenous. He stripped her of her clothing, and she shoved down his briefs. Then they were naked, skin to skin, heart to heart, staring into each other's eyes.

"Ricky," he said gruffly without looking away.

"Here." Ricky pressed a condom into Martin's hand. "Slow and easy. If it gets dark in your head, I'll pull you back."

Martin tore open the condom and rolled it on. With his hips between her legs, he ran his fingers along her slit, spreading her wetness.

She moaned. "Martin."

He shushed her and bit her lips. Then he trailed those soaked fingers over her nipple. "Are you scared?"

"Yeah. I'm scared you won't ever put it in."

He bared his teeth with a growl and drove his hips into hers, filling her up in one long thrust.

Their eyes connected. Their breaths held. Then they burst into movement.

"Goddamn, Tula." He pistoned into her, holding her close and kissing her with a possessive tongue.

She gasped at the wet burn between her legs and flexed upward, chasing his rhythm, desperate to take all of him.

He was magnificently long and thick. Every thrust required effort, working each inch deeper and deeper. Before he buried to the root, he pulled back, slowly dragging all that heaviness away. Then he plunged again.

"You fit this huge thing inside Ricky?" She squeezed her inner muscles, making him groan.

"I didn't hear any complaints." He rubbed his nose along hers and gave her a gorgeous smile. "You're going to take us both."

Her heart rate went wild. "Don't tease me."

He scooped her up into his strong arms and rolled to his back while keeping them joined. With her legs straddling his incredible body, she sat up and ran her hands over the carved grooves of his chest and abs.

He touched her the same way, exploring the rise of her breasts and plucking at her nipples. She twisted her hips, and he looked down to where they connected, his eyes smoldering.

When his gaze lifted, he took in every detail of her shape, his fingers following the path of his eyes.

The intensity of his attention on her sliced up her breaths into little needy gasps. To be desired by such a beautiful, perfectly sculpted man felt surreal.

"What did you look like before six months of training?" She ground down on his cock, delighting in the sound of his groan.

"He looked the same." Ricky ripped open a condom packet with his teeth. "Pretty sure he has endless layers of abs under those abs. If he loses an eight-pack, he has more to spare."

"You should talk." Martin raked his eyes over Ricky's body, lingering on Ricky's cock as he sheathed it in latex.

Now that she knew their history as trained slaves, she understood how these two flawlessly attractive men had ended up together. Evidently, all their vigilante friends were stunningly gorgeous.

"Tula." Martin clasped her neck and pulled her down to his chest. "You've never taken two cocks at once?"

"You know I haven't." Her body caught fire, and her pussy clenched uncontrollably.

"If you keep doing that…" He kicked up his hips, stroking himself inside her. "I'm not going to last."

"I'm not, either."

She stretched toward his sinful mouth, tasting his lips, chasing his tongue, and grinding down on him. He pressed in and out of her, worshiping her with his hands and watching her expression.

He was so damn sexy like this—aroused and attentive and utterly devoted. She lost herself in his passion as they moved in a drugging rhythm.

Their fucking wasn't fast and mindless. Nor was it soft and easy. Every thrust was heavy, intimate, and thrumming with affection. They rocked together, kissing and sucking, driven by an unquenchable thirst for love—to grow it and hold it and never let it go.

She glanced back to look for Ricky, but he was already there, kneeling behind her.

With her chest pressed against Martin's, she arched her spine, lifting her ass for Ricky.

"Jesus." He groaned and bent down, sinking out of her view. "I wish you could see this. The way your pussy wraps around him, gripping him like a glove as he slides in and out."

Spurred by his words and insanely turned on, she undulated her hips and rode Martin's cock with everything she had.

Until she felt a gust of warm breath on her back hole. Then the wet, sliding stroke of a tongue.

"Holy shit." She faltered, tipping on Martin's chest as her breaths sprinted into oblivion.

Ricky's wicked kiss lowered, licking and sucking the place where she and Martin connected. The sensations were maddening, burning across her flesh and revving her pulse.

When the heat of his mouth vanished, she didn't need to look back to see where he went. Martin's fingers bit into her ass, and he released a long, guttural groan.

"He's licking your balls, isn't he?" She grinned.

"Christ, yes. He's—" Martin inhaled sharply, and his body went rigid beneath her. "Ricky, don't."

"What?" She craned her neck, trying to see behind

her.

"Okay, I won't touch you there." Ricky leaned over her back to meet Martin's eyes. "I figured it was off limits, but I needed to know."

"Your ass?" she asked quietly. "You don't want that?"

"No." Martin ran a shaky hand down her arm. "I can't be on the receiving end of anal. Never again."

"That's okay." She gave him a soft smile and spoke against his lips. "If he needs a back door, he has mine."

"I'm going to ruin this pretty little pucker." Ricky pushed his thumb against her rectum, making her shudder. "But tonight, I'm going to share your pussy with Martin's massive cock."

"I'm wildly excited and equally terrified about that," she said. "Is it going to hurt?"

"Probably," Martin said.

"Now I'm just terrified."

"It's not going to hurt." Ricky glided a hand down her spine, massaging her back. "I know what I'm doing, and I'll go slow." He reached between her legs from behind, and his fingers found her, delving inside and stretching along the length of Martin's buried cock. "You're more than wet enough. Fucking soaked."

"I feel you touching me." Martin shifted beneath her and gripped the backs of her thighs. "Touching both of us. It feels unbelievable." He widened his legs, taking hers with him.

In the next breath, a stretch of pressure invaded her pussy. Martin held still, adjusting his hips as Ricky leaned onto her back.

The fullness inside her bloomed into a wicked burn. She writhed through it, gasping as her body throbbed and stretched with the addition of Ricky's penetration.

"How are we doing?" His breathing grew shallow, and the cage of his arms around her began to shake.

"I'm good." She focused on Martin's hooded eyes, his locked jaw, and realized he was too overwhelmed to speak. "We're adjusting."

It was a rough start. With every other thrust, one of them popped out. The positioning of legs and hips took time to perfect, resulting in numerous stops and starts. But once they mastered the alignment and pace, they fell into blissful delirium.

Their hands went everywhere, gripping muscle, bruising skin, pulling one another closer, harder, as their bodies rose and fell like a tide.

Martin kissed her until the connection of lips became sloppy and impossible. She clung to his broad shoulders and panted against his neck as she rode the profound sensations of two cocks inside her.

Then they went wild, fucking into her like flesh and blood machines. She couldn't breathe, couldn't move. All she could do was just lay suspended between them and let their hands move her body up and down, jacking themselves off.

Hipbones ground against her, sandwiching her in. They were so deep, so huge. Muscled physiques, burning skin, vibrating groans, intoxicating male scents, stabbing cocks—they were all around her, inside her, owning her with an intensity that shoved her over the cliff.

"Shit, shit, shit." As the orgasm sneaked up on her, she found Martin's eyes and exploded into panting, trembling ecstasy.

Wave after wave of tingling electricity crashed over her. She ground down on their hardness and screamed their names through multiple octaves.

Martin's pupils dilated. His gorgeous mouth hung

open, and she was gone, swept away by pleasure and love and complete happiness.

As aftershocks shuddered through her, she collapsed between them, laughing breathlessly through the wet strands of hair stuck to her face.

"Fuck, that was hot." Martin brushed the hair from her eyes.

"A hot mess." She sighed, utterly content yet hungry for more. "Will you finish inside Ricky?"

She didn't have to ask him twice.

Their hands caressed and moved her limbs as they repositioned around her. She ended up on her back with Ricky between her legs. He slid into the drenched clasp of her body, lazily stroking as Martin knelt behind him.

Then Martin drove his hips, driving into Ricky's ass as Ricky sank in and out of her pussy.

What a spectacular view. She watched their expressions contort with pleasure, their exhales escaping sharply with relief, and their bodies flexing in their urgency.

Martin circled his arms around Ricky's sweat-slick chest and fucked into him with purpose. Hammering hips, slapping flesh, masculine moans—they consumed her with their strength and stamina.

Ricky turned his neck toward Martin behind him, and their mouths mashed together—all tongue and teeth and volcanic desire. Martin gripped his jaw, pulling him deeper into the kiss as he set the vigorous pace of their fucking.

"Fucking hell," Ricky moaned into his mouth.

"I know." Martin released him and pushed down on his back, trapping him between her chest and Martin's.

There wasn't a sliver of space between them, their bodies pressed together so tightly they couldn't press any closer. Yet they managed to keep their weight from crushing her, using the strength in their arms and legs.

Together, the three of them become one body, one beating heart. They moved in tandem, grinding and rocking in a tumble of limbs, mouths, cocks, and sweat. Skin heated. Muscles contracted, and groans grew deeper as they reached a crescendo.

"I'm going to come." Martin bore down on Ricky, his face tight with emotion as he seized her gaze. "Both of you with me."

"I'm there." Ricky panted and caught her mouth in a frenzied kiss.

He pulled back as he came, his breath caught in his throat, his mouth open in a silent roar. Martin followed him over, pounding hard and losing rhythm.

The intensity and love burning from their eyes took her with them. She sailed into the searing depths of brown and green, her hands tangling in the contrasting shades of blond and black hair, holding them to her and falling apart.

They crumbled into a sweaty, sated pile. The tension in their bodies slowly fled. Heart rates cooled down, and they snuggled into warm skin and soft hair, relaxed muscles and caressing hands.

"I finally have the answer," she breathed.

"What?" Martin's voice rumbled in his chest.

"Ricky Martin is the answer to every question I've ever had about life and death. I've experienced both in your arms."

Their quiet laughter enveloped her in joy. It was an impenetrable moment.

Nothing could touch them. Not time or distance. Not the prison walls or whatever awaited outside.

They held onto the moment with six hands.

They held on as tightly as possible, in every position,

for the next six weeks.

TWENTY-EIGHT

Tula couldn't sleep. The sound of her heartbeat thrashed brokenly in her ears. Pain stabbed in her chest and throat, and if she lay here much longer, she would break down so inconsolably she would ruin the last hours she had with Martin and Ricky.

She'd promised herself she would be strong.

For her.

For them.

Their time in Jaulaso was over, and they'd spent the past few hours making love to her as if every thrust, every kiss, and every breath was their last.

They'd fucked themselves into a coma.

Moving slowly and silently, she slid out from between their hot, heavy bodies.

Martin grunted, reaching for her, and she froze. His hand curled around her hip, clinging to her in his sleep. She waited with tears in her throat.

Eventually, his fingers loosened, and she slipped out of bed.

She dressed in the dark, grabbed a towel and soap,

and checked the time on her phone.

Matias Restrepo had told Martin and Ricky that a military guard would arrive on the ninetieth day with court orders to release them from Jaulaso.

Their ninetieth day started three hours ago.

Hector wouldn't learn about their release until they were gone. She would fake her surprise and pretend like she didn't really care. He believed her relationship with them was just sex and manipulation.

That was all it was supposed to be.

She never expected to fall in love.

She'd been very careful to hide her feelings from Hector. He'd sent her to do a job, and it was compromised the moment she learned he'd lied to her.

To survive the next three years in his prison, she would have to fake every interaction she had with him. His organization thrived on loyalty. Traitors and dissenters were killed without mercy.

The lights were off as she crept into the corridor and soundlessly shut the door.

She wanted to be clean for them when they said goodbye. Not just her body. She needed to cleanse her state of mind.

The Mexican government would honor the deal that was made for their release. In fact, the government was the only entity that had the power to reduce her sentence. Maybe Martin and Ricky could've negotiated for her if they had the intel on Hector that the government wanted. But they didn't.

She faced three years of separation from them. She needed to accept that and purge the bitterness that had been gnawing at her for weeks.

She would say goodbye, absorb their promises, and do what she could to survive the rest of her sentence.

Her trudging gait carried her through the empty corridor and into the dark stairwell. When she entered the ground floor, she glared at the closed door across the hall.

Was Hector asleep in there? Was he dreaming about the women and children he extorted for a business he considered unprofitable?

Maybe his involvement in that operation was so hands-off he didn't know his cartel was kidnapping people and selling them into slavery.

She grimaced. That sounded really naive, even in her head.

With a glance up and down the hall, she found it vacant as usual at three in the morning. One thing she could count on in Area Three was that its residents partied hard and crashed even harder.

Thirty steps from the stairwell, she passed her old cell. Garra had given it to another inmate weeks ago. Not that she cared. After Martin and Ricky left, she would stay in their cell, wrap up in the lingering scent of them, and pass the rest of her time replaying the best three months of her life.

A one-minute walk took her out of the cellblock and into the corridor that housed the showers. She stepped into the bathroom and peeked around the corner.

Empty.

The light in there stayed on at all hours, and she used it to find a clean place to store her towel and clothes.

As she reached for the button on her jeans, she heard a terrified squeal.

The squealing cry of a child.

A horrible coldness trickled down her spine, and her senses went on high-alert.

She used to wake to the sound of a crying child when she slept in her old cell. But she hadn't had a nightmare since she started sleeping with her guys.

Was she having some kind of traumatic flashback?

The cry sounded again, farther away, and the echo lingered, hitting her circulation with electric shocks. The hairs raised on her arms. Her blood turned to ice, and a paralyzing chill trailed goosebumps across her skin.

She wasn't half-asleep or drunk on tequila. She was wide awake, totally alert.

This wasn't her imagination.

Where did the cry come from? The vents in the ceiling? The empty corridor?

Her heart banged in her chest as she approached the door and peered out.

Not a soul in sight. No sound. No crying child.

It wasn't uncommon for the families of the inmates to visit Area Three. Sometimes, those families included children.

Did a kid get trapped in here? The prison guards did a head count on every person who came and went in the prison. How in the fuck could a child have been missed?

She stood on the threshold to the hallway, her feet frozen in ratty sneakers as she waited, listened.

Then she heard it.

A faraway, muffled shriek. The horrifying sound hiccuped into a convulsion of sobs before abruptly cutting off.

Terror struck her gut and locked up her joints.

Someone was hurting that kid.

She ran in the direction of the cry, down the hall and around the corner. The next corridor veered into a part of Area Three she rarely ventured.

Doors led to closets and maintenance rooms housing electrical boxes and machinery that kept the prison operational. No one wandered into this area unless something was broken.

At the next turn in the corridor, she stopped.

Up ahead was a door to another maintenance room. Only this one stood slightly ajar. The broken chain on the hinge must have swung, preventing it from closing all the way.

Pain throbbed in her molars from clenching her jaw, and the strength in her legs threatened to abandon her. The instinct to turn back and run straight to Martin and Ricky made her tremble uncontrollably. But she couldn't leave.

One of the inmates was hurting that child.

She didn't make a sound as she approached the door. She had no weapons, no fighting skills, and her muscles were so taut with fear she could barely move one foot in front of the other.

This might've been the stupidest thing she'd ever done, but she didn't intend to enter that room. She was just going to put her ear there and listen.

She reached the opening with a painful knot in her stomach. Her teeth chattered, and her entire body coiled to spring at the smallest sound.

Holding her breath, she leaned in.

Silence.

She strained her hearing, her gaze darting behind her every second, as she tried to listen over her thundering heart.

A distant footstep drifted from behind the door, then another, followed by the heaving of breaths. Grunting. Panting. The sound of metal scraping against concrete.

All the heat in her face rushed to her feet. None of those noises should be associated with a child.

She looked back down the hall, the impulse to run pulling through her with eye-watering force.

Turning back, she touched the door and gave it the

smallest push. The hinges didn't squeak. She pushed again, giving her enough room to wriggle in.

A maze of sewer pipes greeted her. Narrow and long, short and wide, they stacked in various sizes and rows and ran the length of the vast dark space. Some connected at joints and elbows. Others vanished into the ceiling and floor. Most of the pipes were the width of her body.

The sounds of grunting drew her toward a large pipe that ran parallel with the ground. Ducking behind it, she followed it around a bend toward the noise.

The beam of a flashlight shone through the plumbing, aimed at something twenty feet away. She couldn't see through all the pipes that separated her from whatever was breathing on the other side.

But there was a gap underneath.

Her hands slicked with sweat as she lowered to her knees. Chills gripped her spine and crawled over her scalp. She was so fucking scared.

Breathing silently through it, she dipped her head beneath the lowest pipe and stared across the floor to the other side.

Her heart stopped, and her mind fractured in horror, refusing to accept what her eyes couldn't look away from.

Long dark hair floated in a puddle of red. A tiny mouth hung open in a soundless scream, and glassy dead eyes stared right at her.

Bile hit her tongue, and her insides filled with blistering poison.

Only the upper half of the little girl was in view. She couldn't have been older than thirteen as she lay dead and nude in the blood that poured from her torn-out throat.

Tula was too late. Devastation reared up in her chest, crushing her heart.

Who had done this? How could someone kill a child?

The body jerked, followed by a grunt.

No, no, no.

The body rocked again, and again, being pushed by something she couldn't see.

Tremors wracked her limbs as she crawled alongside the pipe until the rest of the child came into view.

A man knelt between lifeless legs.

Rutting.

Raping.

Fucking the dead body.

Saliva rushed over her tongue. Vomit rose, and tears hit her eyes in a combustion of horror and fury. She clapped her hands over her mouth to silence the scream clawing in her throat.

She knew that slim, masculine frame. Knew the linen pants he wore. Knew how soft that thin cardigan felt beneath her hands when she danced with him.

Everything her mother had said about Hector La Rocha was true.

Only this was worse. So fucking worse.

He wasn't alone. Someone stood behind him, holding the flashlight. Watching. Allowing this despicable, gut-wrenching thing to happen.

The overpowering and agonizing feeling of terror, shock, dread, and revulsion incapacitated her. The utter fear of being caught by him immobilized her lungs, her legs, and the blood in her veins. She was afraid to breathe, petrified to make a sound.

The girl was gone. Dead. There was nothing she could do. She needed to get out of there. If he saw her…

The godawful groaning sounds of him finishing sent her scrambling backward in a flailing of arms and legs. She landed on her back, her clammy hands pressed to her mouth and nose, held in a frozen state of hell, and praying they hadn't heard her.

"This one was with the batch we smuggled in from Texas," the man with the flashlight said in Spanish.

She would recognize that slimy voice anywhere.

Simone.

"How many?" Hector stood and zipped his pants.

That sound... God, the ghastly sound of his zipper would forever haunt her.

Stiff and sickened with grief, she edged alongside the pipe, heading toward the door.

"Two dozen. It's getting harder to smuggle them through the border towns. We need new routes."

Realization slammed into her, redoubling her heart rate.

All those cries she heard over the past two years, the screams that had woken her from sleep...

They were real.

There had been other children, and she'd ignored them.

She'd let them die.

She would be next if she didn't get the fuck out of there.

Rising on silent feet, she swayed through bouts of dizziness. Nausea threatened. Her nerves stretched, overtaxed to the point of breaking as her bladder quivered to release.

Push through it and go!

Instinct took over. Self-preservation shoved her toward the door. All pain and thought vanished as her mind narrowed to one imperative.

Survival.

She moved on impulse, out the door, down the hall,

around the bend. The compulsion to look back tingled between her shoulder blades, but she ignored it, kept going, started running.

As her legs flew into a sprint, everything came flooding back.

The lifeless eyes. The jerking body. The sound of the zipper.

She gagged, and the violent hacking doubled her over.

Keep going. Run!

If she'd stayed in the sewer room, she might've picked up something valuable from their conversation. She might've heard names and locations of the men running the operation.

She might've been killed.

How did he sneak the children into the prison? What did he do with the bodies? Did he bring them in on a schedule? Could she track it and figure out a way to stop him before he did it again?

The questions fell behind her as she ran into the stairwell. But she couldn't outrun the toxicity of what she'd just witnessed. It boiled inside her, bubbling in her stomach. She made it to the second flight of stairs before her guts emptied in a spew of vomit and tears.

Her knees crashed onto the step, and she heaved great sobbing waves of anguish, puking all over the stairs.

When there was nothing left, she pushed away from the mess and wiped her mouth.

What was she going to do?

How would she look Hector in the eyes and pretend she couldn't see the bloody, gruesome wasteland of his soul?

She needed Martin and Ricky. Her heart demanded she run to them, tell them what happened, and let them console her as she fell apart in their arms. She was desperate for them. They would take this burden from her and make it easier to breathe.

Her chest constricted.

They were leaving in a few hours. If she unloaded this on them, they would sabotage their departure. They would find a way to stay and keep her safe.

Her mind spun through the horrid details of Martin's childhood. After everything he'd been through, he would never let a monster like Hector La Rocha live. If she told him about this, he would go on a killing spree and get himself killed.

Even if she could convince him not to retaliate, how could she put this on their shoulders and send them off without a resolution?

They had come to Jaulaso because they already knew Hector was evil. Telling them what she just saw didn't gain anyone anything.

She only had a handful of hours left with them. She didn't want to spend it rehashing the horrors of what she'd just witnessed. She had the next three years to do that.

But if she didn't tell them, she would be tainting their final moments with dishonesty. She would have to slap on a smile, pretend nothing was amiss, and send them off with kisses and hope.

It was an impossible decision.

She forced herself to her feet and returned to their cell. The short walk didn't give her enough time to shake the trembling from her body.

The deepest shivers would never go away. She would never escape what she saw tonight.

But she could do something about it.

The seed of an idea sprouted as she silently opened the door and slipped into their cell.

Darkness slammed into her, pressing in on all sides. She felt it on her skin, the contamination of Hector's depravity infecting her pores.

"Tula?"

Ringing invaded her ears, disorientating her as she stumbled in the blackness.

"Tula? What are you doing?" The distant voice was smothered by a heavy fuzz of violence.

Grisly images flashed behind her eyes. Long black hair. Pools of blood. Tiny fingers. The zipper.

She swayed in the nightmare, drowning in the pain, trying to keep her head above her and her feet beneath her.

"Tula? Tula?" Warm arms came around her, competing with the coldness. "Are you okay?"

Martin held her up, his presence a beacon in the dark. Then Ricky pressed in behind her, his mouth falling to her neck, anchoring her to him.

This was what she needed. What *they* needed. For the next few hours, she couldn't let anything take this from them.

She knew what she had to do.

She'd promised herself she would be strong.

For her.

For them.

"I had a nightmare." She pressed a kiss to Martin's hard chest.

"Come back to bed."

"Just a sec. I want to brush my teeth." She slipped away, fumbling in the dark for her toothbrush.

"Why are you dressed?" Ricky lit a candle, illuminating the room in a soft glow.

"I was going to take a shower."

"Do it tomorrow."

Today was tomorrow.

Their last day together.

"Okay." She turned away before they saw the plastic smile that wasn't working on her face.

They were half-asleep with exhaustion. That was the only reason they hadn't detected her dishonesty.

Lying to them made her feel sick, but it was the only way she could protect them.

As she brushed her teeth and stripped her clothes, her mind picked up and discarded a dozen ways to deal with Hector La Rocha.

Maybe there were smarter, safer solutions to end his depravity, but there was only one outcome she wanted. The seed of her idea bloomed into a plan.

Right now, though, she only wanted to think about the two people who mattered most to her. She was going to savor every second they had left together.

Then, once they were safely out of Jaulaso, she would iron out how, where, and when.

She was going to kill Hector La Rocha.

TWENTY-NINE

Saying goodbye was the most excruciating thing Tula ever had to do.

She stood between Martin and Ricky in the privacy of their cell and peppered desperate, tear-soaked kisses over their faces and hands.

They were already dressed, seconds from walking out the door.

From the moment she'd crawled back in bed with them early that morning, they'd been saying goodbye.

They said goodbye while moving inside her body. They said it with growly, pain-stricken words. They said it with their eyes as they memorized her features and collected her tears with their lips.

Three months with them hadn't been enough.

A lifetime with them wouldn't have been enough.

"You need to go." She pulled them closer, protesting her own command.

"This is fucking bullshit!" Martin wrenched away and tore his hands through his hair. "We haven't thought through every option. There must be a way—"

"We've beaten this to death." Tears slid free, and she swatted at her cheeks. "You can *not* stay here. Giving up your freedoms helps no one. There's no reason—"

"There's one reason." Ricky cupped her face. "And you're the only reason that matters."

"We're sticking to the plan." She dug in deep and shoved back her shoulders. "You're walking out of here today, and that's final."

There would be no communication. No phone calls.

Over the past two years, she'd only used her phone to contact the U.S. consular. She checked in regularly to monitor the status of her sentence and nag him about an early release.

La Rocha Cartel monitored the call logs of all cell phones in Jaulaso. If she veered from her pattern and called a number she'd never dialed, it would raise suspicion. Even if she called an untraceable number or a reception desk at some random business, Hector would know about it.

She couldn't do anything that might cause him to second-guess her. Especially now that she knew how cruel and truly sadistic he was.

Once he discovered Martin and Ricky's charges had been dropped, he would know something nefarious was going on with them. Drug trafficking charges didn't just go away. Not in Jaulaso.

Martin and Ricky wouldn't be safe in Hector's city. The instant they walked out of here, they would have to leave Ciudad Hueca.

There would be no visits from them. No calls. No letters. No packages. Any contact would make Hector suspect she'd taken sides with them.

They would be heading back to the Colombian headquarters of the Restrepo Cartel, where they lived.

Only the residents knew the location. It was a secret they couldn't share.

She would never be able to find them.

They promised to come to her when she was released. She wanted to believe them, but her plan made that impossible.

When they left, she would have to forget them. At least, whenever she stepped out of this cell. Her pain would be trapped in this room, hidden from the rest of the world.

Ricky embraced her in a rib-crushing hug. "We're going to get you—"

"No more promises. Just hold me."

He tightened his arms and kissed her deeply. His breaths shook as painfully as hers, but they kept the tears at bay. They'd cried enough.

Martin moved in, tugging her away from Ricky. His kiss was harder, angrier, more punishing. Every lick commanded she stay safe. Every bite confessed how much he hated leaving, and every sucking pull laid claim to her heart.

They owned her. No matter what happened, she would always be theirs.

As they opened the door and stepped into the hallway, her entire world pulled away, and she was left standing outside of it. Alone. They knew it, too, given the way their shoulders tightened, and their faces hardened.

The pain was unwieldy, like a blanket made of boulders had been draped over her shoulders. It weighed her down and pinned her in place, making it physically and emotionally exhausting to stand beneath.

They glanced back with love and fear, hope and grief filling their parting expressions.

No words were needed. Everything had already

been said.

Except the one thing she'd held back.

She told them with her eyes.

I love you.

If she ever saw them again, she would tell them with her voice and every part of her being.

She shut the door before they took the steps that would carry them away.

Her forehead dropped against the doorframe. Her breath perished in her chest, and her fingers slid helplessly up and down the wall as she tracked the sounds of their retreating footfalls.

Then she couldn't hear them at all. She couldn't feel the warm glow of their love pulsing through her body. She was too cold. So unbearably frigid. Her heart actually ached. It ached so ruthlessly it felt as though she were suffocating beneath the colossal pain.

They were still in the building. If she ran, she could catch them before they exited the stairwell.

Then what? More kisses? Another goodbye? It would never be enough.

She pressed her feet firmly to the floor and mentally traced the path they would take through Jaulaso. She imagined herself at their sides as they walked out of Area Three.

No one would stop them. They weren't members of La Rocha Cartel.

They would reach the front of the prison and leave with their escort. A prison guard would notify Hector as that happened.

But they would already be gone.

Safe.

Far away from her.

Her grief sat right beneath her sternum, next to her

heart. It expanded with ungodly pressure as her body took deep sighing breaths in an attempt to draw more oxygen. Panic rose with swelling agony, and her chest tightened, fighting a looming anxiety attack.

Martin and Ricky had coached her through this. She could hear their voices in her head telling her to relax and stay calm. They knew the next few hours would be the hardest, and they'd reminded her over and over to not break down.

A knock would sound on her door soon. Meetings would follow. Interrogations about where they went and what she knew.

She would endure it with a disappointed expression fixed on her face while she slowly died inside.

But she had a plan.

What Martin and Ricky didn't know was that she wouldn't be finishing her three years in Jaulaso.

Killing Hector La Rocha wouldn't be easy. If she somehow succeeded, she would have to flee Jaulaso before his body was discovered. Timing would be critical.

Pushing down her grief, she grabbed her phone and dialed the U.S. consular. He answered after a few rings.

"This is Petula Gomez." She pulled in a deep breath and released it.

"Petula." He sighed, exasperated. "Nothing has changed with your sentence."

"I'm not calling about that."

In 1977, the United States and Mexico signed a prisoner transfer treaty. Since that time, some American and Mexican prisoners have been transferred to their respective countries. She'd already been sentenced, which made her eligible to transfer to a prison in the United States.

All she had to do was plead guilty and hope to hell

Hector didn't discover her intent to desert the cartel.

"Start the process to send me back to the U.S." She strengthened her voice. "I'm ready to plead guilty."

The consular had been advising her to do this since day one. She hadn't listened to him because she always had Hector's protection in Jaulaso.

And she had her pride.

She was innocent, serving a sentence for a crime she didn't commit. A guilty plea would mar her criminal record forever.

After two years in Jaulaso, she didn't give a goddamn fuck about her pride or her record. She just needed to get out and didn't care what it took.

"I'm confident the U.S. Department of Justice will concur with your request," he said. "Once everything is signed off, arrangements will be made for your transfer."

"How long will it take?"

"You'll be in U.S. custody within a month."

PART THREE

THIRTY

The knock on the door came an hour later. An hour that Tula had spent shoving her pain so far down beneath her bones she could no longer feel it.

She moved stiffly to the door, expecting Garra on the other side. But when she opened it, he wasn't alone.

Garra stepped back to make room for Hector to enter.

The air tried to rush out of her lungs, but she held it in and arranged her features into a mask of pleasant surprise.

He stood two feet away, infecting her precious sanctuary with his pedophilic, child-killing pestilence.

His black hair combed back neatly with silver streaks at the temples. The cardigan was gone, but he wore his signature button-down shirt, open at the collar.

She couldn't think about his pants or the things he did when he wasn't wearing them.

Please, leave.

She didn't want him here. Not in the place she'd shared with Martin and Ricky.

His dark eyes took her measure, the depths warm and gentle, camouflaging the sickness that festered within.

What were his true intentions with her? Had any part of the past two years been real? Or was it all manipulation?

He'd sent Garra to collect her DNA in a violent, repulsive way. He required her to sit through his meetings but kept his human trafficking operation concealed from her. Then he tasked her, his only daughter, to seduce his enemies, not knowing if they would kill her or hurt her. All the while, he protected her from the other inmates, learned English through her instruction, and danced with her. Why?

Her mind delivered the sound of a zipper to her ears, but she didn't react, didn't look down. She blocked out the reminder of who he was and assumed her role.

"Have you seen Martin and Ricardo?" She craned her neck around him to glance into the hall. "They said they were going to get food, but they never returned. I was just on my way out to find—"

"They're gone." His eyebrows knitted together as he studied her.

"What?" She squared her shoulders with feigned indignation. "You had them killed? You said I had time to—"

"No," he tsked. "They left Jaulaso. The military dropped their charges and released them."

"Oh." She slumped onto the mattress and blew out a breath. "Shit."

"You don't know anything about that?" He cocked his head, his expression soft and concerned.

"No." Her fingers trembled, and she flexed them. "What does it mean? Are they working with the military? Like undercover or something?"

"That's my assumption."

"Oh, God." She pressed her face into her hands and made a noise she hoped sounded like a self-loathing groan. "I failed you."

"Petula." He lowered onto the bed beside her, sending her nerves into a shrieking fit of horror. "You kept them distracted. Whatever secrets they came to steal from me remain safely guarded. *They* failed. Because of you."

There was so much truth in that it fucking hurt. If they hadn't become entangled with her, if they hadn't chosen her over their mission, they might've succeeded.

They could've taken down Hector's entire human trafficking operation if they'd learned where his officers were hiding. But she'd gotten in their way.

She'd distracted them just like Hector had wanted.

"I don't feel like I was any help at all." She stared down at her hands, playing coy as she worked up the courage to meet his eyes. "They got away."

When she finally lifted her head, she stared at him through a one-way window. She could see his ugliness, his unadulterated evil. But he couldn't see her. The utter fear she felt in his presence, the grief of losing Martin and Ricky, her plan to kill him—all of it was invisible to him.

Because she was his daughter. Their genetic connection made him partial to her. He *wanted* to trust her.

She would manipulate that trust until her transfer went through. Then she would kill him with it.

He watched her for a moment, his head tipping with curiosity. She held still, her facial muscles slack as she thought about the gooey goodness of grilled cheese, her favorite passage in *The Hellbound Heart*, the tattered stubs of her shoestrings—anything except the images of him with that little girl.

Disgust raged beneath her schooled features,

seething under her skin and cooking her from the inside out.

"You liked the gringos," he said.

She loved them.

Losing that love felt like a straitjacket constricting her body. She would never adjust or grow comfortable in it. She would never be able to take it off. It would forever bind her and prevent her from holding anyone and anything. Maybe it would eventually make her insane, and she would welcome the madness because a reality without them hurt too damn much.

"They were attractive." She shrugged. "I mean… I had a good time *distracting* them, I guess." She glanced around the room. "But it'll be nice to have my privacy back. Can I keep this cell?"

"If you'd like." His gaze drifted to Garra, who waited outside the door. Then he returned to her. "I put an alert out. The entire city is on the lookout for the gringos. If they attempt to contact you—"

"I'll castrate them," she deadpanned.

He laughed, just like she knew he would, and the air around him settled into affectionate trust. She felt like she was going to throw up, but at least he hadn't noticed.

"I'll let you know if they contact me," she said. "In the meantime, I'm probably just going to hang out in here for a while, read some books, and enjoy my alone time. Is that okay?"

He inclined his head. "As long as you delight this old man with a dance every now and then."

The shudder that rose up was so powerful she had to clench her core muscles to stifle it.

"Of course." She stood with him and followed him to the door. "I'm sorry they got away. I hope you're not too disappointed in me."

"You never disappoint me, my girl." He touched her chin in a featherlight caress of fingers and filth.

"Thank you."

He entered the corridor and breezed past Garra, vanishing around the corner.

Garra remained, and his eyes moved over her like lie detectors. She gave him the same treatment, questioning every crease in his brow and twitch in his bearded jaw.

Did he know about Hector's depravity? He was the most loyal man in the cartel. It was safe to assume he knew about and guarded every skeleton in Hector's closet.

"I will watch over you again," he said in Spanish.

"No, you will not. Did Hector tell you to—?"

"No." He glanced down the hall and looked back at her. "I don't want you wandering around alone. I know you feel safe—"

"I've never felt safe. Not in Jaulaso, and definitely not with you."

He inhaled sharply. "Fine."

As he turned away, she shut the door and locked it.

Her hand lifted to her face where Hector had touched her, and all the pain she'd pushed down over the past hour came roaring back.

She clawed at the stabbing burn in her chest and buckled over, gasping for breath. Her knees gave out as she hurled herself toward the sink, landing against it.

With the faucet on, she shoved her face under the spray and frantically scrubbed away the feel of Hector's fingers.

He was so fucking vile and sick, and he was related to her. How could that be? How could she share DNA with something so atrociously inhuman?

She turned off the water and stared at the yellow stains in the sink. She was alone. Martin and Ricky were gone, and she had to continue on without them. She had to carry the weight of Hector's sins without their protection or help.

It was too late to tell them about the things that happened to her last night. She'd made a decision, and she couldn't take it back. She would never be able to curl up between their bodies and cry through the horrors she'd witnessed.

The safe, happy world she'd lived in with them was gone. That place would never return to her. They could never come back here.

They were gone.

Gone.

Gone.

Their absence swallowed all her attention, smothering her entire existence in desolation. She felt it in her face, throbbing through her gums and consuming her sinuses. Tears burned from her swollen eyes. Her throat filled with lava. The pain spread through muscles, arteries, and organs, weakening everything in its path.

She dragged heavy, useless limbs to the bed and buried her nose in the blankets, breathing in their masculine scents and seeking out the indentations of their body prints in the mattresses.

Mattresses that had been clawed by passionate hands. Walls that had been dampened by the press of sweaty bodies. Bedding that had tangled and twisted in the throes of hunger.

Surrounded by remnants of their time together, she rewound their love scenes, remembering them inside her and clinging to the blissful sensations. She knew them inside and out, and she would never forget.

Ricky's panty-melting smile, the commanding rumble in Martin's voice, the way they stared at each other so intimately and possessively, and how that captivating eye contact eventually included her—all of it tattooed across her soul.

She lost herself in the pain.

She grieved them with her whole body.

Once the sobbing began, she couldn't stop. She fell into the black abyss and didn't try to climb out. Curling up in the darkness, she cried through the rest of the day and into the next one.

No one knocked on the door or tried to invade her isolation. She wouldn't have let them in. She was in no position to show her face.

A few cans of soup and early-morning showers got her through that first week. The two times she ventured out at three in the morning, the sounds of a crying child haunted her. But the corridors remained silent and empty.

Over the next few weeks, she pulled herself together long enough to inject her presence into Area Three.

At night, she walked the halls, listening for children and monitoring the vacant sewer room.

During the day, she watched the inmates from her favorite bench in the yard and swallowed her fear during visits with Hector in his cell.

On the surface, she was the woman she'd been for the past two years—aloof and unapproachable, present but not involved. She sat on the outskirts of the common areas with her nose in a book, just like she'd always done.

But on the inside, everything had changed. She couldn't understand how the world could go on around her when her life had completely stopped.

Life had abandoned her the moment Martin and Ricky walked out that door.

She tried not to dwell on it, but it was a splinter under her fingernail that couldn't be removed. Sometimes the pain dulled, but it never went away. She couldn't think of anything else except for that damn splinter, stuck in a place it didn't belong. Her entire body felt it. She couldn't pull it out, couldn't chop it off. She couldn't escape it.

Three weeks later, she received the green light on her transfer to the United States. It didn't ease the agony of her loss, but it gave her some focus.

In six days, the U.S. Bureau of Prisons would begin her transfer to a federal correctional institution near her home. She was going to a satellite prison camp for female offenders in Phoenix, Arizona.

She knew the date and time of her departure.

She knew when Hector was going to die.

THIRTY-ONE

The morning of Tula's transfer, she waited in the stairwell across from Hector's cell. Her heart hammered in her stomach, and her legs burned to run.

She'd managed to keep her scheduled departure a secret. In fact, the whole transfer process had been shockingly easy.

Too easy.

Something felt off, but she couldn't put her finger on it.

A late phone call to the consular last night confirmed everything was in order.

She could just go now. Run straight out of Area Three and head to the front of the prison. Her ride would be here in a few hours. She could find a place to hide and wait it out.

Maybe she could contact the Mexican military and tell them Hector was smuggling children into the prison. But part of her suspected they already knew.

They'd tortured her for information on the cartel, desperate to bring down the whole organization. Then they framed her.

She didn't trust them.

But if she ran now, how many children would be raped and murdered while she served the rest of her time in the States?

This was the only way.

Right on time, Garra appeared at Hector's door to walk his boss to the showers. She slipped out of view in the stairwell, listening to their voices and tracking the retreat of their footsteps.

Then she waited through a minute of nerve-wracking silence before she sneaked into his cell.

Over the past few weeks, she'd cataloged the placement of everything in his quarters. It took her five seconds to locate the knife under his pillow. Another five seconds to slide it into the narrow space behind the record player.

In under a minute, she was out of his room and strolling back to her cell with deliberately slow steps.

Then she waited for an hour—hands drenched in sweat, fingers trembling uncontrollably, and pulse pounding in her head.

Once she stepped out of this prison cell, she would never return. If she lived through the next part, she would head straight out of Area Three without looking back.

One more glance around the room filled her with unbearable sorrow. She had to leave it all behind. The signed novel of *The Hellbound Heart*. The candles that illuminated so many nights of pleasure. The box of men's clothing that was scented by them. A distinctive fragrance that would forever haunt her.

It was okay. She could do this. It was just stuff, and this cell was just an empty space they'd left behind.

Time to go.

No amount of detachment or determination could overpower the terror that owned her body as she walked back to Hector's cell. Maybe this would've been a good time to square things up with Jesus, but she didn't think the Lord and Savior would be on board with what she was about to do.

By the time she reached Hector's door, she'd built a sturdy wall around her emotions. But she wore her fear like an invisible cloak. Ice-cold and unshakable, it clung to her skin and drained all her warmth. She felt it with every breath, but she couldn't see it.

If prison life had taught her anything, it was how to keep her weaknesses hidden beneath a veneer of tattoos and cool reserve.

Or maybe it was an inherited skill that had been passed down in her blood. Hector had mastered the art of concealing depravity beneath a soft cardigan and layers of affection.

He answered her knock on the door, wearing a pleased smile. "Petula."

"Are you up for getting your feet stepped on?" By some miracle, she'd evaded all dancing and touching for the past month.

"I thought you'd never ask. Come in."

As they exchanged their usual greetings, she chewed blistering gashes on the insides of her cheeks.

Drawing this out wasn't an option. Her nerves unfurled with every miserable heartbeat. At any second, he would detect her distress.

"Can I select the song today?" she asked.

"Go ahead."

She floated to the record player on numb legs and pulled an album from the stack. Her hands shook as she set up the record, her mind focused on the knife she'd hidden behind the turntable.

Was it still there? Would she be able to grab it before he stopped her? Would she chicken out at the last minute?

"Which song did you choose?" He approached her, staring too closely at her tingling face.

Fuck, she'd forgotten to look at the album.

Her tongue twisted through the saliva pooling in her mouth. "You'll see."

She adjusted the needle but didn't place it on the vinyl. The next few seconds had to be timed flawlessly.

Deep breath.

"Ready?" She positioned her stance beside the record player, turning her body just right as she opened her arms.

He stepped into her space, pervading her senses with the gruesome echoes of a dark sewer room.

His hand clasped her hip. His other reached for her fingers.

"I'll start the song." She angled toward the turntable and twisted her ankle just right to make it look clumsy.

Her tripping step distracted him away from her hand as he caught her fall. In that blur of a moment, she bypassed the needle on the player and wrapped her fingers around the hilt of the knife.

Her pulse exploded as she swung.

She'd sat in the prison yard for two years, listening to inmates talk about the most lethal ways to kill a man. She would've never considered the armpit as a target. Evidently, neither did Hector.

He saw the knife coming and shielded his core. She put all her strength behind the thrust as she stabbed upward into his armpit. With the blade still pointed up, she yanked it back toward her, making sure she severed the main artery there.

Blood spurted instantly, but instead of falling, he attacked.

His hand caught her throat, and she shoved him off with a surge of ferocity. The blood loss made him weaker, and his injured arm didn't work.

As he shuffled to stay upright, she stabbed him again in the same spot. And again. She must've hit cartilage or bone the second time because the knife stuck, slipping from her fingers as he stumbled backward.

He stared at the protruding weapon in his shoulder, his eyes wide with shock. "Why?"

"You're pure evil. You don't belong here. Not in this world. Not among *children*."

His hip bumped into the table, knocking it aside, and he dropped to the floor.

The vicious pounding in her chest overpowered her relief. She needed answers.

Kneeling beside him, she squeezed his throat and held him immobile. "I know what you do in the middle of the night."

His eyes blinked rapidly, and he slapped an uncoordinated hand at the knife in his shoulder. Half of his shirt was red, and the puddle beneath him was growing. The artery in the armpit supplied blood to his extremities and sat close enough to the heart to drain him quickly. He didn't have much time.

"Give me the locations of the commanders involved in the smuggling of those kids."

"I sent you to the gringos as a test." The cords in his neck strained beneath her hand, and his English grew sloppy with his pain. "I didn't care about them. I needed to know who *you* were." He switched to Spanish. "I challenged your loyalty to see who you would pick. Them or me." His eyes watered with tears. "I thought you chose *me."*

"You sick son of a bitch," she seethed. "If you wanted to test me, all you had to do was tell me you were raping and killing children. You would've found out real quick where my loyalties lie."

He held still, staring up at her, eyes locked. A twitch skipped along his clenched jaw that had nothing to do with the knife in his shoulder. He was disappointed with her. Furious. Flames roared in his gaze, ready to ignite everything around him.

Well, fuck him, because her rage blazed hotter. The inferno inside her wasn't explosive or out of control, but it burned mighty and strong at the end of a two-year wick.

The acidity of her wrath resided in her stomach, waiting to be spat from her mouth in a string of venomous words. But she wasn't going to say them. She was going to stab all her hurt and disgust into his dying body.

She slapped a hand over his mouth and yanked the blade from his shoulder. His jaw worked beneath her palm, roaring without sound. His back bowed and spasmed, and more blood flowed from his wounds.

With the knife secure in her fist, she let her fury flood out all at once. The blade came down, fast and relentless, over and over into the lower quadrants of his abdomen.

Though he was screaming, her hand trapped the noise as her other jabbed and twisted the blade, gouging countless holes, goring and mangling. To draw out his death, she avoided the liver, spleen, and big veins that were higher up.

He probably only had seconds left, but she wanted to make fucking sure he felt every single one of them while staring into her eyes.

Her arm moved like a disembodied appendage,

separated from her soul. What she felt wasn't human. It wasn't *her*. The mindless need to kill brutally and ruthlessly… It warped her mind and laced her veins in fire. She was intoxicated with it. And terrified.

She dropped the knife and stared down at the mutilated remains of his lower abdomen. The bloodbath sickened her and thrilled her.

"Vera Gomez," he whispered.

Her heart stuttered. "What?"

"Your sister." A macabre smile pushed through his agony-soaked expression. "She smuggles them for me. All the pretty little girls."

Her breath stopped and restarted as her mind tried to separate the information. "You found her? She's alive? Wait… She works for you? She would never—"

His mouth formed words, but no sound came out. His eyes lost focus, blinking slowly as he stared at nothing. Death moved in, stealing the answers she desperately needed.

"Where is she?" She slapped his slack face, knocking his head to the side. "Answer me!"

"With…" His tongue lolled in his vile mouth, dying with his words. "Your brothers."

He fell silent. No breath. No movement. Eyes glazed and unseeing.

Dead.

Hector La Rocha was dead, and her sister was alive.

Vera's alive.

A sob of relief burst from her throat. She gulped down the next tearful exhale and pushed to her feet, teetering and stunned to the bottom of her stomach.

Vera was smuggling children? She was the one Martin and Ricky were looking for? And the Mexican military…

They arrested Tula because of mistaken identity.

Vera wasn't mixed up in this. She would never do anything to harm innocent people.

She couldn't think about this right now. Blood was everywhere, trailing a gruesome path from the record player to his prone body. It splattered her black shirt, coated her hands, and clotted in her hair.

She needed to get out of there.

Racing to the sink, she scrubbed off the evidence. Clothes, skin, hair—all of it received a furious rubbing until only a few damp spots remained on her shirt.

She didn't spare a glance at the body as urgency propelled her to the door. The scariest part wasn't over.

She still had to walk out of Area Three without raising suspicion. With any luck, Hector's death wouldn't be discovered until she was on her way to the United States.

The corridor would be busy at this hour. The moment she stepped out there, she would have to put on her game face. Business as usual.

A few deep breaths helped her steady her hands. Then she opened the door.

Garra and Simone stood a few feet away. Their conversation fell silent, and both heads turned in her direction.

She glared at them—because that was what she would normally do—while reaching behind her, blindly trying to find the handle and close the door.

In two long strides, Garra was in her space. His hand went to her cheek, and he pulled back a red-smeared thumb.

"What did you do?" he whispered angrily.

Her fingers caught the door behind her, pulling it closed as Simone crowded in, pushing it open.

"That's blood." Simone examined her up and down before angling his head to see into Hector's cell.

Her stomach dropped, and her knees wobbled.

The body lay around the corner, but the goddamn evidence was on her face. She couldn't talk her way out of this. She needed to run.

"I got a bloody nose." She tried to squeeze past them, but multiple hands caught her arms and dragged her back inside.

The door shut with finality, closing her in and sucking all the air from her lungs.

"Get your hands off me!" She kicked and thrashed as they hauled her toward the crime scene. "Let me go!"

And there it was. Hector's body lay in a pool of red, eyes open, with a hundred mangled knife wounds in the abdomen.

"Holy Mother of God." Simone stared at the bloody corpse, stunned. Then his tawny face turned red-hot. "You did this."

"Garra." She twisted in his arms, prepared to beg for mercy from the only man in Jaulaso who might actually listen. "Please, let me explain."

His nostrils flared, and his fingers bit into her back.

Desperation drove her hand to his hair. She gripped hard, touching him for the first time as she put her face in his. "Please, don't hurt me again."

Something moved in his eyes, a soft pulse at the centers, that seemed to humanize his entire expression. He opened his mouth to speak, but his attention darted to Simone behind her.

As she turned, Simone drew a large knife from his boot and lunged for her.

She had no time to react before Garra shoved her out of the way. She landed on her back beside Hector's body, her breath frozen as Garra crashed into Simone.

They went down in a tumble of fists, rolling across the floor with the knife swinging around them. She scrambled back and dug in her feet to run. Until her gaze snagged on the blade beside Hector's leg.

She didn't think beyond the need to kill Simone. He'd held the flashlight, watched the violence. He needed to die.

With a surge of adrenaline, she grabbed the knife and spun toward the fight.

Simone was bigger, stronger, and had the upper hand as he flipped Garra onto his back and fell on top of him. She saw her chance and raced toward them.

Holding the knife with the sharp edge angled down, she stabbed it deeply and firmly into the back of Simone's neck. When his body jerked, she yanked hard on the hilt, dragging the blade toward the spine and severing everything in its path.

Simone collapsed on Garra's chest, covered in blood and instantly dead. She pressed her fingers to the pulse point in his neck, just to be sure.

Fuck.

She'd just killed another cartel member.

Garra didn't move beneath the body as he watched her closely, his eyes stark and unblinking. Then his lips pulled back with a hiss, exposing blood-stained teeth.

"You're hurt?" She couldn't see much of him beneath Simone and all the blood.

"Yes."

"Are you going to kill me?"

"Never." The intensity of his conviction pulled her to her knees.

She shoved the body, and Garra released a roar of agony. As the weight fell away, she saw the knife.

Buried to the hilt in Garra's stomach, the eight-inch blade had gone all the way through him. He would be dead within minutes.

Against all logic, an ache of compassion swelled in her throat.

"Some letters came for you." He heaved a breath, choking on a mouthful of blood. "Forms you needed to sign to complete your transfer."

"What?" A fresh wave of fear crashed over her.

He knew about her desertion? For how long? Had he alerted the cartel? Would they be waiting for her as she tried to leave?

She bent over him. "What did you do?"

"I hid them from everyone. Forged your signatures and sent them back to the consular."

"Why?" Her head jerked back. "Why didn't you tell me?"

"I didn't want you to know I…"

"What?"

"I love you."

She blew out a breath. Didn't matter that he was dying. She couldn't pretend to give a fuck about that sentiment. "Do you know what Hector was doing to children in the sewer room?"

He looked away and coughed out a string of blood. "I didn't condone it and never helped him with that."

Disgust burned in her gut. "How did he get them into Jaulaso?"

"They're drugged. Put inside crates. Brought in with shipments of firearms."

Firearms? Hector and his men had conversations about those shipments in every meeting. Had they been talking about trafficking humans right in front of her?

She clenched her hands. "You did nothing to stop it.

Makes you just as guilty as the rest of them."

With a slow nod, he closed his eyes and let his head loll.

"You're not dying yet." She gripped his jaw and forced his narrowed gaze to hers. "Where's my sister?"

"With your brothers, but you can't—" A gulping breath rolled his eyes into the back of his head.

"Garra!" She shook him until he refocused on her.

"Can't go after Vera. Hector's sons… They'll know what you did. They'll avenge him."

"They know who I am? They'll recognize me?"

"Yes. Stay away. They'll kill you." His hand fell to his pants and flopped around his hip. "The bag…my pocket. Take it. Show it on your way out."

His eyes closed, and his breathing slowed to a stuttering wisp. She was losing him.

"Where is Vera? Give me a location. A town. Anything."

He parted pale lips but didn't open his eyes. "C-C-Calaaa—" The rest of it died on his last breath.

Calaaa-what? Off the top of her head, she couldn't think of a town in Mexico that began with those syllables, but she would have plenty of time later to research it.

Shoving her hand into his pocket, she removed a plastic baggie of heroin. "Show this on my way out?"

Confusion morphed to understanding. The drugs were her ticket out of Area Three. Unlike Martin and Ricky, she was a cartel member. She would need a reason for leaving the area.

"Thank you for helping me." She patted Garra's lifeless chest and shoved to her feet.

She ran to the sink, cleaned away the blood, and double-checked her face.

Then she left. Out the door, through the corridors,

and into the common area. Her body operated on a flood of adrenaline, racing her heart and pushing away the fear.

An armed inmate stopped her at the door to the exit. "Where are you going?"

"Delivering something for the boss." She pulled the baggie from her pocket and held it up.

He gave it a glance and nodded.

Then he opened the door.

Sunlight baked her eyes as she stepped into the outdoor courtyard and hurried to the other side. It'd been two years since she walked this path, naively following the prison guard that Hector had sent for her.

Only one month ago, Martin and Ricky crossed this same yard.

Where were they now? Did they miss her? Would they try to find her? How would they even know where to look?

She had no way to contact them. No way to tell them she was leaving.

None of this was a revelation. When she made the call to process her transfer, she knew it meant she would never see them again.

As she entered the central part of the prison, she dropped the bag of heroin on the floor and made her way through the filthy halls.

She'd killed Hector La Rocha.

Vera was alive.

She was returning to Arizona.

All of this should've lifted her spirits and carried her faster to the door. But it was overshadowed by longing and heartache.

She should've never fallen in love. But she did. Times two.

Nothing would ever compare to the three months

she had with them. They were the touchstone of human integrity. A taste of a full and vibrant life. They were the real deal. Her deepest sorrow. Her greatest happiness.

She'd carried two-hundred dollars into Jaulaso.

Two years later, the only thing she carried out was a broken heart.

THIRTY-TWO

It had been there for three months—this exhausting, unstoppable anger that kept Martin awake at night. He lay in bed at the Restrepo headquarters and twined his fingers through Ricky's hair, trying to quiet his raging thoughts.

They'd been in Colombia for three fucking months, and no one could tell them anything about Tula. They didn't know if she was protected by La Rocha Cartel, unharmed, or still alive.

Hector La Rocha was dead. It was all over the news two months ago. The reports claimed he was brutally murdered in his prison cell, along with his closest men, Garra and Simone. As for who had done it? That mystery was still being investigated.

Maybe it was an inside job by one of the inmates in Area Three. It could've been an attack by the González Cartel or one of the enemy gangs.

But deep down, Martin knew.

Tula had found a way to kill the cartel boss. If Martin weren't so fucking angry with her for risking her life, he would've been beaming with pride.

Three dangerous men.

Murdered.

He couldn't begin to imagine how she'd done it or what had prompted her. But whenever the scenario played out in his head, he couldn't see past his blinding rage and fear.

Just because she wasn't listed among the dead didn't mean the cartel hadn't retaliated in the two months that followed. There had been multiple prison riots since Hector's death. Chaos had erupted in fires, gunfights, and prisoner breakouts.

The news didn't report the names of the casualties from the Jaulaso riots, and none of Martin's resources had been able to obtain that information.

Everything was on lockdown. The entire city was up in arms over the death of their leader, and the Mexican government was scrambling to keep the prison contained. There were talks about shutting Jaulaso down.

Where was Tula during all this? He couldn't stop imagining her holed up in that foul cell, alone and unarmed, while the prison burned down around her.

He gritted his teeth to the point of breaking. His shoulders ached with endless tension. Animosity saturated his blood with acid—burning, seething, poisonous.

He was infuriated with the Mexican military for putting an innocent schoolteacher in Jaulaso. He was outraged with the Mexican government for ignoring his pleas to release her. He was pissed at Matias Restrepo for refusing to negotiate another deal that would send Martin back to prison.

And he wanted to strangle Cole Hartman for making promises he had yet to keep.

When he and Ricky left Jaulaso three months ago, they went straight to Cole. The retired military-spy-secret-agent—whatever Cole was—had been able to spring Van and Lucia out of a Venezuelan prison within one week. Yet he couldn't give Martin a single update on Tula after three months.

Cole said the turmoil in Jaulaso had delayed his progress, but he would find her and get her out. He just needed time.

There was fuck all Martin could do about it, and that was the root of his fury. He was enraged with himself more than anything. He shouldn't have left her.

The only thing keeping him from mentally snapping was the man in his arms.

Ricky carried his own anger with a quiet intensity that Martin envied. Even in his devastation over leaving Tula, Ricky had been able to wrap a blanket of calmness around Martin and cool them both down before they lost their shit.

He used that same calmness to control Martin's unhinged aggression during sex.

Martin was nowhere near cured of his PTSD. Hard, rough fucking triggered him every time, but Ricky never gave up on him. He'd figured out how to battle Martin's demons with a soft rumbling voice, sensual caresses, and assertive eye contact. Didn't matter how deep in the past Martin fell, Ricky always pulled him back.

Even now, as his best friend slept beside him, he felt his rage give way to the patience that seemed to radiate from Ricky's presence.

Black hair lay in tousled waves on Ricky's head. His tanned skin glowed white in the spill of moonlight from the balcony door. Dark eyelashes, straight nose, square jaw—all his features formed a breathtaking portrait of masculine symmetry.

The seam of his full lips hid a tongue that could

make Martin shoot his load in under ten seconds, and his nude body exuded all the grace, strength, and chiseled perfection of a demigod.

No one could pull off the freshly fucked look like Ricardo Saldivar. Martin had worked him into a hard-earned orgasm only an hour earlier, hoping to fuck them both to sleep.

At least Ricky had found a moment of solace.

But he was awake now, given the irregular pace of his breaths.

Martin shifted closer, touching their foreheads together.

"I miss her." Ricky opened his eyes, locking onto Martin's.

"Yeah." A clamp of renewed anger constricted his chest. "We promised her we'd get her out."

Loving a woman they couldn't see or touch or protect… It was such a goddamn helpless feeling. But breaking a promise to her felt even worse.

"She's fierce as hell." Ricky gripped Martin's neck. "You know as well as I do, she's the reason Jaulaso went up in flames."

"I'm going to redden her fucking ass for it."

Ricky glanced at the clock on the nightstand. It was two in the morning, but he didn't need to ask Martin why he was awake. They hadn't had a full night's sleep since they left her in that hell.

"You know what I miss?" Ricky connected their mouths in a languorous kiss, sweeping his tongue and igniting the heat that burned between them. "I miss her soft hands and lips."

"I miss her sexy little tits." He licked a path down Ricky's throat, nipped at the flex of pecs, and swirled his tongue around Ricky's nipple.

With a shameless moan, Ricky gripped Martin's swelling erection, rubbing in slow teasing strokes. "And the sound of her husky voice when she wants to fuck."

"Especially when she's quoting her favorite books." Warmth spread through his body as he rocked into Ricky's tight fist. "Her nerdy, schoolteacher thing really does it for me."

"Yeah?" Shifting closer, Ricky pumped his hand and stole hungry kisses. "Her smile does it for me. The sweetness in it, the breathy sounds she makes, the wet grip of her pussy…"

Martin captured Ricky's thick cock and touched the hard length the way he used to touch himself. Fast and aggressive, firm and desperate, he jacked Ricky off until their kissing and stroking turned feral.

"Fuck, I miss her tight little cunt." Kicking his hips, Ricky thrust faster into Martin's fist.

"My hand's not as good as her pussy?"

"No." Ricky groaned through a laugh. "But it gets the job done. Really fucking well. Don't stop."

He didn't stop until he took Ricky's cock into his mouth. He sucked ravenously until Ricky undulated and moaned through a body-shaking orgasm. Then he lubed up, flipped Ricky over, and rode Ricky's hot ass into a slow, grinding climax.

They should've been able to sleep after that, but they couldn't. She was a sadness they shared, a pain that laded their thoughts and kept them on edge.

Stretched out on the bed, face to face, they sank into the intimacy of their eye contact.

Martin traced a finger along the carved terrain of Ricky's abs, marveling at the ease in which he could touch his best friend. He'd been so fucking scared he would hurt Ricky irreparably that he'd denied them this pleasure for seven years.

He should've known Ricky had the physical and emotional strength to handle Martin's pain, even when Martin couldn't.

"I love you." He rested a hand on Ricky's face, roaming his thumb along that strong jawline.

"You, too."

They stayed that way for hours, drifting in and out of sleep.

Sometime before dawn, Martin's phone rang on the side table.

His heart rate tripled as he reached for it. But Ricky beat him to it, lunging across his chest and putting the call on speaker.

Martin didn't have to look at the screen to know the call was from Cole Hartman. His knuckles were white from clenching his fists, and his entire body froze in anticipation.

"You better have good news for us." Ricky set the phone on the bed and rubbed his palms on his thighs, his expression taut.

"She's alive," Cole said. "But she's not in Jaulaso."

All the air in the room evaporated. Martin couldn't catch his breath.

"What the fuck?" Ricky jumped off the bed and dragged his hands through his hair. "Where is she?"

"She transferred to a federal prison in the U.S. the day Hector was murdered. That took planning." Cole let that settle in before he asked, "Can you catch a flight to Phoenix, Arizona?"

"Holy fuck." Martin exchanged a startled look with Ricky. "She's in Arizona?"

"Yes. During her transfer hearing, the U.S. Parole Commission reduced her sentence. She's getting released next week, and I'm not the only one who knows this. Someone put out a contract hit on her life."

THIRTY-THREE

"Petula Gomez." The female corrections officer waved her through the final checkpoint. "You're clear to go."

Tula shoved her hands in the front pockets of her jeans and swallowed around a knot of conflicting emotions. Uncertainty and exaltation, terrible fear and utter joy—all of it burned the backs of her eyes as she pushed through the exterior door.

Two years after her arrest, she stepped out of prison as a free woman.

A buzz of electricity exploded inside her. The good kind. The bursting-with-warmth kind that carried more possibilities than she could hold in her chest. Endless paths awaited her feet, but there was only one path she wanted.

The Arizona sun burned into her retinas as she scanned the parking lot of glinting metal.

Were they here?

What if they weren't?

She would have to figure out where to go and how to get there.

She would have to start a life without them. She'd

braced herself for that prospect, but the thought still lanced unbearable pain through her insides.

The scent of asphalt and desert heat filled her lungs. There was no wind, but she felt the wide-open air, vast and alive and all around her.

She swayed beneath the petrifying surrealism of standing outside without walls, bars, or shackles. Hell, she'd been reeling since she left Jaulaso.

She hadn't seen a man, an illegal drug, or a weapon of any kind in three months. Everything was different in federal prison—the rules, the meals, the curfew, the women… Good God, when she'd arrived here, she hadn't been around another woman in two years. She still didn't know how to interact with them.

The differences between this prison and Jaulaso were so extreme she'd spent the last three months in a dazed state of shell shock.

But the biggest shock came last week.

Out of nowhere, someone had deposited funds into her prison bank account. The amount had been more than enough to purchase snacks and nicer prison shoes from the prison commissary.

The anonymous donor hadn't left a message, but she hoped.

She hoped with all the hope that remained in her shattered heart that Martin and Ricky had found her.

If they had, she didn't know how. They would've had to search the U.S. prison databases. How would they even know to look for her in the States?

With her eyes on the parking lot, she wandered down the sidewalk, dressed in the same jeans and t-shirt she wore the day she killed Hector La Rocha.

Her clothes had been in storage, never washed. That meant the black cotton of her shirt retained the bloody specks of Hector's death.

The authorities didn't know she had done it. No one had even questioned her. The news stories called it a deadly dispute within the cartel.

She still couldn't believe she'd killed him.

Her father.

The notorious crime boss of La Rocha Cartel.

The same day it happened, she sat through her transfer hearing, accepted her guilt, and learned her transferred sentence of three years in Mexico converted into only three months in the United States. Transferees didn't always get a reduced sentence, but it happened sometimes. She was one of the lucky ones.

She would never be acquitted of the drug smuggling charges, but it didn't matter.

Nothing mattered more than finding the two men she loved with every breath in her body.

The long sidewalk led her to the parking lot. Cars occupied almost every spot in a sea of steel and glass. Beyond that lay endless desert. She shielded her eyes from the sun and raked her gaze back and forth, searching, aching, panicking.

Nothing moved.

No one was coming.

Just as she was about to let go of the dwindling ray of hope that flickered inside her, the rumble of an engine sounded.

On the far side of the lot, a large SUV pulled out of its spot and slowly motored toward her. More vehicles followed suit—a truck, several sports cars, and a luxury sedan—all scattered through the lot and leaving their parked positions at the same time.

Her pulse careened into a gallop.

Garra had warned her that Hector's sons would

avenge their father's death. Had they found her? Would they try to abduct her or kill her on federal property?

She spun back toward the entrance, knowing she would never make it up that long path in time. Terror consumed her as she bolted into a sprint.

Car doors opened behind her, and footsteps closed in.

"Tula!" The familiar masculine voice pierced shards of light through her tunnel vision.

She faltered, gulping for air as she whirled back.

Two pairs of arms came around her, enveloping her in the strange scents of cologne, aftershave, and woodsy shampoo. None of the fragrances belonged to Martin and Ricky, but her body recognized every chiseled inch of them.

Her hands identified the carved definition in their chests. Her fingers distinguished the differences in the textures of their hair as she pulled their heads toward her. Her gaze found green eyes, brown eyes, and all the gorgeous features that had occupied her thoughts since the day they walked into Area Three.

She melted instantly into the press of their bodies, caressing and grabbing solid muscle while trying to maintain eye contact.

"You came." She choked on a sob and pushed back just enough to reach for their faces. "You're here."

"Tula." Martin shook his head, his voice cracking. "We should've never left."

"Don't say that." She stroked his rigid jaw. "This is love. It slays and conquers and never looks back." The hot burn of tears blurred her eyes. "It's the reason you're here."

As she absorbed the sculpted details of their fierce expressions, the walls inside her ruptured one by one. It started as a tingle in her fingers and toes, crashed through her limbs, and rolled over her in a warm powerful tide, washing away her doubts and fears.

Life had returned to her. They were here, breathing with her, touching her skin, and watching her with the same intense longing that curled her fingers into their clothes.

The universe had given her another chance at happiness, and she wouldn't squander a second of it.

"I love you." She met each pair of eyes as great rushing waves of felicity soaked into her heart, mending it as quickly as it had been broken.

"I love you, too." Ricky tightened his arms around her and Martin, wrapping them in a protective bubble. "So damn much."

Martin tangled a hand in her hair, angling her face toward his. "Fucking hell, I need to kiss you right now, but—"

"Idiots!" a man shouted from inside the SUV. "Get your asses in the car!"

"We need to go." Ricky swept her up into his arms and took off toward their ride.

The urgency in his gait sent a chill across her scalp. "Are we in danger?"

"Yes."

She held tight to his broad shoulders. "Those other cars—"

"They're with us." He slid across the backseat of the SUV with her body tucked against his chest.

Martin followed him in, and the vehicle lurched into motion as the door swung closed. Two men sat in the front seat, but she didn't get a look at them before Martin and Ricky pulled her back into their orbit.

She sat sideways on Ricky's lap as Martin positioned

her legs across his thighs and drifted close, surrounding her with the potency of his full attention.

"I'm so sorry." Ricky ghosted his lips along her temple, his hand resting on her neck. "We couldn't wait for you at the door. We had snipers lined up—"

She inhaled sharply. "In the other cars?"

"Yes."

"Because of Hector's sons? They're coming for me?"

"They have to get through us first." Martin stared into her eyes and slid his fingers across her cheek, touching her with a stunned sort of reverence, like he couldn't believe she was here.

"How did you find me? How do you even know Hector's sons are looking for me?"

His gaze drifted to the driver, sitting directly in front of him.

The man's brown eyes greeted her in the rearview mirror. His profile revealed a straight nose and trimmed beard that failed to hide the dimple in his cheek. He was handsome, like jaw-droppingly stupid handsome, but a dangerous air circulated around him, raising the hairs on her arms.

"That's Cole Hartman," Martin said.

"You're the military guy." She held his gaze in the mirror, recalling everything Martin and Ricky had told her about his specialized skills and connections in the criminal world. "You're the one who found me?"

"Yes, but before last week, we thought you were still in Jaulaso." He glanced at the road, the side mirrors, and returned to her. "The prison's on lockdown, including all information on its inmates. We didn't know if you were alive or dead."

Ricky's body went stiff beneath her, drawing her attention to the pain he couldn't conceal in his eyes. Martin wore a similar expression, his features bearing the exhaustion from months of stress.

Guilt cleaved through her. "I'm so sorry. I should've told you my plan. The night before you left… I slipped out to take a shower and saw something really…heartbreaking." Her chest squeezed, trapping her next breath. "I'll tell you everything, but not here. Not right now. It's going to hurt to relive it, and I…"

Ricky touched his lips to hers. He didn't try to silence her with a kiss. He just held his mouth there and let their breaths coalesce and shudder together.

"Whenever you're ready. We're not going anywhere." He ran his nose along hers. "Never again."

"I won't let you go. Never again." She closed her eyes, exalting in the connection.

When he leaned back, her attention fell on the other man in the front seat. With model-worthy features, red hair, and a tall, muscled frame, he fit the description of the mechanic roommate Martin and Ricky had always talked about.

"You must be Luke," she said to him.

"Good guess." He twisted around to give her a wink. "They must've told you I was the best looking.

"The best-looking redhead." She grinned.

"The *only* redhead." Cole veered onto the interstate, heading toward the city. Then he found her gaze in the mirror. "I have eyes and ears in the cartel underworld. One of the inmates in Jaulaso contacted Hector's sons and told them you transferred to the States. When they put a contract out on your life, my informants notified me. That's how I found you." He tapped his fingers on the steering wheel. "If you have any information on them or La Rocha business—"

"My sister is alive, and she's with them."

She walked them through the day she killed Hector—how she did it, everything that was said, and the clues Garra gave her before he died.

"They smuggle children inside crates with their weapon shipments." She clenched her hands. "I think, all along, they were discussing their human trafficking operation right in front of me. They just always referred to it as *firearms*. So while I was in the women's camp, I wrote down everything I remembered from those meetings."

She pulled a small journal from her back pocket and squeezed her fingers around it. Two years of memories filled the pages—conversations, smuggling routes, towns in North, Central, and South America that began with *Cala*, as well as the details of that haunting night in the sewer room.

"Give it to Luke." Martin nodded at the redheaded vigilante. "He's leading the next phase of the mission."

"Vera's part of that phase." She clutched the notebook to her chest. "Until I have evidence of her guilt, I won't turn against her."

"I won't kill her." Luke held out his hand, waiting for the journal.

"I'm going with you."

"No." Martin put his face in hers. "There's a contract out on all three of us. We aren't going anywhere near Hector's sons until the situation is neutralized. We'll be involved in the operation. In the *background*. Understood?"

Her pulse quickened. "There's a contract on you and Ricky?"

"Yes. They connected us to you. How could they not? We lived among La Rocha Cartel members for three months. Everyone saw the three of us together."

She sucked in a breath and turned back to Luke. "What will you do if you find her?"

"I'll shackle her." He lifted a shoulder. "Haul her ass into the Restrepo headquarters for questioning."

The arid landscape of Phoenix, Arizona blurred past the windows. She was only minutes from her old apartment. That was where she'd been, sitting on the couch and looking forward to summer break, when Vera called. It was the last time she'd talked to her sister.

"Please, don't kill her." She relinquished her journal to Luke.

"I promise."

"Aren't you going to ask where we're going?" Ricky caressed a hand through her hair.

"I don't care where, as long as we go there together."

Whatever lay ahead could be her greatest challenge yet. There would be tears and laughter, fighting and fucking, and everything in between. A lasting relationship with one man was hard enough. But with two? It would be twice the work, twice the joy.

She couldn't wait.

Five miles from her old neighborhood, Cole drove through the wealthiest part of Phoenix. Mansions sat on estate lots, boasting their own lagoons, lush green yards, and wrought iron gates.

When Cole pulled up to one of those gates and punched in a passcode, she straightened on Ricky's lap.

"We're going to stay here for a few days." Ricky kissed her shoulder.

"Is it safe? I assumed we would head to Colombia where you live."

"We will." He turned her to face him. "You've been locked up for two years. Taking you to Matias' headquarters might feel like another prison. We thought you would want to experience some of the places and things you loved here before we dragged you away."

"You're right." A watery breath heaved up, clogging her voice. "Thank you."

"But we won't be alone here. Most of the group came with us, along with some of Matias' men. They're here to keep us safe."

As Cole drove through the gate, the cars from the prison followed in behind him. Towering stone walls surrounded the driveway, with security fences and armed men blocking every alcove and path.

Jesus, they weren't fucking around. This place was a fortress.

"Who owns this property?" she asked.

"It belongs to the Restrepo Cartel." Martin gripped her hand, twining their fingers together. "We're safe here."

Sitting between him and Ricky, she'd never felt safer.

The next hour involved a tour through the ten-thousand-square-foot mansion and introductions to the men and women who made up the Freedom Fighters.

Some of them weren't there. Matias, Camila, Tate, and Lucia were working on another mission in Colombia, and Kate lived on the other side of the world. But she met Josh, Liv, Tomas, Amber, Livana, and the most intimidating presence of them all, Van Quiso.

The massive kitchen buzzed with activity. More food than anyone could ever eat covered the counters. Beautiful people filled the doorways and chairs, and the intimate history between them vibrated through their laughter and lit up their eyes.

They engaged her in friendly conversation and teased Martin and Ricky about their seven-year foreplay.

For a group of ex-traffickers, ex-slaves, and vigilante murderers, they were surprisingly affectionate and gentle. But those were traits she no longer trusted. If it weren't so abundantly clear that Martin and Ricky loved these people, she would've been looking for the nearest exit right about now.

Even so, her nerves felt raw and wired. She wasn't used to so many aromas of food, the constant touching from strangers, and the extravagance of her surroundings. It was too much all at once.

The only thing holding her together was the comfort in the possessive hands that never left her lower back and hips. Their eyes never left her, either. Martin and Ricky watched her as if she might vanish right in front of them.

"This is the grilled cheese from the bakery near your apartment." Ricky guided her to the bags of takeout on the table. "We tried to remember all the restaurants you talked about and—" He tilted his head, squinting as he studied her. "You're overwhelmed."

"A little."

"A lot," he said.

"Yeah."

He grabbed a bag of grilled cheese, signaled Martin, and led her upstairs.

THIRTY-FOUR

Tula stood beside a king-sized bed in a master bedroom fit for royalty. Tufted fabrics, rich woods, and elegant decor—the opulence of her surroundings overwhelmed her senses and made her uneasy. Hell, a standard bed in an ordinary room would've put her on edge. She wasn't used to any of this.

She'd eaten the grilled cheese with Martin and Ricky. It tasted just as delicious as she remembered, but it sat heavy in her nervous stomach.

After the quiet meal, she'd changed her clothes in the bathroom, slipping on jean shorts and a dark tank top over a burgundy satin bra and panties set, just like the one she'd described to them all those months ago.

Bags of new clothing and beauty products filled one corner of the master suite. Martin and Ricky had shopped for her, brought in all her favorite foods, and set up house in this mansion to help her adjust and keep her safe.

They'd thought of everything, and she was grateful beyond words. But she didn't need any of it.

She just needed *them*.

Most of her anxiety resided in all the things left unsaid. Months of keeping her emotions locked up weighed on her chest.

This luxurious master suite with its over-sized mattress had all the makings for a sinful night of passion. She wanted that desperately, craved a carnal reconnection with them, but more than that, she needed to give them her ugliest memories.

"Tula." Martin lifted her chin with a finger, anchoring her with that simple touch. "Tell me what you need."

"Hold me while I tell you the rest?"

His expression softened, and an approving grunt sounded in his throat. Then he lifted her and settled them into bed.

Ricky slid in on her other side. They kicked off their shoes, tangled their legs with hers, and for the next two hours, listened to her talk through every decision, every emotion, everything she experienced from the moment she heard that little girl cry until now.

They held her tight between their warm bodies, kissed away her tears, and asked questions. By the time she finished, she felt like a different person. Lighter, more relaxed, finally free.

"Thank you for telling us." Ricky pulled her against his chest and played with her hair. "I'm so fucking sorry you went through that alone."

"I'm not alone now. Thank you for listening."

Tension seeped from her muscles, replaced by a drugging sense of peace. His hand continued its caress, his fingers running from roots to ends, over and over in hypnotic strokes.

Within minutes, she dozed off.

She woke sometime later, sprawled on her stomach

with Ricky curled up against her side. The sun had set beyond the window, and sitting in a chair a few feet away, Martin watched her with an intensity that made her shiver.

He'd barely spoken a word since she'd started talking hours earlier. She knew he was compartmentalizing everything from the perspective of someone who had suffered at the hands of a pedophile.

Her heart ached for him. "Tell me what you're thinking."

"I'm going to beat your ass."

"Oh." Her neck stiffened, and a tingle of heat flushed her skin. "Because I lied to you about leaving the room that night?"

"You lied to us, risked your life *multiple* times, and executed a dangerous plan that you deliberately prevented Ricky and me from weighing in on."

"I was protecting you. If I told you that night what I witnessed and what I intended to do, what would you have done? Where would the three of us be sitting right now? It wouldn't be *here*."

His jaw flexed. "You could've died."

"I didn't."

"Come here."

Her heart skipped at the unbending tone in his voice, and she obeyed instantly, willfully, desperate to close the distance between them.

The bed shifted behind her with Ricky's movement as she climbed off to stand before Martin. He unfolded his powerful frame from the chair, rising to his full, towering height.

The coils low in her belly thrummed to life. Breath drawn, blood circulating, she lifted on her toes, gripped his shoulders, and rested her brow against his.

"I fucking missed you." The sublime heat in his

words heightened the featherlight caress of his fingers as he slid them around her neck.

"Same. So much the same." She savored the brush of his exhale against her lips and the vibration of his nearness humming across her skin.

An undivided moment of calm caught and held. Breaths fused. Promises issued without voice, and hands began to roam.

It was a slow perusal. The finger he trailed along the neckline of her tank top sought out her collarbone beneath. She traced the taut sinews in his neck and the lines of his whiskered jaw. He stroked the rise of her breast, and she raked her hands through his soft blond hair.

Every touch was a sacrament, every caress a solicitation for more. Through it all, they held an impenetrable stare, eating each other with their eyes, wanting, panting, the need in their bodies growing voracious.

Sliding her palms beneath his shirt and up his torso, she adored the twitching of chest muscles and the heart that beat within. He stripped off her top, and his arms folded around her back, drawing her in close and walking his fingers up and down her spine.

Her entire being shook, mourning the months they missed together and aching to release the tension that had built up during the painful separation.

He pulled his head back to regard her, his chin lifted and eyes drawn to her lips. She couldn't formulate a thought beyond her desire for this man and the one closing in around her back.

Ricky's hands slid over her, exploring her flesh where it greeted the satin of her bra. Then he and Martin touched her together, their movements unhurried yet earnest. The skimming of knuckles, the scrape of trimmed nails, the glide of warm palms—every stroke removed a piece of her clothing and sent shimmers of pleasure between her legs.

When she was finally nude, all the heat inside her had knotted into a bundle, her chest barely coping with the heave of her breaths. Her thighs trembled, and her skin burned and shivered. If they didn't kiss her soon, her nerve endings were going to tear themselves apart.

How the floor beneath her feet vanished, she didn't know. One moment she was standing between them, and the next she was on the bed, face down on Ricky's chest with Martin bent over her back.

As Martin angled his face over her shoulder, she held her breath, ready for his kiss. But he bypassed her and slammed his mouth against Ricky's.

Masculine tongues rolled together, the tips of their lips barely touching as they licked and grunted and rocked their hips with hers between.

They were a union of testosterone and passion housed in muscle and bone. Watching them kiss was a privilege. Witnessing the love they shared in their eye contact was a precious honor, and they were giving her this intentionally, wickedly teasing her and making her wait.

Their kissing was explosive yet intimate as they stared into each other's eyes and murmured indiscernible words. Then those eyes turned to her.

Ricky grabbed her first, his tongue plunging past her lips. She was already gone, spinning with lust, and overcome by the protective feeling of them surrounding her. Broad frames, flexing legs, grinding hips, rock-hard strength… They wore their hunger in the tense lines of their perfect bodies.

Ricky took her mouth possessively, expertly as

Martin licked a tingling path across her shoulder and along her neck, stripping her of all self-control.

Her nerve endings responded to his tongue, and her body answered his devotion with a rush of wet heat between her legs.

With a hand in her hair, Martin tore her mouth away from Ricky's and joined it with his own. The deep intensity of his kiss detonated into a throbbing fire.

His fingers turned bruising, his lips punishing as he claimed her, destroyed her, and put her back together. He was so wild and consuming she had to tilt her head away to gulp down some air.

Then the heat of his body left her back. His hands grasped her knees, positioning them on either side of Ricky's hips and forcing her ass upward.

With her chest pressed to Ricky's, she swiveled her neck, bringing her gaze to Martin's vibrant green eyes.

There was no warning in his expression before he slammed a hand against her bare backside. The impact drove a yelp from her throat and sweltering sting through her buttocks.

She stared down at Ricky, shocked, wheezing, and insanely turned on.

"So fucking hot." His brown eyes pulsed around dilated pupils.

"Does he spank you like this?"

"Not enough."

Martin struck her again. And again. And again. His searing blows landed on every inch of her quivering, red-hot flesh, from her hips to the backs of her thighs.

Then his mouth was there, licking the hurt and blowing tender breaths on the fire he'd ignited.

His lips moved lower, deeper, invading her soaked pussy and teasing her anus. He kissed her thoroughly while Ricky took her mouth, their tongues curling and laving her at both ends.

She whimpered against the stimulation, wobbling on boneless legs as she tried to maintain her straddled position over Ricky.

Martin reached between her thighs and tackled Ricky's jeans. Ricky lifted just enough to tear off his shirt, his expression dazed with need.

Their movements grew frenzied, stripping clothes and scooting across the bed. The whole time, she stared into Ricky's eyes, hovering over him and stealing kisses between his panting breaths.

"I need you." She gripped the bulges of his biceps, her knees pressed into the mattress on either side of his trim waist. With her butt in the air, her pussy clenched uncontrollably, dripping, aching to take him in.

"Martin. Condom." Ricky tipped his back, his eyes glued to hers as he gripped his cock between the spread of her thighs. "Hurry."

"No condoms." She held out a hand behind her, staying Martin. "Nothing between us. Whatever happens, happens. As long as we're together."

"Inside you bare?" Ricky stroked himself between her legs, pulling hard on his steely length as he moaned against her mouth. "God, yes, Tula. I've never had sex without a rubber."

She glanced back at Martin, finding him gloriously nude and staring at the exposed wetness of her center. "You're not on the pill."

"No."

He took his erection in hand, lazily rubbing from root to tip as he exchanged a look with Ricky.

In the next heartbeat, he was on her, mounting her backside and pushing inside her with a long, throaty growl. She felt him harden and throb against her inner walls, and holy fuck, it was incredible.

Ricky's body began to shake beneath her as Martin fell into a fast, rhythmic thrust of hips. She collapsed against Ricky's chest beneath the force of Martin's storm, her pussy stretching and contracting around the delicious glide of his cock.

Ricky's fist worked beneath her, and she caught it, slowing his strokes, grinding into him, and gasping at the friction of his hardness against her clit.

His neck went taut, straining in his desperation, his eyes never looking away. "Need inside you."

"Not yet." Martin curled a hand in her hair and slammed into her over and over, panting and grunting. "Swear to God, Ricky. You're going to come the instant you're inside her. She feels so fucking good. Hot and tight and creaming all over my dick."

His growly words pushed her toward her tipping point. She shifted her hips, angling them higher to take more of him.

With a moan, he rammed his heaviness harder inside her, driving deeper, faster, hitting a crescendo. Then he leaned in and reached between her legs to join his hand with Ricky's and hers around Ricky's cock.

Together, they stroked him into a gasping furor of curse words.

"Fuck, fuck, fuck!"

"Don't come." Martin set the pace of their hands, in sync with the sliding thrusts of his cock inside her.

"Give me your mouth, *querida,*" Ricky said.

She pressed her lips to his, willing to give him everything he demanded.

Ricky's guttural sounds of need filled her mouth, and Martin stretched over her to join the kiss.

Their free hands roved her skin. Their bodies rose and fell against her, three tongues connecting, retreating, and uniting again as they lost our breaths together.

They took her heart with every touch, and in return, they gave her theirs. Happiness swelled so fully in her chest she wanted to scream with every ounce of breath that dwelled in her lungs.

The only thing that would make this better was if they were both moving inside her.

"Need you both." She groaned into Ricky's neck.

"Greedy girl." Martin smacked her hard on the ass and pulled out of her pussy.

Before she caught her next breath, Ricky worked himself inside her.

"Oh, God!" He dug his fingers into her hips. "Feel that?"

"I feel you deep." She wrapped her arms around his magnificent body that was so warm and strong as he unleashed his hunger. "So deep in places no one has ever been."

He stared at her blearily, high on the pleasure, and she melted into his molten brown eyes.

Martin already had the lube and rubbed a cool smear of wetness between her ass cheeks.

Ricky's hand slipped down her throat, danced around her collarbone, and settled into a possessive hold on her breast. Martin caressed her other tit as the head of his lubed dick found her rectum, rubbing a slow circle against the ring of muscle.

She gasped and arched into the pressure, and he went inside, gliding in inch by thick inch as her name fell from his mouth.

Sensations vibrated and throbbed through every pleasure point, causing her ass and pussy to clench around their beautiful cocks.

Martin grunted an agonized sound, and Ricky's breath cut off. She sank her nails into Ricky's shoulders and turned her head, shifting her gaze between theirs, holding that contact, her entire world.

Then they moved, pushing and pulling her against them as she pressed into their thrusts.

The warmth of their skin met hers, and three bodies morphed into a single being.

Three hearts without walls.

Fused into a single soul without bars.

Lost and found.

Locked up and freed.

Together, they became an unbroken forever.

THIRTY-FIVE

Bogotá, Colombia
One month later

The clinking of dishes and the scent of grilled meats accentuated the tranquil ambiance in the elegant dining room. Ricky savored the last bite of his syrupy, spicy tri-tip steak, but not as much as he savored the two people at his table.

Tula sat across from him with Martin at her side, their postures distinctively dissimilar as they stared at him.

Tension tightened her shoulders. Her fingers curled into the linen tablecloth, and her pouty lips made him so fucking hard he had to cover his lap with a napkin.

Martin reclined in his seat with imposing confidence, his bright green eyes fixed on Ricky as he subtly worked his hand between her legs.

The dining room hummed with conversations. Servers in black suits glided from table to table. Restaurant patrons whispered and laughed softly among themselves, and around the perimeter stood a discreet security detail, provided by Matias Restrepo.

During their few days in Phoenix, he and Martin had taken her to restaurants, movie theaters, strolls through the park… They fit in as many dating excursions as they could before boarding Matias' private jet. When they arrived in Colombia, they moved her into the suite he and Martin shared at the Restrepo headquarters.

The three of them spent the past month helping Luke and the others follow up on the information Tula had compiled in her journal. With Cole Hartman's assistance, they *think* they located the main headquarters of Hector's sons and their human trafficking operation.

Tula's sister hadn't been found yet, but one of Cole's informants claimed Vera had been recently spotted with Hector's sons.

Luke, along with a team of Matias' men, were in Mexico now, checking out the alleged headquarters. Ricky, Martin, and Tula had flown there with him to drop him off. On the way back, they stopped in Bogotá to give Tula a proper night on the town.

"Why can't we just sit here and have a nice meal together?" Her gaze darted through the dining room as her cheeks heated with the quickening of her breaths.

From Ricky's angle, it looked like Martin's hand was just resting on her lap beneath the table. But her restless shifting and breathy little noises were dead giveaways. Martin's fingers had found their way beneath her dress and deep inside her cunt.

"If you wanted to just sit here, you should've picked a couple of boring guys." Ricky leaned across the table and arched a brow.

"I didn't pick you. You picked me." Her nipples hardened beneath the burgundy satin of her cocktail dress.

"Is that how you remember it?" He looked at Martin.

"I succinctly recall," Martin said, adjusting his black tie, "Tula coming to us and asking to be our friend."

She made a gulping sound and gripped Martin's arm as he played with her pussy. "I liked your American accents."

"That's not the only thing you like." Ricky turned in his seat at the sound of music.

Across the dining room, a man sat behind a black piano and tapped the keys into a slow, hypnotic song. Couples floated to a small dance floor, swaying to the melody.

He and Martin had coaxed her into dancing a few times in the privacy of their bedroom. She'd been reluctant at first, but they were determined to replace her memories of Hector with new experiences.

Ricky waited until his erection calmed down. Then he stood and offered her his hand.

Martin slid his touch away as she glanced at the dance floor and sucked in a breath. And another. Straightening the front of her dress, she slowly stood and accepted Ricky's hand.

Burgundy satin hugged her body from tits to thighs. Her long black hair fell in sexy waves around her arms, and a touch of smoky color darkened her brown eyes.

She was the most gorgeous creature he'd ever seen, standing beside the man who loved him as deeply as they loved the woman they shared.

Ricky didn't know what the future would bring beyond her sister and the Freedom Fighters. But it was their adventure to take. The three of them together. Hand in hand.

So he laced his fingers with hers, met Martin's eyes, and took the next step.

"Let's dance."

The DELIVER series continues with:

UNSHACKLE (#7)
Luke's story

DOMINATE (#8)
Tomas' story

COMPLICATE (#9) - ***the final book***
Cole's story

LOVE TRIANGLE ROMANCE

TANGLED LIES TRILOGY

One is a Promise

Two is a Lie

Three is a War

DARK COWBOY ROMANCE

TRAILS OF SIN

Knotted #1

Buckled #2

Booted #3

DARK ALASKAN ROMANCE

FROZEN FATE

Hills of Shivers and Shadows #1

Cage of Ice and Echoes #2

Heart of Frost and Scars #3

DARK PARANORMAL ROMANCE
TRILOGY OF EVE
Heart of Eve
Dead of Eve #1
Blood of Eve #2
Dawn of Eve #3

STUDENT-TEACHER / PRIEST
Lessons In Sin

STUDENT-TEACHER ROMANCE
Dark Notes

ROCK-STAR DARK ROMANCE
Beneath the Burn

BILLIONAIRE REVENGE
Dirty Ties

OLDER WOMAN / YOUNGER MAN
Incentive

DARK HISTORICAL PIRATE ROMANCE
King of Libertines
Sea of Ruin

New York Times, Wall Street Journal, and *USA Today* bestselling author, Pam Godwin, lives in the Midwest with her husband, cats, retired greyhounds, and an old, foul-mouthed parrot. She traveled the world for seven years, attended three universities, married the vocalist of her favorite rock band, and retired from her quantitative analyst career in 2014 to write full-time.

Her interests veer toward the unconventional: bourbon, full-body tattoos, and tragic villains. Equally peculiar are her aversions to sleeping, eating meat, and dolls with blinking eyes.

EMAIL: pamgodwinauthor@gmail.com

www.ingramcontent.com/pod-product-compliance
Lightning Source LLC
Chambersburg PA
CBHW020245030826
48979CB00030B/2627/J

* 9 7 8 1 9 6 6 5 3 7 0 0 7 *